MUSLIMS

MUSLIMS
The Real History

Ali Mahmood

Published by
Rupa Publications India Pvt. Ltd 2018
7/16, Ansari Road, Daryaganj
New Delhi 110002

Sales Centres:
Allahabad Bengaluru Chennai
Hyderabad Jaipur Kathmandu
Kolkata Mumbai

Copyright © Ali Mahmood 2018

The views and opinions expressed in this book are the author's own and the facts are as reported by him which have been verified to the extent possible, and the publishers are not in any way liable for the same.

All rights reserved.
No part of this publication may be reproduced, transmitted, or stored in a retrieval system, in any form or by any means, electronic, mechanical, photocopying, recording or otherwise, without the prior permission of the publisher.

ISBN: 978-93-5304-112-0

Sixth impression 2023

10 9 8 7 6

The moral right of the author has been asserted.

Printed in India

This book is sold subject to the condition that it shall not, by way of trade or otherwise, be lent, resold, hired out, or otherwise circulated, without the publisher's prior consent, in any form of binding or cover other than that in which it is published.

In gratitude to Billo, my wife, for her advice, criticism, patience and support during the five long years spent in the preparation of this book.

Contents

Introduction ... ix

1. The Prophet Muhammad ... 1
2. Inheritors of The Prophet's Legacy ... 14
3. The Umayyads ... 38
4. The Rise of the Abbasids ... 57
5. The Golden Years of Islamic Civilization ... 67
6. The Decline and Demise of the Abbasids ... 74
7. The Rise of Egypt ... 83
8. Muslims in Spain ... 104
9. The Tide Turns in Spain ... 115
10. Genghis and Tamerlane ... 124
11. The Delhi Sultanate ... 147
12. The Great Moguls ... 163
13. The Rise and Fall of the Safavids of Iran ... 198
14. The Rise of the Ottomans ... 214
15. The Decline of the Ottomans ... 230
16. The Birth of Modern Egypt ... 251
17. Saudi Arabia: The Rise of a World Power ... 264
18. The Afghans ... 276

19. The Genesis of Modern Iran	292
20. Jinnah Creates a Muslim Homeland	299
21. Europe Eclipses the Muslim Empires	305
22. The Muslims Fight Back	312
23. Pakistan and the War on Terror	362
24. The Periphery	373
25. The Muslim World Today	401
Epilogue	417
Acknowledgements	419
Bibliography	421
Index	429

Introduction

'The ink of the scholar is more holy than the blood of the martyr.'

—The Prophet Muhammad

When The Prophet Muhammad left Mecca for Medina, he had less than a hundred followers. Within a century after his death, the Muslims had conquered all the territory from the Atlantic Ocean to China, and the empire of Islam led the world in science, education, medicine, culture, commerce and war. This empire dominated the world for a thousand years. The two empires that followed after the seventeenth century were, in comparison, short-lived—the British Empire lasted for 200 years and its successor, the American Empire is in decline after only sixty years.

Between the seventh and the seventeenth centuries, Muslim power shifted from the Arabs to the Persians, the Turks and the Moguls. The capital of the Islamic empire moved from the sands of Mecca and Medina to Damascus, Baghdad, Cairo, Cordoba and Istanbul, as new dynasties replaced the old—the Umayyad, the Abbasid, the Fatimid—followed by Tamerlane, the world conqueror, and the three gunpowder empires—the Ottoman, the Safavid and the Mogul. The golden centuries of the world of Islam flourished while the Dark Ages made life nasty, brutish and short in Europe. The great libraries of the caliphs in Cordoba and Baghdad ran to half a million books while the great European collections did not even reach a thousand volumes. The Qanun, or Laws of Ibn Sina, dominated medicine in Europe for 500 years and Ibn Firnas demonstrated flight at the age of seventy—600 years before Da Vinci drew his sketches—but never risked an actual attempt to fly.

The thousand years of the Islamic Empire were a time of great achievement, great institutions, great cities and most of all, great men. Tamerlane surpassed Alexander as a world conqueror, and Nader Shah outclassed Napoleon as a general who died undefeated in battle. The second Caliph, Umar, and the Indian ruler Sher Shah Suri demonstrated a system of justice in which even their own sons were subjected to the law of the land. Harun al Rashid, whose court in Baghdad inspired the *One Thousand and One Nights*, made his nightly forays incognito into the streets of Baghdad to better understand his people and their lives. When Saladin conquered Jerusalem and Balian, the Christian general reminded him of the cruelty and barbarism of the earlier Christian conquest. Saladin gently but firmly replied, 'I am not of those men. I am Saladin'. He gave away all that came to him as ruler and died penniless without even the money for a decent burial. Akbar the Great, of India, created an empire though he tried but failed to create a religion. Shah Abbas, the greatest Persian king created Ispahan and built the Sheikh Lutfollah Mosque, perhaps the most beautiful mosque in the world. Suleiman the Magnificent, before whom the world trembled, was the pre-eminent sovereign in both Asia and Europe.

This remarkable era is the legacy of The Prophet, and of those he inspired to pursue education, justice and the rule of law. Equality for all meant that merit replaced birth as the foundation of a new aristocracy and Islam gave birth to revolutionary values and attitudes that created a different type of man who is willing to sacrifice and struggle for what he believed to be right, rather than blindly pursue his own selfish interests. It was these values and attitudes that helped the Muslims to reach greatness; but all good things come to an end and it was the loss of these values and attitudes that, in the seventeenth century, brought them crashing down. After one thousand years at the top, the Muslims spent 200 years at the bottom; the former masters of the universe were deprived and humiliated by their new lords from the West. They became a people without hope.

The Europeans had guns and technology through which they acquired the wealth of the world and became masters of all for three centuries. What they didn't have was wisdom and restraint, and by the twentieth century their greed turned them against each other in two World Wars, which, over a century, led to 100 million deaths, and weakened them till they no longer had the appetite or resources to maintain their empires, which crumbled. As the Europeans departed, new countries were born in the Muslim world, and new heroes started to pull their nations out of the debris of the past.

Ataturk proved that the West could be beaten in battle; Mossadeq nationalized the Anglo-Iranian Oil Company (AIOC), Britain's greatest international corporate asset; Nasser took back the Suez Canal; Sukarno rejected both US and Russian control and fought to create an unaligned Third World; King Faisal of Saudi Arabia imposed an oil embargo on America; Khomeini removed the Shah, America's regional strongman; the Afghan Mujahideen fought the Union of Soviet Socialist Republics (USSR) to a standstill, till finally the latter ceased to exist; oil money, but most of all, courage, meant that the Muslims didn't have to suffer humiliation any longer. Their fighters remembered the warnings of Khalid bin Walid to the enemies of Islam, that he brought with him men who desired death as ardently as they desired life.

Today, the word 'Muslim' brings up visions of oil, petrodollars, jihad, or terrorism, and veiled women. These have become the key issues that define the relationship of the Muslim world with the West. But we need to look beyond the sensational headlines and breaking news and consider who the real Muslims are—the silent moderate majority, or the aggressive fundamentalist minority; the suited doctors and heart surgeons in the West, or the turbaned executioners of the

Islamic State of Iraq and Syria (ISIS) with their slave girls captured in war?

Today a war is being fought, by Muslims against Muslims, to determine the future face of Islam. But behind the scenes, manipulators in the West provide the money, armaments and support in stoking the fires of conflict.

1

The Prophet Muhammad

'He was Caesar and Pope in one; but he was Pope without the Pope's pretensions, Caesar without the legions of Caesar, without a standing army, without a bodyguard, without a palace, without a fixed revenue; if ever any man had the right to say that he ruled by divine right, it was Muhammad, for he had all the power without its instruments and without its supports.'

—R. Bosworth Smith

Muhammad, The Prophet of Islam, is recognized by Muslims and non-Muslims alike as the most influential man in human history. He was supremely successful on both the religious and the secular level, and both as a religious and a political leader.

Muhammad was born in 570 AD in Mecca, at that time a backwater, while the two great empires of the day were the Persians and the Byzantines, the eastern remnant of Rome's empire. His father, Abdullah, died before he was born, and his mother, Amina, died when he was six years old. Thus, he grew up as an illiterate orphan. When he tried to explain his religion, Islam, to the citizens of Mecca, he was ridiculed and attacked. By 622, the year of the Hejra, when he moved to Yathrib (Medina), there were hardly a hundred followers of Islam. However, over the next eleven years, he built up his community, conquered Mecca, and died in 633 AD.

Within twelve years of the death of Muhammad, his successors, inspired by his teachings, his values and his example under the leadership of the first two Caliphs, Abu Bakr and Umar, conquered the Persians and the Byzantines and created the most important empire in the world. Within a hundred years this empire stretched from the Atlantic Ocean to the borders of China. The empire of Islam dominated the world for a thousand years, as compared to the British Empire of 200 years, and the American Empire of today which, after just sixty years, seems to be in serious trouble.

Shortly after birth, Muhammad's mother gave his custody to a Bedouin woman who brought up Muhammad in the desert. After a few years he returned home, but the death of his mother left him an orphan. His grandfather, Abd al-Mutalib, looked after him with love and affection, but two years after the death of his mother, he too died, passing the young boy into the protection of his father's brother, his uncle Abu Talib, the father of Ali.

Muhammad's family was prominent, and drew their livelihood from selling water from the spring, Zam-Zam, to the pilgrims who were drawn to Mecca by the presence of the Kaaba. Mecca's economy centred on pilgrimage and trade, and the leading citizens of Mecca were prosperous as a result. There was little agricultural activity due to shortage of water and the desert environment. Muhammad, as a young orphan, lacked the status of his prosperous uncles, Abbas, the banker, and Hamza, the famed warrior, and spent his time looking after the livestock. Often alone in the desert, he started to think about his world and started to be affected by issues of truth and social justice. At an early age, his sensitivity and selflessness showed him to be unusually considerate towards and concerned about others. With no opportunity for schooling, Muhammad grew up illiterate, unable to read or write.

Abu Talib was a member of the syndicate that financed and controlled the Meccan caravan cartel, and he inducted his nephew, Muhammad, as his deputy on the long caravan journeys. Muhammad proved an able apprentice and quickly earned respect and trust as his experience and knowledge of the business grew. As his importance to his uncle grew, so did his confidence, and he requested the hand in marriage of Fakhita, the daughter of Abu Talib. Talib did not recognize the career prospects of his nephew, and declined the match, preferring to marry his daughter into a more elite and rich family of Mecca.

The life of Muhammad is fully documented. The first sources are the *Quran* and the Traditions, and the most important collection is possibly that by al-Bukhari. The first biography was written by Ibn Ishaq, and the first most complete history was the massive account by al-Tabari, running to thirty-nine volumes. These provide the basis for the numerous biographies that have followed. Perhaps the best modern biographies by Western authors are those by Barnaby Rogerson and Lesley Hazleton—easy to read, and exciting as a story.

Muhammad then joined the service of Khadija, a prosperous widow who was to become his first wife. She had been married twice before, and the death of her husband had left her wealthy with a share in the caravan cartel. Ibn Ishaq describes her as 'a merchant woman of dignity and wealth; a determined, noble and intelligent woman.' Despite the age difference—Khadija was forty to Muhammad's twenty-five—she decided he was the man for her, and proposed to him saying, 'I like you Muhammad, because of our relationship and your high reputation for trustworthiness and good character and truthfulness.' For twenty-four years, they were happy together, till the time of her death. For twenty-four years Muhammad remained loyal and devoted to her in a monogamous marriage of simplicity, shared values and a common struggle. Khadija was to become his first follower. They had four daughters and two sons, both of whom died in infancy. She was the most important woman in his life, and many years later, after her death, his young favourite, Aisha, was to confess that Khadija was the only woman of whom she was truly jealous.

As Muhammad entered his fortieth year, he seemed to have it all—a loving family, wealth and respect. But despite his apparent success, he was tormented with discontent. Then, in Ramadan in the year 610, when he retired into solitude, he experienced revelation, as an angel came to him saying, 'Muhammad, I am Gabriel and you are the messenger of God.'

Thus began the third chapter of Muhammad's life. The first chapter was of Muhammad the orphan, the second of Muhammad the successful family man, the third was of Muhammad's struggle in Mecca to introduce Islam, and the fourth was to be the Medina period of final success when Muhammad combined spiritual with political leadership as he added the roles of head of state, general and statesman to his religious and spiritual work.

SPIRITUAL AND POLITICAL LEADER

Muhammad threatened the vested interests of the Mecca elite, for whom religion was a major income source due to the heavy stream of pilgrims. Big business and the Mecca power networks were determined to stop him. Muhammad would not back down, so the establishment came down hard on him using the standard tactics of insults, social boycott, physical threats soon escalating into assassination attempts, torture, trade sanctions and economic pressure. Muhammad decided that for the safety of his followers, he would have to leave Mecca.

Muhammad started the quiet evacuation of the Muslims but did not himself leave until an assassination threat made staying too dangerous. In the stealth of night, he left with his friend Abu Bakr, using his cousin Ali as a decoy in his own bed. Discovering Ali, the would-be assasins asked him where Muhammad was, but defiant, he replied, 'Do you expect me to keep watch over him? You wanted him to leave and he has left.' When the would-be assassins discovered the ruse, they were angry and frustrated and set off in hot pursuit to catch up with Muhammad on the route to Medina. Muhammad and Abu Bakr hid in a cave and escaped discovery due to a spider's web which covered the entrance to the cave, leading his pursuers to conclude that no one had entered.

Slowly and carefully Muhammad negotiated with community leaders in Medina, the terms of his move to their city and the pattern of integration of his Mecca group of Muslims with their new hosts and allies. In the twentieth century, several leaders have sought safety from persecution by fleeing from their home or country—Lenin in Switzerland, Khomeini in France and Mao in the mountains during his Long March. Muhammad's move to Medina was different from the start, he was not just a private citizen in exile from his home town, but an arbitrator of disputes and a leader and founder of a new religion which spread quickly among the people of Medina. He would not see Mecca again for the next seven years.

Whereas Islam had threatened the commercial interests of the Mecca capitalists by attacking the religions that attracted the pilgrims and their cash, the Medina economy was basically agricultural, with farms spread over a twenty-mile long water basin. The disputes and discord of the Medina tribes were healed by the spirit of brotherhood that Islam fostered among the Muslims, and Islam now grew quickly. Furthermore, Muslim unity created a balance to the dominance of the Jewish tribes with their greater wealth and education. During his early days in Medina, Muhammad was prominent but not predominant. His power grew as he quickly demonstrated that despite his idealism, he was also a practical strategist, more than able to hold his own in the power politics of the time.

At first, the Muslims at Medina were poor; their homes, mud huts, and even their simple mosque was as much a community centre as a place of prayer. They earned their living as labourers, farmers, and a few of them, as petty tradesmen. Earlier, Muslims had prayed turned towards Jerusalem. But after The Prophet's night journey to heaven, Muslims started praying turned towards Mecca.

Islam differed from the other religions of the time in two ways. Firstly, it imposed a higher degree of discipline on its followers—intoxication, gambling and other licentious behaviour was forbidden whereas prayer, hygiene and community life were encouraged. The culture of Islam created a dedicated Spartan group of men ready for any hardship in pursuing the objectives of Muhammad. It is interesting that the prohibition of intoxicants progressed in three stages:

- verse 216 of sura 2: 'The sin in them is greater than the benefit.'
- verse 46 of sura 4: 'O believers, do not come near the prayer while you are drunk!'
- verses 92 and 93 of sura 5: 'Keep away from them! Then, perhaps, you will become more prosperous.'

The second major difference between Islam and the other great religions, Christianity and Judaism, is the imposition of the two new duties of zakat and jihad (holy war). No comparable obligations are imposed in any other religious system. Muhammad's purpose was to organize a state, and that required an army and public finance. The Islamic taxes paid for a combat-ready army which became the key to the expansion of Islam that followed.

In accordance with the custom of the time, Muhammad and his supporters started to raid the trade caravans of Mecca. At first they were not very good at it, and most of their targets escaped than were captured. But with good leadership and after acquiring experience, they started to meet with success. Raiding gave them slaves and hostages for ransom, and their wealth grew.

The antagonism with Mecca escalated as raids led to three battles. The first, at Badr, was a great victory for the Muslims despite the fact that their small force of 300 was outnumbered three-to-one by the Meccans. The original plan was to capture a large and rich caravan from Mecca, guarded by a small contingent of barely seventy guards; but news leaked out, the caravan escaped and a thousand-strong force came to protect the caravan. The larger Meccan army eyeballed the Muslims, warning them to back off. To their surprise, the Muslims did not retreat; they attacked, and in a short time, routed the Meccans, killing Abu Jahl, the hard-line Meccan leader. A ragged group of Muslims, outcasts and freed slaves, had defeated the elite army of the tycoons from Mecca. The tide had turned. The field was rich with booty and captives for ransom, including the son of Abu Sufyan, and Muhammad's uncle, Abbas, the rich banker. Muhammad's own son-in-law, the husband of his daughter Zaynab, was among those captured, and when Zaynab sent her necklace, which had been her wedding gift from Khadija, as ransom, Muhammad broke down in tears and sent both his on-in-law and the jewels back to her. Muhammad returned from the victory at Badr to personal tragedy. His daughter, Roqayya, Uthman's wife, had died. Muhammad gave his last daughter, Um Kulthum, to Uthman as wife to replace her sister, and was reported to say, after her death, that he so dearly loved Uthman that had there been a third daughter, he would have given her in marriage to him also.

A month after the battle of Badr, there occurred 'The Affair of the Qaynuqa'. The Qaynuqa was one of the three Jewish tribes who felt their power threatened by the new politics of Medina. Muhammad was also disappointed that despite the similarities in the two religions, the Jews had shown no inclination to convert to Islam. One high spirited Qaynuqa man had harassed a Bedouin girl by ripping off her skirt. A passing Muslim intervened to rescue the girl, and in the brawl the Jew was killed, as was the Muslim. The opposition to Muhammad was led by Abdullah ibn-Ubayy, who took the side of the Jewish tribe, and in the play of power politics, severe action was taken against the Qaynuqa, who were ordered to leave Medina, taking only what they could carry. The leftover property of the Qaynuqa was to be divided among the Muslims. The exiles from Mecca had now in turn, exiled others.

The second battle was at Mount Uhud where an army of a thousand Muslims was defeated by the 10,000 troops of Abu Sufyan and his allies. In this battle, Abu Sufyan showed that he was a better leader than the boorish Abu Jahl. Cool and competent, his strategy was faultless, unlike the manic aggression of his wife, Hind. Hind wanted revenge for her father and her brother who were both killed by the famous warrior Hamza, the uncle of Muhammad. She had promised freedom to Wahshi, the Ethiopian slave whose skill with the javelin was unmatched. Like a panther, Wahshi stalked Hamza till he found the moment to hurl his javelin and slay his prey.

A key role in winning the battle was played by the brilliant young commander of the Meccan cavalry, Khalid bin Waleed. Later, Khalid was to become a Muslim, join Muhammad's army and earn renown as 'The Sword of Allah' and the conqueror of Syria.

Muhammad himself was badly injured as a savage blow to the head split his lip, broke his nose and gashed his forehead. Believing him to be dead, the Muslims fled. However, Muhammad was not dead, but the seriousness of the wound caused him severe pain and splitting headaches for the rest of his life.

As the victorious Meccans plundered the dead and dying, the savage Hind searched out the body of Hamza, ripped out his liver, and screaming with joy, stuffed it into her mouth and ate it. All were shocked, including her husband, Abu Sufyan, who disowned her savage act of revenge: 'Some of your dead have been mutilated. I neither commanded this nor forbade it, and it neither gave me pleasure nor saddened me.' He ordered a return to Mecca, saying, 'Wars go by turns. This has been our day for your day.'

The Muslims were disheartened after the defeat at Uhud, but unforeseen events changed the mood. Some members of the second Jewish tribe, the Banu'n-Nadir, planned to assassinate Muhammad, and the Muslims retaliated, leading to the expulsion of the tribe and the plunder of their property. The excitement of battle with the Banu'n-Nadir, victory and the booty that resulted, revitalized the enthusiasm of the Muslims.

The third encounter was 'The Battle of the Trench' when Abu Sufyan attacked Medina in 627. Muhammad defended Medina with a trench which was an innovative tactic that stopped the Meccans and resulted in an impasse with only a handful of casualties. It was suspected that the last Jewish tribe, the Qureyz, was secretly preparing an alliance with Abu Sufyan. A few hours after the Meccan army left, the Qureyz were declared enemy and besieged.

Defeated, the Qureyz were subjected to the judgement of Saad ibn-Muad, who had been wounded in the battle and was dying. Saad pronounced his terribly harsh judgement: 'The men shall be killed, the property divided, the women and children made captives.' And it was done. For three days the killing continued, as hundreds were executed and the trenches filled with the bodies. Among those killed was a beautiful Jewish girl who was a friend of Aisha and sat talking to her till her name was called out. She walked, smiling to her death. Aisha described the scene: 'I have never met a more beautiful, good-tempered and kind-hearted woman. When she rose to walk to the execution ground and I told her that they would certainly kill her, she answered, with a smile, that staying alive did not matter to her.'

WIVES OF THE PROPHET

Muhammad had a number of wives—nine at the time of his death. Till Khadija died, she was his only wife, but after her death he had several other marriages:

- Sawda, a widow, who could look after his home and daughters
- Aisha, the daughter of Abu Bakr, and his young favourite
- Hafsa, the daughter of Umar, an educated intellectual and recently widowed; she was a fervent Muslim and assembled the first written *Quran*
- Umm Salama, whose heroic husband had died; beautiful and graceful, she was wooed by Umar and Abu Bakr, both of whom she refused
- Zaynab, Muhammad's beautiful and sophisticated cousin, who was forty years old to his sixty; she was married to Zayd, his adopted son but she divorced him and married The Prophet, subsequent to a Quranic revelation that released them
- There were two other Zaynabs. One was the daughter of a bedouin sheikh, who was also a widow. She lived in The Prophet's household for only a year before her death. Another

was a seventeen-year-old beautiful Jewish girl whose father, brother and husband had all been executed by the Muslims. She was renamed Safiyah
- Jowayriya, the beautiful captive, whom Muhammad offered to ransom and marry
- Umm Habiba, the daughter of Abu Sufyan, an important political marriage which made Abu Sufyan the father-in-law of The Prophet, and warmed the relationship between the former enemies
- Maymuna, sister-in-law of Abu Sufyan and maternal aunt of Khalid bin Waleed; after this marriage, Khalid became a Muslim, joined Muhammad and led the Muslim army to victory and conquest, earning the title of 'Sword of Allah'; Maymuna was also the sister of the wives of The Prophet's uncles, Abbas and Hamza
- Maria the Copt, who bore The Prophet a son, Ibrahim, who died in infancy
- And others—Fatema, Hend, Asma, Habla and Omm Sharik

The Prophet's special marital privileges are set out in sura 33 of the *Quran*. He was permitted more than four wives, the maximum allowed to other believers, and after his death, no other men could marry his widows.

The Prophet's wives gave him joy, comfort and important political connections. But at times, they were also a source of problems. The famous 'affair of the necklace' when Aisha was lost in the desert, and was rescued by the young Safwan, created a controversy and a scandal. When he asked Ali for his advice, Ali replied that there was no shortage of women for The Prophet to marry. The matter was finally settled by the Quranic revelation in sura 24 which established Aisha's innocence. In fact, those who were guilty of spreading the scandal were themselves punished with lashing.

Nine wives meant bickering and rivalry. Finally, when jealousies grew out of hand because of The Prophet's affection for Maria the

Copt, he locked himself on the roof and refused to meet any of them. Panic prevailed, because his marriages supported an important power network in the politics of Mecca and Medina. Finally, he agreed to see Umar, and explained that he was not divorcing any of the ladies but he would not go near them for a month.

HIS FAREWELL PILGRIMAGE

Muhammad's final move on Mecca began with his declaration that he would perform the pilgrimage of Umrah, and he set out with 700 men. The Meccan army blocked him, and the Truce of Hudaibiyyah was negotiated to the effect that for the next ten years, there would be no armed confrontation and the raids on the caravans of Mecca would stop, but the Umrah of The Prophet and his group would be deferred till the following year. So the next year, in February 629, The Prophet, with 2,000 of his followers, entered Mecca. There was no opposition as Mecca's top military commanders, Khalid and Amr, were now Muhammad's generals and Mecca's leader, Abu Sufyan, was now Mohammad's father-in-law. When Abu Sufyan rode out, he was seated on Muhammad's white horse. With him was Muhammad's uncle, Abbas, the banker.

The short meeting was almost relaxed. Muhammad had built bridges by his marital alliances to both Abbas and Abu Sufyan, who accepted Islam, saying, 'I testify that there is no god but God and Muhammad is his messenger.' And it was over. Mecca surrendered, an amnesty was declared and past sins forgiven. Even Wahshi, the Ethiopian slave who had killed Hamza, converted to Islam and was spared. He tells his own story:

> After the battle of Uhud, I continued to live in Mecca for quite a long time until the Muslims conquered Mecca. I then ran away to Ta'if but Islam soon reached that area as well. I heard that however grave the crime of a person might be, (God) forgave him. I, therefore, reached Muhammad with Shahadatayn on my

lips. Muhammad saw me and said, 'Are you the same Wahshi, the Ethiopian?' I replied in the affirmative. Thereupon he said, 'How did you kill Hamza?' I gave an account of the matter.

Wahshi was forgiven but Hind was livid, and abused and publically humiliated her husband for his surrender, but finally she submitted and was forgiven and her past sins forgotten. So much so that Muhammad even took her son, Muawiya, as his own secretary, in recognition of his capabilities. Muawiya was later promoted to the rank of governor of Syria, became the fifth caliph, and went on to found the first dynasty of Islam, the Umayyad.

Another man lucky to escape death was Abdollah bin Abi Sarh, a foster brother of Othman, who kept him hidden for several days, and then brought him to Muhammad for pardon. When Abdollah professed Islam, Muhammad was silent. He later explained, 'His Islam was not voluntary but from fear.' But he was spared, and years later, Othman, during his caliphate, appointed Abdollah as commander of the Arab invasion of North Africa and later, governor of Egypt.

Muhammad then entered the Kaaba, accompanied by Bilal, Othman and his adopted grandson, Usamah. Paintings of Mary and child and of Abraham were protected, but all else was removed, and the idols were destroyed.

In the year that Muhammad conquered Mecca, the Emperor Heraclius defeated the Persian Empire in a series of dazzling campaigns and took Jerusalem, returning the true cross to its home. At that time, Heraclius's victory seemed the more important, but history was to show that it was Muhammad who was to change the world forever.

After fifteen days, Muhammad left and returned to Medina, which was to remain his home and his capital till the time of his death. In 632, Muhammad made his farewell pilgrimage—his last visit to Mecca—and established the ritual of the Haj forever. He made his farewell sermon to the crowds, which encapsulates some of the main principles of Islam:

- Regard the life and property of every Muslim as a sacred trust.
- Return the goods entrusted to you, to their rightful owners.
- Hurt no one so that no one may hurt you.
- God has forbidden you to charge riba (interest). Your capital, however, is yours to keep.
- You will neither inflict nor suffer inequity.
- You have certain rights with regard to your women, but they also have rights over you. Treat your women well and be kind to them for they are your partners and your committed helpers.
- Every Muslim is the brother of another Muslim, and Muslims constitute one brotherhood.
- Do not stray from the path of righteousness after I am gone.
- I leave behind me two things—the *Quran* and my example, the Sunnah—and if you follow these you will never go astray.

Muhammad returned home, and in June, collapsed with a splitting headache and a fever which burned him for ten days. He lay in the room of his beloved wife Aisha, where he died, his head on her lap. His last words were, 'Lord, grant me pardon.'

2

Inheritors of The Prophet's Legacy

Sayings of Abu Bakr:

'If you want to control other people, first control yourself.'
 'Without knowledge action is useless, and knowledge without action is futile.'
 'Do not follow vain desires; for verily he who prospers is preserved from lust, greed and anger.'

People were in shock and couldn't believe that Muhammad was dead. Umar was ranting that he would kill anyone who claimed this. But soft, gentle Abu Bakr calmed them down:

> O people. To those who used to worship Muhammad, Muhammad is dead. But for those who used to worship God, God is alive and can never die. Muhammad is but a messenger; messengers the like of whom have passed away before him. Will it be that, when he dies or is slain, you will turn back on your heels?

While Abu Bakr talked of the religious implications of the death, the Medina leaders called a meeting to discuss the political implications, and to select a successor to lead the community. They did not invite the emigrants from Mecca, the Muhajireen. They wanted a leader from among their own. Abu Bakr and Umar entered the meeting and argued that the Muslims were much more than just a Medina community, and only a Quresh would be acceptable, to which the Medina group replied that there should be two leaders, one from Medina and one from Mecca. Abu Bakr proposed Umar and Umar proposed Uthman; fighting broke out. Umar then took the hand of Abu Bakr and pledged allegiance, proposing him as the successor. One by one, everyone accepted; the power struggle was over and Abu Bakr was the new leader.

ABU BAKR: A MAN OF DECISION

Abu Bakr was well qualified to take on the mantle of leadership. He was the first adult male Muslim, an old friend of The Prophet, a businessman who had made a small fortune in trade and had spent most of it in the service of Islam, and a gentle, kind and wise man whose daughter Aisha was the favourite wife of The Prophet after the death of Khadijah. He was a respected elder of the community and a sheikh.

The next day, at the mosque, the succession was formalized as the congregation acclaimed Abu Bakr as the successor, Khalifat Rasul Allah and the deputy of Muhammad. His acceptance speech was stunning in its humility and democratic approach:

> I have been given the authority over you, although I am not the best of you. If I do well, help me; and if I do wrong, set me right. Truth consists of loyalty, and disregard for truth is treachery. The weak among you shall be strong in my eyes until I have secured his rights, if God wills it. Obey me for so long as I obey God and His Messenger. But if I disobey God and His Messenger, you owe me no obedience.

All accepted, except one—Ali—who abstained from taking the oath of allegiance. Ali, the first to accept Islam after Khadijah, the cousin of The Prophet, as close as a son, the son-in-law who had married Fatima, who had lain as a decoy in the bed of The Prophet when the assassins came for him in Mecca; Ali the pure, the brave, who many believed to be the best choice for successor. Ali was not even invited to the deliberations and remained in Aisha's room with the body of The Prophet which he washed and buried where it lay. The seeds of dissention had been sown.

There is no doubt that Ali deserved better treatment than he received. His Shia supporters maintain that he was bypassed and excluded from the new power elite led by Abu Bakr and Umar. Fatima, his wife, was denied a substantial part of her small inheritance. The Messenger of God died without leaving a dinar, a dirham, a sheep or a camel to his name, but they did expect to inherit some land he owned, which Abu Bakr denied them, ruling, 'We do not have heirs; whatever we leave is alms.'

At the centre of power were the two fathers-in-law of Muhammad, Abu Bakr and Umar, and the two sons-in-law, Uthman and Ali. All four, in turn took the caliphate. Abu Bakr's supporters argued that his seniority favoured him—he was sixty to Ali's thirty; his age not only meant wisdom and experience, but also attracted those whose own ambition did not relish waiting out Ali's longer life expectation. They also argued that Islam was not a heredity monarchy. Ali's close relationship as cousin, son-in-law and almost-adopted son of The Prophet worked against him in the democratic egalitarian mood of the time.

With Muhammad gone, the tribes of Arabia decided to break free, not so much from Islam and Islamic practice, as from the taxes that Medina demanded. This rebellion led to the Ridda Wars, the war of apostasy. Abu Bakr took a hard line. He may not have been much as a warrior, but his Islamic fervour was unmatched. In the Battle of Badr, he had come face to face with his son in combat. Years later, his son confessed, 'Dear father, I found you twice under my sword at Badr, but I could not raise my hand because of my love for you.'

Abu Bakr replied, 'If I had had the chance, I would have killed you.'

What Abu Bakr lacked in the ability to fight, he more than made up for in his judgement of men. He selected as his commander, Khalid bin Walid, who was to prove one of the greatest generals in history. The great generals of Europe—Caesar and Alexander—were infantry generals, and Napoleon was an artilleryman. But their achievements in battle were at least matched or even surpassed by the three great generals of Asia—Sebotai, commander of the armies of Genghis Khan and his heirs; Tamerlane (Timur), who created one of the world's largest empires in a lifetime of conquest; and Khalid, whose victories laid the foundation of the empire of Islam. Sebotai, Timur and Khalid were all cavalrymen whose speed and tactics made them invincible.

Khalid was the Achilles of the Muslim army. Flamboyant and an expert both in personal combat and in the skills of command, he was a key figure in defeating The Prophet and the Muslim army at Uhud and later, after his conversion, earned the title of 'Sword of Allah' for his success as commander of the Muslim armies. Khalid led the Muslims to victory in the Ridda Wars, brought all of Arabia under Muslim control in just two years, and then in 637, won the historic Battle of Yarmuk where he totally destroyed the 80,000-strong army of Heraclius, the powerful Byzantine emperor.

Khalid was dramatically described by Amr ibn al-As, the other great Muslim general: 'He is a master of war; a friend of death. He has the dash of a lion and the patience of a cat.'

Abu Bakr, an ardent admirer of Khalid, heaped praise on him unreservedly: 'Women will no longer be able to give births to the like of Khalid bin Walid.'

When Khalid was appointed commander by Abu Bakr, he addressed Abu Ubaydah with humility, 'But for the necessity of obeying the orders of the Caliph, I would never have accepted this command over you. You are much higher than me in Islam.' Abu Ubaydah replied with grace, 'I have received with gladness the letter of Abu Bakr appointing you commander over me. There is no resentment in my heart, for I know your skill in matters of war.'

But Khalid was flawed by arrogance, cruelty and lack of diplomacy. When the false prophet, Mustafa Kemal, amassed a large army at Aqraba against Khalid's troops, the latter scored yet another victory and the field ran red with slaughter. Mustafa Kemal himself was killed by a spear hurled with deadly accuracy by the Ethiopian marksman Wahshi, who later boasted, 'With this spear, I killed the best of men and the worst of men: Hamza and Mustafa Kemal.' The prisoners were ruthlessly executed by Khalid in a three-day massacre remembered as 'The River of Blood.'

Abu Bakr, however, seemed to have no flaws. He dressed simply, lived plainly and accumulated no wealth. He spent his savings in the service of Islam, took only a small salary and when he was short of money he even milked his neighbour's cow for extra cash. He was fair and just, and was democratic in his government style. He was much loved and respected. His instructions to the Muslim armies were lessons in morality and compassion:

> Do not betray; do not carry grudges; do not deceive; do not mutilate; do not kill children; do not kill the elderly; do not kill women. Do not destroy beehives or burn them; do not cut down fruit-bearing trees; do not slaughter sheep, cattle or camels except for food. You will come across people who spend their lives in monasteries; leave them to what they have dedicated their lives... Now advance in the name of God.

But in less than three years, death overtook him. He was sixty-three when he died, the same age as The Prophet. But unlike The Prophet, who did not designate a successor, Abu Bakr clearly named Umar as the man to follow him as the second Caliph.

UMAR: A MAN OF ACTION

> 'His food consisted of barley bread or dates, his drink was water; he preached in a gown that was torn or tattered in twelve places; and a Persian satrap who paid his homage as

to a conqueror, found him asleep among the beggars on the steps of the mosque of the Muslims.'

—Edward Gibbon (About Umar ibn Khattab, in
The History of the Decline and Fall of the Roman Empire)

'Submit to Islam and be safe, or agree to the payment of Jizya, and you and your people will be under our protection, else you will have only yourself to blame for the consequences, for I bring the men who desire death as ardently as you desire life.'

—Khalid bin Walid (In his letter to the
Persian governor, before invading)

Sayings of Hazrat Umar:

'Tribute is better than booty; it lasts longer.'
'The art of warfare depends on wisdom as well as the use of force.'

Umar was a hard man. He was hard on others, and even harder on himself. This stern, austere puritan was amongst history's greatest leaders. Strategist and administrator without equal, he built a civilization and created an empire that endured for a thousand years. For his beliefs he was willing to pay any price. His justice was absolute—no privilege, no favour, and equality for all before the law. When his son was found drunk, the law was mercilessly applied—his son was lashed; eighty strokes without remission. The lashing killed the boy.

Money, luxury and even comfort meant nothing to him. He spurned beds, tents and mattresses but would sleep on the desert floor under his patched cloak. He allowed himself two new garments a year, one for summer and one for winter. When he was asked to fix an allowance for himself on his appointment as Caliph, he formed a committee with the clear instruction that his salary should be fixed at a level equal to the average income of his people.

Once when he went to review his victorious army, his four great generals respectfully rode out to greet the Caliph, who was still wrapped in his tattered old cloak. Expecting praise for having destroyed the army of the Byzantine Empire, and having conquered Syria and Palestine, they were shocked at Umar's rage at their smart outfits: 'Do you come to me dressed like that? Have you changed so much in just two years? You all deserve to be dismissed in disgrace!' In reply, Khalid tore apart his parade cloak to reveal his armour, dented and slashed in four years of continuous fighting for the faith. But with Umar, there was no such thing as a good excuse; he was only interested in the bottom line.

When Umar took over as Caliph, Ali acknowledged his authority, and in a move for reconciliation, he married the youngest widow of Abu Bakr and adopted her son, the young half-brother to Aisha. He also gave his daughter, Umm Kulthum, in marriage to Umar, which cemented their relationship as father-in-law and son-in-law. Umar was not just the father-in-law of The Prophet, he was also his grandson-in-law! With Ali on board, Umar's authority was absolute and he could focus on implementing his vision.

Umar's style of government set the blueprint for Muslim leaders through the centuries that followed. The empire was divided into provinces ruled by governors, and the provinces into districts ruled by sub-governors—in all, a hundred top administrators, all carefully selected by Umar himself. Umar believed in hands-on administration—not just making the policies, but also making sure that implementation was up to the mark. His famous secret night forays into the streets set the example for Harun al-Rashid, the famous Abbasid ruler who also features as one of the main characters in *One Thousand and One Nights*, and even in current times, for Sheikh Mohammad of Dubai and Shahbaz Sharif of Pakistan, both top quality administrators, whose night-time personal checks on implementation are a recognized part of their government style.

Umar developed his institutions of government—the standing army, the police, the system of jurisprudence and justice, the administrative courts to control the bureaucracy, the Diwan or treasury to organize payment of state grants to deserving citizens, and his famed intelligence service to ensure that the Caliph knew all that was going on. His methods have inspired Muslim rulers across the centuries. Saladin, the hero of the crusades, was inspired by his humility and selflessness; Sher Shah Suri, in medieval India, was motivated by his justice; the oil rich Arab kings and sheikhs followed his system of distributing wealth to their people; and his intelligence network has wide imitation.

Above all, Umar is remembered for his conquests. It was under his rule that the Muslims spread out of Arabia and defeated the two great empires of the time—the Byzantines who controlled the eastern remnant of the Roman empire, and the Sassanids of Persia, with their vast lands and fabled wealth. The conversion of all of Arabia to Islam had created a new problem—the Umma or Muslim brotherhood closed the door on the traditional activity of raiding that provided supplementary income in a land devoid of agriculture, for a Muslim was forbidden to covet the property of, or harm another Muslim. Economic necessity pushed the Muslims to look beyond Arabia and luck ensured that their timing was perfect. The two great empires had exhausted themselves with never-ending warfare, and small, new Muslim armies cut through them like a hot knife through butter. The Muslims had no new military technology, but their commitment and passion were unmatched. Where others retreated in the face of danger, the Muslims welcomed martyrdom in battle as a sure way to heaven. The Muslim generals quickly acquired an expertise that established them as lords of war as they blazed their way across the pages of history—Khalid bin Walid, Amr bin al-As, Sa'ad bin Abu Waqqas, Uqba bin Nafi, Tariq bin Ziyad and Mohammad bin Qasim. But above all, it was luck and perfect timing, for it was the time for the old era to end and a new age to begin.

THE CONQUEST OF SYRIA

When Umar became Caliph, one of his first acts was to remove the commander-in-chief of the Muslim army, Khalid bin Walid. This came as a surprise since Khalid had already established his reputation as the unmatched expert in the art of war. Khalid was a hero of battle and the Muslims believed that they could not lose as long as they were led by him. Umar wanted to establish that it was not Khalid, but God who gave victory. It was also felt that Khalid's arrogance deserved a comeuppance. Umar and Khalid had fallen out many years before, when they met in the ring of the Mecca Wrestling Championship as young men. Khalid, the young 'Achilles', was dwarfed by the giant Umar, who towered above him and was recognized as the favourite to win. But as the signal to start the match sounded, Khalid moved like a panther and threw Umar. A loud crack was heard as Umar's leg bone snapped, and the fight was over; Khalid was the new champion. Umar walked with a limp for the rest of his life as a reminder of his defeat.

Khalid was replaced by the revered Abu Ubaydah. Khalid was undoubtedly the better general, but Abu Ubaydah was the more respected Muslim. But even after his demotion, Khalid continued to play the key role in battle due to the wise acquiescence of his commander-in-chief. Khalid was the star in the taking of Damascus, the hero of the battle of Yarmuk and a leading player in the conquest of Homs and Chalkis. In the battle of Maraj al debaj, he killed the son-in-law of Heraclius and took his daughter captive. Heraclius wrote to him, 'You have killed my son-in-law and captured my daughter. You have won and got away safely. I now ask you for my daughter. Either return her to me on payment of ransom or give her to me as a gift, for honour is a strong element in your character.' Khalid, true to style, replied, 'Take her as a gift, there shall be no ransom.'

Khalid accepted his dismissal and humiliation with grace and settled in Chalkis, where he died. Eventually, Umar relented and admitted that he had been wrong about Khalid: 'May God bless the soul of Abu Bakr, he knew men's character much better than I. He put Khalid in the right place.'

Yarmuk was the Waterloo of Heraclius's Byzantine Empire. A month of fighting minor engagements culminated in a decisive battle. At Waterloo, rain had given an unexpected advantage to Wellington's army; at Yarmuk, a sandstorm gave the advantage to the Muslim army. Khalid captured the old Roman bridge, cutting off the chance of retreat by the Christians, and a mighty slaughter followed. It was more than defeat; it was total destruction—the 20,000 Muslim army, with Khalid in charge of the tactical command, had destroyed the 80,000-man army of Heraclius; Syria and Palestine were taken.

But Jerusalem resisted and the patriarch, Sophronius, insisted that he would surrender only to Omar himself. The Caliph arrived not as a conqueror but as a pilgrim, his eyes humble with respect. When the prayer was called, he declined to pray in the church but instead moved out into the porch. He later explained that he had done this to spare the Holy Sepulchre, which would otherwise have been converted into a mosque. The Covenant of Umar guaranteed Christians and Jews freedom of religion.

During its long history, Jerusalem has been destroyed twice, besieged twenty-three times, attacked fifty-two times and captured forty-four times. Omar's conquest of Jerusalem stands in stark contrast to the savage reconquest by the Crusaders, centuries later, with scenes of slaughter and cannibalism described by a commander of the Crusaders in a letter to the Pope: 'In Ma'arra, our troops boiled pagan adults alive in cooking pots; they impaled Muslims on spits and devoured them grilled.' Jerusalem was taken for the second time by the Muslims under Saladin, whose conquest has again gone down in history for its chivalry, kindness and concern for the conquered when he paid from his own money, the ransoms of prisoners who were unable to arrange the funds for their release.

In response to Sephronius' demand to surrender personally to Umar, the Muslim general Shurahbil suggested that Khalid impersonate Umar since he looked a bit like him. But Khalid's fame worked against him and he was recognized; Sephronius refused to negotiate.

Three years after Yarmuk, in 639, famine and plague struck. Damascus became a danger zone, so Umar wanted Abu Ubaydah safe and out of there. Knowing his chivalrous nature and that he would never leave his people, Umar veiled his purpose and simply ordered him to come 'on an urgent affair'. But Abu Ubaydah was not fooled and chose to stay and share the danger with his people. Both he and his son died of the plague, as also did Yazid, the able son of Abu Sufyan.

The famed poet, Omar Khayyam, described the world as a 'chequer board of nights and days, where destiny with men for pieces plays'. It was the destiny of Abu Ubaydah and Yazid to die of the plague. It was the destiny of Muawiya to fill the vacancy and be promoted to commander. He went on to become the fifth Caliph and the founder of the Umayyad dynasty.

IRAQ AND IRAN

In the East, a complicated succession struggle after the death of the great king, Chosroes, in 628, finally put Yazdgard on the Persian throne in 632, the year when The Prophet had died. He was assisted by his fabled general, Rustam, a fine warrior, astute and intelligent, who inflicted a terrible defeat on the Muslims at the Battle of the Bridge, where the commander of the Muslims was killed by one of Rustam's elephants.

But nothing could break Umar's determination, and he sent a new commander, Sa'ad bin Abi Waqqas, who had fought beside The Prophet at the Battle of Badr. Sa'ad led the 30,000-strong Muslim army at the battle of Qadisiya, to meet the Persian force of twice as many soldiers under the battle-hardened General Rustam. The luxury and rich clothes of the Persians made a vivid contrast with the poor ragged Muslims, contemptuous of wealth, unsophisticated and fearless. The defeat at Qadisiya broke the back of the Persian

Empire. Rustam was killed, but the emperor, Yazdegerd, fled with what remained of his army. He was to resist the Muslim onslaught for another twenty years, until finally he too was killed.

Umar directed operations from Medina in his own unique style. When Hermuzan, a captured Persian commander was brought to him dressed in all his finery and jewels, Umar was sleeping in the corner of the mosque in his usual simple clothes. The Persian, surprised, asked, 'Where are his guards?' He was told, 'He has none.' They sat to talk, and when Umar asked the Persian his view of events, he replied that God had switched sides and now favoured the Arabs. Umar replied that the real reason was that previously the Persians had been united, while the Arabs had not.

As the Muslim armies swept through the vast lands of Persia, there was little resistance from the local population. The peasants had little affinity with the aristocrats at court, and the Muslims were not seen as a danger or a threat. They did not massacre townspeople and villagers, they did not seize their houses or their lands, they did not interfere with their religions or customs, and they did not even settle among them. They demanded only that taxes be paid, and that people did not aid their enemies. There was no forced conversion to Islam and the Muslims built themselves new garrison towns, Kufa and Basra, where they lived separate from the locals. This kept the locals safe from plunder and the Muslims safe from corruption and decadence. Umar discouraged farming and forbade property acquisition. The new deal gave greater religious freedom and lower taxes. People were comfortable with the change.

However, one man who was less comfortable with the change was the commander, Sa'ad bin Abi Waqqas, who was overworked and swarmed by commotion and people in his new palace in the city centre. To secure some privacy he built a wooden door with a lock. When Umar heard about this, he had the door burned down, and reprimanded Sa'ad for putting a barrier between himself and his people. Elitism and the VIP culture were out; equality and humility were in!

EGYPT

Today Egypt is a relatively poor, overpopulated Muslim country of 85 million people. In the sixth and seventh centuries, when the Muslims arrived, Egypt was a rich Christian nation where the plague had reduced the population to 3 million. The man who conquered and changed the destiny of Egypt was the remarkable and brilliant Amr ibn al-As, general, administrator, adventurer and romantic. If Khalid was the Achilles of the early Islamic conquests, Amr was the wily Ulysses.

Amr's mother was a slave girl of stunning beauty. She became a renowned concubine with several important and powerful lovers. Some called her a prostitute, and many questioned who Amr's true father was. He was bold in battle, astute in strategy, cunning as a fox and ever ready to gamble for the highest stakes to seize the opportunity. Always the negotiator, he agreed to become a Muslim and join Muhammad 'on condition that my past sins be pardoned and he give me an active part in affairs.' When the Muslim armies burst out of Arabia in conquest under Umar, Amr decided that it was Egypt that he wanted and he set out with a small force of 4,000 men to conquer it. Umar, fearing that the risk was too great, sent a letter suggesting they turn back if they had not yet entered Egypt, but Amr guessed what was written in the letter, and refrained from opening it, till they were in Egypt and it was too late to turn back.

Amr, with his small force, conquered Egypt and resolved that he would keep it at all cost. Egypt was his destiny. He captured Babylon; and when he took Alexandria, 'Queen of Cities', he sent his excited letter to the Caliph, 'I have taken a city of which I can only say that it contains 4,000 palaces, 4,000 baths, 400 theatres, 1,200 greengrocers and 40,000 Jews.'

Amr wanted to make Alexandria his capital, but Umar was firm in his order that the Muslim troops stay away from big city temptations. Amr had put down his camp at Fustat. The story goes that he had left his tent standing because a small bird had built its nest and Fustat became the new Muslim capital, till the Fatimids built Cairo nearby. Umar also strictly forbade the victorious Muslims from taking any land from the locals—even Amr was refused permission for land to build his palace. The Egyptians were happy to exchange their Byzantine and Persian masters for the Muslims. They appreciated the fairness, justice and security that the new rulers gave them.

Amr's problems came rather from home. Umar sent his agents to curb Amr, with his blunt message: 'I have had enough experience of dishonest officials and my suspicion has been aroused against you.' Uthman dismissed him and gave the governorship to his foster brother and ordered Amr back to Medina. Ali gave the governorship of Egypt to his stepson, Muhammad bin Abu Bakr. But Amr came back and defeated him. Muhammad was killed, his body sown up in the skin of an ass and he was thrown into a fire. His sister Aisha, the widow of The Prophet, was inconsolable, cursed Amr in her daily prayers and never again ate roast meat.

But Amr always found his way back. He was governor of Egypt under Umar, governor under Uthman and governor under Muawiya.

Amr did not stop at Egypt. With his young nephew Uqba bin Nafi, they moved through North Africa, conquering as far as Tripoli. Later, Uqba went much further, earning the title of Conqueror of Africa.

Egypt was not Amr's only claim to fame. When he was moved out of Egypt by Uthman in 647, he allied himself with Muawiya as his most valuable advisor and general. He led Muawiya's army against Ali in the civil war for the caliphate, and played the key part with his devious strategy as arbitrator, turning the decision against Ali. If Ali had denied him his Egypt, he would deny Ali the caliphate. After defeating Muhammad bin Abu Bakr, he again took the seat of governorship. He died in office.

In two years, Amr had not only conquered Egypt twice, but he had presided over a massive political change, which was as permanent as it was swift. Christian Egypt became Arab–Muslim Egypt, with a new language, new religion and a new culture. But the seeds of harmony were sown to ensure that the Copts and Muslim could live together in peace for a thousand years. Amr was not an oppressive predator in Egypt; rather he followed the advice of Umar: 'Tribute is much better than booty; for it continues, whereas the spoil soon vanishes as if it had not been.'

MEDINA

Even as the empire spread, power lay in Medina, the seat of the Caliph. The power of the armies and the victorious generals was overshadowed by the immense power of the Caliph himself. Sa'ad, the hero of Qadisiya, was removed for cutting short the customary prayers. Amr, the master of Egypt, was publically humiliated and his honesty questioned. And the great Khalid, was removed from command and tried, for bathing in wine! In the time of Umar, it was dangerous to be a hero and dangerous to be a victorious general who was also popular.

The source of Umar's total power was his legitimacy. He was the sole candidate nominated by Abu Bakr, and every act of his demonstrated his total commitment to Islam. He was untainted by love of material possessions or personal desires. It was accepted that self-interest played no part in his decisions and all obeyed him without question or reserve. He embodied the principles of justice, simplicity and Islam.

By this time, the economy of the Arabs was imperial. As in other empires that followed, income was not determined by productivity but by the importance given to the individual by the empire. The revenues of the Muslims were derived from conquest, from tribute, plunder, and taxes on the conquered. These revenues were spent on administration costs, military expenses and a stipend for the Arabs. The revenues were vast, but every last dirham in the treasury was always spent—Umar did not believe in building up reserves. The register of those entitled to a stipend was known as the Divan, which listed the categories of those entitled—ordinary soldiers (200 dirhams each), veterans from the Ridda Wars (3,000 dirhams), survivors of the battle of Badr (5,000 dirhams) and wives of The Prophet (10,000 dirhams; except Aisha who received 12,000 dirhams). The Arabs were a favoured nation, and the citizens of Mecca and Medina—the original Muslims—a privileged super-class. Every conversion meant one less person to tax, and one more person to subsidize; this was enough reason to discourage aggressive conversion to Islam.

In 644, after ten years as Caliph, Umar was stabbed and killed by a Persian slave named Abu Lulu in the mosque, as he started his prayers. There was no reason for the assassination, and the slave killed himself. Before he died, Umar appointed a committee of six to select the next caliph from amongst themselves. The two most prominent members of the committee were the two sons-in-law of The Prophet, Ali and Uthman.

UTHMAN: A MAN OF COMPASSION

Even before Umar passed away, the electors were in such heated discussion that Umar asked them to stop and let him die in peace. Once the burial was done, the negotiations continued. Of the six electors, Talha was away travelling, Ali and Uthman were candidates, and Zubair and Sa'ad each supporting one or the other; so the decision lay with Abd al Rahman, who offered to stand down as a candidate if they agreed to abide by his decision. He selected Uthman as the third Caliph.

There were two main reasons for selecting Uthman. Firstly, his age (at seventy, he was a respected elder and, Ali being much younger, could follow later). And secondly his character—soft, as compared with the rigid idealist, Ali. After ten years of Umar's hard rule, the public mood was for the relaxed government style that Uthman offered rather than another tension-ridden period of empire-building under Ali.

Uthman was an easy man to like. Handsome, charming and generous, he was born with a silver spoon. He inherited millions and multiplied them. An astute businessman, he had the golden touch. If

Ali was the son-in-law of The Prophet, Uthman had also married two of Muhammad's daughters. He was not much of a warrior, but his skill in administration and the business of government were recognized and respected. He was literate and cultivated and stood out amongst the early Muslims who were passionate but poor.

The third Caliph was already an old man when he took office, and was eighty-two when he was assassinated. His twelve-year rule was divided into six good years and six bad years. His luck changed at the end of the first six years when he lost the ring of The Prophet which slipped off his finger and fell into a well.

Uthman quickly changed the austere social structure that the intense Umar had maintained. Clothes became more fashionable; houses more palatial; and a new aristocracy emerged, more focused on money than religion. Under Umar, all the Muslims of Mecca and Medina were equals, a privileged but disciplined elite. Under Uthman, his relations, the Umayyads, were more equal than others. Under Umar, law stood above all; under Uthman, mercy trumped law. Soon after Uthman's accession, Obeidallah, the son of Umar, seeking to take revenge for his father's assassination on mere suspicion alone, rashly killed a Persian prince and a Christian slave, without any evidence of their guilt. In his trial, Ali proposed death for killing a Muslim without justification but Uthman allowed money-compensation in lieu of blood, and then paid the money himself on behalf of Obeidallah. Where one of Umar's sons had been killed by the punishment that Umar enforced, the other was spared by Uthman's clemency and refusal to punish.

In the first six years, Uthman streamlined the administration, improved the revenue system, built up the treasury and reserves, developed infrastructure and continued the conquests. Herat, Merv, Balkh and Kabul were taken. The Persian King was killed and the first written *Quran* was finalized.

The one flaw in Uthman's style of government was his favouritism of his Umayyad relatives, some of whom were very unsavoury characters but nevertheless got all the top jobs. His half-brother

Abdallah was given Egypt, despite the fact that he was excluded from the general amnesty granted by The Prophet after the conquest of Mecca. His cousin Marwan was appointed the powerful Secretary of State, despite the fact that he was a last minute convert whose father had been exiled by The Prophet. Walid ibn Uqba, another half-brother, was given Kufa, and had to be removed for coming to the morning prayers smelling of alcohol; he was sentenced to eighty lashes, but no one could be found ready to administer the punishment, so he was forgiven. Two Umayyad sons-in-law were given command of Kufa and Basra, another Umayyad was made Inspector of markets in Medina, and most powerful of all, Muawiya, was governor of Syria. The Umayyads had it all, and people didn't like it. Resentment, jealousy and discontent spread like cancer through the Muslim communities, and particularly through the garrison towns—Fustat in Egypt, and Kufa and Basra in Iraq—where the soldiers watched the Umayyads accumulate vast fortunes with the conspicuous consumption of the new super-rich.

Amr, the wily general, tried to persuade Uthman to change his ways: 'O Prince of the faithful, you have subjected the whole nation to the Beni Umayya. You have gone astray and so have the people. Either make up your mind to be just or give up the job.' Ali also tried to reason with the Caliph, but it was no use. Uthman defended himself: 'I have done my best; and as for the men ye blame me for, did not Umar himself appoint Mughira to Kufa, and if ibn Aamir be my kinsman, is he the worse for that?' 'No,' replied Ali, 'but Umar kept his lieutenants in order, and when they did wrong, he punished them; whereas you treat them softly because they are your kinsmen.' Even Muawiya, appointed by Umar, but controlled totally by his master, grew bold with Uthman, who could never command the authority and respect of his predecessor.

The influential family members amassed fortunes by feeding off the ever growing state treasury. Handouts, land grants and interest-free loans to finance their acquisitions fired the resentment of ordinary people against the cronyism and nepotism surrounding the Caliph.

Conspiracies and rebellions grew.

In 656, dissidents from the three garrisons of Fustat, Kufa and Basra marched on Medina. The rebellion had begun. The rebels from Egypt demanded that Mohammad, the young son of Abu Bakr, be given the governorship. Under pressure, Uthman agreed and the rebels prepared to march home. It seemed that Uthman had defused the crisis.

But an unexpected twist of events showed that when fate intervenes, the plans of men are like dust in the face of a storm. A rider coming from the palace was seized by the returning rebels, who, when searched, revealed a letter with the Caliph's seal addressed to his governor in Egypt demanding the arrest and execution of the rebels. The column turned back to Medina to confront the Caliph about the double-cross. It is suspicious that the other two columns, from Kufa and Basra, turned back for Medina at the same time. Was this a strategy further hidden conspiracy?

Uthman denied knowledge of the letter, and whatever his weaknesses, he was never a liar. The rebels shouted insults at the Caliph, calling him a liar and an incompetent old man. They demanded that he resign; if he refused, they would kill him.

Uthman behaved calmly and with dignity; but he refused to resign. The mood in the city was ominous; the situation simmering with pent up rage. The next Friday, as he spoke in the mosque, the Caliph was attacked with stones and knocked unconscious. He was carried home, where he was barricaded in by the rebels. As the assassins moved in for the kill, Uthman did not resist, but peacefully read his *Quran* as he waited for the inevitable.

The assassins burst into the room of the Caliph, Mohammad bin Abu Bakr among them. Mohammad seized the Caliph's beard, crying, 'The Lord abase thee, thou old dotard.' 'Let my beard go,' Uthman replied calmly, 'I am no dotard, but the Caliph whom they call Uthman.' And the swords were plunged into him as into Caesar, centuries before, and as into Becket, centuries later. The blood of the Caliph of Islam drenched red the pages of his *Quran*. His young wife,

Naila, threw herself on her husband to protect what was left of his body and a sword sliced off two of her fingers. Again and again, the assassins plunged their blades into the body of the Caliph, till finally he lay dead. Then they departed for the treasury. That night, the Caliph was buried, not in the graveyard but in a field—a neglected Jewish burial ground.

ALI: A MAN OF IDEAS AND WORDS

Sayings of Ali bin Abi Taleb:

'Have love for your friend up to a limit for it is possible he may turn into your enemy some day; and hate your enemy up to a limit for it is possible he may turn into your friend some day.'

'Every breath you take is a step towards death.'

'Do not raise your children the way your parents raised you; they were born for a different time.'

'One who acquires power cannot avoid favouritism.'

'One who comes into power often oppresses.'

'Be generous but not extravagant; be frugal but not miserly.'

'There is no wealth like knowledge, no poverty like ignorance.'

'Do not be hard lest you be broken; do not be too soft lest you be squeezed.'

'A poor man is like a foreigner in his own country.'

'A wise man first thinks and then speaks; a fool first speaks and then thinks.'

'Avarice dulls the faculties of judgement and wisdom.'

Abu Bakr was a man of decision; Umar, a man of action; Uthman, a man of compassion; and Ali was a man of ideas and words. Ali was honourable, brave, sincere, honest, selfless and wise; but by worldly standards, his career was not a great success. Expected to succeed The Prophet, he was passed over time for twenty-four years, till he finally became Caliph in 656. His rule lasted less than five years and was scarred by civil war, strife and division till his assassination. Great men need luck; Ali was unlucky.

In his short rule, Ali fought a civil war against Aisha, Talha and Zubayr; he fought an insurrection by Muawiya, the Umayyad governor of Syria, who became Caliph; and battles against the Kharijites, the religious fanatics, one of whom finally killed him. Through it all, the stigma of the regicides who had killed the caliph, Uthman—despite his innocence—haunted him.

When he was made Caliph, Ali was fifty-five years old and no longer the young hero of the early battles of Islam. He had put on weight, was balding and after the death of Fatima, The Prophet's daughter, had taken many wives from whom he had twenty-six children.

When Ali took the caliphate, the immediate pressure was to punish those guilty of the assassination of Uthman—the regicides. But it was easier said than done. Ali was helpless: 'Just now they are beyond our power.' So he denounced the work of the regicides as high treason, but could not take steps to punish them.

His first mistake was the decision to change the governors, the powerful administrators who controlled the territories of the empire. The wily Moghira was a master strategist of political manoeuvre; he advised Ali to hold off at least till he had consolidated his position. The practical son of Abbas, a valued supporter of Ali, pleaded to at least keep Muawiya in place for the time being: 'When thou art firmly seated, depose him if thou wilt.' 'Never,' replied Ali. 'He shall have naught but the sword from me'. 'Thou art brave,' Ibn Abbas replied, 'but innocent of the craft of war; hath not The Prophet himself said, "What is war but a game of deception?"' This decision, to go after Muawiya, was to divide his territory and cost him his caliphate.

When Ali demanded Muawiya's resignation, Muawiya made no reply. The bloodstained shirt of Uthman and the severed fingers of his wife stirred emotions to a frenzy in Damascus, with the demand for punishment of the regicides. They now blamed Ali for the murder. An army of 60,000 was ready to take revenge against Ali, who had no option but to announce an expedition against Muawiya.

Seeing an opportunity to unseat Ali, Talha and Zubayr made their move. Though they had sworn allegiance to the new caliph, each harboured his own ambitions for the crown. It was not difficult to enlist Aisha to their cause. She preferred Zubayr rather than Ali as Caliph. They proceeded with their army to Basra.

Ali tried to negotiate, but was unsuccessful. The rebels demanded vengeance against the executioners of Uthman. The two armies joined the battle; Ayesha, on a camel, stirred them on. Zubayr and Talha were both killed, but Ayesha fought on, fearless, as arrows rained down on her, one wounding her arm. Finally Ali sent her brother Muhammad to persuade her to stand down. Over 10,000 Muslims died in the Battle of the Camel—a tragic day. Ali forbade loot or taking of prisoners. Friend and foe alike mourned Zubayr, who had saved the life of The Prophet on the field of Uhud. Aisha retired to Medina where she spent the rest of her days. She remained a celebrity and a source of hadith, dying at the age of sixty-six.

In Egypt, Muawiya outplayed Ali. Cays was Ali's representative in Egypt, a capable and loyal lieutenant. Muawiya tried to win him over, but he was committed to Ali. Muawiya next kindled Ali's suspicion of Cays, and Ali sacked him and replaced him with Muhammad bin Abu Bakr. Muawiya then made an ally of the great general Amr, who was only too ready to return to Egypt and defeat Muhammad and the pro-Ali forces. Muawiya's influence spread over Syria, which included Palestine, Jordan, Lebanon and also the rich province of Egypt.

In Kufa, Ali prepared his army, which was 50,000-strong. In Damascus, Muawiya was ready with an even larger army led by the wily general Amr. They met on the field of Siffin. Once again, Ali tried to negotiate a compromise; once more, Muawiya demanded punishment of the regicides. Negotiations failed and the armies joined in the battle. Ali was a great and brave war general, and after weeks of fighting, victory seemed within his grasp. Muawiya, searching for a way to avoid defeat, suggested to Amr a match of champions, to which Amr countered that Muawiya should challenge Ali. But Muawiya was no fool, and pointed out that in such bouts, Ali always killed his challenger; he was not ready to fight him. Amr then suggested a ruse, that their lancers enter the fray with leaves of the *Quran* fixed to their spears, crying 'Let God decide'. This provided justification to cease fighting and the troops endorsed the call for arbitration. Each side would appoint an arbitrator and the two arbitrators would decide the matter according to the principles of Islam.

Pandemonium prevailed and Ali's troops insisted on Abu Musa as their arbitrator. Ali was shocked—Abu Musa was in disgrace for his disloyalty. Muawiya chose Amr. The odds were already stacked against Ali. Even the document agreeing to arbitration was worded to show parity; it ignored the fact that Ali was the Caliph and Muawiya, merely one of his governors. By cunning, Amr had already turned defeat on the battlefield into victory on the negotiation table.

As they waited for the arbitration to unfold, uncertainty prevailed throughout the empire. Finally, at Duma, Abu Musa and Amr met before a large crowd of spectators to decide the future of Islam. Several names were discussed as compromise candidates, but all were rejected. Then Abu Musa proposed that both Ali and Muawiya be deposed and the people elect whoever they will as Caliph. Amr agreed, and the two umpires came before the spectators to announce their decision. Abu Musa spoke first, saying that in the interests of keeping the peace, he proposed both Ali and Muawiya be deposed. But then to his surprise, Amr announced, 'He has deposed his fellow and I too depose him. But as for Muawiya, him I confirm.' Abu Musa was thunderstruck: 'What could I do? He agreed with me, then swerved aside.' But the damage was done. There was no going back. In the words of Omar Khayyam,

> 'The Moving Finger writes;
> and, having writ,
> Moves on: nor all thy Piety nor Wit Shall lure it back to cancel half a Line,
> Nor all thy Tears wash out a Word of it.'

There were now two caliphs—Ali in the East; Muawiya in the West. Back home, there was more trouble brewing for Ali. The Kharijites had stopped their battle at Siffin when Amr sent the *Quran* on lances into the fray and they had imposed Abu Musa as arbitrator on Ali, despite his obvious unsuitability. Now they protested the dual caliphate, saying they would follow only God's lead. They were determined to create true Islamic government or to die in the attempt. Disorder and dissention led to skirmishes and battle, with many fanatics killed in the clashes. The majority was slain, but some survived and these few were determined to take revenge.

Ali and Muawiya settled into a working accommodation, but the fanatics now decided that they must kill both caliphs and also Amr. The conspirators planned the triple assassination for a Friday when all three leaders were to lead the prayers—Ali in Kufa, Muawiya in Damascus and Amr in Fustat in Egypt. The assassins prepared swords dipped in deadly poison and slipped into the mosques.

Amr sent a substitute to lead the prayers. The substitute was killed, Amr escaped and the assassin was caught and killed. Muawiya was stabbed and the poison went into his bloodstream, but timely and expert medical help saved his life and he survived and recovered. Ali, unlucky as always, was stabbed and the wound was fatal. Before dying, Ali told his son Hasan, 'If I die, his life is forfeit; but see that thou mutilate him not, for that is forbidden by The Prophet.' Since he was clearly dying, they asked him if he wanted his son to succeed him. He replied, 'I do not command it, neither do I forbid it.' He died aged sixty, after a hard life of devotion to honour, a wise and noble man, but a sad reminder that personal virtue and capability are not enough if luck is lacking.

3

The Umayyads

'When his friends expressed surprise at the vastness of his gifts to his opponents, he told them, "A war costs infinitely more".'

—Muawiya

'Al-Hasan (Ali's son) succeeded him, and God knows, he was no man for the job: money was offered to him and he accepted it. Muawiya intrigued with him, and said "I'll appoint you my successor after me", and that deceived him, and he divested himself of the office he held and handed it over to Muawiya.'

—al-Tabari

The rivalry between the Hashemite and the Umayyads endured for three and a half centuries. The two families were cousins and both descended from the patriarch Abd Manaf, whose sons Abd Shams and Hashim fathered the two branches of the family. The Umayyad branch was the more successful—richer and more powerful. However, all that changed with the Prophethood of Muhammad, who had emerged supreme. But despite the wars and the antagonism, they were not simply enemies. Muhammad had given two of his daughters in marriage to Uthman, a prominent Umayyad, who became the third caliph, and had himself married the daughter of Abu Sufyan, the Umayyad leader. Muawiya, the founder of the Umayyad dynasty was the brother-in-law of The Prophet.

Muhammad bore no grudges; he believed in merit. Despite Hind's atrocious behaviour on the battlefield when she rapaciously ate Hamza's liver, he had no hesitation in empowering her son Muawiya and giving him a key job in his administration. It was not just tragic but also ironic that his Umayyad cousins slaughtered his family at Karbala in their brutal power struggle. Almost a century later, the Hashemites had their revenge when the Abbasids, descended from The Prophet's uncle, Abbas, invited the Umayyads—almost a hundred of them—to dinner, and clubbed them to death; their corpses, together with those wounded but not dead, were covered with a huge carpet and the banquet continued amidst the stench of the dead and the groans of the dying. The Abbasids showed that if the Umayyads were cunning, they were more cunning. With the Abbasids, the Hashim branch of the family moved away from its tradition of piety and demonstrated that they could be as worldly wise and ruthless as success required.

The Umayyad dynasty was significant for four reasons:

- It established monarchy and dynasty over the Islamic revolution.
- It replaced passionate religious fervour with worldly values, ambition for power and wealth, and love of luxury.
- It converted the empire of Islam into the empire of the Arabs, in which Arabic and privilege for the Arabs became a dominant and then a divisive feature.
- It saw the second great phase of conquest, establishing the empire from the Atlantic to the borders of China.

Fourteen caliphs ruled the ninety-year Umayyad dynasty, but seventy years of this period covered the rule of just four of these—Muawiya I, Abd al Malik and Hisham (twenty years each), and Walid (ten years).

Muawiya I was the founder and also the greatest of the Umayyads. The dynasty was a result of his determination to leave the empire to his descendants. But his descendants, the Sufanyids (named after his father Abu Sufyan), were to endure only four years after his death. He was unlucky to have a useless son and heir in Yazid, and a weakling of a grandson in Muawiya II, who hardly ruled for a few months.

Marwan, a cousin, followed as Caliph. He was a cunning man, who was also determined to found his own dynasty. This meant sidelining Khalid, Yazid's son, to clear the way for his own son, Abd al Malik. He devised the clever strategy of marrying the widow of Yazid and indicating that he would promote her son Khalid as crown prince. But his wife, suspecting his sincerity, smothered Marwan with a pillow as he slept. Thus, Marwan secured the dynasty but lost his life after a brief rule of nine months.

Abd al Malik ruled for twenty years and was followed by four of his sons, earning him the title 'Father of Kings'. His eldest son, Walid, ruled for ten years, resulting in stability and constant policy for thirty crucial years, during which Umayyad conquest and empire reached its heights.

The Muslims were blessed with great generals. In the early days, it was Khalid bin Walid, Amr bin al-As, Sa'ad bin al Waqqas, and now Al Hajjaj; Qutayba and Mohammad bin Qasim in the East; and Uqba bin Nafi, Musa bin Nusayr and Tariq in Africa and Spain. The Umayyads conquered North Africa, Spain, Central Asia, Sind and Multan in India, and from the Atlantic Ocean to the borders of China. These great warriors lived through the constant danger of battle, but too often fell victim and met their deaths due to the vicissitudes of politics and intrigues back home in Damascus.

The one misfit amongst these worldly caliphs was Umar II, who was pious, saintly and a true believer. In his three-year rule, he reversed many of the prevailing policies, and was so revered that even the Abbasids who wiped out the Umayyads and desecrated their tombs, honoured Umar's grave and respected him as a saint.

The last significant Umayyad caliph was Hisham, who also ruled for twenty years. He was a capable man, who left the treasury full, but was unable to stop the decline of the dynasty, which seven years after his death, was destroyed by the Abbasids. But alone, of all the Umayyads, his descendants survived in power. It was his grandson, Abdur Rehman, who escaped the treacherous Abbasid massacre and was the founder of the dynasty of the Umayyads in Spain.

After the death of Ali, the fourth caliph, Muawiya became the dominant power; but Kufa Hasan, Ali's eldest son, was unanimously proclaimed Caliph, continuing the double caliphate. Muawiya sent his army to Kufa to deal with the problem. Hasan prepared his supporters to meet them and sent an advance guard of 12,000 men to stop Muawiya's troops. When reports reached Hasan's main force that his advance guard had been defeated, the troops mutinied and attacked his pavilion. Hasan wrote to Muawiya, agreeing to negotiate terms of abdication.

Muawiya prepared to do what he did best—negotiate. The Hasan–Muawiya treaty was drawn up; the main terms being:

- Hasan to cede power and retire from politics, with the condition that the caliphate would return to him or his brother Husain, in the event of Muawiya's death
- The ritual cursing of his father, Ali, was to stop
- Muawiya was not to use public tax revenues for his private expenses
- Hasan's followers to be guaranteed immunity and security
- Hasan to retire to Medina and get a hefty cash settlement of 5 million dirhams together with the revenue from one district in Persia

Muawiya, now with a monopoly of power, could focus on building the empire of Islam; Hasan, financially secure and free from the entanglement and danger of power politics, could get on with his preferred pursuits—religious studies and married life. His followers called Hasan the great peacemaker, for having ended the conflicts that weakened the Muslim community. Those less committed to him, called Hasan the great divorcer; it is said that he ran through seventy or ninety marriages before he died at the age of forty-five.

Hasan certainly promoted stability by the great peace. When provoked by those who agitated for renewed conflict, he replied, 'If Muawiya was the rightful successor to the Caliph, he has received it. And if I had that right, I too have passed it on to him. So the matter ends there.'

But danger lay in wait for him where he least expected it—at home. His wife Ja'da poisoned him, it is said, on the instigation of Muawiya who was not too keen to pass the crown back to Hasan when he died. With Hasan dead, she went to Muawiya, who gave her 100,000 dirhams, but not the husband of her choice—his son Yazid; he was not ready to risk the life of his beloved son with a woman who had just murdered her own husband!

MUAWIYA

'I apply not my sword where my lash suffices, nor my lash where my tongue is enough. And even if there be one hair binding me to my fellowmen, I do not let it break: when they pull, I loosen, and if they loosen, I pull.'

—Muawiya

Dynasties and empires are at their most fragile at times of succession. For thousands of years, the best way to transfer power from the outgoing to the incoming ruler has been the subject of active debate. Today the fashion is democracy, with elections as the mechanism for succession. In the early days of Islam, there was no fixed road to succession. The Prophet was chosen by God; Abu Bakr was chosen by acclamation; Umar was nominated by Abu Bakr on his deathbed; Uthman was selected by a committee of electors; Ali was acclaimed in the turmoil following the assassination of Uthman; Muawiya became co-Caliph with Ali as a result of arbitration, and then became sole

Caliph as a result of Hasan's abdication; and Yazid was imposed as successor by his father, creating Islam's first dynasty.

Succession has resulted from merit, guile, force and finally, dynasty. Muawiya has been criticized for replacing the democratic politics of Islam with dynasty and kingship. To be fair to him, this trend was also visible in the party of Ali, his adversary; the Shia believed that the family of The Prophet, the Alids, had a divine right to rule.

The Prophet had been the first to recognize Muawiya's talent, and had started him on his career; Umar promoted him to the governorship of Syria; his power grew under Uthman and finally his strategy and guile won him total power from Ali and Hasan. He was an outstandingly capable ruler, politically adept, generous and scrupulous in his enforcement of justice, who believed in merit and loyalty rather than family. His rule as Caliph for twenty years was a time of prosperity at home and conquest abroad. Though a pious Muslim, he did not aggressively push conversion since he well realized that the more the number of converts, the less the tax revenue for the state. He was comfortable with Christians who were valued by him in his administration and even at home—his wife, Yazid's mother, was a Christian.

In twentieth-century communist China, Madame Mao had a Gang of Four which proved to be a major disaster. In the first century of Islam, Muawiya's 'gang of four' proved an unmitigated success—Amr bin al-As, the wily Odysseus of early Islam who ruled Egypt; Mughira, the unprincipled one-eyed rogue who was governor of Kufa; and Ziad, the hard hearted ruler of Basra. These, together with their boss Muawiya, constituted the political genius of the time.

Ziad was the son of a slave girl; his father was reputed to be Abu Sufyan. Earlier, in the time of Umar, when Mughira was accused of adultery and three witnesses testified against him, Ziad, the fourth witness, saved his life by saying he had seen the lovers together but had not seen penetration! This saved Mughira's life and tied Mughira to Ziad with a special bond. Ziad was appointed governor of Basra by Ali, and had proved the ablest administrator of the day. But even after the death of Ali, when Muawiya was Caliph, he remained loyal and devoted to the memory of Ali. Mughira finally persuaded him to switch loyalties. To cement his commitment, Muawiya publically recognized Ziad as Abu Sufyan's son, and as his own brother.

Ziad was a tyrant who ruled Basra and Kufa through terror and draconian measures; when faced with protests, he cut off the hands of fifty dissenters to show that he meant business. Ziad coveted control of Mecca and Medina, and the people of the two holy cities prayed for God's protection from this cruel tyrant. Whether it was God's intervention or just bad luck, Ziad developed a dangerous boil on his hand which killed him, keeping the twin cities safe from his harsh rule.

It was said of Muawiya that he was slow to anger and had absolute self-control. This aspect of his character was highlighted by Nizam al-Mulk (who was, for thirty years, the chief minister of the Seljuk kings), in his *Book of Government or Rules for Kings*, a Muslim equivalent of Machiavelli's *The Prince*:

> One day when he was giving audience and all the nobles were in his presence, a young man came in wearing tattered clothes; he greeted Muawiya, sat down in front of him and said, 'O Commander of the Faithful, I have come today with an urgent request; if you promise to grant it I will tell you what it is.' Muawiya said, 'Anything that is possible I will grant.' The youth said, 'Know that I am a poor man and have no wife; and your mother has no husband. Give her to me in marriage, so that I may have a wife, she a husband and you gain the reward.' Muawiya said, 'You are a young man and she is an old woman; so old that she has not a single tooth in her head. What do you want her for?' He said, 'Because I have heard that she is plump and I have always liked plump women.' Muawiya said, 'By Allah, my father married her for the very same thing, and it was the only virtue she had. Anyway, I will speak to my mother about this, and if she is willing, I am certainly the best procurer for your purpose.' Muawiya showed no sign of agitation and remained completely calm.

Considering that the mother in question was the liver-eating Hind, the young man must have been a glutton for punishment or a serious pervert!

Muawiya was a master of administration; he streamlined the chancery, developed infrastructure, built up the postal service, and made the Syrian army into a powerful fighting machine. Under his rule, the empire expanded into North Africa, Khurasan in Eastern Persia, and Afghanistan and Bokhara in Central Asia. But as he turned the theocratic state of Islam into a temporal monarchy, puritan passion was replaced by worldly considerations; wealth, power and luxury became the focus of life; wine, women and song replaced prayer. Times had changed.

Muawiya was not just a good judge of his friends, he was also a good judge of his enemies. At the end of his prosperous reign, an old man of seventy-five, he advised his son Yazid to beware of three of his opponents—the two Abdullahs, sons of Umar and Zubayr; and Husain, son of Ali. 'It is Abdullah, son of Zubayr, that I fear the most for thee. Fierce as a lion, crafty as a fox; destroy him root and branch.' His warning proved only too correct—Abdullah set up the rival caliphate in Mecca and Medina where he ruled for a decade and almost brought down the Umayyad dynasty. Abdallah said of Muawiya, 'Truly the son of Hind deployed dexterity and mental resourcefulness as one will never see after him.'

YAZID

Yazid, the frivolous and dissolute son of the great Muawiya, ruled only three years, but in that short time earned eternal disrepute and hatred for the assassination of Hussein at Karbala, the sacking of Medina, the city of The Prophet, and the siege of Mecca in which the Kaaba was set on fire and seriously damaged. His early death saved Mecca from further destruction and shame.

When he took over as Caliph, several important Muslims refused to acknowledge his right to rule; the two most important of these dissenters were Hussein bin Ali and Abd Allah bin Zubayr. Hussein was the first to move. On promises of support from Kufa, he set out with a small group of his family and close friends, men, women and children. They were stopped at Karbala on the instructions of the governor of Iraq, Ubaydallah, whose father Ziad, the son of the slave girl, had been Muawiya's powerful governor of Iraq. The slaughter was merciless; the family members killed with Hussein included two of his sons, six of his brothers, two of his nephews, Hassan's sons and six other descendents of Abu Talib, the father of Ali. Seventy heads of those slain were taken to Ubaydallah's palace, together with women and children. As the proud governor turned the head over with his staff, an aged voice was heard, 'Gently... it is The Prophet's grandson.'

The head, together with Hussein's sister, and his surviving children were sent to Yazid in Damascus. Yazid disowned responsibility and reproached Ubaydallah for the massacre. The head was returned to Hussein's sister for burial with the body, forty days after the massacre on the tenth of Muharram 61 (10 October 680). Ever after, the tenth of Muharram and the fortieth day (the return of the head) have witnessed the passionate outpouring of grief by Shia Muslims, the world over. In 687, Ubaydallah was killed—late and inadequate justice for the martyrdom of Hussein.

Opposition to Yazid centred in Mecca and Medina under the leadership of Abd Allah bin Zubayr. As more and more territories accepted Abd Allah and rejected Yazid, the Umayyad position grew precarious. Medina condemned the degenerate ways of the Umayyad court with its 'singing girls and pet monkeys'. Yazid sent in his troops who sacked and plundered Medina and then moved against Mecca. Abd Allah refused to submit and the siege of Mecca began. Catapults hurled rocks on the city and the Kaaba was severely damaged by the fires that raged. But before Mecca was taken, news came of Yazid's death, and hostilities ceased. The Syrian army returned home, leaving Abd Allah in control of Mecca. He was generally recognized as the true Caliph, as Umayyad authority collapsed. Abd Allah bin Zubayr split the caliphate and ruled as rival to the Umayyad caliphs for a decade, till Abd al Malik sent in his formidable general, al Hajjaj, for the second siege of Mecca in which Abd Allah was killed.

THE RISE OF THE MARWANIDS

Yazid's young son Muawiya II was weak and sickly. Knowing that he was dying, he addressed his people, saying that like Abu Bakr, he would have appointed a successor but there were none of Umar's calibre; that like Umar he would have nominated electors, but he did not see any men fit for such a task; so he left them to choose a successor for themselves. The family wanted Khalid, a younger son of Yazid, but those who wanted stronger rule, supported Marwan, a cousin. Marwan was chosen as Caliph on the condition that Khalid would succeed him. In his short reign, Marwan had two notable achievements: being killed by his wife, who smothered him with a pillow, and securing the caliphate for his son, Abd al Malik, 'The Father of Kings', who ruled for twenty years and was followed, in turn, by four of his sons. The remaining eleven caliphs of the Umayyad dynasty were all Marwanids, descendants of Marwan.

Abd al Malik was a competent ruler. In his twenty-year rule (685–705), he consolidated the power of the Umayyads, stamping out rebellion. Together with his right-hand man, al Hajjaj, the hard and very capable general and governor of Iraq, he controlled the eastern part of the empire. He spread the use of Arabic as the language of administration, government and business. He strengthened the treasury by his efficient tax collection system. He built the Dome of the Rock in Jerusalem. He created stability to ensure that his family, the family of Marwan, remained above internal challenge, till it was ultimately destroyed by the Abbasids. His son Walid continued his father's policies; he also retained al Hajjaj as his key lieutenant over the expanding eastern empire.

Al Hajjaj is one of the most unusual and most interesting characters of the time. Exceptionally competent, but incomparably cruel, this teacher of the *Quran* developed into the top administrator and politician, effectively the minister of defence. Intelligent and tough, he was a feared and hated tyrant, who throughout his career, remained fiercely loyal to the Umayyads. He is said to have been responsible for 100,000 deaths. In 694, when he was given charge of Kufa, he made his famous introductory speech to the citizens: 'I see heads which have become ripe for plucking, and I behold blood between the turbans and the beards.' His actions more than lived up to his words.

Never the diplomat, Hajjaj, on taking command, decreased the pay of the Iraqi troops, which did not endear him to them. He was faced by resentment and even a mutiny by the well-equipped 'Army of the Peacocks', which was so serious that the Caliph, in his negotiations with the mutineers, even offered to remove Hajjaj. But victory in battle ended the mutiny and saved Hajjaj.

When tax revenues fell off, imposing financial pressure on the government, Hajjaj's technique for dealing with the problem was as high-handed as ever. He rounded up the Mawalis, converts to Islam, and forced them to pay the taxes of unbelievers. This certainly raised the revenues, but also raised the level of resentment seen by converts as contrary to Islam's promise of equality to all Muslims.

But Hajjaj created the stability that the empire so badly needed. When he was sent to deal with Abdullah bin Zubayr, the rival caliph in Mecca, he was ruthless in his attack. Without pity, he bombarded Mecca. Eight years earlier, Yazid had ordered the siege of Mecca; now under Abd al Malik, Mecca was again under attack. Resistance continued for some months, but then the people of Mecca started to desert; even two of Abdullah's sons went across to Hajjaj. Abdullah went to his aged mother, Asma, the daughter of Abu Bakr, who told him to die as a hero should. 'That,' he replied, 'is what I thought. But I wished to strengthen my thought with thine.' He put on his armour and charged towards his death. Hajjaj had the body impaled as a warning to others, but Abd al Malik in shame, ordered that it be given to Asma for burial.

THE GENERALS AND THEIR CONQUESTS

It is the conquests of the Umayyads that have earned them their glory as a great dynasty that made a major contribution to Islam. These conquests substantially obscured their glaring weaknesses and failings—the falling moral standards, the massacre of Husayn and The Prophet's family at Karbala, the attacks on Mecca and Medina, the burning down of the Kaaba, and the cruelty and greed. These conquests were the achievement of a series of great generals who were brave, resolute and skilled in the art of war.

In the East, Hajjaj was the leader. He selected the generals and tried to micro-manage them. Qutayba bin Muslim was his most important protégé—appointed and fully supported by Hajjaj, as governor of the far Persian province of Khurasan, and then conqueror of Transoxonia, the lands of Afghanistan, Central Asia, Bokhara, Samarkand, Khwarezm and Fergana. Despite the fact that these were the bloodiest and toughest of the wars of conquest, Qutayba was the man for the job. As much a diplomat and negotiator as a battle general, he united the Arabs of Khurasan in a jihad that offered them the chance to serve God and grow rich. Ever willing to work with local kings and chiefs, he preferred pacification to conquest. His practical and reasonable approach was seen when he captured a Buddhist shrine and found two pearls the size of pigeon eggs. On being told by the monks that two birds had placed them there—a miracle—he commented wryly that this showed the foolishness of Buddhism! He was equally ready to use persuasion, bribery or force; after conquering Bukhara, he built a great mosque, but locals were not willing to come to prayers, so Qutayba offered two dirhams a head to persuade them. The *Quran* was read in Persian, the local language.

For over a decade, Qutayba was the virtual ruler of the Far East, accountable only to Hajjaj. Then in 714, Hajjaj died; a year later, the Caliph, Walid, died. Qutayba was in trouble. In the contest for succession, Hajjaj and his associates had supported the son of Walid, but the new caliph was Walid's brother Suleiman, who now went after the old guard with a vengeance. The witch-hunt was on. Qutayba knew that his time was up. When he was summoned back to Damascus, rather than risk returning, he decided to make a stand. He assembled his troops and tried to rally them to support his rejection of the authority of Damascus. But his appeal for loyalty was met with a stony silence. Qutayba totally lost his cool, and later admitted, 'When I spoke and not a single man responded, I became angry and did not know what I was saying.' He became uncontrolled in his insults, comparing his men to wanton slave girls, mangy camels and even the backsides of wild asses. There is a saying: 'Speak when you are angry, and you will make the best speech you will ever regret.' For Qutayba it was over; there was no going back. He lay on his couch, awaiting the end: 'Let it be, for this is God's will.' Qutayba was killed, his brother was killed, all his family members were killed; their bodies crucified. The Persians of Khurasan were amazed; no one had ever achieved as much as Qutayba—was this his reward? So ended the story of Qutayba and with it, ended an era in the Muslim conquest of Central Asia.

Hajjaj's nephew, the seventeen-year-old Muhammad bin Qasim, was an ambitious and capable young man who was given a chance to go and conquer the new territories in India—Sind and Multan. He set out on the perilous and difficult journey through Baluchistan and Mekran, with a small force. In a series of dazzling campaigns, he established Muslim rule in the western provinces of India. As Muhammad bin Qasim and Qutayba continued their Eastward conquests, Hajjaj spurred them on with the promise that whoever reached China first, would be the governor of that fabulous empire.

But with the change of caliph in Damascus, Muhammad bin Qasim's meteoric career was cut short. Some say he was summoned back to Damascus where he was tortured and killed; others say that he was sewn into the hide of a cow and was dead when he reached Damascus. He was twenty when he was murdered.

But what is disaster for one man, is a blessing for another. The new governor of Fars, Kerman, Mekran and Sindh was Yazid bin

Muhallab, the very same man whom Hajjaj had arrested and tortured, driving a rod into his leg. When Yazid had cried out in pain, his sister, the wife of Hajjaj, had screamed in sympathy. Hajjaj had turned to her and divorced her on the spot.

In the West, the conquests started with Amr bin al-As, whose repeated reconquests of Egypt were necessitated by political reversals back home in the capital. Amr was to die honoured in office as governor of his beloved Egypt, unlike so many of the outstanding generals. Even the great Khalid bin Walid, the first of Islam's generals, ended his days in disgrace. Amr sponsored his nephew, Uqba bin Nafi, recognized in history as the conqueror of Africa. Uqba stormed through North Africa, taking the countries of Libya, Tunisia, Algeria and Morocco. When he reached the Atlantic, he rode his horse into the sea, disturbed that there was no more land to conquer and shouted, 'O Lord, if the sea did not stop me, I would go through the lands like Alexander the Great, defending your faith and fighting the unbelievers.' Uqba saw his conquests as a jihad to spread the faith, and he was disgusted with the attitude of the Berbers whom he tried to convert: 'The people of this country are a worthless lot; if you lay into them with the sword, they become Muslims but the moment your back is turned, they revert to their old habits and religion.' Ever victorious, Uqba sent home treasures and tribute, including many young Berber girls of outstanding beauty that he captured in war, 'the likes of which no one in the world had ever seen.' Due to politics back home, Uqba was sacked from the governorship of the country he conquered, and arrested. But he made a spectacular comeback when in 680, Muawiya died and Yazid reappointed him, arresting his rival instead. Uqba died in battle—a martyr, as he had desired.

Two names are remembered for the conquest of Spain, known to the Muslims as al Andalus-Musa bin Nusayr and Tariq bin Ziyad. Musa's father was a freed slave who had been captured in war. Musa rose through merit, and with the support of his patron Abd al Aziz bin Marwan, the brother of the Caliph, and was appointed governor of Iraq. Tax revenues were found to be missing; Musa was blamed and told either to pay or to die. Abd al Aziz had faith in Musa's integrity and paid the money, saving his life. He later had him appointed governor of Ifriqiya. In North Africa, Musa did not impose Islam by force, but respected Berber traditions and won their respect. Many Berbers converted, including, it is reported, Tariq bin Ziyad, who became Musa's trusted lieutenant.

The conquest of Spain was the result of an accident. It was never planned; in fact, Tariq, responsible for the conquest, was reprimanded and struck by a whip by his boss, Musa, for having acted without authority or even permission. Spain was ruled by the Visigoths, and the commander of their army was Count Julian. When Julian was departing for Africa to hold the frontier against the advance of the Muslim armies, he left his beautiful daughter, Florinda, at court. King Roderic saw her, raped her and made her pregnant and she wrote to her father begging him to come and get her. Julian was enraged and went to Tariq, offering to take the Muslim army into Spain as revenge. Tariq sought instructions from Musa, and was given permission to take an exploratory force of 7,000 men to see the lie of the land. Tariq passed through a rocky island, known thereafter as 'the rock of Tariq' or Jebel Tariq (Gibraltar) and entered Spain. Like a hot knife through butter, they cut through Spain in no time, and conquered the southern part of the peninsula. Musa was consumed by jealousy, and was vicious in his criticism of his subordinate. But later they reached an accommodation; Spain offered more than enough glory and booty for all.

But glory turned to dust when Musa and Tariq were summoned back to Damascus. The Caliph, Walid, died; the new caliph, his brother Suleiman, stripped Musa of his rank and confiscated all the booty. Musa's two sons had been appointed governors of Spain and Africa by their powerful father; both were assassinated. His sons' heads were sent to the Caliph who callously asked Musa if he recognized them; Musa replied with dignity that it belonged to someone who had always been a true Muslim. The seventeenth-century historian, Ibn abi Dinar, wrote, 'Musa, who had conquered half the inhabited world, who had acquired so many riches, died in poverty, begging alms from passersby, after having been abandoned by the last of his servants. Overcome by shame and misery, he wished for death, and God gave it to him.' He added, 'The details of Musa's death give my contemporaries, who are poorly read, a striking example of the vicissitudes of human life.' So ended the story of Musa, the son of a freed slave, and Tariq the Berber, the first non-Arab commander of the Muslim conquests.

As death or disgrace removed the great Muslim generals from the scene, the pace of conquest slowed. In France, the historic battle of Tours saw the end of the Muslim advance into Western Europe, when Abd al Rehman, the Muslim general, was killed in the fighting. The following morning, when the French leader Charles Martel readied his troops for another day of battle, there was silence in the Muslim camp—the tents were empty; the Muslims had gone. European historians see Tours as one of history's most important battles that saved Europe from Islam.

In the East, the Arab and the Chinese armies met at Talas. In Tours, the Muslims lost the battle; in Talas, they were victorious. This was the last time that the Chinese armies reached so far west. Though not appreciated at the time, Talas was to be a turning point in history. It was here that the Arabs captured the artisans that produced a new Chinese invention—paper—and took home this strange new technology. Within two centuries, the superiority of paper over parchment, and Islam's emphasis on knowledge, resulted in libraries of half a million books in the Islamic world at a time when the greatest libraries of Christian Europe had less than a thousand.

The three caliphs who followed the long rule of Abd al Malik were very different from each other—Walid, Suleiman and Umar. Walid's interest was art, culture, architecture; Suleiman's, the harem; and Umar's, religion. The conversation at court changed accordingly—in Walid's time, it was culture and construction; in Suleiman's, it was the beauty of slave girls; but with Umar, it was austerity and Islam.

The empire reached its height under Walid, the most powerful and illustrious of all the caliphs. There was prosperity at home and conquest abroad. But all good things come to an end, and with Suleiman, decay set in. Suleiman's rival for the throne had been the son of Walid, who had been the candidate of Walid's close associates. Those who had been the privileged under the caliphate of the elder brother, were now in trouble. Dismissal, imprisonment, torture, and even execution, erased them from the power elite. The generals and governors who had built the empire, now met destruction instead of their well-deserved reward.

After the caliphate of two of Abd al Malik's sons, Walid and Suleiman, the crown passed to a cousin, Umar II, who was descended from Umar the Great. It was well-known that the great Umar used to go out in secret, among his people, to understand their lives. On one such trip, he overheard a milkmaid refusing to obey her mother's orders to sell adulterated milk. The mother repeatedly urged her, 'Mix in the water. Caliph Umar is not watching.' The girl replied that though Umar was not watching, Allah sees everything. The next day, Umar sent an officer to buy milk from the girl, and learnt that she had kept her resolve; the milk was not adulterated. He summoned the girl and her mother to court, told them what he had seen and offered to marry her to his son, Asim. She accepted, and from this union was born a girl, Layla, who became the mother of Umar II.

Throughout his life, Umar II lived up to the high moral standards of his grandmother and great grandfather. Unlike the rest of the Umayyads, he was pious, religious and selfless. His lifestyle was simple and austere. He made his wife return to the treasury the costly jewels gifted to her by her father, the Caliph, Abd al Malik. On his death, her brother, the new caliph, offered the return of her jewels, but she declined, mindful of her husband's wish. Umar II's justice was surpassed by none.

At that time, the burning issue was the resentment of non-Arab converts, the mawalis, who were denied equal treatment with the original Arab Muslims, in contradiction to the principles of Islam. The tax advantages of being a Muslim threatened to create a flood of converts that would diminish state revenues and bring about a serious financial crisis. Umar dictated that there should be no differentiation in Islam between Arab and non-Arab and that there should be no obstacles to acceptance of Islam by mawalis. These policies stepped up the level of conversion to Islam, as more and more people joined the faith.

But after two and a half years, Umar became sick and died. The throne went back to the sons of Abd al Malik—first Yazid II, and then Hisham. Yazid II was another serious harem man, and the empire had started its downward path in his short four-year rule. Hisham was better. He was a decent man who kept extravagance under control and built up the treasury but was unable to stem the decline. The rebellious mood grew as Alids, Abbasids, Shias, Persians and Turks defied the authority of Damascus. In 743, he died; the following year saw three caliphs come and go in quick succession.

Walid II, the nephew of the dead caliph, Hisham, was overjoyed at the news of his uncle's death. At last he could inherit, and have all the money, wine, women and song to his heart's content. He threw his cousin, the son of Hisham, into prison where he was beaten and shamed. He seized and emptied the treasury. His behaviour was scandalous. As his popularity plummeted, another of his cousins, Yazid III, marched on Damascus, seized what was left of the treasury and killed Walid. Yazid III was a son of the late caliph, Walid I, but was the first caliph in Islam born of a slave mother. His weak legitimacy was further eroded by the murder of his cousin, and resistance to his rule was now led by Marwan II, another cousin.

The dynasty was on its last legs, and there was little that Marwan, the last of the Umayyads could do. Two factions, the Qays and the Kalbs, were jealously antagonistic to each other. Numerous princelings, many the sons of previous caliphs, all claimed equally royal blood and stood ready to rebel or conspire. The non-Arabs resented the privilege of the Arabs. The Shia hated the Sunni. The Kharijites and the Hashemites, and both the Alids (descendants of Ali) and the Abbasids (descended from The Prophet's uncle, Abbas), were irrevocably opposed to the Umayyads, and were determined to bring them down. And in the distant Persian province of Khurasan, a shadowy revolutionary general, Abu Muslim, launched his bid for power.

It all came to a head at the battle of the Zab, after which Syria lay at the feet of the Abbasid victors, Damascus surrendered, and the Caliph, Marwan, fled for his life. In Egypt he was caught in a church, where he had sought refuge; he was overpowered and killed and his head was sent to Salih, the local commander of the Abbasids, who cut out the tongue and threw it contemptuously to a cat.

4

The Rise of the Abbasids

Today, Khurasan is the eastern-most province of Iran. In the second half of the eighth century, it was much more. At the time of the Muslim conquests, Khurasan spread over Afghanistan and Central Asia. It was a long way from Damascus, and the authority of the Umayyads diminished even as the distance increased. Merv was its capital city. Though insignificant today, for a while during the Middle Ages, Merv became the greatest city in the world. It was from Khurasan that the Persians and Arab settlers rose up in revolt against the Umayyads with the new leadership that became the Abbasid dynasty.

The Khurasani army of revolution was led by a freed slave known as Abu Muslim who disdained power for himself and proclaimed that he would restore the caliphate to the family of The Prophet. But it was unclear who or which branch of the family he supported. Many believed that the Alids would be designated. As events turned out, it was the family of Abbas (an uncle of The Prophet) who would take the leadership. Though on the fringe at the birth of Islam, with criticism that uncle Abbas had been, at best, a late convert—if he had converted at all—the Abbasids made up for their lack of legitimacy by their ruthlessness and cunning.

As the revolution exploded, the Abbasid family was hidden

in Kufa by Abu Salama who emerged as the local leader of the Hashemite cause. Three months after the occupation of Kufa by the Hashemite troops, Abu Salama supported Abbas in his coup. Abbas went into the great mosque and addressed the people, praising them for their support to the family of The Prophet, demonizing the fallen Umayyads, offering financial rewards and declaring his mission to root out all opposition, for, 'I am the Great Revenger; my name Saffah, the Slaughterer.' And slaughter he did—both of his enemies and of his friends. One of his early victims was Abu Salama who had supported him in his coup.

His primary target was the family of the Umayyads. Extending an olive branch, he offered them an amnesty and invited them to a banquet of reconciliation. Ninety members of the family accepted the invitation. As they settled down to the feast, the attendants suddenly attacked them with clubs. Most were killed in this savage attack; some lived, though mortally wounded. Carpets were thrown over the dead and dying, and the feast continued with wine and laughter. The slaughter of the family of The Prophet at Karbala had finally been avenged by the slaughter of the Umayyads. But one young Umayyad prince who had not attended, escaped the slaughter—Abd al Rehman who fled to Africa and then Spain, where, after five difficult and dangerous years, he found sanctuary and founded the great Umayyad dynasty in Cordoba. The Abbasid caliphs endured for 500 years. The Muslims in Spain ruled for 800 years.

The killing did not stop here. At Basra, the victims were cut to pieces and their bodies cast in the streets to be eaten by stray dogs. Even those that tried to find sanctuary in Mecca and Medina were not spared. In Syria, the tombs of the caliphs were desecrated and the corpses mutilated. Throughout the empire, amnesty was offered as a ruse; those who fell for it were slaughtered. Even the solemn word of the Caliph was merely a trick to deceive.

In less than five years, Abbas, having secured power for his family, died of smallpox. He designated as his heir, his brother Abu Jafar, who ruled as the Caliph, Mansur, from 754 to 775.

Mansur was a complicated, cunning and eccentric man. He was a political genius, deep and dangerous, in the style of a Mafia godfather. It was he who consolidated the empire for the five-hundred-year dynasty that followed him. When his brother, the Caliph, died, three strong men controlled power in the Abbasid state—Mansur, the new caliph; Abu Muslim, the champion of the new dynasty; and uncle Abd Allah, the strongest general in the Abbasid family. Abu Muslim controlled the armies of Khurasan. Abd Allah had led the defeat of the last Umayyad caliph and was considered by many, including himself, as the best choice for Caliph. Mansur persuaded Abu Muslim to attack Abd Allah, who was defeated in battle and imprisoned, where he died in captivity seven years later. Mansur then persuaded Abu Muslim to visit him in his camp where he was murdered in the tent of the Caliph by the royal guards. These fast, bold and risky decisions left Mansur as the single strong man in the empire. Mansur won over Abu Muslim's commanders with financial inducements. Seduced by promises of wealth and power, they gave their loyalty to the Caliph who had murdered their leader.

The Shias, resentful at having been bypassed in the power struggle that brought the Abbasids to power, rebelled under the leadership of Muhammad, the great grandson of Hasan bin Ali, known as 'The Pure Soul' in Medina. Mansur's advisors were not worried: 'Praise God! He has begun his rebellion in a place where there is no money, no men, no weapons and no fodder. Stop provisions coming from Syria and he will starve where he is.'

Muhammad and his brother were killed and the rebellion contained. For as long as he ruled, Mansur continued his secret witch-hunt of potential Shia troublemakers. He gave to his daughter-in-law, Rita, the keys to a secret room in the palace which was only to be opened after his death, and which, even then, only she and her husband Mahdi were permitted to enter. Inside the secret chamber were laid out rows of corpses—men, women and children—all, identified by labels in their ears. Mahdi, now Caliph, was shocked to see the bodies. He was trying to mend relations with the Alids and these corpses could destroy his peace overtures. He had the bodies secretly burned.

Having settled with his enemies, Mansur, over the last twelve years of his life, concentrated on building a capital and an efficient government machinery. For his capital city, he chose a green field which became Baghdad. Within the first century of its creation, Baghdad was to become the greatest city in the world, the city of the *One Thousand and One Nights*. To streamline his government administration, he selected a remarkable man, Khalid the Barmakid.

Barmak was a physician who had lived at Balk, near the river Oxus. When the great Qutayba conquered these lands, Barmak's wife was taken as a slave and concubine by Abdallah, the brother of Qutayba. They had a son, Khalid, known in history as Khalid the Barmakid. Khalid's exceptional ability was soon recognized by the Caliph; he became Mansur's chancellor, and for three generations, Khalid, his son Yahya and grandsons Fadl and Jafar, effectively ruled as a family of viziers whose power and wealth matched the caliphs' until their tragic destruction at the hands of Mansur's grandson, the Caliph, Harun al Rashid.

Mansur was a thoughtful and wily eccentric who would squat for hours, scratching the ground with his cane, while he worked out his strategies and plans. He was a systematic and obsessive administrator who involved himself in detail. To crush Muhammad the Pure Soul, and his brother Ibrahim, he himself came to Medina. Ziyad, a notable of Medina, was woken in the middle of the night and frogmarched to Mansur, who was squatting on the ground, poking around with an iron rod. Ziyad was told that the Caliph had been like that all night. After a long silence, the Caliph raised his head, looked at Ziyad standing there and snapped, 'Where are Muhammad and Ibrahim, you son of a bitch?' 'May God kill me if I don't kill you. Get out!' said Mansur.

Mansur was pious and served no wine at his table. Stern, austere and disciplined, he rose at four in the morning, worked long hours and slept by ten at night. He was an eloquent orator; he liked to be informed and spent hours daily reading and evaluating intelligence reports. Notorious as a miser, in contrast to his stylish and fashionable son, he explained that he had grown up in poverty whereas his son had only known wealth and prosperity.

The legacy of this brilliant and dangerous man included the great metropolis of Baghdad, a highly efficient bureaucracy, a powerful army and a treasury sufficient to cover the expenditure of the next ten years. Persian influence had grown; the Arab empire had been converted into an international Islamic empire.

PEACEFUL TRANSITION

On the death of Mansur, the crown passed peacefully to his son Mahdi—mild and generous; a very different man to his father. Soon, wine, women and song replaced the dour austerity of Mansur's court. But Mahdi was no idle playboy. He could be hard—cutting off the hands and feet of rebels in Khurasan before beheading them. And he could be cunning, as shown in his handling of the vizier, Yacub, suspected of sympathy to the Alids. He invited Yacub to dine with him in a beautiful garden in the company of a stunning slave girl, who clearly captivated Yacub. Mahdi told him, 'Take her; she's yours.' Yacub took her, little realizing it was a trap; she was a spy, and later revealed Yacub's secrets, leading to his arrest. He was cast into a pitch dark prison where he remained so long that he lost his sight.

The young Prince Mahdi purchased a slave girl, Khayzuran, in the markets of Mecca. Khayzuran was more than pretty; she was something special. He fell in love with her and married her, and she became a power in the land. Two of her sons, Hadi and Harun, became caliphs, but her passion and favourite was Harun. It is rumoured that she had Hadi killed, smothered by a pillow in the power struggle of the brothers for the throne. With the accession of Harun, her power as the Sultana Valida, or Queen Mother, grew even greater. Her annual income was reputed to be 160 million dirhams, an amount equal to half the tax revenues of the entire caliphate. Her rise from slave girl to favourite wife of the caliph to Queen Mother, showed that Abbasid Baghdad was definitely an upwardly mobile society—at least for a lucky few! Khayzuran was one of the four great ladies of the Abbasid court, along with Zubayda, wife of Harun; Qabiya, mother of Mu'tazz; and Shaghab, mother of Muqtadir.

SUCCESSION BATTLES

The Abbasid formulas for succession created more problems than they resolved. Al Saffah, the first Abbasid caliph, appointed his brother Mansur but stipulated that he was to be followed by Isa bin Musa. Mansur was wily enough to negotiate a compromise, and Isa withdrew his claim on payment of a huge cash settlement. Mahdi decreed that his eldest son Hadi be Caliph, to be followed by a younger brother, Harun. Hadi was crowned, but a year of political infighting between the two groups of supporters was only ended by the death of Hadi. Next, Harun made the mistake of trying to secure a double succession for two of his sons, first Amin and then Mamun. The result was war between the brothers and on Mamun's victory, the execution of Amin. The desire to pass the throne to a son always overrode the desire to honour the wishes of a dead father or brother.

Mahdi died in a hunting accident and was succeeded by his son, Hadi. Harun was shy and retiring, and content to live a peaceful life with his bride, the princess Zubayda, his cousin. In thirteen months, Hadi died in mysterious circumstances. The Harun camp moved fast; Yahya, the Barmakid who had been imprisoned by Hadi, was released; Jafar, Hadi's son, was arrested; and Harun was proclaimed Caliph. The effective coup d'état was orchestrated by the Barmakids who dominated power so totally in the new government of Harun al Rashid that the next ten years were known as the 'Decade of the Barmakids'. Yahya and his sons, Fadl and Jafar, controlled an efficient administration supported by effective tax collection. Jafar was the closest friend of the Caliph, his advisor, drinking partner and constant companion. They were the greatest family in the realm with wealth and luxury that rivalled the Caliph.

In the year 802 AD, Harun went on pilgrimage to Medina and Mecca with his sons, Amin and Mamun, and other important notables. After distributing largess, he got on with the real business—settling the succession of his two sons in the event of his death. Detailed formal agreements were drawn up, witnessed, signed and hung up on the walls of the Kaaba. Amin's mother, Zubayda, was a blue-blooded royal princess and he was given the first right to succeed as Caliph. He was to be followed by his brother Mamun, who was designated heir to Amin. While Amin ruled as Caliph, Mamun would control the great province of Khurasan and would also have important powers in the central government. Though Amin could not question Mamun's succession, he did have the right to nominate Mamun's successor. The agreement went into great detail; Amin was not to entice Mamun's officials away from him and Mamun was not to aid any of Amin's enemies. Harun seemed to have thought of everything. But it all went wrong. The urge for power and the intrigues of supporters who staked their ambitions on one brother or the other, led to war, and with the victory of Mamun, the murder of Amin. Harun's great plan for stability of the empire resulted in instability. History has little regard for the plans of men.

The Barmakids had ensured Harun's accession and had run government efficiently for him for seventeen years; but now after his return from Mecca, things changed. The love affair was over. At court, little signals exposed the family's fall from grace; if the venerable Yahya wanted a drink of water he had to ask several times. Then suddenly, the Caliph struck. Yahya and Fadl were arrested, never to be released for as long as they lived. Jafar, Harun's favourite, was murdered and his corpse displayed publically to highlight his disgrace. In a moment, the greatest family in the realm was totally destroyed. But why?

It was never explained, but many theories were whispered. Was it just resentment in Harun's heart for his dependence on his old mentor? Was it Jafar's unauthorised release of an Alid prisoner and his lying to Harun about it? Or was it because of Abbasa, the beautiful and beloved sister of the Caliph?

The two people that Harun loved most were his beautiful and witty sister, Abbasa, and his flamboyant friend, Jafar, the Barmakid. He was happiest in their company, spending the evenings drinking, dining and enjoying their brilliant conversations. But he was bothered by social convention that frowned on the unmarried princess spending her evenings with an eligible male. So Harun was inspired by a brilliant idea—he would get them married. But it was not to be a normal marriage; this marriage was only for public display. The couple was allowed no intimacy, no sex. This worked for a while, till attraction led to passion between Abbasa and Jafar. The young husband and wife were drawn into a secret and illicit affair. A child was born to them, but sent to Mecca and hidden. And then they were exposed; their secret was revealed to Harun who was enraged. Harun ordered the murder of his sister, her child and her husband. Jafar's father and brother were imprisoned; their wealth confiscated. The Barmakids, the greatest family in the realm, were destroyed—a tragic reminder of the fickleness of fortune.

The court of Harun al Rashid is the stage setting of the story of Scheherazade in the *One Thousand and One Nights*. It was a time of culture, romance, brilliance and above all, extravagant luxury. Ambassadors of kings from Asia and Europe marveled at the splendours of Harun's lifestyle. The style and glamour of the Queen, Zubayda, and of Ulayyah, Harun's fashionable sister, were well known. They gazed with wonder at palaces adorned with jewels, and at wedding extravaganzas where a thousand magnificent pearls were showered on Mamun, Harun's son. At one banquet, Harun was served a dish of exceedingly small slices of fish; his brother, the host, explained that the slices were actually fishes' tongues, a very expensive delicacy. But it was not just the conspicuous consumption of the nouveau riche; even slaves and concubines were highly educated, as illustrated by the story of the slave-girl Yawaddud, whom Harun was willing to purchase for the princely sum of 100,000 dinars after she passed with flying colours a searching test in medicine, law, astronomy, philosophy, music, mathematics, poetry, history and the holy *Quran*! Harun's son Amin, who followed him as Caliph, preferred girls who looked like young boys, and had a collection of female pages with boyish haircuts dressed in boy's clothes. The poet laureate was the gay and shocking Abu Nuwais—he preferred boys that looked like girls!

But all good things come to an end. At the age of forty-seven, Harun fell sick and died. The state had never been more prosperous or secure. Amin was crowned in Baghdad, and Mamun took control of Khurasan. Very soon, Amin's advisors conspired to replace Mamun, the crown prince, with Amin's son. Both their future security and the ambitions of the elite at court were at stake. Estrangement between the brothers developed into hostility. The stage was set for war. Baghdad was for Amin; distant Khurasan and the Persians were for Mamun, whose mother had been a Persian slave girl, gifted to Harun by Zubayda.

Amin looked like a sure thing. The great Baghdad army backed him; he controlled Iraq, the richest province of the empire. The Abbasid family and the nobles supported him. Even Mamun's wife, children and personal wealth were in his custody in Baghdad. Mamun—far away in distant Merv, the capital of Khurasan, supported by the Persians—seemed to have little chance. If his Persian advisors would leave him in peace, he would have happily accepted the situation and given up resistance to his brother, the Caliph.

But events forced him into war. Amin sent a powerful army of 50,000 crack troops against his brother, led by Ali bin Isa, the ex-governor of Khurasan. Mamun raised a small force of only 3,000–4,000 men, to put up a hopeless resistance under a young Persian aristocrat named Tahir. It looked like a suicide mission but the young Tahir was a man favoured by destiny, and against all odds, won at the battle of Rayy, with Ali killed by a lucky arrow. The family of Tahir was to become the most powerful in the land, after the royal Abbasids.

Even after defeat at Rayy, Amin still looked the stronger of the brothers, but then the holy cities, Mecca and Medina, turned against him, shocked that he had gone back on the oath of succession displayed on the walls of the Kaaba by Harun, their father. It was sacrilege which cost the Caliph his legitimacy and lost him the moral high ground.

Tahir, now recognized as an expert in fast moving warfare, cut through the territories of the Caliph, till he stood at the gates of Baghdad. A long and terrible siege followed. The Caliph was captured, thrown in a dungeon and murdered. All the prosperity brought by earlier caliphs had been destroyed.

Even after the death of Amin, the civil war did not end for six years. The vizier, Fadl ibn Sahl, was determined to keep Mamun and the capital at Merv, leading to resentment and revolt in Iraq, Syria and Egypt. Mamun tried strategy and guile to retain control; he even announced Ali Ridha, a descendent of Ali and Fatima, as his heir to attract support. But even this did not convince anyone, since the Caliph was considerably younger than his chosen successor, and also enjoyed the best of health.

Finally, Mamun moved back to Baghdad and set about rebuilding the empire. Harun's time was the epitome of luxury and style. His son Mamun presided over the greatest flowering of learning and knowledge. His House of Wisdom, the 'Bayt al Hikma', collected the scholars of the age and the greatest library of the time.

5

The Golden Years of Islamic Civilization

Sayings of The Prophet Muhammad, Peace Be Upon Him:

'Go in quest of knowledge even unto China.'
'Seek knowledge from the cradle to the grave.'
'Verily the best of God's servants are just and learned kings; and verily the worst are bad and ignorant kings.'
'One hour's meditation of the work of the creator is better than seventy years of prayer.'
'The pursuit of knowledge is a divine commandment for every Muslim.'

The reign of Harun al Rashid and his son Mamun established the dominance of the Muslims in knowledge, science, education and civilization. While Mamun collected the greatest minds of his time in his Bayt al Hikma—university, library and centre of mathematics, algebra, physics, astronomy, medicine, architecture and translation—in Europe, the great Emperor, Charlemagne, was merely learning how to write his name. Imitators followed in other Muslim capital cities—Cordoba, seat of the Umayyads of Spain, had its Dar al Hikma; and Cairo, the capital of the Fatimids, was the home of al Azhar, the world's first great university. From Central Asia to Spain, Muslim civilization was on a different level to Europe.

It started with translation. The Greeks had created an advance in knowledge without parallel in the Mediterranean. The other two great centres of knowledge were China and India. But these three great civilizations were separated by both distance and language. Muslim conquest removed the geographical barriers, and translators in the new Bayt al Hikma removed the barriers of language. The most influential of the translators was Hunayn ibn Ishaq, a physician who revived the science of medicine by translating the forgotten Greek texts into Arabic. The Caliph, Mamun, paid Hunayn in gold the weight of the books he translated. Another Caliph, al-Mutawakkil, appointed him as his personal physician, but for a time, imprisoned him for refusing to poison an enemy in return for great riches as a reward. After a year in prison, when brought before the Caliph and threatened with execution, he replied that he was prevented from preparing the poison because of his religion and his profession. He was restored to honour. The century of translation brought Aristotle, Plato, Hippocrates, Galen, Euclid and Ptolemy onto the library shelves in Baghdad.

The Prophet Muhammad placed great importance on cleanliness and hygiene. Five times a day, before each prayer, Muslims had to wash. The clothes of the early Muslims may have been patched and out of fashion, but they were clean. Hygiene and health were two sides of the same coin. The great medieval capital cities, Baghdad, Cordoba and Cairo, had garbage collectors, public baths and a new type of institution—hospitals—whose doors were open to rich and poor alike, regardless of their ability to pay. The early Arab philosophers of medicine studied the translations of Hippocrates and Galen and quickly moved beyond them.

Greek medicine had been built on the work of Galen, who had dissected live pigs for his experiments on anatomy. He had operated on humans, even piercing the eye to remove cataracts. Thousands of miles away, the medicine of India followed a different course, and further still, in China, acupuncture and other remedies developed along yet different paths. The primitive Europeans had no medicine to speak of; they lived in a world of superstition and witchcraft.

PIONEERS IN EVERY FIELD

The two greatest pioneers of medicine in the world of Islam were al-Razi and ibn Sina. Both are recognized in the West as among the most important contributors to the development in the field of medicine. The portraits of al-Razi and ibn Sina hang in the School of Medicine in the University of Paris. Al-Razi was the first great Muslim doctor. He recognized that every disease has a specific cause—it is not a punishment of God. He rejected superstition as a rationalist who questioned everything. In his *Shukuk ala alinosor* (*Doubts about Galen*), he writes, 'It grieves me to oppose and criticize the man Galen, from whose sea of knowledge I have drawn much.' He understood how greatly health was influenced by behaviour and diet.

All over the Middle East, pharmacies named after ibn Sina are common. Ibn Sina was the greatest Muslim pioneer of medical science. His great work, *al Qanun fi al Tibb* (known in the West as *The Canon*), remained the bible of medicine longer than any other work, and between the twelfth and seventeenth centuries, was the chief guide to medical science in the West. Ibn Sina (also known as Avicenna) was a child prodigy who could recite the *Quran* at the age of ten, started the serious study of medicine by the age of thirteen, dramatically cured the Emir while still a teenager, read Aristotle's *Metaphysics* forty times as a young man and memorized it word for word. He had to flee when the Turks conquered the area where he lived, refused job offers from the great and mighty Sultan Mahmud of Ghazni and lived through a period of insecurity till he settled in Isphahan. He developed over 700 new drugs.

The Muslims led the world in medicine, with great doctors

rising in Spain, Cairo, Central Asia, Iran and Baghdad. They worked alongside great Jewish doctors such as Maimonides, in an environment of tolerance. One happy story of interfaith cooperation is about the Christian king of Leon, Sancho the Fat. Sancho ate and ate till he was grossly obese. His subjects, disgusted with his obesity, deposed him. Sancho went to the Muslim ruler in Spain, who had a renowned Jewish doctor, Hasday ben-Shaprut, and asked him to help him lose weight. The Caliph received Sancho as an honoured guest, put him under the expert care of Hasday, and Sancho was reduced to a respectable size. Sancho returned to Leon where he was reinstated with honour by his people—a Christian king treated by a Jewish doctor in the court of a Muslim caliph.

The genius of the Muslims covered mathematics, algebra, trigonometry; their work laid the base for the twenty-first century world of electronics and computers. One of the greatest names was ibn al-Haytham who has been compared with Einstein in the twentieth century. But perhaps the greatest of the great was al-Khwarizmi, the mathematician, from whose name the term 'algorithm' was created—to describe a set of numerical calculations critical to software design, modern engineering, computers and smart electronics. Al-Khwarizmi's greatest contribution to mathematics and science was the simple 'zero' which he learned from the Hindu mathematicians of India. The introduction of the zero revolutionized all calculation, created the decimal system and made simple what till then had been impossible.

The imam, Mowaffak, was a renowned teacher in Nishapur, in Khurasan. According to legend, anyone who studied under his guidance would know good fortune later in life. Three young boys came to study under him, and aware of the legend, they decided to swear an oath that whoever of them became successful, he would help the other two. The first of the boys became a vizier, or prime minister, to the Seljuk sultan. In fact, for thirty years, he was famous as the greatest vizier of the Islamic world. His madrassahs were state-of-the-art educational institutions of the time. He also wrote *Siyasatnama*, the book of government for kings, which was perhaps a better manual for rulers than Machiavelli's *The Prince* written centuries later. His name was Nizam al-Mulk.

Nizam al-Mulk invited his two friends to court and asked them what he could do for them. The first, Hasan al-Sabah, was politically ambitious and was made a minister. Soon he turned against his patron and led the Ismaili Assassins in a war of terror against the government. The Assassins murdered Nizam al-Mulk and his Sultan and became a terror in the empire—the prototype of the suicide bombers of today. Their style was public assassination, often during Friday prayers at the mosque, in which the assassin willingly gave up his life to enter paradise as a martyr.

The other young man had no such ambitions. He was in love with a slave girl, Darya, and just asked for a simple life under the protection of his patron and friend. His name was Omar Khayyam and he wrote poetry. His *Rubayat* is still read centuries later, with its simple verses:

> Here with a Loaf of Bread beneath the Bough,
> A Flask of Wine, a Book of Verse—and Thou Beside me,
> singing in the Wilderness—
> And Wilderness is Paradise enow!

Khayyam was a good poet, but he was a truly great mathematician. His calculations on the calendar showed the number of days in a year to be 365.24219 858156. In the twentieth century, scientists, aided by atomic clocks, Hubble telescopes and computers have calculated the number of days in a year as 365.24219 0—a difference of only fractions of a second. Through his study of the stars, Khayyam demonstrated that the Earth revolves on its axis, as opposed to the conventional wisdom of the time, that the heavens orbit the Earth. With the passing of centuries, Hasan al-Sabah is forgotten, Nizam al-Mulk is forgotten, even the great mathematical genius of Omar Khayyam is forgotten, but his *Rubayat* lives on.

Today, the great cities of the world are London, New York and Paris. In the golden years of Islamic civilization, the cities that amazed the world were Baghdad, Cordoba and Cairo. As centuries passed, these were replaced by Agra and Delhi, home to the Moguls of India; Isfahan, the seat of Shah Abbas; Istanbul, the capital of the Ottomans; and Samarkand, the city of Tamerlane the conqueror. In the tenth century, Baghdad, together with its suburbs, had a population of 2 million, every house had adequate water supply, the roads, parks and gardens were regularly swept and all refuse was removed and the streets were lighted with lamps. At that time, London and Paris were dirty slums of hardly 25,000 people, where disease was rampant, illiteracy universal and the townsfolk stank unbathed. For Europe, these were truly The Dark Ages. New York was just a Native American encampment. On the other hand, Cordoba, the capital of Muslim Spain, competed with Baghdad; the Caliph's personal library contained 600,000 books at a time when the largest library in Europe had less than one thousand.

Astronomy was another area where Muslims excelled. Abbasid astronomers calculated the diameter of the Earth at 7,909 miles against an actual figure of 7,932 miles. Instruments such as the astrolabe were refined by the Muslims, and state of the art observatories were set up. In recognition of the important role played by the Caliph, al-Mamun, the Almanon crater in the south-central region of the moon was named after him.

In the fifteenth century, the Renaissance genius Leonardo Da Vinci conceived many new inventions; the most spectacular of these, credited to him, is a flying machine. Leonardo was born in 1452 AD. Six hundred years before Leonardo was born, in 852 AD in Cordoba, a Muslim stuntman, Armen Firman, jumped off a building in front of a crowd, to demonstrate flight. It didn't work, and he fell to the ground, where he escaped with minor injuries. The crowd laughed at his folly. However, one man watching with interest was a middle-aged scientist and philosopher named Abbas ibn Firnas, who was skilled in mechanics and mechanical devices.

Ibn Firnas went home fascinated; he would study and solve the problem of flight. He would develop a new science—aeronautics.

After twenty-three years, at the age of seventy, he was ready, and he summoned the townsfolk of Cordoba to show them flight. Ibn Firnas jumped. He flew for ten minutes, with the ease and grace of a bird, and he proved that man could indeed fly. Finally, he started his descent. But now trouble hit him; he was coming down too fast. 'My God,' he thought, 'forgive me; I forgot the tail' (it was the tail that allowed birds to slow their descent and land safely). He hit the ground hard, broke his ribs, but survived. He had done it; he was the first man to fly. But somehow, his name has been lost in history and his well deserved credit was given to another who played with the idea—but never risked actual flight—600 years later.

6

The Decline and Demise of the Abbasids

Sayings of Nizam al-Mulk:

'A king should avoid favouritism and disproportionate rewards.'

'A king must subdue hatred, envy, pride, anger, lust, greed, false hopes, lying, avarice, malice, violence, selfishness, impulsiveness, ingratitude, and frivolity; he must possess the qualities of modesty, gentleness, clemency, humility, generosity, staunchness, patience, gratitude, pity, love of knowledge and justice.'

The long and bloody civil war had reduced the empire. The long absence of the Caliph, Mamun, from Baghdad had weakened stability. He now needed to move from Khurasan to Baghdad, but there were still serious obstacles to his return. His vizier, Fadl, was determined to keep him in Khurasan, and Mamun's appointment of the Shia, Aly Rida, as his successor, had led to revolt in Baghdad with his uncle, Ibrahim, saluted as Caliph. But chance or—as some whispered—assassination, cleared the way. Fadhl was found murdered in his bath, and Aly Rida died eating grapes.

With Mamun back in Baghdad, the pretender, his uncle, Ibrahim, went into hiding, but was finally found eight years later disguised as a woman and he was taken, an object of ridicule in his female attire, to the court of Mamun, who cried, 'Bravo! Is it you, Ibrahim?' He appealed for mercy and it was granted. Mamun was equally forgiving and gracious to all those who had opposed him. It was a time of reconciliation and forging of unity.

Mamun was known for his tolerance and open-mindedness. Even Christians and Jews felt secure, and many benefitted from the opportunities available to the elite. Jews predominated in banking and Christians were famous as doctors of medicine. Surprisingly, the one group which was persecuted by a new inquisition was the orthodox Muslim traditionalists. The debate of the time was between the traditionalists (who maintained that the holy *Quran* was eternal and therefore immutable) and the Mutazilites (who believed that it was created, and therefore could be reinterpreted by reason to adapt to changing times). The Caliph, Mamun, sided with the Mutazilites, who ceded greater authority to him, and started the persecution of the traditionalists who were seen as the party of opposition to the government. Their leader was Ahmad ibn Hanbal (founder of the Hanbali School of Jurisprudence) who was imprisoned and tortured but held firm to his beliefs. The flexibility of the Mutazilite doctrine supported the free flowering of intellectual enquiry that took place under the patronage of Mamun.

Other than the Sunni–Shia divide, there are four major schools of Islamic jurisprudence—the Hanafi, the Hanbali, the Shafii and the Maliki. Hazrat Ali, the leader of the Shia, was assassinated, as was Imam al Shafii. Imam Abu Hanifa, the founder of the leading Hanafi School, met a dramatic death at the hands of the Abbasid caliph, al-Mansur, when he refused the Caliph's offer that he become the chief judge of the state. Abu Hanifa declined saying he did not regard himself as fit for the job; al-Mansur lost his temper and accused Abu Hanifa of lying, to which he replied, 'If I am lying then my statement is doubly correct. How can you appoint a liar as chief qadi?' He was thrown into prison and tortured till he died in the year 767. Imam Ahmad ibn Hanbal, founder of the Hanbali School, was also imprisoned and tortured, but was finally released by a later caliph, with honour. Only Imam Malik ibn Anas, the founder of the Maliki School, lived and died peacefully in Medina, a respected elder at the age of eighty-four. Three of the four great 'Righteous Caliphs'—Umar, Uthman and Ali—were assassinated and practically the whole Umayyad clan was murdered at a feast hosted by the Abbasids, whose last caliph in Baghdad was, in turn, killed along with his family, by Hulagu, grandson of Genghis Khan. It was dangerous to be a leader in those times.

But despite the occasional murder, his use of inquisition and torture and the execution of his brother Amin at the end of their war for the caliphate, Mamun can be considered, comparatively, a reasonable, tolerant and humane leader who rebuilt the glory of the empire and took Abbasid rule to its heights. He died at the age of forty-six of a fever. His brother Mutasim, who was with him at the time, succeeded him as Caliph.

THE END OF AN ERA

It was not just presence at Mamun's deathbed that confirmed Mutasim over Abbas, Mamun's son, as the successor. Mutasim had a strong-arm; over the years, he had been building up a personal bodyguard of Turkish slave soldiers, which made him a dangerous man to oppose. Mutasim had, for years, been buying slaves which he built up into an elite fighting force. These 'Turks' did not come from Turkey, but from Central Asia—the areas of Uzbekistan, Kazakhstan, Turkmenistan—the steppes of the twentieth-century USSR. They were tough, hardy nomads, used to living in tents and moving with their herds of animals.

They introduced a new style of warfare—war on horseback by expert archers, who, from childhood had lived on horseback, and could take severe hardship and deprivation. Their support made

Mutasim a force to be reckoned with.

In the twentieth century, the Americans used a new type of soldier against the USSR—the Taliban—who later were to turn against their masters. So too, the Turks, introduced by Mutasim into the Abbasid praetorian guard, were to become the nemesis of the later Abbasids. These Turks, together with the Mongols from the grasslands of the steppes of Central Asia, were to conquer the major part of the world; their great conquerors Genghis Khan and his grandsons Hulagu, Mongke and Kublai, together with Tamerlane and his descendants, the Great Moguls of India—Babur and Akbar—and finally the Ottoman Turks who reached their zenith under Suleiman the Magnificent, were to rule for almost a thousand years from the Atlantic Ocean to China, and up through much of Europe to Moscow.

In Baghdad, the Arabs and Persians did not like these rough and rude intruders who were fast becoming the new elite. Recognising this, Mutasim decided to move to a new capital, Samarra, which he would build sixty miles north of Baghdad. This had two advantages—first, it isolated the Caliph and his Turkish guard from the undercurrents of Baghdad politics; and secondly, it allowed him both to use the vast tracts of newly valuable land at Samarra as grants to promote the loyalty of his army and to make vast profits through this new speculative opportunity.

From Samarra, the Caliph conducted a series of successful wars, while he continued his late brother's policies of supporting the Mutazilites and the Alids. The elite were divided into two groups—the Tahirids from Khurasan who also controlled Baghdad, and the Turkish slaves. Discontent between the groups led to a conspiracy to kill Mutasim and put Abbas, the son of Mamun, on the throne. Plied with drinks, the conspirators revealed their secrets and the conspiracy was exposed. They were killed in a purge, including Abbas, who was given tasty and salty food, and then denied water to drink till he died. Mutasim's reign was a time of stability and prosperity. He was an easygoing man, physically strong with a great interest in military matters, but not an intellectual. It is said that he was illiterate, which is surprising for an Abbasid prince; but clearly he had no interest in reading. He did, however, appoint as tutor to his son, the great mathematician and philosopher al-Kindi, considered by scholars of the Italian Renaissance as one of the twelve greatest minds of the Middle Ages.

Mutasim's new Turkish slave army ensured that he would rule till his death, and even after his death, the Turks protected his son Wathiq, who also ruled without challenge. But the damage was done and it was these hard soldiers from the East that destroyed and brought down the great Abbasid dynasty after the death of Wathiq.

A succession of caliphs suffered and died at the hands of the new Turkish terror, their own bodyguards. Mutawakil, the tenth Abbasid caliph, was assassinated by the Turkish troops on orders from his son Muntasir. Mustain, the twelfth Abbasid caliph, who was elected by the cabal of Turkish generals, tried to abdicate in favour of his brother, Mutaaz, but was killed together with his wife. His head was brought to Mutaaz, who was playing chess and casually remarked, 'Lay it aside till I have finished the game.' Mutaaz also put his brother Muyyad to death to eliminate the competition, but it didn't help; he was captured by his Turks who demanded 50,000 dinars to release him. He appealed to his mother, the fabulously rich Qahiba, who refused to help her son, saying she did not have the money. The twenty-four-year-old Caliph was denied food and water till he died. Qahiba, the Queen Mother, kept her treasure, but lost her son.

Mutahdi, the fourteenth Abbasid caliph, was chased by his Turks onto the roof where he was caught and killed by crushing his testicles. Al Murtada, the seventeenth in the line, ruled for only one day before he too was deposed and killed. Muqtadir, the eighteenth Abbasid caliph, was twice deposed by his Turks, but survived as a total puppet with no power, till finally, after over two decades of drunkenness, sensuality and extravagance, he was killed by his troops; his head impaled and his body left lying where he was slain. During his reign, the Abbasid Empire was truncated with Abdur Rahman III becoming Caliph in Spain, and the Fatimid dynasty establishing itself in Egypt—

the period of the triple caliphate. Qahir, the brother of Muqtadir, who became the nineteenth Abbasid caliph, within two years was deposed and blinded with red hot needles, then imprisoned for eleven years where he was tortured to extract his treasure. When finally released, he was reduced to begging for his food. Muttaqi, the twenty-first of his line, was blinded and later killed. His brother, Mustaqfi, the twenty-second caliph, was also blinded, so that at one time, three blind ex-caliphs could be seen wandering helpless, dependent on whatever handouts they could receive.

Blind and helpless, the caliphs were passed from one set of masters to another. Without dignity, they lived as servile puppets for the next two centuries, first under the Shia Buyids, and then under the Sunni Seljuks. Finally, in 1258, a new conqueror, the Mongol, Hulagu, grandson of the great Genghis Khan, hit Baghdad, killing not just the Caliph but slaughtering the entire population and destroying the city and its environs. The rule of the Abbasids in Baghdad ended.

The early Muslims were hardy men, who lived simple lives, without luxury. Every Muslim was a soldier, whose duty was jihad. But by this time, success and conquest had turned the tough warriors into a luxury-loving elite, who paid mercenaries or slaves to fight on their behalf. These Turkish slaves finally took power from their masters, the caliphs. To save themselves from their new 'masters'—the cruel Turk slaves—the caliphs welcomed the Shia Persian Buyids, who proved to not be saviours, but a new set of oppressors. Once again, they waited for new saviours and the Ghaznavids (Turks from Central Asia) replaced the Persian Buwayids. The Ghaznavids were ousted by the Seljuk Turks, and when the Seljuks proved too oppressive, the Caliph welcomed the Khwarezm Shah, the latest in the line of conquerors from the East. The Caliph then made his biggest mistake. He invited the emerging conqueror, Genghis Khan, to save them from the Khwarezm Shah. Genghis destroyed the Khwarezm Shah and his grandson, Hulagu, destroyed Baghdad, creating his new dynasty, the Il-Khans.

Even as the Persians, Turks and Mongols in turn took control of the Abbasid Empire and its caliphs in Baghdad, the Umayyads resurrected an empire in Spain, and the Ismaili Fatimids, sweeping across North Africa, established their capital at Cairo. As the old Abbasid Empire grew more and more feeble, the new dynasties in Spain and Egypt grew increasingly stronger. These new empires expanded as the old empire contracted. Three ethnic groups, each with its own experience and skills, controlled different functions in the empire—the Arab Muslims and their ulema were in charge of religion and law, the Persians were charge of the administration and bureaucracy and the Turks provided the army and the generals.

Spain was isolated by its distance but the rest of the world of the Muslims was hit by two attacks—from the West came the crusaders, determined to win back the holy lands of Palestine; from the East came the Turks and Mongols, first to take over and then to destroy. The crusaders were the lesser evil, and were the concern of the Muslims of the West, in Syria and Egypt. The Mongols in the East were the truly unstoppable disaster. Through these calamities, another problem added to the instability of the times—the Ismaili Assassins spread terror with their suicide killers whose dramatic murders could hit anywhere, threatening Saladin in the West and killing Nizam ul Mulk, the brilliant vizier of the Seljuks, in the East.

THE LEGACY ENDURES

Even as the power of the caliphs eroded, the myth of the caliphate endured. For the caliphs were not mere kings; they were there, in theory at least, to protect and promote Islam. Descended from the family of The Prophet himself, they had, in the minds of the Muslims, a legitimacy that superseded kingship or force of arms. Their mandate was Islam, the greatest legacy of Muhammad. So a strange phenomenon developed; their conquerors dominated the caliphs, controlled them as puppets, blinded and even killed them but accepted their sovereignty and used them to confer legitimacy on their new dynasties.

The Turkish slave generals who usurped power from the Abbasid caliphs, lacked legitimacy, both because they had started their lives as slaves, and also because they belonged to a completely different ethnic group or race. By keeping the Abbasids on as titular caliphs, they sidestepped the obvious resentment they would have faced if they had replaced them totally. This held even truer for the Buyids who were not only from a different race, but also from a different sect—the Shia—whereas the majority of the citizens were Sunni. The Seljuk Turks also recognized the advantage of retaining a caliph, and so did the Mamlukes of Egypt; and so the tradition of Abbasid titular sovereigns conferring legitimacy, endured for 500 years till the last caliph, Mutawakkil, was carried off to Constantinople by the great Ottoman conqueror, Salim the Grim. Mutawakkil, tired of living as a captive in poverty, resigned and retired back to Egypt, after which the Ottomans claimed the caliphate.

EXTRAORDINARY LEADERS ON THE HORIZON

The three dynasties that ruled through the decline of the Abbasids, each produced a remarkable leader. The greatest Buyid, Adudal Dawla, consolidated the small and divided kingdoms of the Buyid family, created an empire and finally took the title of Shahinshah. He was not only the greatest Buyid, but also the most illustrious ruler of his time. He married the daughter of the Caliph, and married his own daughter to the Caliph. He had an able Christian vizier, Nasr ibn Harun, and promoted science and learning. He built famous hospitals and other public works.

The greatest Ghaznavid was Sultan Mahmud of Ghazni, son of Subuktigin, who is remembered as a military hero by the Muslims. The Pakistan army has named its Ghaznavi missile after him. He was a passionate Muslim and saw himself as a Ghazi waging jihad against the Hindus. He made seventeen raids into India, smashing idols, destroying temples and taking massive booty back to embellish his capital, Ghazni, which became one of the great cities of the world.

His raid on the temple of Somnath has passed into legend, with his smashing of the idol, to discover a vast treasure hidden therein. The love of his life was his slave, Malik Ayaz, whom he made King of Lahore. Ayaz was no beauty, but it was his character that attracted Mahmud. He was precocious, once telling Mahmud that he was a greater king than Mahmud, because love had made Mahmud into the 'slave of his slave'. It is said that Mahmud, to avoid temptation, lest he allow the relationship to sink into sin, once cut the locks of Ayaz, determined to keep his relationship platonic. Many such stories are told of this love.

The greatest of the Seljuks was Alp Arslan. He was a soldier, whose pride and passion was war. He left the civil administration in the hands of his Persian vizier, Nizam al-Mulk, as did his son Malik Shah. Nizam al-Mulk was the greatest vizier of the Muslim empires, and his legacy includes his famous schools which became the blueprint for the universities that followed in Europe. His treatise on government, the *Siyasatnama,* has become a classic on the art of government. Alp Arslan defeated the Byzantine emperor Romanos at the pivotal battle of Manzikert. Romanos was taken prisoner and brought before Alp Arslan, who asked, 'What would you do if I was brought before you as prisoner?'

'Perhaps I would kill you,' replied Romanos.

'My punishment is much heavier,' said Alp Arslan, 'I forgive you and set you free.'

Alp Arslan was an outstanding archer, but his excellence was to prove the death of him. In battle, when an assassin came forward with a dagger to attack him, he ordered his guards to hold back, thinking to make the kill himself; but his foot slipped, the arrow missed its mark and the assassin plunged his dagger into his heart. As he lay dying, the great warrior advised his generals, 'Do not let your vanity override your good sense.'

7

The Rise of Egypt

Balian, the Christian leader at Jerusalem, said to Saladin, 'When the Christians captured Jerusalem, they massacred every Muslim in the city walls.' Saladin replied, 'I am not of those men. I am Salahudin.'

'By a single warrior on foot, a king may be with terror, though he own more than a hundred thousand horsemen'.

(From an Ismaili poem in praise of the Assassins)

As the Abbasids grew weaker in Baghdad, Egypt took the centre stage in the world of Islam. For over 500 years, three dynasties—the Fatimids, Saladin's Ayubids, and the Mamluk slave dynasty—ruled Egypt and dominated the Muslims.

By the middle of the tenth century, the Buyids controlled the Abbasid Empire, retaining the caliphs as mere titular puppets. The Buyids were Shias from Persia. In the second half of the tenth century, the Fatimids, who claimed descent from Fatima, the daughter of The Prophet, took Egypt and created their empire in the West. The Fatimids were Ismaili Shias. For the first time, Shias ruled the major part of the umma of Islam. Even the holy cities of Mecca and Medina fell under Shia control.

It was a time of tumult and change with remarkable men—Hakim 'the Mad'; the great Saladin, hero of Jerusalem; and the warrior Baybars who defeated the invincible Mongols at the battle of Ayn Jalut. It was a time of the first female rulers in Islam, the Fatimid Princess, Sitt el Mulk, and the Sultana, Shajar al Durr, who presided over the end of the Ayubid dynasty and the birth of the Mamluk era. It was the age of the Crusades, the Assassins and the World Conqueror, Genghis Khan.

The story of medieval Egypt started with Ahmad ibn Tulun, a slave from Farghana in Central Asia who was gifted to the Caliph, al-Mamun, in Baghdad. Ahmad was sent to Egypt with the Abbasid army as lieutenant to the governor. He established his independence from his Abbasid masters, and stopped sending vast tribute to Baghdad, preferring to spend the money in Egypt. He was a good ruler, and Egypt prospered. He died leaving a treasury of 10 million dinars and a fleet of a hundred ships. But, as so often happens, this capable ruler was succeeded by a mediocre son, whose only memorable achievement was to arrange the marriage of his daughter Qatr al-Nada (Dewdrop) to the Caliph in Baghdad, wasting an absolutely enormous amount of money on the wedding.

Once more the Caliph's army conquered Egypt, reducing the country by plunder and extortion. The invaders grew rich as the Egyptians grew poor. Then another capable governor, Muhammad ibn Tugh al-Ikhshid, arrived and re-established stability. In Baghdad, the caliphs had lost effective power as their own foreign soldiers deposed, blinded and killed them. The governor moved away from the control of his masters, ruling in their name but ignoring their authority till he died, and once again, incompetent sons replaced a competent father. For twenty-two years till the end of the dynasty, Egypt was governed by their tutor, a black eunuch named Abu al-Misk Kafur (also called Musky Camphor).

In 967 AD, a low flood of the Nile led to famine as 600,000 people died of starvation. When there were no more animals to slaughter, parents started to eat their children. In 968 AD, Kafur died and a plague spread. In 969 AD, the Fatimid army conquered Egypt.

THE FATIMIDS

In the Maghreb region of Mediterranean Africa, at the start of the tenth century, Abu Abdullah drove out the Aghlabids, rescued Ubaidullah al Mahdi Billah and installed him as the first Fatimid caliph. Within two years Ubaidullah, succumbing to paranoia, assassinated Abu Abdullah in a move reminiscent of the murder of Abu Muslim after he brought the Abbasids to power.

The Buyid takeover had weakened the Abbasid caliphs and the Maghreb was a long way from Baghdad. This combination of decline and distance, gave the new Fatimid dynasty of North Africa free reign to establish a growing empire. Much closer to home, in Bahrain, another Shia group, the Qarmatians, effectively cut Baghdad off from the Hejaz. In 906 AD, they killed 20,000 pilgrims en route to the holy cities of Mecca and Medina. In 928 AD, they sacked the holy cities, desecrated the waters of Zam Zam with corpses, and stole the black stone from the Kaaba, which they only returned on the payment of ransom after twenty-two years.

The fourth Fatimid caliph, al Muizz (953–975 AD), seized the opportunity created by the power vacuum in Egypt which had, in quick succession, suffered famine, plague and the death of the strongman Kafur, sending his able general, Jawhar the Sicilian, to annex this rich land. In 969 AD, Jawhar defeated the Egyptian army, conquered Egypt and founded the new capital city of al Qahirah (Cairo). Within the next three years, Jawhar added Syria and Damascus to the Fatimid territories.

In 973 AD, when the situation in Egypt was stable and safe, Muizz made his triumphant entry into Cairo, and the good and able Jawhar, retired to the sidelines, never to be heard of again. A series of remarkable caliphs followed, Aziz and Hakim, and then Muntasir, who ruled almost sixty years during a period when Fatimid wealth and power reached its peak. The golden age of the Fatimids was the result of a century of capable rulers, luck and a set of policies that valued and promoted merit, tolerance, trade, production, education and culture. These policies created wealth which reached the people of Egypt rather than being siphoned off to a luxury loving elite in distant Baghdad. Without a doubt, the Fatimids were equally addicted to luxury and excess, but at least the money spent at home, was circulated in the local economy. Gold from Ghana boosted the value of the currency and the surplus harvests of the generous Nile River, combined with the tribute paid by vassal states to an expanding empire, ensured new heights of prosperity. The economy was masterfully handled by Yaqub ibn Killis, a converted Jew, who acted as finance minister both under the Caliph, Muizz, and his son, Aziz. Yaqub made Egypt the centre of international trade, connecting the Middle East to India and the Far East.

Muizz was a great man of varied talents. The Fatimid conqueror of Egypt can also be credited with the invention of the fountain pen. His demand for a pen which would not stain his hands or his clothes is recorded in detail by his historian Qadi al-Numan al-Tamimi:

> We wish to construct a pen which can be used for writing without having recourse to an ink holder and whose ink will be contained inside it. A person can fill it with ink and write whatever he likes. The writer can put it in his sleeve or anywhere he wishes and it will not stain nor will any drop of ink leak out of it. The ink will flow only when there is an intention to write. We are unaware of anyone previously ever constructing a pen such as this. I explained, 'Is this possible?' He replied, 'It is possible if God so wills.'

In 996 AD, Muizz died. His able and charismatic son, al-Aziz, 'generous, courageous with a propensity for clemency', became Caliph and continued the policies of his great father. He retained his father's financial guru, Yacub bin Killis, whose tax reduction and trade promotion maintained the high growth rate of the economy. He built a powerful navy. Aziz was reputed to be the wisest and most beneficent of all the Fatimid caliphs of Egypt. But he made one serious mistake which was eventually to cost the Fatimids their dynasty. To balance the power of his Berber and Sudanese battalions, he imported Turkish soldiers to strengthen his defence capability and his internal security. Clearly, he had not studied with care, the history of the Abbasid caliph, al Muntasir, who had gone down this same road. Those who will not learn from the mistakes of others are destined to suffer the same consequences. Just as they had done in Baghdad, the Turk mercenaries eventually took Egypt from their masters, and their dynasty, the Mamluks, ruled for two and a half centuries.

After two great caliphs, came Hakim, the sixth Fatimid caliph, and the sixteenth Ismaili imam, who was definitely the most controversial ruler of the medieval Islamic world. For 15 million Ismailis, he is the ideal supreme ruler, divinely ordained and chosen; for 2 million Druze, he is the incarnation of God; Western historians have named him 'The Mad Caliph' and see him as an eccentric tyrant given to killing those around him on a whim. Hakim was volatile and unpredictable. At times, he was tolerant with Christians and Jews but intolerant of Sunni Muslims; then he would reverse his policies as his pendulum would swing to the opposite extreme with the destruction of 30,000 churches and humiliation of Christians forced to wear heavy iron crosses about their necks, and Jews with wooden calf heads dangling from their necks.

On the positive side, he was generous and was a dedicated patron of education who founded the famous Dar al Ilm, the House of Knowledge, in Cairo. He was renowned as an effective administrator who was ruthless in dealing with his officials with an obsession to eradicate corruption and immorality.

On the other hand, he was vicious and ordered murder casually on a whim. His atrocities were terrible. It was rumored that he invented novel forms of torture. Reputed to have executed as many as 18,000 people—many innocent—he, once when walking past a public bath, heard the happy sounds of women bathing inside, and immediately ordered it to be sealed, leaving all the women to perish within. Once he cut off the hands of a musician, then sent him a thousand pieces of gold to make up for it; then feeling he had been too kind, he cut off the man's tongue. He ordered the killing of dogs and the burning of chessboards. Stanley Lane-Poole, the historian, writes of him:

> *Officials were tortured and killed like flies, arms were hacked off, tongues cut out, every kind of barbarity inflicted... General Fadl had the misfortune to enter the royal presence when Hakim was busily engaged in cutting up the body of a beautiful little child whom he had just murdered with his own knife. Fadl could not restrain his horror but he knew the consequences: he went home, made his will and admitted the caliph's headmen an hour later. He had seen too much.*

He believed women should stay indoors in their homes, and to prevent them from going out, forbade shoemakers from making shoes for them. Christian women were ordered to wear shoes of different colors—black on one foot, red on the other. Many thought it strange, but perhaps no more strange than the fashions of today when women proudly wear Christian Louboutin shoes, black above and red below.

Al-Haytham, one of the greatest scientific geniuses of his time, made the long journey from Central Asia to Cairo and offered his services to Hakim. He would build a dam at Aswan to harness the Nile. But try as he did, success eluded him, and knowing the reputation of the Caliph, he began to fear for his life. He feigned madness to escape the wrath of the Caliph, himself considered unstable if not mad. He survived but the dam at Aswan was shelved for 1,500 years till in the twentieth century, President Nasser showed it could be done.

His spy network gave him a profusion of information that he used to promote his supernatural reputation. His extreme austerity and unusual ways added to his myth. His complicated relationship with his intelligent and beautiful sister, Sitt el Mulk, created tensions, with accusations of her improper lifestyle. For some years, he forbade the pilgrimage to Mecca, and his elevation by the new Druze religion to divine status, made many question whether he was a true Muslim. In a fit of rage, he ordered that old Cairo be set on fire and for three days, watched it being burned and pillaged till he ordered a stop. Finally, one night he walked into the desert, alone, as was his habit, and was never seen again. It is rumored that his sister conspired to have him murdered, but nothing was ever proved. His end was as strange as his life.

Hakim's son, Zahir, was proclaimed Caliph, but since he was only sixteen, his aunt, Sitt el Mulk, effectively ruled as regent. She restored good order and set the kingdom back on the road to prosperity, but after four years, she died.

Zahir was a pleasure-loving self-indulgent young man, with a sudden cruel streak which proved him his father's son. He once invited all the young girls of the palace to a party and they came dressed in their finest clothes. The doors were locked and 2,660 girls were starved to death; their bodies lay unburied for six months. A few years later, Zahir himself died a victim to the plague.

The young Muntasir became Caliph at the tender age of seven and ruled for sixty years. The long period of his rule was volatile; he inherited an empire with fabulous wealth at its height, but when a terrible famine hit Egypt, he was reduced to living on the charity of two loaves of bread a day. The empire eventually recovered and he ended his days in comfort after a roller coaster of ups and downs.

While the Caliph was a mere child, power was exercised by his mother who had started her life as the black slave of a Jewish slaver. She was not the smartest of rulers, and the empire contracted to little more than Egypt as the dominions broke away. But once Muntasir took over the reins of government, peace and prosperity were substantially restored, despite the interference of his dominating mother.

To counter the power of the Turkish troops that had been imported by Aziz, Muntasir's Sudanese mother had imported her own black army from the Sudan. Jealousy between the two armies led to disorder, and the Turks finally took control of the capital, raised their own wages by twenty times, and started to plunder the wealth of the Caliph, forcing him to sell his treasures to them at a fraction of their value. They treated the Caliph with contempt.

At the same time, Egypt was hit by a terrible famine which lasted for seven years, draining what little was left of the fabulous wealth of Egypt that Muntasir had inherited. All the animals were slaughtered and eaten, then the stray dogs and cats, and finally when no more animals of any kind were left, people started eating each other. Using hooks on rope, they 'fished' for passersby, catching them, dragging them up and cooking and eating them. One lady vividly tells of her own horrible experience, in Paton's *A History of the Egyptian Revolution*:

> My flesh being plump, I was seized and dragged into a room covered with marks of blood and exhaling a smell of dead bodies. I was then thrown, naked, flat on my face, and my hands and feet tied; and after the excision of cutlets from my hips, they were roasted and eaten. The men having indulged in wine to excess, fell senseless with drunkenness on the floor... (I escaped). My wounds have now healed, but my body is still furrowed with deep scars.

The famine was followed by a terrible plague. Rich and poor alike were desperate for food, the price of which rocketed even as the price for houses and jewelry plummeted. A house was exchanged for twenty pounds of flour; an heirloom necklace for a mere handful of flour. The army of the Turks forced the Caliph to sell his priceless treasures for a pittance—an emerald necklace valued at 300,000 dinars was purchased by a Turkish general for 500 dinars. And the fabulous library of the Caliph, famed for its collection of 2,400 illuminated *Qurans* and its autographed copy of Tabari's history, was looted with rare manuscripts, used to fuel fires, and ornate leather bindings used for repairing the shoes of the Turkish slaves.

Muntasir was finally saved from the Turkish terror by Bedr el-Gemali who had started life as an Armenian slave but was now the most powerful general in Syria. Bedr arrived and was received cordially by the Turks, but secretly each Turkish general was marked as victim to one of his officers. In the morning, each of his officers appeared with a Turk's head in his hands. In one night, the problem was resolved and the Caliph was back in control. Bedr was ruthless in establishing his authority throughout Egypt and up to Aswan. He brought back so many captives that a slave girl could be bought for a dinar. For the next twenty years, till he died, Muntasir ruled an Egypt of peace and plenty.

After Muntasir, the decline of the Fatimids continued, irreversible. The days of glory were over, and finally, the great Saladin extinguished the dynasty and ended the era as gently as he would have snuffed the flame of a candle at the end of an evening.

SALADIN

'Win the hearts of your people and watch over their prosperity; for it is to secure their happiness that you are appointed by God and by me... I have become as great as I am because I have won men's hearts by gentleness and kindness.'

—Saladin (On his deathbed; his advice on kingship, to his son)

Salah ad-Din Yusuf ibn Ayyub, known to the West as Saladin, had a privileged youth. As reward for services rendered, Saladin's father had earned a governorship. His uncle, Shirkuh, was a highly placed general. Saladin, while still a teenager, had been an aide of Nur al-Din and had learned his values and attitudes from his God-fearing master. Unlike so many who are born to privilege, Saladin was to become the most respected and admired ruler of his age.

Saladin was a slender man with a dark complexion, a Kurd born in Tikrit, also the birthplace of Iraq's notorious Saddam Hussein. Surprisingly, he was not a great general and always preferred diplomacy and negotiation to fighting. He was indifferent to the trappings of power; his food, clothes and home were simple. His small house was in stark contrast to the Caliph's palace of 4,000 rooms that he inherited together with its library of 120,000 books and sacks full of jewels (including an emerald four-fingers long and a ruby over 2,400 carats) which he gave away. He kept nothing for himself. He was chivalrous to a fault, enjoyed chess and loved polo, which gave him opportunity to indulge his passion for horses. He loved to spend his evenings with his friends, scholars and poets, where the discussion was free, without protocol or flattery. He was a family man, whose wife gave him sixteen sons. His brothers were his most important lieutenants. There was nothing low, vain or petty in his character and all his life he impressed others by his example.

Saladin was kind and generous to all, and fortune, in turn, was kind and generous to him. His effortless rise is a story that defies belief.

Almost unwillingly, he went with his uncle Shirkuh's army into Egypt where Shawar, the crafty vizier of the Fatimid caliph, was playing off the Crusaders against the Muslims, sometimes siding with one and sometimes with the other. Shirkuh defeated the vizier, and when he conspired to assassinate Shirkuh, the general killed him and took the vizierate himself. Within two months, Shirkuh died from overeating, leaving the way open for Saladin to succeed him. Saladin was seen by all as young, inexperienced and weak, which made him the perfect choice.

Al-Adid, the last Fatimid caliph, was a sick young man. When Saladin's boss, Sultan Nur al-Din, put pressure that Al-Adid's rule be terminated, Saladin ordered that Al-Adid's name be replaced by the Abbasid caliph's name in the Friday prayer in the mosque, but that he should not be informed of the change: 'If he recovers, he will know the truth soon enough; if not, let him die in peace.' Al-Adid died three days later, unaware of the change in his status. Saladin avoided inflicting pain even on his enemies.

In quick succession, Al-Adid, the last of the Fatimid caliphs, died, followed by Sultan Nur al-Din, Saladin's boss; next to pass away was Amalric, the Christian King and Saladin's most powerful enemy.

THE RISE OF EGYPT | 93

Luck, destiny or divine intervention had removed the five men who could have obstructed the rise to power of the reluctant ruler, Saladin, who now reigned supreme. To further his legitimacy, he married the widow of Sultan Nur al-din.

When Saladin took power in Egypt, the country was rich as a transit hub for international trade between Europe and the East (India and China). But his success, which would have satisfied other young men, was but a stepping stone to fulfillment of his dreams and objectives, to unite the Muslims, to drive out the Crusaders and to retake Jerusalem. Throughout Syria and Egypt, rival groups fought for power and their lack of unity had given the opening to the Crusaders to enter and conquer. Famous as the terminator of the Ismaili Fatimid caliphate, he had earned the hatred of the Ismaili Assassins, the dangerous secretive sect who, from their mountain base, spread terror with their dramatic public assassinations of powerful men. Their grand master was the Iraqi born Rashid al-Din Sinan, the 'Osama bin Laden' of his time.

The Assassins claimed they could kill anyone. Usually when they sent their fidayeen, the victim died. Three times they sent killers to Saladin; three times they failed. Saladin's proverbial luck, which had disposed of those who had stood between him and his destiny, intervened to repeatedly save his life from these ultimate assassins.

- In October 1174, the Assassins forced their way into his tent; they were killed by his guard.
- In May 1176 while he was resting in his tent, an Assassin rushed in and struck him with a dagger. Saladin was saved by the armored mail he was wearing; the assassin and his accomplices were killed.
- In August 1176 when he was riding with his troops, an Assassin dropped out of a walnut tree onto Saladin's horse; but his timing was out and he fell onto the rump and then to the ground where he was trampled and hacked to death by the guards.

As a precaution, Saladin always wore chain mail, and took to sleeping in a tall wooden tower. Finally, an emissary of the Assassins came to see him with a message. Saladin allowed him into the tent, but kept his guards on hand. The emissary refused to deliver the message unless the guards were removed, so Saladin passed the order, but retained his two most trusted bodyguards, saying,

'These two do not leave me. If you wish to deliver your message, do so, and if not, go.'

He said, 'Why do you not send away these two as you sent away the others?'

Saladin replied, 'I regard these two as my own sons, and they and I are as one.' The messenger turned to the two Mamluks and said, 'If I ordered you, in the name of my Master, to kill this Sultan, would you do so?'

They answered yes and drew their swords, saying, 'Command us as you wish.'

Sultan Saladin was astounded and the messenger left, taking them with him. And thereupon Saladin inclined to make peace with him and enter into friendly relations with him. And God knows best.

The Assassins that threatened Saladin lived in the mountains of Syria and were led by Rashid ud din Sinan (the Old Man of the Mountain). These killers were the Syrian branch of the movement that had been created almost a century earlier by Hassan al-Sabbah, Lord of Alamut, his mountain base being Persia. Hassan was an exceptional man, a thinker, writer and man of action, 'learned in geometry, arithmetic, astronomy, magic and other things.' He had converted to the Ismaili doctrine at the age of seventeen, and then disillusioned by Cairo, where realpolitik had replaced the religious mission of the early Fatimids, he moved to the mountain fortress of Alamut, securing his base area in a strategy that was successfully followed by Mao Zedong a thousand years later.

Hassan was ascetic, abstemious and pious; it was said of him that he had no pride or arrogance and emanated calm and good will. Once he secured Alamut, he spent his years studying, praying, and teaching and preparing his new breed of assassins, the prototype suicide killers of Islam, which in the twentieth century, have inspired the suicide bombers who have terrorized both the Christian and the Muslim worlds. These fidayeen were eager to die as martyrs on their dramatic missions where they would publically kill their victims with their daggers and then wait fearlessly for death.

Hassan never left Alamut till his death—in fact, only twice in thirty-five years did he leave his house, and that only to go onto his roof. He killed one of his sons on suspicion of murder. The boy was subsequently discovered to be innocent. He put his second son to death for drinking wine. His wife and daughters left him, never to return. He lived out his life alone with his deadly mission.

Hassan, an Ismaili Shia, was the sworn enemy of the Sunni Seljuks, whose great empire under the flag of the powerless Abbasid caliphs, had reached its peak under Sultan Malikshah, and his brilliant vizier, Nizam ul-Mulk. Hassan was determined to kill the vizier, and one of his assassins approached the great man with a petition, and while he was reading it, dispatched him with his dagger. Forty days later, Sultan Malikshah also died and the affairs of the realm were thrown into confusion. Nizam ul-Mulk's two sons were also attacked by assassins, and one was paralyzed in the attack. The Seljuk kingdom splintered as brothers and sons fought for control.

Saladin, after neutralizing the Assassins and uniting the Muslims, could now focus on his life mission of defeating the Crusaders and retaking or liberating Jerusalem. The two great armies met at Hittin, where Saladin won total victory. The Christian King and his generals were taken as prisoners and so many soldiers were sold into slavery that the price of a slave plummeted to an all-time low.

Now, finally, Saladin prepared his assault on the holy city of Jerusalem. One of the Christian knights who had survived the disaster at Hittin was Balian; he approached Saladin with a request for permission to travel through the Muslim lines to bring his wife and children out of Jerusalem, to safety. Saladin agreed on the condition that Balian stay in Jerusalem only one night and not take part in the fighting. Balian gave his oath to abide by this condition. In Jerusalem,

Balian was touched by the sad plight of the Christians. Clearly, it was his duty as a Christian to stay and take command. So Balian wrote again to Saladin explaining his dilemma. The reply amazed the Christians; not only did Saladin release the knight from his sworn oath, he even arranged for the man's wife and children to be escorted to safety. And so Balian stayed to prepare a heroic, though hopeless defense.

Saladin tried his best for a peaceful capitulation of Jerusalem. He offered extraordinarily generous terms but the Christian leaders were determined to fight; then after two weeks of siege, the city surrendered. The Christian conquest of Jerusalem in 1099 had culminated in a disgraceful massacre with looting, rape and even cannibalism. The Muslim conquest almost a century later, in 1187, was in stark contrast, a display of chivalry, mercy and restraint. In Jerusalem, Saladin not only won his place in history as one of the greatest heroes of Islam, but also earned the admiration and respect of even his foes as a man of exceptional humanity, morality and honor. Saladin set ransom money for the Christians to buy their freedom. The amount was not high—ten dinars per man, five per woman and one for each child. For the poor who could not raise even this moderate sum, Saladin himself, together with his brother, paid the ransom money, earning the undying gratitude of those they freed. In contrast, Heraclius, the head of the Church in Jerusalem, paid his own ransom of ten dinars and was allowed to leave with a cartload of treasure belonging to the Church. The patriarch never offered to pay for a single man—unlike Saladin, he valued the money more than the Christian souls which were his responsibility.

The loss of Jerusalem triggered the third Crusade, whose most famous knight was Richard, King of England, the Lion-Heart. Richard was a tough fighter who had taken the crown from his father by force on the battlefield. From the moment he arrived in the Middle East, he took the offensive. He took Acre and when Saladin was not fast enough to meet his demands, he slaughtered 3,000 Muslim prisoners. He inspired terror amongst the Muslims. Richard took the other coastal cities and now threatened Jerusalem itself. But it was not to be. Dissention within the Christian ranks, followed by conspiracy of his brother John, back in England, forced him to abandon the war and set back on his journey home. Departing, he promised that he would be back to take Jerusalem; Saladin replied with grace that if he had to lose his land, he would rather lose it to Richard than anyone else.

Many are the tales of chivalry between these two remarkable men—how Saladin sent ice water to relieve Richard's fever, and the time when he sent a horse to Richard when his steed was killed in battle, leaving him a helpless target. Richard negotiated with Saladin's brother for a settlement and even offered his sister Joanne in marriage to create a united kingdom in which Jerusalem would be the wedding gift to the newlyweds and would be open to Christians and Muslims alike. Finally, a three-year truce was signed. Richard never made the pilgrimage to Jerusalem, and Saladin never made the pilgrimage to Mecca. Saladin died, honored but poor. Careless of wealth, he had given away fortunes. His own wealth, when he died, was not enough to pay even for a simple funeral.

After his death, infighting erupted between his sons and finally his brother took control. But with the new century, came famine and plague with a death rate so high that one property changed hands forty times in a single month. In 1240, al-Salih Ayyub, who was ruling Damascus, was invited by the emirs in Cairo to take over from his brother whom they had ousted. He returned and became Sultan, but lived in insecurity, fearing conspiracy from his family and from the powerful emirs. To protect himself, he created a new regiment of Turkish slaves, known as Mamluks, who were to save his kingdom but destroy his dynasty.

Al-Salih died in his tent in 1249, preparing to tackle a new Crusade under the leadership of the French King, Louis IX. His wife, Shajar al-Durr, concealed the fact lest demoralization set in, and had his son established on the throne; he was to be the last of the Ayyubids. Shajar al-Durr followed a great line of women who have affected the history of Egypt—six women pharaohs including the great Hatsheput; the manipulative femme fatale Cleopatra, who had married, first, her own brother, then Julius Caesar and finally Mark Antony; and more recently, Sitt el Mulk, who had ruled as regent after the death of her brother, the Fatimid caliph, al-Hakim.

THE MAMLUKS

Shajar al-Durr was a beautiful lady. She was also intelligent, strong and irresistible. She started her amazing career in the harem of the Caliph and moved into the bed of al-Salih, and after giving him a son, became Queen of the great Egyptian empire. After the death of the Sultan, she moved from regent to Sultana, as the choice of the powerful Mamluk amirs who held effective power. For eighty days she ruled on her own, till her former master, the Caliph, sent a message to the Mamluk generals: 'If you have no man to rule you, let us know and we will send you one.' When the generals chose Aybak as commander-in-chief and Sultan, she married him, retaining him as her subordinate, and keeping to herself the keys of the treasury.

Aybak, the first Mamluk sultan, was a happy man—husband of a beautiful queen and ruler of a great empire, he even had a sexy young mistress. But when he prepared to marry the new object of his desire, fate, in the person of a jealous wife, intervened. She had him murdered in his bath. She, in turn, was beaten to death by the palace slave girls, ending the career of this remarkable lady, the former slave girl who was the last queen of the Ayubid dynasty and the first queen of the Mamluks.

In the Christian world of the West, enslavement was the greatest disaster that could hit any man. Treated as animals, the black slaves of America lived in sub-human conditions, tormented by cruel domination and the lash. The best that a black slave could hope for in America was to become a 'house nigger' or 'Uncle Tom'. Slavery was the fate of anyone with a 'black' skin.

However, the Prophet had enjoined kind treatment of slaves on the Muslims. Slaves ate with their masters and lived almost as members of an extended family. In the West, slavery was racial; there was no escape for anyone with a black skin. In the world of early Islam, slavery was religious—no Muslim could be enslaved, conversion to Islam offered a release from slavery. In the Muslim umma, enslavement was a career opportunity that frequently led to power and glory, just as the great universities of the West, Oxford, Cambridge, Harvard and Yale, are today. In the history of the Middle East and Asia, slaves who became kings and even slave dynasties, are commonplace. But even here, the Mamluk slave dynasty of Egypt that ruled for over 250 years, stands out as unique.

The Mamluks were a race apart from the subjects that they ruled. They spoke a different language, followed different values and cultures and lived as a military oligarchy interested in only what they could take, not what they could give to the people and land that they ruled. The explosion of science that had been the amazing achievement of the Muslims, now faded, but architecture and building reached new heights. Their rule has been divided into two dynasties—the Bahri Mamluks and the Burji Mamluks—after the location of their barracks. The Bahris were housed in the Nile River (bahria) and the Burjis in the citadel (burj). Together they ruled an empire from their headquarters in Cairo for 270 years. The tradition of foreign rule continued in Egypt—the Fatimids had come from the Maghreb; Saladin was a Kurd; and the Mamluks were slave mercenaries from Central Asia.

After the murder of Aybak in his bathtub, Qutuz took control, first as regent for Aybak's son, then after deposing him, as Sultan himself. But it was not a good time to be a king in the Muslim world. Sultan Qutuz could not look forward to a leisurely rule with wine, women and song; instead, he was faced with the conquering armies of Hulagu, the grandson of Genghis Khan. Hulagu sent envoys; Qutuz had them executed—not the best way to start a relationship with the family of the World Conqueror. It looked like a bad move; a big mistake. But luck intervened. Thousands of miles away, Mongke, Hulagu's brother and boss, died. Taking revenge for Qutuz's bad behavior and conquering Egypt fell on Hulagu's priority list. But getting back to headquarters to join the negotiations on succession of the leadership of the empire of Genghis Khan was clearly much more important. Hulagu departed with his main army, leaving his general, Kitbuqa, in command of a small force of 20,000 men.

The armies met on the field of Ayn Jalut in 1260. On both sides the Turk and Mongol cavalry, the finest fighters of the age, readied for battle. The Mongols were led by an experienced general hardened by many battles in many campaigns. The Mamluks were led by a great general who was to become a legend, the blond, blue-eyed, Baibars. At Ayn Jalut, the unstoppable Mongol advance was stopped, the unbeatable Mongol army was beaten and Kitbuqa was captured and taken to Qutuz, who reviled him. Kitbuqa boldly replied that one year's births among the people and horses of the Mongols would make good the losses of that day and then the revenge of the Great Khan would be terrible; he asked to be beheaded without hearing any more insults, and that was immediately done. The hero of the day was the Mamluk general, Baibars. The victorious general had high expectations of reward and honor, but Qutuz disappointed him. Baibars, always a man of action, killed his Sultan and the murdered Sultan was succeeded by his murderer.

Akbar was the great Mogul; Suleiman, the great Ottoman; and Baibars was the greatest of the Mamluks. He started his life as a slave sold for the small sum of 800 dirhams but was returned because of a defect in one of his eyes. A giant of a man with immense strength, bold and resourceful with a wicked sense of humor, he became a legendary hero to the Egyptian people. He was a brilliant general who defeated the Mongols, drove out the Crusaders, and conquered Nubia in North Africa. He was an outstanding administrator who built canals, harbours and other public works and created a state-of-the- art postal service. He was a visionary statesman whose alliance with The Golden Horde, a branch of the Mongol family which held the kingdom in Southern Russia, was crucial in countering the massive power of the Il-Khans, his greatest enemy. He also signed commercial treaties with several European powers.

Within a year of becoming Sultan, he made cunning moves to reinforce his legitimacy. He invited to Egypt a survivor of the family of the Caliph, who had been wiped out by Hulagu's destruction of Baghdad, and installed the feeble survivor as Caliph of Islam. The Caliph, in turn, appointed Baibars as the legitimate Sultan. Egypt was to remain home to these powerless caliphs till the sixteenth century when the Mamluks were defeated by the Ottoman conqueror, Salim the Grim. After a brilliant rule of seventeen years, he died drinking poison intended for another. Where Saladin had defeated the Franks, Baibars defeated not only the Franks but also the superpower Mongols; where Saladin started from privilege, the son of a governor, Baibars started as a slave, the lowest of the low. Though Saladin has greater international fame, Baibars has greater achievement. But Saladin remains the greater man—kind, honorable, trustworthy and selfless. In contrast, Baibars was treacherous in his tactics and had no qualms in promising amnesty to a city if it surrendered, and then slaughtering and plundering the victims of his deceit once he entered with his army. Saladin believed in 'honor above all' where Baibars believed that the end justifies the means. Both were great men who deserve their place in history.

After a two year interlude in which two of Baibars' young sons were placed on the throne, Qalawun, a capable Mamluk general, took power. Within a year he defeated the Mongol army at Hims, showing once again that the Mamluks were more than a match for the Mongols in battle. Maybe the hardy warriors of the Steppes had grown soft in their conquest of Persia. Until the time of Qalawun, it was rule by the strongest; power was up for grabs and the leader was he who outfought the other contenders. After Qalawun, it was family rule—five sons followed each other, then nine grandsons and two more generations, till the end of the Bahri dynasty.

Amongst a host of powerless and irrelevant sultans, al-Nasir was important, both for his long reign lasting almost sixty years and for his achievements. He again defeated the Mongol army, this being the fourth time they had lost to the Mamluks; but he was a big spender with his love for luxury and beautiful buildings and his massive public works, including a canal to link Alexandria with the Nile, which required a workforce of 100,000 men. To raise money, he increased the tax burden, and he imposed harsh punishments on those who raised the price of bread and other basic necessities to manage the economic crisis. But soon civil war, famine and plague added to the general misery and the days of his family's continued rule were numbered.

The rule of the Burji Mamluks lasted 134 years as an example of bad government by degenerate, wilful and corrupt sultans who took office through intrigue and assassination, regardless of their origins or birth. Only Barquq was born of a Muslim father; the rest were from the slave pen. Al-Muayyad was a drunkard; Barsbay spoke no Arabic; Inal was totally illiterate; and Yalbay was both illiterate and insane.

Homosexuality was common among these treacherous, bloodthirsty and degenerate sultans. Their greed and cunning in profiteering from the poor was equal to the corruption in modern Third World democracies. Barsbay banned the import of pepper and cornered the market, selling at an exorbitant profit; he banned the planting of sugar cane to create a monopoly for himself.

Famine and plague reduced the population to a third. Terminal decline of the Mamluk dynasty set in. The India trade was lost due to the new route round the Cape of Good Hope discovered by the Portuguese explorer Vasco da Gama. New conquerors entered the arena—the great Tamerlane from Samarkand and the Ottoman, Salim the Grim. The Mamluk and Ottoman armies met at Marj Dabij in 1516. The Mamluks followed the old beliefs of honor and personal valour in battle; the Ottomans followed the new technology, artillery, guns and long-range weapons. Strength and bravery was of no use against the new style of warfare mastered by the Ottomans, who inflicted total defeat on the Mamluks. It was the end of the dynasty; Egypt now was reduced to a mere province of the Ottoman Empire.

Salim departed for home, taking with him the puppet caliph, who was later alleged to have transferred his office to the Ottoman.

The line of the caliphs who claimed descent from The Prophet was extinguished; the new caliphs henceforth were Turks who had come from Central Asia, their original home thousands of miles from Arabia. The Turks had conquered the Arabs. But as Muslims, they were no less than the Arabs and part of the brotherhood of Islam.

8

Muslims in Spain

'Brothers in Islam! We now have the enemy in front of us and the deep sea behind us. We cannot return to our homes, because we have burned our boats. We shall now either defeat the enemy and win, or die a coward's death by drowning in the sea. Who will follow me?'

—Tarik ibn Ziyad, conqueror of Spain

'You may weep like a woman for what you could not defend like a man.'

—Ayesha, mother of Boabdil, the last king of Granada (her statement to her son, when they went into exile)

The eight-hundred-year long Muslim rule in Spain began with the rape of a beautiful young girl, reached its height due to the love affair of a queen and met its destruction due to the jealousy of his wife when the king fell in love with a Christian slave girl. True, that it was not just the emotions of women that created or destroyed this magnificent era, but they were certainly the spark that lit the fires that in turn, led to the birth, height and death of

Muslim rule in Spain.

At the start of the eighth-century, Roderick, the Visigoth king, ruled Spain. His able general, Count Julian, protected the kingdom, keeping the Muslims of North Africa at bay. When Julian departed for Africa with his army, he left behind at court, under the protection of the King, his beautiful young daughter, Florinda. Roderick was a selfish, pleasure-loving and immoral king and was fired with lust when he saw the beautiful Florinda. He raped her and she became pregnant. She confessed to her father, who now developed a cold hatred for his king and was determined to take revenge. Nevertheless, he hid his feelings when he came to get his daughter. He had dinner with Roderick, who asked him to bring some special hunting falcons back from Africa. Julian replied that he would bring him such hawks as he had never in his life seen before. The hawks he brought back were the Muslim warriors who conquered Spain.

When Julian offered to take the Muslims into Spain, Musa the governor of the western regions was suspicious. Was it a trap? He allowed his Berber general, Tarik, to take an exploratory force of 7,000 men to Spain, with instructions to be cautious—this was not to be an expedition of conquest but one of reconaissance. Tarik crossed over from Africa to Spain, stopping midway at a rock which was named after him—the rock of Tarik.

Having crossed, he burned his boats to show his men that there was no retreat; it was victory or death. The small Muslim army resolutely faced the much larger Spanish force and achieved complete and total victory. Spain was conquered and remained under Muslim rule for almost eight centuries. Despite the clear orders of Musa, his boss, (who was now green with envy at Tarik's glorious conquest), Tarik pushed on. Cordoba was captured by a force of 700 men, with hardly a blow, and left in the keeping of the Jews, who declared themselves allies to the invading Muslims.

Hearing of Tarik's astonishing victories, Musa, the governor of the western region, rushed across to Spain, eager to get his share in the glory. Tarik met him with deference and respect, but in return, was struck by Musa with a whip and insulted for going beyond his orders. Tarik was imprisoned but later released by the Caliph. Once again, a victorious Muslim general received punishment rather than praise for a historic victory.

Within ten years, after consolidating their position in Spain, the Muslims entered France. The new governor, Abd-er Rahman, resolved to conquer all of Gaul. But fate stepped in, and against all odds, the Muslim army was defeated in the year 733 at Tours, by Charles Martel, known thereafter as 'The Hammer', and Europe remained Christian, saved forever from the Muslim onslaught. The Muslims retreated within the borders of Spain, consolidating their kingdom, where they enjoyed peace and prosperity for 300 years.

THE BIRTH OF ANDALUSIA

The Muslims spread over the fertile south which covered two-thirds of Spain and named their land 'al-Andalus'. The Spanish Christians retreated to the cold, bleak and arid north. Andalusia was a land of rivers and valleys, perfect for cultivation, to which the Arabs applied their techniques of agriculture and irrigation. These farms laid the foundation for the wealth of Andalusia. The Muslims governed mildly, justly and wisely. Low taxes and a high level of religious freedom kept the people content. It was a happy time.

The only discontent was among the Berbers, who resented the fact that though they were the spearhead of conquest, they had been denied the best lands and opportunities. Resentment led to rebellion and the Arab emir, Abdel Malik, invited the Syrian troops to come to his assistance. The Syrians defeated the Berbers, but instead of departing, they killed Abdel Malik and set up their own chief in his place. Dissention from party factions and rivalries led to instability and anarchy.

At this time, Abd al-Rahman, the last surviving Umayyad prince who had escaped the massacre of his family by the Abbasids, arrived in Spain. The five years of his flight for survival as he fled from Syria through Africa, had turned the boy into a man. Hardened by adversity, he had become expert in the arts of strategy and negotiation. He was now an accomplished warrior and statesman. Still a young man in his twenties, Abd al-Rahman was full of hope and ambition, despite the destruction of his family. He was brilliant, resourceful and brave, blind in one eye and devoid of the sense of smell. Prompt and decisive in action, troubled by few scruples, his policy was always equal to any crisis. He was a man of destiny and that destiny was Spain.

Prince Abd al-Rahman met the army of the emir at the river Guadalquivir. He was untried in battle, and some of his soldiers from Yemen made sarcastic remarks about the fine stallion of the prince and that such a fine horse would make an excellent escape from the battlefield in defeat. Abd al-Rahman rode up to the Yemeni chief, who was seated on a mule named 'Lightening'. Complaining that he found his stallion difficult to ride, he offered to swap him for the mule. The chief, delighted but confused, accepted the offer and respect for the prince replaced scorn as his authority was restored. Abd al-Rahman won the battle, and Spain.

The Arab elite in Spain rallied around the Umayyad prince who had arrived. The troops of the governor deserted and joined Abd al-Rahman and within a year, Andalusia was his. Baghdad sent an army against him and he was besieged for two months till he led his small troop of 700 men against the army from Baghdad. They threw their scabbards into a fire, swearing they would never put their swords away till they had secured victory. His victory was total; he put the severed heads of the generals from Baghdad in a sack, and with labels in their ears, sent his bloody gift to the Caliph, al-Mansur, who asked his courtiers, 'Who is the Falcon of the Quraysh?' The courtiers first replied 'You', then 'Muawiya', but each time the Caliph said 'no'. Finally, he gave the answer: 'The Falcon of the Quraysh is Abd al-Rahman. Thank God there is a sea between that man and me!'

Al-Mansur also paid homage to his enemy in Spain, thus:

Wonderful is the daring, wisdom and prudence he has shown!

> To enter the paths of destruction, throw himself into a distant land, hard to approach and well defended; there to profit by the jealousies of the rival parties, to make them turn their arms against one another instead of against himself; to win the homage and obedience of his subjects; and having overcome every difficulty, to rule supreme lord of all! Of a truth, no man before him has done this!

Many tried to take Spain from Abd al-Rahman. Even the Emperor, Charlemagne, made his bid through an alliance with three rebellious Arab chieftains, but none could dislodge the emir, who ruled for thirty-two years and then passed Andalusia to his son. But the years of struggle changed the young dreamer into a formidable tyrant, cruel and cunning, suspicious of everyone and deserted by his friends. Protected by his devoted personal bodyguard of 40,000 Africans who oppressed the population, he ruled by fear rather than love. But he ruled well and laid the foundation for the stability and prosperity of the great civilization that followed him. In establishing his dynasty in Spain, Abd al-Rahman had proved himself the equal of Charlemagne, the mightiest ruler of the West, as he had proved himself the equal of al-Mansur, the mightiest ruler in the East. His dynasty was to last for two and a half centuries.

Abd al-Rahman was succeeded by his son Hisham, and then his grandson al Hakim. Hisham was a kind, just and God-fearing man, who was much loved. He loved to hunt, and built the bridge of Cordoba; but as the rumours spread that he had built the bridge only to facilitate his hunting, he swore never to use the bridge and never used it for as long as he lived. A soothsayer had predicted that Hisham would die in eight years, and strangely, in exactly the eighth year he passed away.

The new emir was his son Hakim, an energetic man who enjoyed life, particularly his wine, women and song. This turned the ulema against him, and a coup was attempted, but the conspiracy failed. This was followed by rebellion but once again Hakim defeated his foes. He crucified 700 of the ring leaders, upside down, and exiled thousands who fled to Egypt, Morocco and Crete. When Toledo caused him trouble, he ordered a dinner to which hundreds of the notables were invited; as each guest entered, he was executed and his body thrown into a ditch. After 'the slaughter of the ditch', Toledo behaved and there was no further trouble. After a twenty-six-year rule, he passed a stable throne to his son Abd al-Rahman II.

Abd al-Rahman II, like his father, loved luxury and style but lacked his father's strength and resolution. He was ruled by four people—his wife, a eunuch slave, a religious scholar and a singer. His wife was busy in unsuccessful conspiracies to secure succession for her son Abdullah, one of the forty-five sons of the emir. The singer, Ziryab, was more than just a singer; he was an arbiter of fashion, a man renowned for his exquisite taste, an interior decorator, a master of etiquette. Ziryab had made a name for himself in the court of the Caliph, Harun, in Baghdad, where it was said that after hearing him sing, the audience was willing to listen to no other. But one day he made the mistake of outshining his master and was given the choice of death or exile. He chose exile and moved to Spain, where the emir, Abd al-Rahman II, was determined to create a court and a city to rival Baghdad. Together, they started the transformation of a provincial headquarter into the greatest and most civilized city in Europe.

There, then, occurred the strange drama of the suicides in Cordoba of forty-four Christian martyrs—strange, because the Christians had no grievance and were allowed freedom of worship and fair opportunities in business. They lived in a time of tolerance where Jesus was given due respect by the Muslim authorities, as a prophet of God. The Muslims considered them quite insane. One by one, these would-be martyrs courted death by publically abusing The Prophet. The kadi, or judge, was a kindly man, and tried to persuade the suicidal martyrs to behave, but they were determined and left him no choice in his judgement. One of the most prominent of the martyrs was a beautiful young girl, Flora, born of a Christian mother and a Muslim father, and herself brought up as a Muslim.

She suddenly declared herself Christian and joined the hysterical chorus of abuse on The Prophet. Though the penalty for her actions, according to law, was clearly death, the kadi ordered only a beating and imprisonment to teach her a lesson and then told her brother to take her away and talk some sense into her. But she was beyond sense, and determined to die, and finally succeeded in securing her own execution.

The decline started when the seventh emir, Abdullah, had his brother poisoned and took the throne. He was unable to control the uprisings and disorder in his kingdom, and the Umayyad dynasty seemed to be in serious trouble. Abdullah, suspecting disloyalty, instigated one of his sons to kill the other. He then had the surviving son murdered, leaving himself childless. The triple murder left only one candidate for succession—a grandson, also named Abd al-Rahman—who was to prove himself not merely the saviour of the dynasty, but also one of the greatest kings of this epoch in the known world.

The Andalusia that Abd al-Rahman III inherited was torn by rebellion and strife. The great kingdom created by Abd al-Rahman I had shrunk to a mere city. The Berbers no longer accepted central authority, the Christians were in revolt and governors of the big cities declared themselves independent and refused to recognize the emir as their king. This anarchy was the inheritance of the twenty-three-year-old son of a Christian slave girl, whose father had been murdered by his uncle on the instigation of Abdullah, his miserable grandfather. But adversity creates strength, and when the times cry out for a saviour, great men of history are born to put things right and rebuild great civilizations. Such was the destiny of Abd al-Rahman III.

REBUILDING A GREAT CIVILIZATION

Abd al-Rahman III set about recovering the territories of Andalusia which had declared independence of Cordoba. These he won back in a series of campaigns, despite some serious setbacks. On one occasion, his army was smashed by the Christians, and he barely escaped with his life. But he persevered against his enemies in the north (the Christian kingdoms) and his enemies in the south (the Fatimids of North Africa). Getting back control of Andalusia took him eighteen years, from 912 to 929 AD. Throughout this period of reconquest, Abd al-Rahman showed his scrupulous honesty and justice. His decisions were fair, his taxes reasonable and his administration gave prosperity and opportunity to all. He did not break his promises, and even his enemies could trust his word. Authoritarian by nature, he was dictatorial in his style but all agreed that he was a benign dictator whose period of rule was the golden prime of Muslim rule in Spain. His economy flourished through a green revolution in agriculture, a growth of industry and an expansion of trade. His lieutenants were men of humble birth who had been elevated and empowered by him alone and owed everything to their emir. He reduced the power of the Arab aristocracy of Andalusia, whose ambitions had been only a source of problems.

By this time, the caliphs in Baghdad were the powerless puppets of their own Turkish slaves, and could hardly be taken seriously. In Tunisia, the Shia Fatimids had claimed the caliphate and were the new and fast growing power spreading across North Africa into Egypt, where they set up their capital in Cairo. Abd al-Rahman III met the changing international scene with a bold and innovative move; making full use of his Umayyad ancestry he too declared himself Caliph of Islam. The period of the triple caliphate had begun; the world of Islam now had three caliphs—in Baghdad, Cairo and Cordoba. He ruled as Caliph for another thirty-two years till his death in 961 AD at the age of seventy. After a rule of almost fifty years, he had transformed Spain. Where he had inherited disintegration and anarchy, he left behind stability, prosperity and civilization as a testament to his genius. On his death, a paper was found in his own handwriting, saying that in the fifty years of his great reign he had known only fourteen days of happiness.

His successor Al Hakim II was a scholar, more interested in his books than in his job of governing the state. His famous library of

400,000–600,000 books kept him busy, not just in collecting the books but also in reading. He also founded one of the earliest universities (University of al-Karaouine of Morocco in 859) which was followed by the al Azhar University of Cairo and the Nizamiyah of Baghdad. Muslims led the world in education at that time, and al Hakim led the development of Muslim education.

Where al Hakim's library was famous, his harem was notorious, not for the number of its occupants but for their gender. Al Hakim ran a male harem; he was homosexual. This created a problem of how to produce an heir. But a solution was found. A Christian concubine, Subh, was dressed and groomed as a boy with the very masculine name of Jafar. She aroused the Caliph's interest, produced a son and heir, Hisham II, became sultana and finally, on the death of her husband, became regent for her young son, the new caliph. Subh, for all her posing as a male for the Caliph, was very feminine in her own romantic inclinations. She found a very handsome and intelligent young man whom she employed to look after her affairs, and with whom she then had a passionate affair. She promoted his career, till finally, after the death of her husband, he became the prime minister of the realm. He was named al Mansur, and is renowned in history as the greatest prime minister in Muslim Spain, under whom, Muslim rule in Spain reached its golden prime. Dressed as a man, Subh produced her son, the Caliph; dressed as a woman, she produced the last great ruler of Muslim Spain.

When al Hakim died, his widow Subh became the most powerful person in the realm, as guardian to her teenage son, Hisham, now Caliph. She empowered three men, who now ruled as a triumvirate—Mansur, her lover; General Ghalib, the commander-in-chief; and the old vizier, al-Mushafi. But history has always shown that triumvirates are but an interim arrangement until the strongest destroys his two rivals. In this way, Caesar had eliminated Pompey and Crassus, and an earlier al-Mansur, the Abbasid in Baghdad, had destroyed his uncle Abdullah and the revolutionary Abu Muslim.

Both in his rise to power and as and absolute ruler, al Mansur used his charm, generosity and guile to win popularity and remove competition. But he was more than just a pretty face; the extent of his iron willpower was once shown in the Council of Viziers, the cabinet, when the discussion was disturbed by the smell of burning flesh—al Mansur's leg was being cauterized with a red hot iron while he was calmly debating the affairs of state. His carefully planned and brilliant strategies ensured that he never failed in his endeavours. His two rivals soon met their death—the vizier in prison; the general in battle. Efficient administration promoted higher agricultural production, trade and industry, leading to prosperity for all, but al Mansur wanted more and this he secured by his endless wars and battles against the Christians of the north. In twenty years, he conducted fifty-seven campaigns, in which he conquered many Christian towns and captured huge amounts of plunder and booty to reward his soldiers. He was a river of wealth to his followers. Though al Hakim had left reserves of 40 million dinars at the time of his death—a huge amount—al Mansur needed more to finance his massive building projects, his expensive and ever expanding army, and his generosity in rewarding his friends and bribing his enemies.

When a conspiracy against him was discovered, instigated by the religious conservatives, he responded with restraint and diplomacy. He prepared a list of all the books that offended the religious sensibilities of the conservatives and had these publically burnt, boosting his popularity even further. The rightists never conspired against him again.

THE END OF THE CALIPHATE

But even as he reached the pinnacle of Muslim rule in Spain, he had sown the seeds of the future destruction of the caliphate of Cordoba. His great army had inducted thousands upon thousands of hardy Berber troops from North Africa, together with entire regiments of Christian mercenaries and slaves. Just as the mercenaries of ancient Rome had destroyed its civilization and the Turkish troops of the Abbasids had usurped their empire, these foreign Berber troops were to replace the caliphate of the Umayyads in Spain. The great vizier died in 1002 AD; anarchy followed.

Power passed into the hands of the military, which installed and removed caliphs at will. Within the next twenty years, the crown changed hands nine times, caliphs were appointed, removed and then reappointed in a series of short realms. Abd al-Rahman V was dragged out of his bathroom and slaughtered in front of his successor, Muhammad III al-Mustafki, who himself had to flee, disguised as a singing girl, but was caught and killed.

Muhammad III had a daughter, Wallada, a blond, blue-eyed beauty with intelligence and style, and a poetess of renown. Her father had no sons, so she inherited all the property—and there was a lot of property. Wallada was a rich girl. She decided to build an academy where poetry was taught together with the arts of love. Wallada wore transparent tunics and scorned the hijab. The mullahs hated her, but she couldn't care less. She started a passionate affair with Zaydun, another poet who was the love of her life. But their affair broke up over his sex life, which included males and finally, a black slave girl of whom Wallada was very jealous. She then started an affair with the vizier, ibn Abdus, who imprisoned Zaydun and confiscated his property, after which she moved in with the vizier and stayed with him till his death. Hell hath no fury like a woman (in this case, Wallada) scorned. When she died on 26 March 1091, it was the end of an era—the same day, the Almoravids entered Cordoba.

The last Umayyad caliph in Spain was Hisham III. He was thrown into a cold dark dungeon. The rebellious viziers held a public meeting in which they declared the end of the caliphate in Spain. When the news was brought to the deposed caliph, he was shivering in the dark as he held his infant daughter close to keep her from freezing; his only concern was to arrange for some light and a bit of bread for his starving child.

9

The Tide Turns in Spain

'I have no desire to be branded by my descendants as the man who delivered al-Andalus as prey to the infidels... I would rather be a camel driver in Africa than a swineherd in Castile.'

—Al-Mutamid, King of Seville (His statement to his son Rashid, explaining his invitation to Yusuf ibn Tashfin, the Almoravid, to save them from the Christians)

'I am not and will not be a ruler of heretics.'

—Philip II of Spain, who destroyed Islam in the country

As dissention split the Muslim empire in Spain into city states, known as the Ta'ifa kingdoms, the Christians in the north found a new unity under Alfonso VI of Leon and Castile. The tide had turned. Muslim power was now in retreat; Christian power was rising. Some of these city-states were conquered; in others, the rulers survived as vassals of the Christian King. Seville replaced Cordoba as the leading Muslim city of Spain.

The last king of Seville was Al-Mutamid, a charming, happy man and a great poet. It was poetry that brought him together with the love of his life, Itimad, whom he married. Itimad's whims were notorious, but the King loved her passionately and tried always to fulfil her desires. One winter, it snowed, and the Queen sobbed that her husband was cruel not to allow her to see such a beautiful sight every year. The King ordered that the landscape be planted with almond trees, whose white blossoms could be mistaken for snow.

Al-Mutamid was a popular king, and his territory expanded. Cordoba was encompassed into his kingdom. But he could not hope to resist the rising Christian power. Finally, despite being warned that the Almoravids were even more dangerous than the Christians, he decided to invite Yusuf ibn Tashfin, the Almoravid leader, to save Spain from Alfonso. It was a decision that would lead him from the pinnacle of happiness and power to the depths of poverty and humiliation.

The Almoravids from Morocco were founded by Abdallah ibn Yasin, a spiritual leader whose madrassa was known as Dar al Muratabin. Fired by puritan zeal, they had already taken Morocco. In battle, they preferred death to defeat. Their commanding general was Abu Bakr ibn Umar. Abu Bakr put his cousin Yusuf ibn Tashfin in charge of the government while he went off to war. He also gave Yusuf custody of his favourite wife, Zainab. Abu Bakr died in battle in the Sudan while Yusuf enjoyed kingship with Zainab, who had happily switched husbands, in Marrakesh. Yusuf, with his army of 20,000, annihilated the huge army of Alfonso at the battle of Zallaqah, shipping home 40,000 heads as a memento of his victory. But he was encouraged by religious fatwas to take over from the Taifa kings, whose moral laxity, bad governance and high taxation had made them unpopular and lost them their legitimacy. The Almoravid conquest stopped the Christian Reconquista for almost a century. Yusuf ruled till his death in 1106 AD when he was hundred years old.

Al-Mutamid was banished to a remote desert village in the Atlas Mountains, where he lived in destitution, tormented by the sight of his beloved wife and daughters spinning wool for a paltry living. When rebellion took place in Spain, he was kept in chains. Languishing in fetters, forgotten and ill, his beloved Itimad dead, he passed away in 1095 AD at the age of fifty-five. A hundred years after his death, the historian, Ibn al Abbar wrote, 'Everyone loves Al-Mutamid. Everyone pities him. Even now he is lamented.'

Even as the mighty Almoravids seemed invincible, a religious scholar, Ibn Tumart, back home in Morocco, started preaching opposition to the establishment. The son of a lamplighter in the mosque, this ugly little man was to provide the inspiration that led to the greatest empire of the time. He lived the life of an ascetic, opposed to music, alcohol or other laxity, and set himself up as the Mehdi. He acquired a passionate following which combined religious fervour with the force of arms. Ibn Tumart died passing power to the son of a potter, Abd al Mumin, the warlord and strategist who defeated the Almoravids in battle, killing 30,000 of them in a purge. Abd al Mumin went on to conquer Algeria, Tunisia and Libya, penetrating up to Egypt. Andalusia too, fell to his disciplined army. He established the greatest empire of North Africa and finally declared himself Caliph of Islam in a glorious rule, as he constructed great mosques and new cities.

CHRISTIAN CONQUERORS AND THEIR CONQUESTS

The dominance of Abd al Mumin's dynasty in Spain stopped the Christian Reconquista for another century, as the tolerance and moderation of the early Muslim rulers in Spain was replaced by a hard suppression that only fuelled the will to resist. Where the soft policies of the Spanish Umayyads had won the support of the Christians and Jews, the Almohad intolerance only made them more determined to resist. This pattern was to repeat itself in Mogul India where Aurangzeb's hard line policies against the Hindus precipitated the decline of the empire of the Great Moguls. Time and time again, toleration and inclusion was to strengthen the stability of empires; intolerance and exclusivity were to prove the precursors of decline. Emperors who would not learn from the experience of history would suffer its repeat.

For fifty years after the death of Abd al Mumin, the Almohads ruled in splendour. Their reputation travelled as far as England, where it is recorded that King John, the brother of Richard the Lion-Heart, sent an embassy to the Almohad caliph, al-Nasir, offering to hold England under tribute to him and to exchange the Christian faith for Islam. Then in 1212, they suffered a disastrous defeat at Las Navas de Tolosa at the hands of a united Christian force. Legend has it that of the 600,000-man Muslim army, only one thousand escaped with their lives. The Almohads were completely and totally defeated; all of Muslim Spain lay at the feet of the Christian conquerors.

In 1236 AD, Cordoba fell; in 1238 AD, Valencia; and then Murcia and Seville in 1243 and 1248. All that remained was Granada, where Muslim rule survived by capitulating and collaborating as vassal to the Christian overlords.

The kingdom of Granada survived for two and a half centuries as a Muslim island in the sea of Christian rule in Spain. Comprising only 3 per cent of the territory, but protected by the natural fortifications of the mountainous terrain and its excellent rulers, Granada flourished, building a civilization that compared favourably with Cordoba in its heyday. Its kings combined diplomacy with strength; under their able administration, commerce and industry flourished. The silk trade reached new heights and Granada prospered and grew wealthy.

Two women, Isabella and Isabel, were instrumental in the final fall of Granada. In 1469, Isabella, the prim Catholic queen, married Ferdinand, uniting the two most important Christian kingdoms, Aragon and Castile. A year later in 1470, the young and beautiful Spanish aristocrat, Isabel de Solis was captured by the Muslims and held for ransom. But her family refused to pay in punishment for her rebellious attitude towards her father, so she was passed as a slave to Abu al Hasan, the King of Granada. The old king fell for her instantly and offered to make her his queen if she converted to Islam. Despite being wild, Isabel was a practical girl, and 'queen or slave girl' was an easy choice. The first wife of the King, Aisha, was consumed by jealousy. She conspired against her husband and using her son, Muhammad al Abdullah (known as Boabdil), she split the kingdom, which was thereafter ruled by two kings. Isabella united Spain to create Christian victory. Isabel, who took the Muslim name of Zoraya, divided Granada resulting in Muslim defeat.

After two centuries of living as vassals to the Christians, the new king of Granada, Abu al Hasan, known to the Christians as Alboacen, refused to pay the tribute. 'Tell your sovereigns that the kings of Granada who used to pay tribute are dead; our mint now coins nothing but sword blades,' he declared boldly, starting on a trail of battle and conquest. But when his son Abu Abdullah, also known as Boabdil, turned against him, and became a client of the Christians, life became difficult. For a while, he locked his son and his first wife in a section of the Alhambra, but Boabdil escaped and with Christian support, set himself up as a rival king in a fort not far from his father. With the Muslims of Granada divided—some supporting the father, and some, the son—the old king now blind, passed power to his valiant brother Ez Zaghal and died. Ez Zaghal, as Muhammad XII, proved no less determined than his brother. When advised to compromise with the Christians, he proudly replied, 'I was sent here not to surrender, but to defend.'

But handicapped by civil war against his own nephew, he finally capitulated as the siege of his city led to starvation, with the Jews and Muslims reduced to eating horses, dogs and rats. On 1 January 1492, Christian soldiers entered Alhambra. Ferdinand and Isabella were hailed as the heroes of Christendom, their glory further enhanced by the voyages of Christopher Columbus to America.

Muhammad XII abdicated, sold his lands and withdrew to Africa where he was blinded and spent the rest of his days in misery and destitution, forced to wear a badge: 'This is the hapless King of Andalusia.' Boabdil, after losing his state, retired to Fez, where he died in 1533–34. A century later, his descendants were still objects of charity, counted among the beggars.

GLORY OF THE MUSLIM CIVILIZATION ENDS

The Kingdom of Castile became a world empire. Ferdinand and Isabella were the most powerful king and queen in Europe. Their children married into the royal houses of Europe:

- The eldest daughter, Isabella, married the King of Portugal, and when he died, married his uncle who succeeded him.
- The son, Juan, married the Princess of Austria, Margaret.
- A daughter, Joanna (the Mad), married Philip (the Handsome), son of the Holy Roman Emperor, Maximillian. Two of her sons became Holy Roman Emperors in turn.
- Another daughter, Maria, also married the King of Portugal after her sister died. (Portugal was important to Spain and could not be allowed to slip out.)
- And finally, another daughter, Catherine (of Aragon), married Arthur, Prince of Wales and heir to the throne of England, and after his death, she was passed to his brother Henry VIII.

The plundered wealth of the Muslims of Spain, supplemented by gold from the Americas, made this family the richest and most powerful dynasty in Europe. Victory was sweet.

Victory for the Christians was defeat for the Muslims and Jews. The first to come under attack were the latter, of whom there were many and who had made Spain their preferred home in all of Europe under the tolerant Muslim rule. They were given a simple choice by Isabella and her deadly inquisitors, Torquemada and Ximenes de Cisneros: 'Convert or leave.' But exile did not mean an easy exit; they could take no gold or silver with them, nor other valuables; the distress sale of their lands and homes meant ruinous prices, and much of this money was extorted from them on their escape. Many were killed, their women raped and their young children taken from them to be brought up as Christians. Fifty thousand converted, 100,000 chose ruin and exile and the rest were lost in the dustbin of history, as the deadly Inquisition went about its terrible torture and genocide.

Bayezid, the Ottoman emperor, was astonished at the Spanish kings 'who could throw out a people as clever as the Jews'. Next came the turn of the Muslims.

Hitler and his Nazis removed 6 million Jews from the map of Europe. Isabella and her family removed 6 million Muslims from the face of Spain. The twentieth-century holocaust took a decade. The sixteenth-century Inquisition took over a century. This was because the problem of the Muslims was a lot more complicated. Hitler wanted the wealth of the Jews, and this could be easily secured by simply exterminating them. The Muslims in Spain were the wealth of Spain, whose economy needed them even if Isabella and her husband decided to remove them. The Muslims were the best workers, the most productive farmers, the most skilled artisans, and in the twelfth century, comprised one in every six of the population; the economy of Spain could not survive without them. So even as the Inquisition worked to eliminate the Muslims, the barons and powerful Christian feudal lords not only argued against the policy of the crown, but even defied the Inquisition, and protected their Muslim vassals.

But leaving economics aside, both Nazi Germany and the Spanish Inquisition believed that the non-Christians were an inferior bestial species with contaminated blood. Both genocides were seen as a purification exercise. Inter-religious mingling was seen as impure and dangerous. Extremist rabbis recommended disfiguring Jewish women who had intercourse with Christians or Muslims. Muslim men who slept with Christian women could be drawn and quartered and the women burned alive, while Christian men who slept with Muslim women were forced to run naked through the streets.

The most important figure in the Spanish Inquisition was the fanatical confessor of the Queen, Ximenes de Cisneros, a hard-liner who made even the modern day Taliban look gentle by comparison. His horror of the female sex was so intense that he refused to sleep under the same roof as women. When cleaning up the morals of the clergy, he dismissed priests living openly with 'wives' or concubines, hundreds of whom left Spain with their companions. He was made

Archbishop, and set about converting the Muslims by his methods that even his fellow Christians gently described as 'not correct.' His enthusiasm in the conversions of Granada allowed him to boast, by 1500, that, 'There is now no one in the city who is not a Christian, and all the mosques are churches. The entire kingdom will convert.'

Those that could afford to go, went. The poor, who could not afford that, converted, or at least pretended to convert. The converts, called Mozarabs, professed themselves Christians, but knew little or nothing of Christianity, and privately dressed, lived and followed their traditional customs and beliefs. They lived in fear of the authorities who used the new laws on religion to extract bribes from them, and of the resentful Old Christians, many of whom tormented them. Year by year, their faith and their numbers eroded, as these pathetic and pitiful New Christians lost all hope that this nightmare would pass. This was a time of taqqiya, or dissimulation, which was permitted to Muslims in periods of persecution.

Charles, the grandson of Isabella, was ambitious. Already holding two crowns as Charles I of Spain and Charles V of the Holy Roman Empire, he ruled most of Europe. Only France remained beyond his control, and England, where his aunt, Catherine of Aragon, was queen to Henry VIII. Acknowledged as the greatest king in Europe, he was overshadowed by the Ottoman, Suleiman the Magnificent. Spain feared that Suleiman would invade, and the Barbarossa brothers, whether pirates or commanders of the Ottoman fleet, struck terror into the Spanish. The Moriscos in Spain were a potential fifth column of Muslim support, so Charles tightened controls over the New Christians. They were forbidden to dress, eat or follow their old customs; not just their beliefs, but even their very culture was to be eliminated. Spies and informers would betray the slightest deviance; refusal to eat pork or drink alcohol was a certain giveaway which would meet with the most severe punishment. Public baths were destroyed, since the Muslim habit of bathing was frowned upon; they were forced, under fear of torture and death, to adopt the dirt of their masters.

Under Philip, the weak son of Charles, persecution intensified. All promises of the State proved to be lies and mere strategies to manipulate the Moriscos. The Church gave the authorities licence to disregard oaths made to heathens. The Muslims rebelled, but were crushed, as 20,000 were killed and 50,000 enslaved.

By 1570 AD, it was all over. In 1609, King Philip III signed an edict denouncing the remaining Muslim inhabitants of Spain as heretics, traitors and apostates. Later that year, the entire Muslim population was given three days to leave Spanish territory, on threat of death. In a brutal exodus, they were forced to pay for even the right to drink from the rivers on their route. Over the next five years, some 300,000 Muslims were expelled and ruined. By 1614, Muslim Spain had ceased to exist. In the century following the fall of Granada, 3 million Muslims had been removed from Spain.

Spain, one of the greatest powers of the world, that entered its golden age in 1600, was in decay by 1650 and in ruins by 1700. By that time, 90 per cent of the nation was illiterate. The glory of the Muslim civilization was dead. The legacy of the Moors and the wealth of the Americas was consumed by war, extravagance and bad government. With its population reduced from 30 million in the golden age of the Muslims, to 7 million, its industrial skills forever lost and its deteriorating farmlands abandoned, Spain was not just illiterate but also bankrupt.

Four centuries later, on 11 March 2004, ten bombs exploded on four trains in Madrid, killing 191 people and wounding 1800, in retaliation for the Spanish participation in the war in Iraq. The bombing took place two days before the general election. The new government withdrew the Spanish troops from Iraq. The perpetrators of the bombings listed the loss of al Andalus as one of the justifications for the bombings.

10

Genghis and Tamerlane

Sayings of Genghis Khan:

'I am the punishment of God... If you had not committed great sins, God would not have sent a punishment like me upon you.'

'The greatest happiness is to scatter your enemy, to drive him before you, to see his cities reduced to ashes, to see those who love him, shrouded in tears, and to gather into your bosom, his wives and his daughters.'

'Heaven has abandoned China owing to its haughtiness and extravagant luxury. But I, living in the northern wilderness, have not inordinate passions. I hate luxury and exercise moderation. I have only one coat and one food. I eat the same food and am dressed in the same tatters as my humble herdsmen. I consider the people my children. I take an interest in talented men as if they were my brothers. We always agree in our principles, and we are always united by mutual affection. At military exercises I am always in front and in time of battle I am never behind. In the space of seven years, I have succeeded in accomplishing a great work, and uniting the whole world in one empire.'

'These are the Four Dogs of Temujin. They feed on human flesh and are tethered with an iron chain. They feed on dew. Running, they ride on the back of the wind. On the day of battle, they devour enemy flesh. Behold, they are now unleashed and they slobber at the mouth with glee. These four dogs are Jebe, Kublai, Jelme and Subotai.'

(The Secret History of the Mongols)

'Tamerlane, Lord of Samarkand, having conquered all the land of the Mongols and India; and having conquered the Land of the Sun, which is a great lordship; also having conquered and reduced to obedience the land of Khwarezm; also having reduced all Persia and Media, with the empire of Tabriz and the city of the Sultan; and having conquered the Land of Silk, with the land of the Gates; and also having conquered Armenia the Less, and Erzerum, and the land of the Kurds—having conquered in battle the lord of India and taken a great part of his territory; also having destroyed the city of Damascus, and reduced the cities of Aleppo, of Babylon and Baghdad; and having overrun many other lands and lordships and won many battles, and achieved many conquests, he came against the Turk Bayazid (who is one of the greatest lords of the world) and gave him battle, conquering him and taking him prisoner.'

—Clavijo, ambassador of Henry III of Castile, to the court of Tamerlane

'Aiming at the right, he struck left, and threatening the brow, he attacked the neck.'

—Ahmed Arabshah, biographer of Tamerlane

In the twelfth century, civilization was changing the two dominant empires of the time—the Muslims in the Middle East and the

Chinese in the Far East. But between these two great empires lay a vast land that had been bypassed by history. Its inhabitants were the nomad Mongols, cut off and isolated by distance, by mountains and by deserts. They lived as they had always lived—on horseback, hunting, grazing their vast herds of horses, in tribes without cities, without permanent homes and without writing or reading, unaware that the world outside had changed and they had been left behind.

Yesugai was chief of one of the small tribes that roamed the steppes. He was a reasonable man except when he saw something that he really wanted. One day when out hunting, he came across a man and a woman and knew that he really wanted her. This meant trouble, because it was not done to take another man's woman; but he was determined. Her name was Hoelun. Her husband, Chileidu, hesitated—should he fight, or should he run? But Hoelun was a practical girl, and she told him to run before he was killed: 'There are plenty of girls who can perch up on the box and drive a wagon. When you find one, call her Hoelun. But stay alive.' She tore off the shift over her head and threw it to him: 'You can take the smell of me with you.' Yesugai took the woman and married her. They had a son, and they named him Temujin. He would later be known as Genghis Khan, the World Conqueror.

When Temujin was a small boy of nine years, his father decided to get him married. A young girl, Borte, was selected as his bride, and as was the custom of his time, Temujin was left in her home to be brought up in her family. His father advised his in-laws, 'My son, Temujin, is afraid of dogs. Do not let him be frightened by the dogs.' Perhaps Temujin had been afraid of dogs when he was three, but not now; as a man, he was afraid of only his mother Hoelun, and to a lesser extent, his wife Borte. *The Secret History of the Mongols* says that '*Borte was beautiful, though in later years Genghis Khan came to prefer the Lady Hulan. Borte had a great deal of dignity, which is an excellent quality, but a man can have too much of it as a daily diet.*'

Temujin was a child when his father died and he, together with his brothers, was brought up by his mother, an exceptional woman.

Survival was not easy, and adversity turned the helpless and illiterate child into a warrior who created the greatest empire in human history, a lawmaker whose Yassa gave his people a code that endured long after his death, and a leader whose wisdom and discipline inspired and transformed his followers. Genghis had total belief in his vision and destiny. He had an uncanny ability to recognize the potential of exceptional men and bind them to loyally serve him. He imposed a system based totally on merit and justice; it did not matter who you were or where you came from. His greatest general Subotai was not even a Mongol; his 'Four Dogs', who became legends in battle, were not even from his tribe.

During their wilderness years, the little family of Genghis and his mother were deserted by all those who had followed his father. Later, when Genghis grew powerful, many came back; Genghis bore them no resentment; even at this tender age, Genghis understood that too much cannot be expected of most men, and loyalty has its limits.

The family survived by hunting and fishing. One day, Genghis caught a fine fish, but his half-brother stole it and ate it. Genghis and his brother Kasar were disturbed and concluded, 'How can we go on living together, if he behaves like this?' So they killed him. Even among the Mongols, it was unusual for a boy of eleven to kill his half-brother, and that too over a fish!

The brothers grew up lean, hard and hungry as outcasts. When he was fourteen, Genghis was captured and locked into a big wooden collar, called a kang, which made it difficult for him to escape. But his captors knew that Temujin had a magical ability to persuade and seduce, and ordered that he be passed from tent to tent, to prevent him from developing sympathy with his jailors. But Genghis did escape, and when a posse was sent out to recapture him, he showed that he could do what was least expected: Realizing that it was futile to flee with no horse, no food and a kang round his neck, he sneaked back into the village and appealed to the family that had been his recent jailor. His entreaties were successful and in this way, he was saved; many years later he rewarded his saviors with the two privileges of not paying taxes and sharing the emperor's cup. One of his saviors became an important general and was known as Chila'un Bahadur, the strong prince. All who helped Genghis were rewarded; all who resisted him were destroyed. Temujin had a charisma and a magnetism that made others follow him.

When riding to recover his horses that had been stolen, he came across a young man, Bo'orchu, swift of decision and careless of danger, who offered to help him. When the horses were recovered, Temujin offered to share them with Bo'orchu, who replied that he would take nothing. Bo'orchu remained a loyal and valued general of Genghis all his life, and like Chila'un Bahadur, became one of the famous Four Coursers of Genghis Khan.

Borte had brought in her dowry a grand sable coat for Hoelun, her mother-in-law. It was the most valuable possession of Temujin's family at a time when they had nothing. When he prepared to go to Toghrul, known later as Ong Khan, one of the most important chiefs of the area, he asked her if he could give her coat to Ong Khan. Without hesitation she agreed; they needed friends more than they needed sable coats. Ong Khan was thrilled with his grand present. Genghis's generosity was a powerful weapon that he used effectively throughout his life.

Of these early allies and followers of Temujin, perhaps the most important were the two brothers, Jelme and Subotai, sons of a blacksmith. They were from the Reindeer People who lived far away in the forests, kept reindeer, and were unfamiliar with horses. Whereas a young Mongol boy learned to ride a horse at the age of three, Subotai could not even ride when he joined the group. The two brothers became part of Genghis Khan's famous 'Dogs of War', and Subotai went on to become the greatest general in history. He conquered thirty-two nations and won sixty-five pitched battles. His achievements surpassed Alexander; and whereas Napoleon saw total defeat, abandoning his army in Egypt and ending his days in captivity on St Helena, Subotai Bahadur never lost a battle and died undefeated at the age of seventy-three. Famed for his speed and mobility, he moved his armies over greater distances faster than had ever been believed possible. His conquests included Korea, China, Persia, Hungary and Russia. Europe was only saved by the death of Genghis Khan which required all Mongol armies to return to Mongolia to elect the successor. His pincer movements to take Moscow and his various tactics and strategies have inspired modern generals such as Rommel in the twentieth century. Subotai had a brilliant military mind and was a master of deception and surprise. He frequently fought and defeated armies much larger than his own. He was a supremely confident risk-taker, always ready to risk all or nothing on the next battle. He possessed the soul of a gambler, which Napoleon considered the most important trait of a great general.

Jelme was not as outstanding a general as his younger brother, Subotai, but one act alone made his contribution comparable. In a battle in 1201 AD, Temujin was wounded in the neck by an arrow. The faithful Jelme sucked the wound until it clotted and saved the life of his friend and leader, who then went on to conquer the world and create the greatest empire in history.

Just as his mother Hoelun had been captured by his father in a raid, Temujin's wife, Borte, was taken from him by raiders; in fact these were from the same family that had lost Hoelen to Yesugai. But whereas Hoelun was never retrieved by her first husband, Borte was recovered by Temujin. But she was recovered with a child in her belly, who was to be her firstborn, Juchi. Temujin accepted Juchi as his own, and gave him the same love, affection and opportunity as to his own sons.

GENGHIS, THE GREAT KHAN

In 1201 AD, Genghis was a vassal of Toghrul, known as Ong Khan, to whom he had given the sable coat. In 1206 AD, he was declared Khan of all the people of the steppes. In these six years, he rose from obscurity to pre-eminence. The chief of a small band of warriors had become the leader of a nation. He learned to make friends who could be allies against his enemies. He learned that even the best of friends could betray him and become an enemy. He learned how greed and jealousy could corrode honour and friendship. He learned to read the hearts and minds of men and he learned the art of binding them to him with the bonds of love and loyalty. And above all, he learned the art of war, which enabled him to conquer the world. In these six years, Temujin became Genghis, The Great Khan. In 1206 AD, when he was proclaimed Khan, Genghis was thirty-nine years old.

The great military strategist Sun Tzu advised, 'Move your enemy forward by promise of advantage; move him back by fear of disadvantage.' Genghis followed this formula of reward and punishment with a passion. He stated his position bluntly, 'All who surrender will be spared; whoever does not surrender but opposes with struggle and dissention, shall be annihilated'. The twenty years that he ruled as the Great Khan, till the time of his death in 1227 AD, were years of conquest. In the East, China, Korea and all the lands till the ocean were conquered; the Jin dynasty of Northern China was destroyed. To his West, the great empire of the Muslim Khwarezm Shah, which included Persia, Afghanistan and Turkestan, was taken. Even his death did not stop the juggernaut, as the great general Subotai continued his relentless march through Russia, sacking Moscow and Kiev. Genghis's sons and grandsons conquered Central Asia and the Middle East, destroying Baghdad and the Abbasid caliphate. Terror was complete; a town would humbly surrender even to a solitary Mongol in the belief that resistance was futile. All knew what the Khan was capable of when his anger was aroused. In revenge for the killing of his father, he ordered that every Tatar male taller than three feet be killed. When he defeated the Taichi'ut, their chiefs were boiled alive. For the Muslims, these were terrible times. Had the Muslim era finally come to its end?

The key to the invincibility of the Mongols was the horse. Every Mongol was a cavalryman, who lived on horseback from the age of three. He fought on horseback, he even slept on horseback; and when he rode into battle, he rode with several spare mounts, so that his horse was always fresh. When there was no food, he would open a vein from the neck of his horse and drink the blood. In the wide steppes where there was always fodder for his horse, he was invincible; the settled territories of cities and farms were less attractive. To an army of a 100,000, with half a million horses, grasslands were as crucial as oil to a modern army.

The Mongols were professional soldiers. No Mongol ever cultivated a field or touched a plow. They had no houses and no settled home. The whole life of a Mongol was war and the preparation for war. Training and discipline made him invincible in battle even when he was outnumbered. To the Mongol warriors, numbers were irrelevant; their strength lay in information, strategy, tactics, mobilization, morale and terror.

But even more important than professionalism and the horse was the leadership of Genghis Khan. His vision, wisdom, determination and uncanny instinct in recognizing the abilities of people as diverse as the general, Subotai, and the sage, Yeliu Chutsai, and binding them with the loyalty he inspired, created a dedicated leadership that endured even after his death. Genghis was never satisfied with merely taking opportunity; he believed in creating opportunity.

No less amazing than his conquests was the 'Yassa' of Genghis Khan, the code of law which this illiterate nomad, who had never seen a city, imposed on the fifty nations that comprised his empire. Through his Yassa, Genghis eradicated crime amongst the Mongols. Theft and adultery,were punished by death; lying and disobedience to an order, were punished by death; spies, false witness, sodomites and sorcerers were punished by death. Through consistent application of the Yassa, Genghis established the rule of law so completely that criminal activity was totally eradicated. It was said that a naked virgin with a sack of gold could pass through the empire with complete security.

Though Genghis advocated religious tolerance, his Yassa stated, 'It is ordered to believe that there is only one God, creator of heaven and earth, who alone gives life and death, riches and poverty, as pleases

Him—and who has, over everything, an absolute power.'

Every man was made to join the army. Women were made to attend to the care of property. The Yassa forbade any Mongol to eat in the presence of another, without sharing his food. Drunkenness was discouraged: 'A man who is drunk is like one struck on the head; his wisdom and skill avail him not at all. Get drunk only three times a month. It would be better not to get drunk at all. But who can abstain altogether?'

Genghis died in 1227 AD, some say from wounds in his last battle, others say after a fall from his horse while hunting. He was buried in an unmarked grave. He divided his empire between his four sons, but his army he gave to the youngest, Tolui. During the lifetime of the four sons, unity prevailed, but after them discord and division set in.

THE WORLD AFTER THE WORLD CONQUEROR

The Western empire of the Crimea and South Russia had been given to the eldest son of Genghis, Juchi, who had died before his father. It was now ruled by Batu the Splendid, Tzar of Russia and leader of the Golden Horde. Another son, Chagatai, inherited Central Asia, but though he was the eldest surviving son, Genghis had indicated his preference for the younger Ogedei to succeed him. Chagatai was hard, given to anger and drank to excess. Ogedei was affable, intelligent and without ambition; everyone loved Ogadei. Tului, the youngest, had no match for bravery and wisdom in war and his wife was the beautiful and wise Siyurkuktiti, known as 'Princess' due to the respect that her character commanded. She gave her sons education and, through them, changed the history of the family of Genghis Khan.

At the first Kuriltai, the gathering after the death of Genghis, to choose his successor, the family and the nobles debated for long hours. Some argued for Chagatai, the eldest, now that Juchi was dead; some argued for Tului, the youngest, who controlled the powerful army. Ogadei, who Genghis had thought most suitable, was relaxed and hardly seemed a candidate for the most powerful office in the world. But finally on the prompting of wise old Yeliu Chutsai, both Chagatai and Tului threw their support behind their father's choice, Ogadei. It was a good choice as the empire flourished and expanded under his compromising approach. Genghis's key lieutenants, Subotai, the great lord of war continued to control the armies and Yeliu Chutsai, the wise advisor, took on greater responsibility in running the administration. The Golden Family was united and harmony prevailed.

During the rule of Ogadei, Yeliu Chutsai ran the empire like a modern day prime minister. But he too passed through difficulties before his authority was established. At one time, Ogedei ordered his arrest for teaching the children of the royal family reading and writing. Later Ogedei ordered his release, but Yeliu refused to come out of his cell in the same way as Socrates in Athens refused to escape after his arrest. The stubborn behaviour of both was to endorse the principal of obedience to the sovereign. Yeliu's greatest contribution was to save the Chinese nation from Mongol genocide. The Mongol conquerors were tempted to kill the Chinese, erase their cities and make China into grasslands for grazing of the huge Mongol herds of horses. Yeliu proposed an alternate policy of taxation to keep a river of wealth flowing to the Mongol headquarters, and his policy was accepted. Yeliu also convinced his boss, Ogedei, that drinking in excess was dangerous to his health; he did this by showing Ogedei an iron vase which had been corroded by alcohol, and warning that if alcohol could do this to iron, it could do worse to his intestines. Ogedei was impressed, but not enough to stop, and alcohol finally killed him. When Yeliu died, his opponents in administration sent guards to search his home to recover the vast treasure that they believed he must have accumulated while in power. But nothing was found; all that Yeliu had collected were an assortment of musical instruments and maps—his passion and hobby.

The empire continued to expand its territory and wealth through three generations—first Genghis himself; then under Ogadei; and finally under Mongke and his brothers Hulagu and Kublai, the grandsons of Genghis. After the death of Ogadei, his widow took power, as was the Mongol custom, to rule as regent till the successor was appointed. Her name was Turakina. She looked like a man, unlovely except to her husband, and the first woman to rule the Mongol empire. She was determined to pass the crown to one of her own children, and emphasized their right to rule. When the kuriltai was called to finalize the succession, Batu, the son of Juchi, who ruled the Golden Horde in the West, refused to come. The sons of Genghis were already dead and so Turakina secured the crown for Kuyuk, the son of Ogadei, weak and sickly, with a love of wine and women.

But Kuyuk's rule was short-lived as he died within two years. His widow tried to retain power for her family but she was no match for the guile of Batu and the Princess, who proved a formidable team. When summoned, Batu again refused to come, saying, 'My foot pains me so I may not ride.' The Princess saw the opportunity and ordered two of her sons, Mongke and Kublai, to go to Batu and enquire after his health. In this way, the new alliance was cemented that took power from the family of Ogadei. The Princess knew she had to move fast; taking her army with her, she rode to Batu; two of Chagatai's sons followed her. She sent back word that the kuriltai would be held in Batu's camp. The ladies of Ogadei's family were cut out and her son, Mongke, was acknowledged as the new Khakhan, the lord of lords.

The members of the House of Ogedei stayed away, but could not resist the outcome of the coup. Batu summed up the situation: 'This thing has been done in such a way that it cannot be undone. Had any other than Mongke been named, the work of the Khanate would have suffered.' He then retired to his beloved Russia, his gout apparently ceasing to trouble him. The Princess wrote to him for advice, 'For two years we have sought to seat Mongke on the throne; yet the children of Kuyuk and Chagatai have not come.' Batu wrote back, 'Set him on the throne and take the head from any living being who turns aside from the Yassa.'

Kuyuk's widow, Ogul Gaimish, conspired to kill Mongke, but she failed and was exposed. She was brought to the Princess, where she was stripped naked and accused. She, however, was defiant: 'How can you look on a body that none but a king has seen?' But she was condemned and put to death, together with her henchmen. Years later, Mongke said of her to the envoy of Louis of France, 'How could that evil woman, viler than a bitch, know the ways of war and peace? How could she settle the great world in quiet?'

In the West today, Mongke is the least well-known Khakhan of the Genghis family; but the empire reached its height under him, and his territories included much of China and the Far East, Central Asia, the territories of Khwarezm, Kazakhstan, Turkmenistan, Uzbekistan, Afghanistan, the Middle East countries of Persia, Azerbaijan, Iraq and Turkey, and most of Russia. He stayed at home to rule, but conquered and administered the vast empire through his brothers, Kublai in the Far East and Hulagu in the Middle East, and through his cousin and ally, Batu in Russia. He was a skilled administrator and a wise leader, who, despite the massive conquests during his rule, preferred reason to force.

Mongke detested luxury, and criticized the extravagance of the women of the royal family. He was not greedy for personal wealth, and reduced the taxes, saying, 'I have it less at heart to fill my treasury than to preserve my people.' With his iron self-discipline, he was untouched by frivolous pleasures as he forged and refined the machinery of world government. He was tolerant of all religions which he treated as the five fingers of his hand. He was scrupulously careful to honour his obligations to Batu, and the latter, in turn, always acknowledged his authority. Their unity was the cornerstone of the stability of the empire.

The eight years of Mongke's rule were a golden period. He died in 1259 of either cholera or dysentery, and with him died the stability of the Mongol empire. Conquests stopped, as the leading players rushed back to join the succession debate. Europe was saved as the Mongol generals withdrew; despite the destruction of Baghdad, the Islamic empire in the Middle East was saved as Hulagu, himself a candidate for succession, departed with the major part of his army, leaving his general, Kitbuqa, with only 15,000 troops to battle Baibars and his Mamluks.

After the death of Mongke, for a while there was civil war between two of the brothers, Kublai and Arik Buka, and when Kublai secured his position as the new Khakhan, he preferred to live in China where he started the Yuan dynasty and adopted the ways of the Chinese that he had conquered. Batu died and was succeeded by his brother, Berke. Hulagu never made it back home to Karakorum, but settled in Persia, where he founded the Il-Khan dynasty.

A strange twist of fate saved the Muslims from destruction from the Mongol onslaught. Berke, the brother of Batu, when travelling through Bokhara, converted to Islam. Returning home, he encouraged his subjects to join him in his new religion which taught that there is one God and Muhammad is his Prophet, and one of the four Mongol empires became Muslim and an ally of the Muslims. Incensed by the sacking of Baghdad, he declared, 'Hulagu has sacked all the cities of the Muslims and has brought about the death of the Caliph. With the help of God, I will call him to account for so much innocent blood.' Now there was a second civil war amongst the Mongols, as Berke allied himself with Baibars and the Muslims, against his cousin Hulagu, son of a Christian mother and married to his stepmother, Dokuz Khatun, also a Christian; even Hulagu's general, Kitbuqa, was a Christian.

Hulagu had been sent by his brother, Mongke, to conquer the Muslims in the West with specific instructions to destroy the Caliph in Baghdad and the Ismaili Assassins in their mountain stronghold. Mongke instructed him, 'Establish the laws of Genghis Khan from Samarkand to the far side of Egypt. Be generous to those who submit to your orders. Humiliate those who disobey.' But only thirty years after the death of Hulagu, his descendant Ghazan also converted to Islam. He had been born and baptized a Christian, but converted partly through belief and partly because of political expediency in stabilizing his regime. He appointed as his vizier, a converted Jew, Rashid al-Din, who ran the administration for twenty years and wrote the official history of the Mongols. Ghazan promoted trade and agriculture and protected the peasants from oppression and plunder; in the words of Rashid, 'Instead of destroying, he built up a civilization.' Now both the Mongol empires of the West, in the Middle East and in Russia were Muslim. They had come to conquer Islam, but instead, Islam had conquered them not through battle but by winning their hearts and souls.

TIMUR: FEARLESS AND FIRM

The next wave of conquest that rode out of Central Asia almost a century later, fought under the banner of Islam and was led by a Muslim conqueror who claimed a connection to the great Genghis Khan—he was Timur Bec, known in the West as Tamerlane, whose ferocity made even Genghis look gentle by comparison. He was described as steadfast in mind and robust in body, brave and fearless, and firm as a rock. He did not care for jesting or lying; wit and trifling pleased him not; truth, even if it were painful, delighted him. He was faultless in strategy, constant in fortune, firm of purpose and truthful in business. Timur's conquests compare favourably with those of Alexander and Napoleon. Alexander died too early to complete or enjoy his empire, and Napoleon died defeated and imprisoned, but Timur never saw defeat and left his vast empire to his heirs. He was an avid chess player, whose intelligence was unmatched and whose strategies in war left him undefeated over his rule of thirty-six years, of which all but two years were spent campaigning in the saddle. He was unmatched as a rider, hunter or warrior. He never laughed and in all his life, he never appreciated a jest.

The historian Yazdi described Timur:

> Courage raised him to be the supreme Emperor of Tartary, and subjected all of Asia to him, from the frontiers of China to those of Greece. He governed the state himself, without availing himself of a minister; he succeeded in all his enterprises. To everyone he was generous and courteous, except to those who

did not obey him—he punished them with the utmost rigor. He loved justice, and no one who played the tyrant in his dominion went unpunished; he esteemed learning and learned men. He laboured constantly to aid the fine arts. He was utterly courageous in planning and carrying out a plan. To those that served him, he was kind.

Whereas Genghis used terror merely as a strategy, Timur enjoyed it. Not satisfied by his trail of towers made from the heads of those he had conquered and slain, on one occasion he even made a tower of living beings, in which thousands of prisoners were piled on top of each other as though they were bricks, and cemented together, their heads facing outwards while they shrieked and moaned till they were dead. Those who lost their lives in Timur's wars are numbered in millions. He conquered every city and every nation to the east and west, limited only by time. After defeating an enemy, he was least interested in taking over the conquered territory. Instead, he would take the best men of talent—scientists, philosophers and artisans—and the most outstanding objects—jewels and historic items—back to his home in Samarkand, which he was keen to make the most amazing city on earth. Often, he would put his conquered enemy back on the throne, provided he accepted Timur's sovereignty and paid tribute.

Alexander was a prince, with all the advantages of inheriting a kingdom from his powerful father, King Philip. Genghis was the son of a chief, who had to endure hard times as a young boy after the death of his father, but his lineage conferred legitimacy and authority on his rise to power. Timur rose from obscurity, without advantage of family or wealth. He was a brigand, who was maimed, according to his detractors, while stealing sheep. His only advantages were his total fearlessness, his brilliant mind and his amazing ability to inspire dedication and loyalty from his fellows.

When Timur was an unknown youth, the strongman of the area was Kazgan, known as the Kingmaker. He became Timur's patron and gave him command of a squadron. Timur's performance won him respect, and the Kingmaker gave him Aljai, one of his granddaughters, in marriage. Timur gave his young wife love and respect, and allied himself with her brother, Amir Hussayn. These were good years, but all good things come to an end. The Kingmaker died, the Mongols returned, his son and heir was unable to hold on to the crown, and Timur and Hussayn's good fortune melted as snow melts in the spring rain.

But adversity could no more hold back Timur than a spider's web could stop the charge of a lion. Timur's wife died, the bond between the brothers-in-law broke, and the two allies became foes. Timur's power grew and Hussayn was killed. The Tatars assembled and chose Timur as Amir. He cemented their allegiance with the most generous gifts, and destroyed dissent by preemptive action. Where other contenders for power claimed legitimacy as descendents of the great Genghis, Timur claimed legitimacy through Islam and by his supremacy in battle. He was a Muslim where the mainstream Mongols were not. But he also married Saray Khanum, the widow of Amir Hussayn; she had in her veins the blood of Genghis Khan, and Timur took the title of 'son-in-law'.

Timur now set upon conquest with a vengeance. He had Samarkand, but all around him were kingdoms greater than his, and Timur could never accept being second-best. To the north lay the Chagatai Mongol kingdom ruled by the descendents of Jochi, the eldest son of Genghis Khan; to the west, the great Muslim powers, Iran, Baghdad, the Ottoman Turks; and further west, the Mamluks of Egypt; to the south, lay India; and finally in the east, the great kingdom of the Chinese Emperor. In 1376, Jehangir, Timur's favourite son and heir, died of a sickness. He was shattered. In the same year, Toktamish arrived, a refugee to the court of Timur. Toktamish was a prince of the family of Genghis Khan, who had escaped when his father was murdered and was now burned with ambition to avenge his father's death and win the crown of the Chagatai Mongol kingdom.

Timur offered a simple choice to his adversaries: surrender and you will be spared, but resist and you will be annihilated. The first great city on his path was Herat, which had suffered conquerors time and time again. Herat had been a major city when the famed capitals of Europe had been small towns, but the Mongol armies had destroyed it, slaughtering almost everyone living there. Herat knew the heavy cost of defeat and surrendered without a blow, giving up its treasures to Timur.

Towns which attempted to resist, were made to regret their mistake; an example to all. At Isfizar, he created a tower of the living, which was a gruesome variation of his usual calling card—a tower of skulls. Zarang felt the full fury of his wrath; it was wiped out. No wall, tree or person remained. Even the irrigation system was destroyed and the green fields were swallowed by the desert.

The richest and most important city of Timur's time, was Tabriz. With a population more than ten times that of London or any other city of Europe, and holding the key to the lucrative trade routes, it was a tempting prize. It surrendered without a battle and avoided the inevitable destruction that was the fate of those who resisted.

Isfahan surrendered to avoid destruction, but destruction was in her destiny. In the night, a rebel group attacked and killed the 3,000-man garrison that had been stationed in the city. Timur was livid and determined to set an example; in the words of the historian Arabshah, 'He ordered bloodshed and sacrilege, slaughter and plunder, devastation, burning of crops, women's breasts to be cut off, infants to be destroyed, bodies dismembered, honour to be insulted.' Every man, woman and child was killed. Seventy thousand lost their lives in the bloodbath. Towers were built with the heads of those killed.

In Shiraz, the poet Hafiz was brought before the conqueror, who asked him how he had dared to equate the value of Samarkand with a mole on a lover's cheek, in one of his verses. Hafiz sidestepped the danger by replying, 'Alas, Prince, it is this prodigality which is the cause of the misery in which you see me.' Timur was amused and was generous in his gifts to the poet.

Suddenly, Timur's conquest of Persia was interrupted by news that Toktamish was invading Timur's territory. This enraged the conqueror, both because he would not tolerate any invasion of his new empire, but also because it was Toktamish who had challenged him. The same Toktamish who had come to him as fugitive from the Mongols; whom he had supported with arms, money and men for years until he was established as Khan of the Golden Horde. But Toktamish, Khan of the Golden Horde, was a very different man from the fugitive Toktamish who had come for Timur's help as a supplicant. Not only was he Khan of a mighty empire, but he was also an outstanding warrior, a general who had learned the art of war under Timur himself. Of all Timur's enemies, he was the one who came closest to defeating the 'conqueror of the world'; of all his foes, he was the warrior that Timur most respected.

Timur hurried back to Samarkand to deal with the problem of Toktamish. His experienced advisors recommended waiting out the winter and preparing for an expedition in spring. Winter was too cold; the snow too deep for the horses, the bitter winds when the temperature fell to -50 degrees, prevented fast movement and threatened frostbite. But Timur liked to do what was least expected; surprise outweighed all other arguments.

Five months passed as Timur chased Toktamish with never a sight of his army. Winter turned to summer, as Timur's tired and hungry troops marched 1,800 miles in pursuit of an invisible foe. Timur battled to feed his 200,000 men and to graze up to half a million horses. Had the expedition been a disastrous mistake?

Then finally the enemy was sighted. Toktamish had a larger army, in better condition and with positional advantage. The Turks had Timur. On the eve of battle, Timur ordered that the best carpets and tents be laid out for a comfortable night. He exuded confidence. The next day, the two armies charged and the fiercest fighting continued for three days. Toktamish, fearing for his life, withdrew. His troops, seeing the banners of their leader gone, broke up in disarray. Flight led to defeat. Timur had shown that when two matched armies fight, it is the courage of the leader that determines victory and defeat. The Mongol army was smashed, but Toktamish, the Mongol leader, escaped.

Three years later Toktamish was back, having prepared another formidable army. The advantage once again lay with Toktamish, but Timur was the lord of war. Timur warned his foe, 'You are acquainted with my victories, and know that peace or war are equally indifferent to me. You have experienced both my mildness and my severity.'

For three days the two armies parried from opposite banks of the river between, looking for the chance to cross. But on the third night Timur disguised the women in his camp as men to fool the enemy that his army had camped down for the night while they secretly sought a crossing. Again the battle was fierce; again Timur held his ground against all dangers; and once again, Toktamish departed the field, saving his own life but leaving his army to destruction. The Golden Horde, was smashed. Once and for all, the Mongol threat was ended; Saray, the capital city of the Golden Horde, was taken, plundered and torched, and its people left to freeze in the snow. Saray ceased to exist; even the lucrative trade route was diverted to the south to ensure that never again would the Mongols taste the wealth that they had known. Toktamish lived a fugitive, never again to threaten his master, Timur.

Timur was no longer young. But neither age nor personal tragedy could hold him back on his relentless march of conquest. Of his four sons, two—Jehangir and Omar Shaykh—had died. The third had degenerated into a perverse drunk, who even tried to dethrone his father, accusing him of old age, weak constitution and infirmity. Timur was enraged by his son's comment that, 'You administer justice, but unjustly.' He removed Miranshah from office. That left only Shah Rukh, and the grandsons.

Next came the turn of India. Timur had to move an army of 90,000 together with almost a quarter million horses across the highest mountains in the world, through ice, snow and precipice. At one mountain, he had to be lowered a thousand feet in a basket, down to where the path resumed. He then battled through the plains, taking Multan and marching on Delhi. By this time he had captured a 100,000 prisoners, who cheered in hope when they saw the army of Delhi emerge from its gates. It was a big mistake; they did not know Timur. He ordered all 100,000 prisoners be killed.

The army of Delhi came onto the field to do battle with the invaders. Their massive elephants and the tanks of the time, created shock and awe among the Turks, who had never seen such beasts. They wondered how to fight them. Timur, as usual, had an answer to everything. His solution was camels with straw tied to their backs and set on fire. The blazing camels charged the elephants which panicked and trampled their own army. Timur took Delhi and with it, the treasure accumulated over centuries. It was over, or so it seemed. The Hindus made a last suicidal stand—burning their homes, killing their wives and children, they charged out to die. Timur's reaction was merciless as he ordered the slaughter of the population. For three days, the massacre continued. For two weeks, Timur plundered everything of value, even a pair of cockatoos, which fascinated him. Then suddenly he gave the order to leave and with him went the treasures of Delhi.

In the Middle East, Timur had already conquered Iran and Baghdad. The dominant dynasty was that of the Ottomans, and their ruler Bayazid, known as the Thunderbolt for his prowess in battle, had been nibbling at Europe. The kings of Europe were terrified and a conquest of Europe seemed inevitable. Timur was not interested in Europe, which he considered a backwater and not worth his time; but he was interested in the Middle East and could not tolerate a rival conqueror there. So once again Timur set out for the West. Bayazid hurried back from his Europe campaign to meet this new threat.

Bayazid had the best infantry in the world, and his crack troops, the janissaries, were undefeated in war. These slave soldiers lived for battle and their discipline and expertise were state of the art. Timur had an army of cavalry—steppe warriors in the tradition of Genghis Khan, but more disciplined, professional soldiers. The future of the world would be decided in one battle to the east of Ankara. Europe prayed for victory for Timur. If Bayazid won, Europe was doomed to being absorbed in the Ottoman Empire.

Bayazid was a truly great general, but Timur was in another class altogether. When Timur approached Bayazid's army, he saw at once that the chosen battleground favoured the infantry and was not suitable for his cavalry. He knew when to fight and when not to fight. He understood that the right time and the right place was the key to winning battles. So he diverted his troops and placed himself between the Ottoman army and Ankara, settling them in the very same camp that Bayazid had vacated to march to battle. For eight days, he seemed to have disappeared; when his new position was revealed, Bayazid's force marched his troops back to save Ankara before it was too late. Timur's only move was to cut off the spring and divert the river, denying water supply to Bayazid's army which arrived exhausted, thirsty and dispirited. By this manoeuver, Timur had as good as won the battle even before the first blow was struck.

The young and confident Bayazid hurled taunts at Timur, who sat, almost bored, on his horse, thinking more of his aching bones than the outcome of the battle to come, which he knew would be sure victory. In answer to Bayazid's challenges, he turned to his trusted generals and in a puzzled tone, asked, 'Does he not know I am Timur?' In three hours it was over: the Ottoman army smashed and Bayazid brought to Timur as a prisoner. Timur was playing chess with his son; he stood to receive the defeated Ottoman and smiled. Bayazid, bold to the end, reprimanded Timur saying that he should not mock one who God has afflicted. Timur replied, 'I smiled that God should have given the mastery of the world to a lame man like me and a blind man like thee.'

Timur threw a banquet to celebrate his victory. The vanquished emperor, Bayazid, was summoned to attend in his royal robes. His behaviour was dour and surly. To liven up the celebration, Timur called in the beautiful Ottoman empress and her ladies-in-waiting to serve and entertain his generals. Bayazid was consumed with rage at the shame of his queen, humbled before the uncouth Tatars. But he was helpless in his confinement, where he died; it is said that he killed himself by beating his head against the walls of his prison.

Timur's historians say he gave Bayazid respect and consideration till the end, even returning Despina, the favourite wife of the Sultan, to cheer him up.

Timur turned back for home; Europe was saved. Why was Timur not tempted by Europe? Europe, like Afghanistan six centuries later, was saved by her poverty—there was nothing there that Timur wanted. No conqueror wants to waste his time in a barren land. Timur took back to Samarkand the treasures of the Ottomans; but one prize that especially pleased him was an old book stained with blood. This was the first *Quran*, which belonged to the Caliph, Uthman, written in his own hand, which he had been reading when his assassins cut his throat, spilling his blood on the Holy Book. In 1868, a Russian general presented the *Quran* to Czar Alexander II who placed it in the imperial library in St Petersburg. But the Muslims prevailed on Lenin to return it to them and it was brought back to Tashkent where it lies till today.

Back in Samarkand, Timur ordered celebrations—two months of feasting, drinking and making merry. He was now a tired old man, almost seventy years of age, stooped, partially blind and frail. From the world, ambassadors and emissaries came to pay homage at his court. But the old warrior had not softened. It was the time of reckoning for those who had abused power while he had been away. The governor of Samarkand himself, who had enjoyed Timur's confidence but had oppressed the people, was hanged. A friend who tried to intercede on his behalf was also hanged and one of Timur's nephews, who offered a large sum to save the condemned man, was tortured, relieved of his wealth and hanged upside down. Merchants were executed for profiteering. No one, however powerful, was above the law.

Then after two months, Timur ordered his army to prepare for war. It was now time for China, the most powerful empire on earth. Kublai Khan's Mongol Yuan dynasty had degenerated and had been ousted by a Chinese peasant warlord, the founder of the Ming dynasty. The great warlord had died, leaving his empire to a weak teenage grandson who was already facing a civil war with his uncle. If ever the time was right to take China, it was now.

Timur set off on the campaign trail, ready to lose everything, or double his empire through this last war. He was old, infirm and unable to speak, and the winter was bitterly cold, but nothing could break his iron will. But age had taken the strength from his exhausted body. He caught a cold which soon turned into a high fever, and he prepared for death, knowing that now he would never reach China. He declared his grandson, Pir Mohammad, his heir, and gave his last words of advice, 'Make justice the guide of all your actions and the empire will long remain in your hands. But if discord and disunity creep in, ill fortune awaits you.'

Pir Mohammad never sat on the throne. Civil war broke out and within a year, he was killed. Finally Shah Rukh, the last surviving son of Timur, took the crown and the remnants of the empire saw stability for a while. Shah Rukh's son Ulugh Beg, who succeeded him, was killed by his own son, who in turn was killed in a year. Within a century, the vast empire of Timur disappeared. His massive structures in Samarkand were destroyed by earthquakes. Nothing remained but the legend. But five generations later, a new empire would be created by a prince descended from Timur's family—a prince named Babur.

11

The Delhi Sultanate

'History in the East does not mean the growth of constitutions, the development of civic rights, the vindication of individual liberty, or the evolution of self-government. These are Western ideas which have no meaning in India'

—Stanley Lane-Poole

'When troopers do not appear at the muster, I order three years' pay to be taken from them. I place wine-drinkers and wine-sellers in pits of incarceration. If a man debauches another man's wife, I cut off his organ, and the woman, I cause to be killed. Rebels I slay; their wives and children, I reduce to beggary and ruin. Extortion I punish with torture and I keep them in prison in chains until every jital is restored. Political criminals, I confine and chastise. Wilt thou say that all this is unlawful?'

—Alauddin Khalji

Muslim rule in India started with the invasion of the Arab army under the young and charismatic Mohammed bin Qasim who met his tragic end sewn inside the skin of an ox, as punishment for a crime he did not commit and a victim to political intrigue back home. Two centuries later, India was repeatedly plundered by the fierce warrior Mahmud of Ghazni, who was attracted to India's wealth but not her climate.

The real conquest of India was the achievement of Mohammad Ghori, who left a viceroy to govern his new colony. This viceroy founded the famous Slave dynasty of India, and from that day till the 'Indian Mutiny' of the mid-nineteenth century, there was always a Muslim king in Delhi.

The viceroy, Qutbuddin Aybek, was the first of thirty-four kings, who ruled over a period of three centuries till Babur, the Mogul, took India. These kings, known as the Delhi Sultanate, fell into five dynasties—the Slave Kings, the Khaljis, the Tughlaks, the Sayyids and the Lodis. The history of the Delhi Sultanate is the story of great and remarkable men who created and built great dynasties, but were followed by weak and degenerate successors. In a repeating cycle, justice, discipline and merit were replaced by self-indulgent orgies of wine, women and song, as strong and capable founders were succeeded by weak and self-destructive heirs. Time and time again, ambitious sultans would conspire to promote the interests of their favourite sons, no matter how unfit for rule. Time and time again, the final arbiter was the sword, which silenced all other arguments.

These Muslim conquerors were a minority group with relatively small armies. Islands in the ocean of Hindu majority, they belonged to a different race, practiced a different religion and subscribed to a different culture. What gave them an edge over the local inhabitants? How were they able to take and keep power for six centuries?

Islam promoted the key values of merit, equality and knowledge, which, combined with discipline, missionary zeal and a conviction of a better world after death, created courageous warriors who feared nothing. But it was also the attitude of the Indians themselves, who were already so divided internally that they saw the invaders as merely another group, no more alien than the numerous and diverse groups that already peopled India. The poor masses of India were practical and unemotional about the reality of their lives; did it really matter who ruled? The power politics of the rich and powerful made no difference to the harsh economic reality of their day-to-day struggles. The caste system of the Hindu religion also led to a fatalism and passivism that left the new conquerors substantially unopposed. But finally it was the military superiority of professional armies, experienced in the art of war, over vast hordes of amateurs without discipline or motivation.

THE SLAVE KINGS

In the world of Islam, slavery was often more of an opportunity than a punishment. Slave dynasties ruled in Egypt, Baghdad and India; and in the Ottoman Empire, slaves were important both in the army, whose crack cadre of janissaries was famous and feared, and in the civil administration. Queens were frequently upwardly mobile slave girls whose road to power started in the bed of the king and ended in the role of Sultana Valida once her son took the throne.

Once, when a courtier offered sympathy to Mohammad Ghori that he had no sons, Ghori replied, 'Have I not thousands of children in my Turkish slaves?' When Ghori conquered India, he left four of these slaves to control the territories of Afghanistan, Bengal, the Indus and Delhi. Of these, Qutbuddin Aybek emerged preeminent, and became the founder of the Slave dynasty of India.

Qutbuddin was a brave and good man, under whose competent rule, peace and stability prevailed. But after only four years he died when his horse fell in a polo game. His son proved unfit to rule, so the crown passed to his son-in-law, Iltutmish.

From an early age, the star of fortune shone on Iltumish, who was without peer in beauty, virtue, intelligence and nobility. But victim of jealousy, he was sold to a slave merchant who took him to the Sultan, demanding the amazingly high price of one thousand gold dinars. This was too much even for the Sultan, who ordered that no one should buy this young slave. Finally a compromise was found, which allowed his sale, provided it was not in Ghazni. In this way, in Delhi, he came into the ownership of Qutbuddin Aybek, who loved him as a son.

Qutbuddin was famed for his generosity, and one night at a banquet, he distributed gold and silver to his courtiers. Iltutmish went out to the soldiers and gave his entire share to them, keeping nothing for himself. Qutbuddin, recognizing the greatness of his slave, gave him his daughter in marriage and elevated him to the highest office. Iltutmish was a man who could be trusted to perform selflessly and loyally.

Soon after taking the throne, Iltumish almost lost it, when Genghis Khan, the World Conqueror, invaded India in hot pursuit of Jalaladdin, the last Khwarezm Shah who had fled to India when he lost his empire to Genghis. Capturing Jalaluddin was a major prize—much more important to Genghis than capturing Delhi. After all, what was Delhi, compared to the great Shah? Genghis had much on his mind, and retired from India as suddenly as he had come. Iltumish breathed a sigh of relief. The storm had passed.

For twenty-five years, Iltutmish ruled successfully. He was as able an administrator as he was a general. Justice, law and order, and the economy flourished even as the territory of his kingdom grew. Grand buildings were constructed, including the Qutb Minar—the tallest building of its time; the Eiffel Tower of medieval India.

But all good things come to an end, and finally the great man lay on his deathbed. When his nobles asked him who was his choice as successor, he replied, 'My sons are given over to the follies of youth; none of them is fit to be king and rule this country, and you will find that there is no one better able to do so than my daughter, Razia.' He died, leaving the nobles, the power brokers of the time, unconvinced. The leading historian Juzjani, wrote, 'She was endowed with all the qualities befitting a king. But she was not of the right sex, and so in the estimation of men, all her virtues were worthless.'

The nobles rejected Razia and instead, crowned her brother, Sultan.

He quickly showed his true nature in an orgy of debauchery while his mother, a low-born concubine of Iltumish, dominated the affairs of state, taking vicious revenge on those in the family who had humbled her in her years as an insignificant servant. She blinded a rival son of Iltutmish and had him murdered. She also conspired to kill Razia. But the people had had enough. They rose in revolt, seized the palace, arrested the Sultana Valida, and executed the Sultan. Razia was enthroned by public acclamation not as Sultana, but as Sultan, the title reserved for male rulers!

Razia put aside her veil, and started dressing and behaving as any confident sultan would. The nobles may not have liked it, but the public were with her, and her performance as a ruler spoke for itself. Her choice of the Abyssinian, Yacut, as her favourite, scandalized the power brokers and finally, seizing an opportue moment, they killed him, imprisoned Razia and appointed her half-brother as Sultan.

Razia was down but not out. She used her charms to captivate her jailor, the governor of Bhatinda, whom she married. Together, they marched on Delhi but their army was defeated. She fled and was found sleeping in a field by a peasant who killed her to steal her ornaments and fine clothes. So died Sultan Razia, a great monarch, wise, just and generous, a benefactor to her kingdom, a dispenser of justice, protector of her subjects and the leader of her armies.

Weak and dissolute sultans, internal rivalries and the terrible Mongols threatening the borders, resulted in chaos. The weak seventeen-year-old Mahmud was crowned Sultan, but he had little interest or aptitude for affairs of state. He spent his time as a dervish, reading the *Quran* and living a frugal and simple life. When his wife requested him for money to buy a slave to help her with the housework, he refused, telling her the treasury belonged to the Muslims and was not for his personal use. But luck favoured him in the person of Balban, an exceptionally capable slave who ran his government for him for twenty years till the death of the Sultan, and then for another twenty years as Sultan himself.

Balban started life with every handicap. Short and ugly, he was kidnapped at a young age and put into the slave market, where he attracted no buyers. But when the Sultan rejected him as a suitable purchase, Balban, ever ready to seize the moment of opportunity, addressed the sultan, 'You have bought ninety-nine slaves for yourself, now buy me for God.' The Sultan agreed, and over the years, Balban rose from slave to malik, from malik to khan, and finally from khan to sultan.

Balban was a great leader who insisted on efficiency. He was ruthless in enforcing discipline and hard work, punishing the tardy and uncompromising in the administration of justice, with no favour to brothers, children, associates or subordinates. He ruled in the name of the God-fearing sultan, Muhammad, for twenty years, and then for another twenty years as Sultan himself. He was a king, bounteous and powerful, in whose time 'an elephant would avoid treading on an ant.' In his forty years of power, he never jested or laughed, and never allowed jest or laughter in his presence.

Balban suppressed the bandits who had made a mockery of law and order, he brought under control insubordinate governors who had eroded the authority of Delhi, and he dealt with the raids of predator Mongols who were ever a threat. By keeping a strong army and at the same time maintaining a good relationship with Hulagu, the grandson of Genghis Khan, he kept the Mongols towards the west of the Indus, leaving Delhi safe from these 'savages descended from dogs, whose stench was more horrible than their colour, whose heads were set on their bodies as if they had no necks, whose chests were covered with lice which looked like sesame growing on a bad soil.'

Balban saved Delhi from the Mongols, but could not save his beloved son Muhammad, who courageously died as a warrior in a battle against them. Balban was eighty at the time, and the death of his son was more than he could bear. By day, it was business as usual, where Balban put on a brave face as he attended to his office duties, but at night he cried in grief, tore his clothes and threw ashes on his head. In two years, he passed away.

As surely as night follows day, great men are followed by weak and dissolute successors. Kaikobad, a grandson of the Sultan, was crowned. He was a young man of excellent qualities who had been brought up carefully and well educated by watchful tutors. When suddenly he was exposed to the temptations of absolute power, he immediately forgot all that he had learned and plunged into pleasure and dissipation of every kind. Vice and immorality spread, mosques emptied as the wine shops filled up. Ladies of pleasure proliferated. Chaos prevailed as Kaikobad, struck by paralysis, was confined to his bed, barely alive. The commander of the army, Jalaluddin Khalji, took control and after three months, sent an executioner to kill the paralyzed Sultan: 'He dispatched him with two or three kicks and threw his body into the Yamuna.'

THE KHALJIS

The new dynasty ruled for only thirty years. The founder, Jalaluddin, was a kind, merciful and God-fearing old man, more concerned with preparing his entry to the next world than improving his prospects in this world. Determined not to spill the blood of fellow Muslims, he pardoned thieves, criminals and even those who conspired to kill him. His clemency and innocence were finally to cost him his life.

Alauddin was the nephew and son-in-law of Jalaluddin. Where Jalaluddin was kind and loving, Alauddin was ambitious and ruthless. The courtiers warned Jalaluddin about his nephew, but the guileless heart of the Sultan relied upon the fidelity of Alauddin—a big mistake!

Jalaluddin went out to meet his nephew who was returning victorious from war, bringing much booty from his conquests. As they embraced, Alauddin gave the signal to an executioner who plunged his sword into the Sultan. With blood pouring from his wound, the Sultan cried out, 'Ah, thou villain, Alauddin! What hast thou done!' Another guard cut off the head of the Sultan, which was presented to Alauddin, impaled on a spear. Setting out for Delhi, he scattered so much gold that the faithless people easily forgot the murder of the Sultan and rejoiced over his succession. On reaching Delhi, he blinded the princes, arrested their mother and secured the throne. Alauddin ruled for twenty years, the most important sultan of the Khalji dynasty and one of the most important and powerful rulers in the history of India.

Having taken control, he moved to show the nobles that he was no longer dependent on their support but they were dependent on his. The turncoat maliks, who had deserted their former master to join him, were arrested, imprisoned, blinded and killed, and their property was confiscated. Only three were spared—three who had never taken money from Alauddin but had remained faithful to his uncle and these brave and loyal men Alauddin rewarded with respect and honour.

The new sultan was an unusual man. Bad tempered, obstinate, hard-hearted and cruel, he was a control freak who kept no advisors and took no advice. Just like the Mogul emperor Akbar, he could not read or write. He worked obsessively for the good of his subjects, unconcerned and unrestricted by convention, legality or religion. He said no prayers and did not even attend the Friday prayer in the mosque. But despite all this, fortune smiled on him and he was remarkably successful in all that he put his hand to.

He was frustrated in only three things that he desired—his attempt to ban alcohol was as futile as the attempted prohibition in America in the time of Al Capone; his desire for the legendary Hindu queen, Padmini, who resorted to suicide to evade his clutches; and the fact that he could not control his first wife, who had the title of Malika-i-Jahan, which was pure torture for a man with an obsession to control everything. It must not be forgotten, however, that he had murdered her father!

When Alauddin took the throne, he was surrounded by problems, conspiracy and internal rebellion, Mongol marauders from the north, shortage of funds and an administration that left much to be desired. Entirely unsentimental and never impulsive, he carefully laid his plans, which he proceeded to execute with his ruthless efficiency. First, he came down hard on those who opposed his government. Two nephews who revolted were blinded by having their eyes cut out with knives, like slices of a melon. When the army revolted, the wives of the leaders were dishonoured and forced into prostitution. Their children were cut to pieces before their mothers' eyes—no tolerance, no mercy.

Alauddin built up his army into an effective fighting machine, time and again routing the Mongols in battle. All fear of the Mongols entirely departed from Delhi. Perfect peace and security prevailed. But feeding an army does not come cheap, so Alauddin decided that the solution was to keep prices of foodstuffs and other essential goods at a low level. This he achieved through a control economy closely monitored by his officials to ensure compliance. Corruption was eliminated and official salaries were raised. If a merchant cheated, fillets of flesh would be cut from his body equal in value to the fraudulently stolen amount—no tolerance, no mercy. His objectives were achieved and soon the coffers of the treasury overflowed with the wealth that was generated.

He tried to work out why so many rebellions were constantly erupting and came to the conclusion that too much money and too much social interaction fuelled discontent and ambition. Through taxation and confiscation, he increased the wealth of the state at the expense of the wealth of its citizens. Through totalitarian control of society, he directed social interaction towards behaviour he considered safe. He discouraged parties where alcohol was consumed, in the belief that drunkenness promotes conspiracy. Taverns were torched. Soon everyone was too busy trying to earn enough with no time or inclination for conspiracies and rebellion. His extensive spy network kept him informed. His strange conclusions seem to have worked very well for many years, and many modern Third World dictators have followed a similar path. In time, success increased his arrogance and megalomania.

Alauddin's policy for the Hindus was severe. He said, 'I know that Hindus will never become submissive and obedient till they are reduced to poverty. They shall not be allowed to accumulate wealth and property.' The historian Barani, wrote, 'As soon as the revenue collector demands the sum due from him, the Hindu pays with meekness, humility and respect and he, should the collector choose to spit in his mouth, opens the same without hesitation, so that the official may spit into it.'

Alauddin was a compulsive workaholic with a knack of selecting capable people and retaining their loyalty. Barani lists ten major achievements of the Sultan as:

1. Cheapness of necessities
2. Invariable success in military campaigns
3. Rout of the Mongols
4. Maintenance of a large army at a small cost
5. Political stability and suppression of rebellions
6. Safety on roads
7. Honest dealings in the bazaar
8. Building works and infrastructure
9. The prevalence of 'rectitude, truth, honesty, justice and temperance in the hearts of Muslims'
10. The flourishing of many great and learned men

He was a brutal dictator of whom it was said, 'No more prosperous times than his had ever fallen to the lot of any Muhammadan sovereign.' But age eroded his health and his power. His favourite, a converted Hindu eunuch named Kafur, grew in strength, and was appointed commander-in-chief and vizier. A capable general, he extended the empire in the south, as practically the whole of the subcontinent was subdued by the army from Delhi. From the war, Kafur brought home for the Sultan fabulous treasures including a diamond whose value was sufficient to feed all the people of the world for two days—this gemstone was known as 'the mountain of light', the Kohinoor. When the great Sultan passed from this world to the next, Kafur took control as regent to a six-year-old son of the Sultan, and started his brutal elimination of potential rivals from the family, arresting, blinding and murdering. Soldiers were sent to blind Mubarak, the third son of the late Sultan. But the young prince bribed them with a valuable necklace he was wearing, and persuaded them to assassinate their leader Kafur instead. Once the eunuch was killed, Mubarak took the throne. But the new Sultan was a degenerate and a debauch, unfit to rule. He courted popularity by reversing the hard policies of his father, and soon the administration, army and economy fell into disarray. Barani describes his short rule,

> During the four years and four months of his rule, the Sultan attended to nothing but drinking, music, debauchery and pleasure, scattering his gifts and gratifying his lusts… He cast aside all regard for decency, and presented himself decked out in the trinkets of a female before his assembled company… Sometimes he made his appearance in company stark naked, talking obscenity.

He executed his three surviving brothers and his father-in-law and was a raging homosexual, whose obsession was a slave who was given the name of Khusrav Khan, who was promoted to dignity and power. But as intensely as Mubarak loved his slave, Khusrav hated his master and planned to kill him.

Mubarak shut his ears to warnings of the treachery being planned by Khusrav. Finally, one night, Khusrav made his move. His henchmen secretly entered the palace. Khusrav was in bed with the Sultan, and seized him by his hair so that the assassins could strike. The Sultan flung him down and sat on his slave as they grappled. An assassin drove his spear through the Sultan, cut off his head and threw the body into the courtyard. The eunuch ascended the throne, killing all who had been close to the Sultan and giving their wives and daughters as concubines to his Hindu supporters. Khusrav now married the widow of the Sultan. The reversal of fortune was seen as a Hindu coup. Positions of power were taken by Hindus: 'Copies of the Holy Book were used as cushions for people to sit on, and idols were set up in the pulpits of mosques… Hindus rejoiced greatly…boasting that Delhi had once more come under Hindu rule.'

The Muslim Turks were not ready to bow before a sultan who

was an Indian-Hindu convert. They rallied under the leadership of the respected general Ghazi Malik, who advanced on Delhi. Barani described the scene: 'So these two foolish, ignorant lads went forth, like newly hatched chickens just beginning to fly, to fight with a veteran warrior like Ghazi Malik...who twenty times had routed the Mongols.' They were quickly defeated and Khusrav was killed.

The noble old soldier, Ghazi Malik, wept over the unhappy fate of the sons of Alauddin and offered the crown to any surviving member of the family. But there were none, and by universal acclaim, the old soldier was crowned as Ghiyasuddin Tughluq Shah. As Barani wryly commented, the murderers of the God-fearing Jalaluddin had met their divine retribution—the entire family of Alauddin had been murdered and most of the conspirators were dead: 'the hell-hound Salim, who struck the first blow, was a year or two afterwards eaten up by leprosy, and Ikhtiyar, who had cut off the head of the Sultan, very soon went mad and in his dying ravings cried out that Sultan Jalaluddin stood over him with a naked sword, ready to cut off his head.'

THE TUGHLUQS

Ghazi Malik, as Ghiasuddin Tughluq, was a fair, noble and just ruler who restored his realm to prosperity and peace. Taxes were reduced, the harvests increased and the people were happy. The mood of the kingdom changed as though the sun had come out from black clouds after a rainstorm. But the Sultan was killed when the roof of a building collapsed on him when returning to Delhi and the throne passed to his son Muhammad bin Tughluq.

Muhammad was brilliant and highly educated with a marvellous memory and a strong personality. He was a man of ideas, impatient to start his great work. He believed himself to be a man of destiny and initiated a program of reforms to build his country. Nothing that he tried, succeeded. His intentions were noble, but his execution was a disaster. Generous to a fault, but cruel and vicious, he earned the hatred of his people. Rebellion was rife, and rebels paid heavily for their treason. His brother was executed; his nephew was roasted alive and his barbequed flesh served to his family.

With dreams of conquering the world, he kept a huge army, but made no use of it. To support his army, he raised the level of taxes. His policies caused an economic collapse which he tried to reverse by currency manipulation. Despite his claim to expertise on currency policy, his monetary experiments were a disaster. He then decided to shift his capital from Delhi to Daulatabad and all the citizens of Delhi were ordered to move. A blind man who refused to move was dragged along the long road to Daulatabad; a month later when they arrived at their destination, all that was left of the blind man was one leg; the rest of the body had been ripped apart along the road. After eight years, Muhammad finally admitted that the move had been a mistake, and he ordered the return to Delhi.

The more he did, the more the mess that he created and the more his subjects hated him. With each year that passed, his frustration grew and his empire decayed. He died in 1351, campaigning against rebels. He had no sons and was succeeded by his cousin, Firoz Shah. After Muhammad's death, India recovered like a sick man after an exhausting fever.

Firoz had been trained in the art of government by his cousin. He now reversed all his predecessor's policies. Torture and murder of Muslims was forbidden. India saw peace and prosperity for the thirty-seven years of his gentle rule. He was ably assisted by his vizier, Maqbul Khan, an illiterate but brilliant Hindu convert. Together they rebuilt the empire. The debts of the peasants were annulled. Taxes were reduced to the levels proscribed by Islam.

Canals and infrastructure were built and the economy flourished. The loyal and hardworking Maqbul Khan was generously rewarded by his sultan, who awarded him an income of a thousand dinars a year for every son that was born to him. Since the vizier had 2,000 ladies in his harem, this grant allowed him to accumulate a sizeable fortune! In return, he administered the kingdom with exceptional skill and wisdom.

Firoz was a devout Muslim, though in private, he enjoyed his glass of wine. He was a father to his people, who took care of the needy and unemployed and refused to dismiss aged officials. He treated the Hindus with kindness. His historians wrote, 'Under Firoz, all men, high and low, bound and free, lived happily and free from care. The court was splendid. Things were plentiful and cheap. Nothing untoward happened during his reign. No village remained waste, no land uncultivated.' He died worn out with weakness at the age of ninety, loved by his people.

But all good things come to an end, and bad times follow good, as surely as night follows day. Internal dissention weakened the kingdom and unimaginable problems arose; at one time, two kings ruled in Delhi at the same time. How would all this end? Natural disaster takes many forms—volcanoes, earthquakes and tsunamis; the disaster that hit the crumbling Delhi Sultanate was Timur.

In his autobiography, Timur describes his decision to invade India:

> About the year 800 A.H. (1398 AD) there arose in my heart the desire to lead an expedition against the infidels and become a champion of the faith…but I was undetermined in my mind whether I should direct my expedition against the infidels of China or against the infidels and polytheists of India. In this matter I sought an omen from the *Quran* and the verse to which I opened was this, 'O Prophet, make war upon infidels and unbelievers and treat them with severity.' My chief officers told me that the inhabitants of Hindustan were infidels and unbelievers. In obedience to the mandate of Almighty God, I determined to make an expedition against them.

He came, he saw, he conquered. He sacked Delhi and slaughtered the population. And then he departed, taking with him the treasures of Delhi and two white cockatoos. He had accomplished his purpose—to kill infidels and seize the treasures of the world. Delhi never recovered till after Babur's invasion.

The day of the Tughluks was over and the empire was falling

apart. The unexpected savior was an Arab general who claimed to be a descendent of The Prophet. This was Khizr Khan who had prudently joined Timur when he invaded India. Khizr now took Delhi as the founder of the short-lived Sayyid dynasty. He was, according to his historian, 'Not enamoured of the trappings of power; he had the substance of power and that was what mattered to him. Although he did not take royal titles, yet he ruled and administered his territories like a king.' He ruled as the viceroy of Timur, and he ruled well. He was generous, brave, merciful, considerate, true to his word and kind. It was said of him, 'The Sayyid was a man with the virtues of Muhammad and the grace of Ali.'

THE SAYYID AND LODHI DYNASTY

The Sayyid dynasty lasted only thirty-seven years under four sultans, the last of whom, Shah Alam, in effect abdicated and moved to a small suburb of Delhi, where he lived happily in obscurity till his death. The most powerful of the nobles in Delhi, was Hamid Khan; he invited an Afghan army commander, Bahlul, to take the throne. Buhlul was a cunning man and on arriving in Delhi, he told Hamid Khan, 'I am a mere soldier and cannot manage even my own fief. You should be the King.' Hamid Khan was pleased, thinking he had found a suitable puppet that he could control. But once the new sultan was secure in his power, Hamid was arrested and was never heard of again. Sultan Buhlul ruled for thirty-nine years as the founder of the Lodhi dynasty.

The ablest of Sultan Buhlul's sons was Sikandar, who was designated as successor; but some of the nobles opposed him because his mother was the daughter of a Hindu goldsmith. Sikandar had many commendable qualities; he was intelligent, God-fearing and benevolent and was famous for his beauty and justice. It was said of him that '(his) zeal for Islam surpassed all bounds' but he did enjoy his secret glass of wine!

Sikandar was succeeded by his son Ibrahim, the last of the Lodhis, who was to lose his throne and his life to Babur at the battle of Panipat in 1526. Ibrahim was a good general with an army of a 100,000 men against Babur's 24,000 soldiers. He also had a thousand elephants, but Babur came with a new weapon that Ibrahim and his men had never seen before—the matchlock musket. It was this new invention that gave victory to the Ottomans and the Moguls, the two rising empires of the day.

The battle of Panipat ended the three-and-a-half centuries of the Delhi Sultanate and gave India to Babur, the founder of the glorious and fabulously wealthy Mogul empire, which flourished till it was finally replaced by British rule in India.

12

The Great Moguls

'Hindustan is a place of little charm. The people are not handsome. They have no genius, no intellectual comprehension, no politeness, no kindness or fellow feeling, no ingenuity or mechanical invention in planning or executing their handicrafts, no skill or knowledge in design or architecture. There are no good horses, meat, grapes, melons, or other fruit. There is no ice, cold water, good food or bread in the markets. There are no baths and no madrassahs. There are no candles, torches or candlesticks. The chief excellence of Hindustan is that it is a big country with plenty of gold and silver.'

—Babur (On conquering India)

'Divine worship in monarchs consists in their justice and good administration. The justice of one hour is better than the saying of prayers all night, and of fasting all day for sixty years.'

—Akbar the Great

'My distress arose from the thought that my son, without any cause or reason, had become my enemy. Sovereignty does not *regard the relation of father and son, and it is said, "a king should deem no one his relation".*

—Jahangir

'First, an emperor ought to stand midway between gentleness and severity. Next, an emperor should never allow himself to be fond of ease and inclined to retirement for these are the most fatal causes of the decline of kingdoms. Next, always plan how to train your servants and appoint everyone to the task for which you deem him fit. It is opposed to wisdom to order a carpet-weaver to do the work of a blacksmith.'

—Aurangzeb

Babur was a true royal with the bluest of blue blood. Descended from Tamerlane on his father's side and Genghis Khan on his mother's side, the two greatest conquerors the world had ever seen, he became King at the tender age of twelve when his father fell to his death in a collapsing building. Immediately, he had to fight for survival, for an empire is not an inheritance and the best title is the strongest sword.

Surrounded by enemies, the young king showed his determination and courage. His greatest comfort and support was his grandmother Begum Isan Daulat, a rock of strength in the tradition of Genghis' own mother and wife. When her husband was captured, she was given as a concubine to one of the officers of the enemy, though her husband Yunus was still alive. She made no complaint, and received her new lord with a smile. But once the door was locked, she and her servant girls stabbed him to death and threw his body into the street. To her captor, she sent a message, 'I am the wife of Yunus Khan. Shaikh Jamal gave me to another man contrary to law; so I slew him; and the Shaikh may slay me too if it pleases him.' Impressed with her courage, Jamal returned her to her husband, with whom she shared a cell for a year till both were released.

Uncles and cousins were determined to snatch the throne from the boy king Babur, and the Begum protected her grandson from the conspirators, who would certainly have taken his throne if not his life. But oblivious of adversity, little Babur dreamt of glory—he would take Samarkand, the seat of his great ancestor Timur, which Timur had made the centre of the world.

BABUR

In 1497, at the age of fifteen, Babur marched on Samarkand and seized the city. Destiny had chosen him to change the world. For a hundred days, he was King of Samarkand. But then he was ousted, only to discover that meanwhile, he had lost his own beloved home at Fergana; even his mother and grandmother were besieged in Andijan. It had all collapsed. He wrote in his memoirs, 'For the sake of Andijan, I had lost Samarkand, but I had lost one without saving the other.' He was now no king at all.

The little boy was shattered. He admitted, 'I was reduced to a sore distressed state, and wept much.' He had lost Samarkand and was driven into exile. Harassed by a powerful rebellion, opposed by his brother and his own army, without a home, he was reduced to a low point in his fortunes. But Babur was Babur—no ordinary boy. He would fight back: 'One or two reverses could not make me sit down and do nothing.'

Babur took Samarkand three times, and lost it three times. He had yet to learn that passion and ambition had to bow down before objective realities. The reality of the times was Shaibani Khan, the Uzbek soldier of fortune who dominated Central Asia when Babur first took his throne. The inexperienced young boy was no match for the great general who was the Lord of Central Asia at that time. Shaibani was the man of the day, but Babur was the man of the future. Unfortunately, the future was slow in coming. Shaibani hounded him, besieged him, starved him and even took Babur's elder sister Khanzada as one of his wives under the terms Babur was forced to concede. Babur was destitute, his army reduced to a couple of hundred men, on foot without horses and armed only with staves. He later wrote, 'It passed through my mind that to wander from mountain to mountain, homeless and houseless, had nothing to recommend it.'

It all looked hopeless. 'I resigned myself to die,' said the young prince. 'I had eaten nothing for two days.' Beaten again in battle by Shaibani Khan, he went into hiding in the wild hills. He had failed and decided that it was best that he depart from Fergana. The best hope for a king without a country is to find a country without a king. Kabul's King, Babur's uncle, had died, his young son had been deposed and a Mongol usurper had seized the throne. Babur would try his luck in Kabul.

Babur was in his early twenties and had just begun 'the use of a razor to my face.' So poor that he could not even afford a proper tent, he made his way south to Kabul. This was the turning point of his career. Till Kabul everything went wrong; after Kabul everything went right—he could do no wrong. He established his little kingdom, while his cousins ruled the more important territory of Herat. But again, Shaibani struck and destroyed the Timurid kingdom of Herat. Now Babur was alone, the last of the Timurids; how long before he too would fall?

But the axe was ready for Shaibani, not Babur. Arrogant in his success, he insulted Shah Ismail, the powerful founder of the Safavid dynasty in Persia. Shah Ismail did not take well to insults; he defeated Shaibani, had his body cut into pieces and distributed around Persia while his skull was embellished in gold as a drinking cup for the Shah. In this way, Babur was finally free of his formidable enemy.

When the wheel of fortune turns there is no limit to the good luck that follows. The Shah now offered Babur an army to take Samarkand. There was, however, one condition: Babur was to lead the Shia army of the Shah, himself dressed as a Shia and with respect to the Shia conventions. Twice Babur had conquered Samarkand at the head of a Sunni army, now the third time he conquered as a Shia. But Sunni or Shia, Samarkand was not in his destiny, and after eight months, he was again chased out of the city of his dreams. Carrying the Shia flag was too great a handicap which made Babur so unpopular that his army of 40,000 was driven out by 3,000, who had the support of the local population.

He returned to Kabul, but now he finally understood that Samarkand and Central Asia was not in his destiny. He started to think of India. He moved slowly, making five forays into India between the years 1519–1524. During the years that he prepared the conquest of India, he became a regular, systematic and deliberate drunkard. He explained that he had sworn to give up alcohol at the age of forty, and since he was nearing this age, he was using his last years to drink his fill. On 25 February 1527, at the age of forty-four, before the decisive battle with Rana Sanga, he finally renounced alcohol, dramatically smashing his cups, and pouring out his stock of wine. He never touched wine again, even though he regretted his decision and complained in a couplet:

'While others repent and make vows to abstain,
I have vowed to abstain, and repentant am I.'

On 21 April 1526, Babur's army of 20,000 faced the 100,000-man force of Sultan Ibrahim Lodhi. Lodhi's army was five times the size of Babur's, but the Moguls had two decisive advantages: firstly, they had the new military technology—guns; but even more significantly, they had Babur, now in his prime, a seasoned and exceptional general. In five hours, an empire was lost and won; Sultan Ibrahim Lodhi was killed and with him fell 20,000 of his army. Babur became Emperor of Hindustan.

The battle won; Babur moved fast. He ordered his son Humayun to Agra to seize the treasury. The next morning he moved with his army to Delhi. When Babur reached Agra, Humayun presented to his father a massive diamond, believed to have been the Kohinoor. Babur valued the stone as sufficient to feed the world for two and a half days, but showed no interest and wrote in his memoirs, 'Humayun offered it to me when I arrived at Agra. I just gave it back to him.'

The Kohinoor, the most famous diamond in history, traced the rise and fall of empires. When Humayun later fled India seeking refuge in Persia, he gifted the stone to his host Shah Tamasp. The Shah in turn, gave it to the Nizam in the Deccan from where it found its way back to the treasury of Shah Jahan. When Nader Shah, the Napoleon of Asia, conquered Delhi, the stone returned with him to Persia. As Persia declined and the Afghans rose, the stone once more turned eastward, finding its new home in Kabul. Ranjit Singh, the Lion of the Punjab, could not leave a prize such as this in the hands of others. The stone came back home to Lahore and in 1849 when the British annexed the Punjab, the Kohinoor passed into the custody of the chief commissioner, Sir John Lawrence, who forgot the stone in his waistcoat pocket for six weeks, till he finally remembered to forward it to his queen in England. Today, it remains the most important piece in the crown jewels of England.

But there was one more battle left to win before India was truly Babur's. The Afghan army had been defeated, but the Rajputs, an even more formidable foe, now prepared to give him battle. On 16 March 1527, Babur met the Rajputs on the field of Khanua. Once again, he was greatly outnumbered. The 200,000-Rajput force was double the size of the Afghan army of Ibrahim Lodhi which he had defeated at Panipat. Their general was the formidable Rana Sanga.

The Moguls were nervous, but then Babur addressed his army. His words put fire into their blood. The coming battle was to be jihad, Muslims against infidels. In honour of the jihad, he dramatically renounced alcohol and rode into battle a Ghazi, a warrior of Islam. The battle lasted ten hours, twice as long as Panipat, and then victory was his. At Khanua, he finally became the unchallengeable Emperor of India. The treasures of five kings fell into his hands; he gave everything away and kept nothing for himself.

Babur had struggled in the wilderness for forty-three years; he enjoyed the fruits of his Indian empire for hardly five. He died on 26 December 1530. The story goes that his dearly beloved son Humayun was dying of an illness and Babur pleaded to God to take him instead of his son. Humayun recovered, Babur died and was buried in a garden at Agra. Thirteen years later in 1543, his remains were transferred to his favourite garden in Kabul where he finally found peace after a life of hardship and struggle.

HUMAYUN

Babur is remembered as a successful hero; Humayun as a feeble failure. But their careers were remarkably similar. Babur lost his kingdom and after a lifetime of struggle, took India; Humayun lost his kingdom and just before he died, took India. Babur had a great enemy, Shaibani Khan; Humayun had an even greater enemy, Sher Shah Suri. The only glaring difference is that Babur had the weak and gentle Humayun as his successor, whereas Humayun had Akbar the Great.

Humayun was kind, cultured, brave, generous—a decent prince. But he was too soft and gentle to make an effective ruler in those hard times. His two great weaknesses cost him his kingdom and almost cost him his life. He was too self-indulgent and always ready to escape to his wine, women and opium to which he was seriously addicted. But even more disastrously, he was too soft on his treacherous brothers, Kamran, Askari and Hindal. Babur, on his deathbed, had told Humayun to never act against his brothers—it was the worst possible advice, which Humayun faithfully followed. When he fled in exile to Persia, the Shah asked him what had brought him to this pass. Humayun replied, 'The opposition of my brothers.' But this was an excuse rather than an explanation—the real reason was his lack of firmness in dealing with their treachery. He paid heavily for loving his brothers too much. Babur's short four-year rule before he died, left his successor a kingdom far from stable. Humayun was threatened by Bahadur Shah in the south, by Sher Khan in the east and by his brother Kamran, who had inherited the kingdom of Kabul, in the north-west. Humayun was a weak and vacillating general who lacked a firm strategy. When he pursued one foe, he would be harassed by another from his rear. When he won a victory, he would waste months in celebrating. While he was busy with women and intoxication, his foes were busy in preparing their counterattacks. The combination of his foolishness, the ability of his enemy and the treachery of his brothers, cost him his kingdom.

Humayun was crowned Emperor at the age of twenty-three in the year 1531. He ruled for nine years till he was overthrown by Sher Shah. He fled into exile in Persia as the guest of the Shah and returned to take India with Persian support after fifteen years in the wilderness. He was no match for his brilliant adversary, Sher Shah, and only after the death of both Sher Shah and his son, who succeeded him, was Humayun able to return and win back his crown. He had ruled for less than a year when he died in an accident, falling down a steep flight of stairs.

The highlight of Humayun's flight from India was his marriage with Hamida Begum and the birth of his son, Akbar, in Umarkot in Sind on 15 October 1542. But the journey was too perilous and the Emperor and his wife continued without an army, at times even without a horse; baby Akbar had to be left behind and was taken to Kabul, where he was entrusted to the care of others in his family. This unsettled period, combined with Akbar's aversion to studies, produced an uneducated and illiterate future emperor, despite the high culture and learning of his father and grandfather, both poets.

When Humayun reached the Safavid court, Shah Tamasp received him as his guest, but it was uncertain how long his welcome would last. The treacherous Kamran offered to cede Kandahar to the Shah in exchange for his brother, but Humayun's charm prevailed. Humayun was generous in his gifts, which included the great Kohinoor diamond, and finally the Shah decided to support Humayun in an attack on Kamran's territories, provided that after victory, Kandahar be handed over to him.

So once more, Humayun was back in India. This time he would take no risks with his brothers. Hindal died fighting Kamran. Askari was captured and sent on pilgrimage to Mecca where he died. Kamran was blinded by the Emperor's soldiers who held him down while stabbing his eyes and then pouring lemon juice and salt to complete the process. The blinded prince was then sent to Mecca on a pilgrimage from which he never returned.

Humayun conquered India with an army of less than 5,000 men. The empire of Sher Shah had crumbled, and the family members were at war with each other. The great general Bairam Khan moved with speed, and Lahore, Delhi and Agra fell to him unopposed. On 23 July 1555, the Mogul throne was once more his.

SHER SHAH SURI

Sayings of Sher Shah Suri:

'If fortune favours me, I can drive these Moguls out of Hindustan.'
'Crime and violence prevent the development of prosperity.'

In 1486 AD, Hasan, a small time jagirdar, had a son whom he named Farid. The young boy showed promise at an early age. He was a bit wild, as the young often are, but he also showed a keen interest in history and the lives of ancient kings. Hasan had lost interest in the faded charms of Farid's mother, and was infatuated with a Hindu slave girl whom he married and who dominated him totally. So Farid went off to study and then took on a small job with the local administration where he earned a reputation for intelligence, fairness and ability.

Hasan called Farid back to administer his two estates and Farid quickly made a success of his new responsibilities. But as his stepbrothers grew older, their mother, the Hindu favourite of Hasan, conspired to get rid of Farid to clear the way for her own sons. So Farid was fired, despite his excellent performance. '(Hasan) bound in the chain of her love and helpless from the force of his affection, was persuaded by her and withdrew his fickle affections from his eldest son.' He explained his unfair dismissal of Farid, saying, 'I know it is not right to grieve Farid, but what can I do?'

In this way, Farid was pushed out by his infatuated father and his ambitious stepmother and set off to seek his fortune. He joined the service of Bihar Khan, the ruler of Bihar, and earned the new name of Sher Khan for killing a tiger, singlehandedly. Sher Khan was undoubtedly a great man with outstanding qualities. He rose from success to success with his ability to create opportunity out of problems, and his reputation grew as both the powerful and the poor recognized his hard work, capability, firmness and sense of justice.

After settling his affairs in Bihar, Sher Khan went to Agra where he joined the court of the Emperor, Babur. He was not impressed by the Mogul government and remarked:

> If luck and fortune favour me, I will shortly expel the Moguls from India, for the Moguls are not superior to the Afghans in battle or single combat, but the Afghans have let the empire of India slip from their hands, on account of their internal dissentions. Since I have been amongst the Moguls and know their conduct in action, I see that they have no order or discipline, and that their kings, from pride of birth and station, do not personally superintend the government but leave all the affairs and business of the state to their nobles and ministers, who act on corrupt motives in every case. Whoever has money, whether loyal or disloyal, can get his business settled as he likes by paying for it. From this lust of gold, they make no distinction between friend or foe.

Sher Khan's closest friends, who heard his views, thought he was crazy.

However, the one man who did not see Sher Khan as crazy was Babur. A keen judge of character, he said to Khalifa, his minister,

> Keep an eye on Sher Khan; he is a clever man and the marks of royalty are visible on his forehead. I have seen many Afghan nobles, greater men than he, but they never made any impression on me. But as soon as I saw this man, it entered into my mind

that he ought to be arrested, for I find in him the qualities of greatness and the marks of mightiness.'

The minister replied, 'Sher Khan is without blame, and does not command a sufficient force to become a cause of uneasiness to Your Majesty.' Sher Khan was sensitive to the slightest signals, and sensing hostility and danger, fled the court. When Babur learned that Sher Khan was gone, he said to his wazir, 'If you had not hindered me, I would have arrested him at once; he is about to do something, God only knows what!'

Sher Khan returned to Bihar, and told his brother, 'I have no longer any confidence in the Moguls, or they in me; I must go to Sultan Muhammad Khan (the ruler of Bihar).' When he arrived, Sultan Muhammad was much delighted, for he admired his great talent. Sher Khan loyally served the rulers of Bihar and his power and reputation grew.

Sher Khan had decided that the empire of India was his destiny, but he was never a man in a hurry. With caution and patience, he built up his strength and finally defeated Babur's son Humayun, at the battle of Kanauj in 1540 AD, nine years after Humayun took the throne. Sher Khan, now Emperor of India, became Sher Shah and because of his obsession with justice, was given the title of Sultan-ul-Adil (the Just Ruler). But Sher Shah was still not satisfied. He was fifty-four years old and lamented, 'Alas, I have attained the empire only when I have reached old age, and when the time of evening prayer has arrived. Had it been otherwise, the world would have seen what I would have accomplished.'

Sher Shah ruled India for only five years but what he accomplished in that time was phenomenal. In the battles and wars on his journey to the throne, he had already proved his ability as a general. He now showed that he was both a leader with vision and also a hard-working administrator who did not leave the details to his subordinates. He was determined to build a better future for all his subjects, rich and poor alike. He believed that true justice was the foundation of good governance, and all should be equal in the eyes of the law.

One day a Hindu shopkeeper presented a grievance before Sher Shah. Adil Khan, the son of the Sultan, had been passing through Agra on his elephant when he looked over a wall and saw the wife of the shopkeeper undressed and bathing. Smitten by her beauty, he 'fixed his eyes upon her' and flirted with her. The shamed lady tried to commit suicide and her husband came to Sher Shah seeking justice. Sher Shah made his decision. He decreed that the punishment must fit the crime, and the wife of his son must disrobe and bathe while the Hindu shopkeeper be given an elephant so that he too could flirt with her while she took a bath. The shopkeeper's honour was vindicated and he declined to embarrass the princess. Sher Shah explained his actions by his dictum, 'Justice alone is the mainstay of government and the source of prosperity to the governed. Injustice is the most pernicious of things; it saps the foundation of government and brings ruin upon the realm'.

Sher Shah left a legacy of great roads, hospitals, civic improvements, fair and efficient taxation, agricultural improvements, and promotion of trade through currency reforms and other measures. Akbar the Great, recognized as one of India's outstanding leaders, who ruled shortly after Sher Shah, benefitted from, and continued, many of his policies.

His enemies said of Sher Shah, 'deceitful and cunning are his ways' and he was ready to do whatever it took to secure his objectives. When stalemated in a siege that carried on for months without an end in sight, he gave his word to Raja Puran Mal that if the Raja would give up the town peacefully 'he would suffer no injury in property or person.' When the Raja came out with his family, Sher Shah broke his word and prepared to attack them. The Raja cut off the head of his beloved wife, his nobles followed suit and charged to their deaths. Under Sher Shah's orders, the daughter of Puran Mal was given to a group of minstrels to be brought up as a dancing girl. Three of his nephews were castrated.

On another occassion, when Sher Shah heard 'exceeding praise' of a dancing girl in the strong fort of Kalinjar, he set out to take the fort and with it, the delightful dancing girl. For a year, the siege continued without result. Sher Shah was a hands-on general, and was himself supervising the launching of rockets when an accidental explosion hit the Emperor and fatally burned his body. In terrible pain, and hovering between life and death, Sher Shah urged his men on to take the fort. The moment he heard that the fort was taken, he passed from this life to the next. The dying Emperor, in his final moments, enjoyed the taste of victory; but he was never to enjoy the dancing girl who had lured him to his final battle.

AKBAR

Within six months of retaking his kingdom, Humayun, always unlucky, fell down the stairs of his palace and died. This accident brought the fourteen-year-old Akbar to the throne. The Mogul kingdom in India was hardly an empire. Covering but a small part of the subcontinent, Akbar's rule was far from stable, with challenges on all sides—the Uzbeks in the north, the Afghans in the east and the Rajputs in the south. Even his brother Hakim ruled Kabul as a separate kingdom, with one eye constantly watching for an opportunity to oust his elder brother.

Akbar was not only young, he was also uninterested in government. He had, from childhood, found reading and writing boring, and whenever his tutors arrived, Akbar would hide or run off to play. He grew up illiterate. Luckily he had someone to look after him and his kingdom at this critical time. The seasoned general Bairam Khan had played a key part in restoring the crown to Humayun. He now secured the throne for Akbar and ruled for him in the early years when Akbar was 'behind the veil'.

Akbar had hardly inherited the crown when he almost lost it. Rebellion in Kabul was overshadowed by the advance of Hemu, the misshapen little Hindu who had already taken Agra without a fight and was already moving to take Delhi. In Delhi, half the Mogul force under Tardi Beg, fled. The remaining army was defeated and Hemu was now master of both Agra and Delhi.

Bairam Khan was a brave and astute general. Fully aware of the risk and the likelihood of defeat if he engaged Hemu in battle, he also understood that if they fled, India would be lost forever. When the amirs advised retreat, Bairam persuaded Akbar to attack. At the plain of Panipat, Babur had won India. Now once again at Panipat, Akbar was to test his destiny. Hemu's troops outnumbered Akbar's small army by five-to-one and more important than numbers, they were a disciplined force hardened in battle. As the battle of the century was joined, victory seemed certain for Hemu, but a chance arrow pieced him in the eye and brought him down. The unconscious Hemu was brought before Bairam and Akbar, as his army broke and fled. Hemu was killed and Akbar's kingdom was secured.

Akbar was the ruler, but it was Bairam who ruled. As each year passed and Akbar grew, he started to resent Bairam's control. He was not born to be a puppet; he was his own man and no one could give him orders. He was married to his cousin Ruqaiya, and Bairam married another of Akbar's cousins, Salima. Perhaps it was Salima that he really wanted, for when Bairam died, Akbar married the young widow who remained a favourite wife for much of his life. Akbar also resented the tight allowance that Bairam sanctioned for him while living a life of conspicuous luxury himself. Bairam believed himself destined to lead, but Akbar knew that he was not born to follow. And even while all believed that Akbar was only interested in fun and games, animals and hunting, the young king was quietly absorbing everything and waiting for his time while the number of Bairam's enemies grew, particularly among the Sunnis who resented the Shia Bairam's patronage of the Shias at court.

At the age of eighteen, Akbar made his move. He was urged on by his foster-mother Maham Anaga, a cunning and ambitious woman eager to see the downfall of the powerful Bairam. Akbar wrote to Bairam in his bold and straightforward style:

> As I was fully assured of your honesty and fidelity, I left all important affairs of state in your charge, and thought only of my own pleasures. I have now determined to take the reins of government into my own hands, and it is desirable that you should now make the pilgrimage to Mecca, upon which you have been so long intent. A suitable fief will be assigned for your maintenance.

After all the moves and strategies were played out, Bairam realized that the game was lost, and came to offer his submission to Akbar. The young king received his former guardian with honour and respect, asking him to decide his future. Bairam elected to go on pilgrimage to Mecca, but was killed en route by an Afghan assassin with a blood-feud. Akbar took Bairam's son, Abdur Rahim, into the palace and personally supervised his education. He became, in due time, the greatest noble in the realm.

Akbar was free of his dominating, though honourable, guardian. He now fell under the influence of his corrupt and conspiratorial foster-mother Maham Anaga who, acting as though she was the prime minister, pushed into high office, her arrogant and conceited son, Adham Khan. Adham, intoxicated by power, misbehaved and annoyed Akbar by holding back the spoils of war for himself rather than sending them first to his emperor as loyalty demanded. In particular, he kept for himself the prettiest women that were captured, and Akbar liked pretty women. When Adham, in a rage of arrogance and jealousy, killed the prime minister and then tried to enter the Emperor's harem, Akbar exploded. He attacked the intruder with the force of an enraged elephant; a single blow of Akbar's fist smashed Adham's face as though he had been felled by a sledge hammer. Akbar then ordered his attendants to throw him down from the terrace and when this did not kill his half-dead foe, he ordered them to throw him down a second time till his neck was broken and his brains dashed out. Akbar went to Maham Anaga and told her what had happened; she merely replied, 'Your Majesty did well.' Forty days later, she died of grief.

Akbar now completely came out from 'behind the veil' and showed his true colours. He was a man of immense physical strength and energy, completely devoid of fear. His legend grew with stories of his killing a tiger singlehanded and his charging an enemy army with a handful of his personal guards and putting them to flight due to the intensity of his attack. But he was also loving and compassionate, regal with the great, but humble with the lowly. Of all the gifts that were presented to him, he was most appreciative of the gifts of the poor, which he received with demonstrations of his gratitude. As a young king he showed a strong appetite for women, food, wine and even opium. He was passionate about hunting, but he also loved animals. An early English traveller wrote, 'The king hath in Agra and Fatepore, a thousand elephants, 30,000 horses, 1,400 tame deer, 800 concubines and such store of ounces (cheetahs), tigers, buffles (fighting buffaloes), cocks and hawkes.' As he grew older, Akbar shed all his passions except one—his passion for conquest, which was to remain with him till his death.

Despite being unable to read or write, Akbar was very learned. His inquisitive mind devoured knowledge, and he would listen carefully while his readers read out books and reports for him. He was not ashamed of his disability, and would say, 'The Prophets were all illiterate. Believers should, therefore, retain one of their sons in that condition.'

An observant historian, Father Daniel Bartoli, described Akbar's self-control:

> Whether by training or innate power, he was so completely master of his own emotions that he could hardly ever be seen otherwise than as perfectly pleasant and serene. He never gave anybody the chance to rightly understand his innermost sentiments or to know what faith or religion he held by... a man apparently free from mystery and guile, as honest and candid as can be imagined—but in reality, so close and self-contained that one could not find the clue to his thoughts.

The empire that Akbar inherited was too small for his ambition. Over the next twenty years, he expanded his realm till the territory under his rule had grown by three times—Bengal, Gujarat, Sindh, Kashmir and Orissa were all absorbed. But war was only one part of his strategy; no less important were his moves to win over the Hindus. For Akbar was fast to recognize and bow down before reality; and the reality was that a small minority of Muslim invaders from Central Asia could not hope to dominate forever the vast Hindu majority of indigenous inhabitants of the subcontinent.

Akbar was a foreigner with no Indian blood in his veins. Three generations later, the Moguls were almost entirely Indian; this was achieved by inter-marriages. Akbar's first two wives were his cousins; his third was a Hindu Rajput princess of Amer (later known as Jaipur). He subsequently added the princess of Bikaner to his growing list of wives. His friend and historian, Abul Fazl, wrote that there were more than 5,000 women in Akbar's harem, and that, '(t)he large number of women furnished His Majesty with an opportunity to display his wisdom.' His son and successor, Jahangir, was born of a Hindu mother, and himself had more than one Hindu princess as wife. The mother of Jahangir's son and successor, Shah Jahan was the Hindu princess of Jodhpur. The famous Nur Jahan, the love of Jahangir's life, who practically ruled the kingdom while her husband wallowed in wine and opium, was actually the twentieth wife of Jahangir.

Akbar's marriages with Rajput princesses were followed by toleration and conciliatory measures towards the Hindus. The jizya tax was dropped, and also the tax on Hindu pilgrims. Akbar even allowed his Hindu wives to practice their religion and Hindus were given equal respect. Famous Hindus at court included Bhagwan Das, Man Singh and Todar Mal, and Akbar's close friendship with Birbal is legendary. Akbar's solution to instability was not just to fight the Hindu majority but to absorb it. He would be the ruler of both the Muslims and the Hindus; all would bind themselves to the Emperor and give him total allegiance. Through toleration and respect, Akbar converted a family of conquerors into a line of emperors with roots in their Hindu empire.

Of all the measures that Akbar took to stabilize his realm, the most revolutionary and the most controversial was the Din-i-Ilahi, a universal religion created by the Emperor as a synthesis of Hinduism and Islam and including the principles of the Parsi and Jain religions. Akbar even stopped hunting and the unnecessary killing of animals which appealed to the Jains, and practiced some of the Parsi rituals of sun worship. Though the Din-i-Ilahi was accepted by ambitious courtiers who wanted to stay on the right side of the Emperor, it did not attract the Hindu or the Muslim mainstream. Many Muslim believers were offended with Akbar's tampering with Islamic tenets and some questioned whether Akbar still remained a Muslim. The Jesuits, whom Akbar also befriended, believed that he was ready to convert to Christianity. Akbar was a great success as a general and as a ruler, but a total failure as a prophet; his new religion just didn't take off.

But apart from in matters of religion, Akbar's rule was a golden time in which the empire expanded, administration was streamlined, tax collection increased the wealth of the state, toleration was practiced and justice was equal for all. Mogul roots in India ensured a stable future for the dynasty. Akbar's years of struggle seemed to be over as he entered old age.

But Akbar was not to enjoy old age and the great achievements of his struggle. His family was to deny him peace till the end. His brother, Hakim, who ruled Kabul, was repeatedly in revolt. Two of the Emperor's sons, Murad and Daniyal, were alcoholics and died of excessive drinking. Salim, who was to succeed his father with the title of Jahangir, rebelled against his father and the last years of the Emperor were spent in complicated manoeuvers against his difficult son.

Jahangir was an alcoholic, subject to great swings of mood. He was also getting impatient to rule as he entered middle age. But perhaps there was more to the breakdown of the father and son relationship, and the strange interplay between them—a mixture of love and hate. Legend has it that Jahangir fell for his father's favourite dancing girl, a beauty named Anarkali, or 'Pomegranate Blossom'; Akbar caught his son giving a flirtatious smile to his lady and reacted violently. Anarkali was condemned to death and entombed in a building in Lahore. Years later, the tomb was converted into a church, and then became a store for government archives. Were the contortions of Jahangir's succession and Akbar's last years determined by father and son both wanting the same girl? God only knows.

Akbar's dearest friends were dead, two of his sons had died of alcohol; only Salim was left, and he had set himself up in Allahabad as an independent ruler and was drinking himself to death. Akbar was too weary to take on his son. But the ladies of the royal house, Salima, Akbar's wife, and Hamida, his mother, persuaded Salim to submit to his father. Salim fell at his father's feet, and Akbar graciously raised him up and took the turban from his own head and placed it on the head of his son. But Salim drowned himself in his drink; the future of the empire looked bleak. Akbar took Salim into a private apartment, slapped his son hard, and locked him in for ten days of 'cold turkey' treatment. The successor was now sober enough to inherit the empire, and before Akbar died, he formally passed his crown to his son.

Akbar the Great was buried in a mausoleum at Sikandra near Agra. Eighty-six years later, a gang of bandits raided the tomb. They stole the gold and silver and other valuables, and dragged out the bones of Akbar, threw them angrily into a fire and burned them.

JAHANGIR

'The business of kings is controlling the world.'

—Jahangir

Akbar was always an emperor; Jahangir remained the perpetual prince. Lacking the gravity or intensity of his father, he was a pampered and spoiled young boy who, though intelligent and brave, grew up willful, indolent, self-indulgent and lazy, and was described as 'the talented drunkard.' Though captive to his craving for both alcohol and opium, he managed to somewhat control his addiction, unlike his brothers Murad and Daniyal. But the empire that Akbar left him was rich and well governed, and Jahangir enjoyed a stable rule in which his subjects saw the highest levels of peace and prosperity of Mogul times. Jahangir was an intelligent and educated man, and had a strong interest in science, though his experiments could demonstrate unnecessary cruelty.

Babur offered his life to God in exchange for his son. Humayun would have happily given his life for Akbar, if offered a choice. Jahangir, in contrast, was the first of his line to rebel against his father, and established a tradition—his eldest son Khusrau rebelled against him, and later Khurram, who was to become the Emperor Shah Jahan, was also to rebel against his father. Shah Jahan's son Aurangzeb rebelled against him. Finally, Aurangzeb's favourite son, Prince Muhammad Akbar, rebelled and even issued an edict deposing his father.

As the Mogul emperors grew too strong for others to oppose them, their only real threats were to come from their own family, resulting in killing and blinding of brothers and sons from generation to generation. Women were to play an important part in Jahangir's life. Perhaps it was a woman who caused the breach between Jahangir and his father, Akbar. For much of his reign, as the Emperor wallowed in intoxication, power was exercised by his beautiful and talented Persian wife Nur Jahan. The complicated twists and turns of his relationship with his son, Shah Jahan, were determined by the harem politics of Nur Jahan, the powerful empress, and her niece, Mumtaz Mahal, the wife of Shah Jahan. Nur Jahan's daughter, Ladli Begum, was used as a pawn in the marriage politics of the royal family, which further complicated succession issues. Women took centre stage in the game of power at the Mogul court.

When Akbar was Emperor, an impoverished Persian courtier, Mirza Ghiyas Beg, fled in disgrace from his country. On the road he was attacked by robbers who stole all he had, so he arrived in Kandahar penniless, sharing a single mule with his wife and children.

In Kandahar, his pregnant wife gave birth to a daughter who they named Mehrunnisa. He was appointed Diwan (treasurer) to the local government in Kabul and due to his astute skills, quickly rose in the administration. Destiny was to favour this Persian family beyond their wildest dreams. Ghiyas, now titled 'Itimad-ud-Daula', became Jahangir's chief minister, his son Asaf Khan became Shah Jahan's chief minister, and his grandson, Shaista Khan became Aurangzeb's closest associate. What the Barmakids had been to the Abbasids, the family of Itimad-ud-Daula was to the Moguls.

But the women of this family were to outshine the men in the power game at the Mogul court. His daughter Mehrunnisa, as a young widow, caught the eye and totally captured the heart of the Emperor Jahangir, becoming his twentieth wife as the Empress Nur Jahan, who ruled the empire while her husband drowned himself in alcohol and opium. His granddaughter, Arjumand, the daughter of Asaf Khan, became the wife of the young prince, Shah Jahan. Arjumand became Shah Jahan's obsession and found her place in history as the Empress Mumtaz Mahal; when she died, her husband was shattered and spent the next sixteen years in building a monument to her memory—the incomparable Taj Mahal; truly one of the wonders of the world.

A few months after Jahangir's accession, his eldest son Khusrav rebelled. His rebellion was quickly crushed and his supporters cruelly punished. Khusrav's men were impaled on stakes as he was paraded on an elephant through their lines. But even though Khusrav was clearly guilty, his father spared him, saying, 'Paternal affection did not allow me to take his life.' He was blinded and imprisoned for fourteen years. Later, he was offered marriage with Ladli Begum, the daughter of Nur Jahan, but he refused.

The fall of Khusrav saw the rise of Khurram, who later became the Emperor Shah Jahan. Khurram was a very competent general whose successful campaigns quickly established his importance. He was also an exceptional statesman and negotiator. His marriage to Asaf Khan's daughter and Nur Jahan's niece, further secured his place in the inner circles of power.

As Jahangir degenerated in his addictions, he happily passed power to Nur Jahan who ruled from behind the veil. Her indispensable intermediary, her brother Asaf Khan, grew in power as her communicator with the world beyond the harem. The two rising stars of Jahangir's court were clearly Nur Jahan and Shah Jahan.

Unexpectedly, Shah Jahan, the admired favourite, rebelled against his father. It seemed to make no sense; he had wealth, power and inevitable succession after Jahangir. What led him to rebellion? Shah Jahan had started to feel insecure. With the decline of Jahangir into his addictions, Nur Jahan had become immensely powerful. Both Nur Jahan and Shah Jahan wanted total power, but only one of them could have it. Nur Jahan had given her daughter Ladli in marriage to Shahryar and the elevation of her imbecile son-in-law could confirm her as the power behind the throne. Shah Jahan and Nur Jahan had become rivals—he was the crown prince, but she was the de facto emperor. Their deteriorating relationship reaffirmed the warning of Hazrat Ali, the son-in-law of The Prophet: 'Have love for your friend up to a limit for it is possible he may turn into your enemy someday.'

Matters came to a head when the great Persian king, Shah Abbas, took back Kandahar from the Moguls. Kandahar was itself by now of little importance, since the sea had replaced the Silk Road as the major trade route; but it had been promised to the Persians in consideration for the support given to Humayun in winning back his crown. Jahangir ordered Shah Jahan to move his army north, but the prince appeared reluctant and laid down his conditions for assuming command of the Kandahar campaign. Jahangir was enraged and ordered that henceforth Shah Jahan should be known as Bi-Daulat, 'The Wretch'. He dispatched his army with his greatest general, Mahabat Khan, to deal with Shah Jahan. The nominal leader of this army was Parviz, an alcoholic prince.

There were three important centres of power, as the health of the Emperor failed. The strongest was Nur Jahan who ruled in the name of her husband, and wanted the succession for her son-in-law, Prince Shahriyar; the most legitimate was Shah Jahan, who had been recognized for many years as the capable crown prince; the rising star, however, suddenly seemed to be Prince Parviz, the new favourite backed by Mahabat Khan, the greatest general in the realm.

Shah Jahan was a general whose ability had been proven by his victories in wars and battles over the years; but he was no match for Mahabat Khan who was backed by the imperial army. For three years, he was chased through the empire, till finally he was forced to submit to his father. In spite of the weakness of his position, he was offered very lenient terms. Shah Jahan, by recognizing reality and submitting, would bide his time and live to fight another day.

After his successful handling of the 'Shah Jahan' problem, Mahabat Khan's stature had grown and he was now the preeminent amir. The other amirs, and the Empress herself, were jealous and apprehensive of his new status. To weaken his power, he and his prince, Parviz, were sent to opposite ends of the empire. Mahabat Khan's reputation was attacked by allegations that he had misappropriated a large part of the booty taken in the campaign against Shah Jahan.

Khan reacted emotionally to this slur on his integrity. He marched to seek audience with the Emperor, with a small army. Without planning or intent, the protest became a coup as the Emperor was taken by his general. The Empress came and joined her husband in his royal captivity. Though Mahabat Khan was lord of the battlefield, he was no match for Nur Jahan in the wiles and strategies that politics required. In just eight months, the Empress regained power for her husband, and the general fled for his life. He joined forces with Shah Jahan, his last refuge.

Nur was back in full control, but Shah Jahan, backed by Mahabat Khan, could not be ignored as the Emperor lay dying, Parviz dead from drinking too much and Shahryar confined with a serious illness. On 7 November 1627, Jahangir passed away. In a moment, Asaf Khan, who had flourished as her brother, converted from supporter to rival as he moved to secure succession for his son-in-law, Shah Jahan. The combination of Shah Jahan, Mahabat Khan and Asaf Khan was invincible. The wheel of fortune had turned full circle.

A young prince was made an interim emperor. Shah Jahan, hastening back to the capital, sent an order to Asaf Khan: 'It would be well if Dawar Bakhsh, Shahryar and the two sons of Daniyal were all sent out of the world.' With one sentence, the emperor-to-be ordered the murder of his brother, two nephews and two male cousins. Years later, his own son Aurangzeb reminded his father of his accession to power when justifying a similar policy of murder which was to be repeated again and again by the later Moguls.

Nur Jahan went peacefully into retirement watching the power that had once been hers, pass to her young niece, Mumtaz, the beloved of the new emperor. She accepted her downfall with grace and dignity and died on 17 December 1645. Perhaps it was a small compensation that her niece, who had eclipsed her, died fourteen years before her on 17 June 1631.

SHAH JAHAN

Shah Jahan was imperial and stately. At an early age, he had shown his intelligence and capability both as a general and as a statesman. He loved beauty in all its forms—jewellery, architecture and particularly women. Arjumand, known as Mumtaz Mahal, was the love of his life, though she was neither his first nor his last wife. She bore him fourteen children in quick succession, seven of whom survived—three girls (Jahanara, Raushanara and Goharara) and four boys (Dara Shikoh, Shah Shuja, Aurangzeb and Murad Bakhsh). Mumtaz was his confidante, advisor and companion, but died in the fourth year of his reign. He was shattered and wept: '(The) Empire has no sweetness; life itself has no relish left for me now.' He, however, consoled himself by building the Taj Mahal, a monument to his love.

But as the years passed, sex became a renewed passion in the aging emperor. He acquired numerous concubines, and was rumoured to have indulged in adultery. The French traveller Bernier even claimed that there was an incestuous relationship that the Emperor had with his beautiful and intelligent daughter, Jahanara, though this may have been been based more on the gossip of the time. Some courtiers justified the possible liaison, saying, 'It would have been unjust to deny the king the privilege of gathering fruit from the tree he had himself planted.'

Shah Jahan had inherited the fabulous empire assembled by his grandfather, Akbar the Great, and matured under his father Jahangir. He was the richest man in the world, and his empire had immense treasure and revenues. He created the most beautiful buildings in the world and the greatest jewellery collection. His peacock throne was itself a treasure house of diamonds, emeralds and rubies—not just beyond comparison but even beyond imagination. But Shah Jahan was unconcerned with the welfare of the ordinary people of his realm, and the discrepancy widened between the wealth and lifestyle of the elite and the wretched poverty of the common people. His administration deteriorated, the standard of justice fell while the revenue collection and corruption grew. But expenditure grew faster than revenue, depleting the massive treasury reserves. Muslim rulers had changed drastically from the early days of Islam when rulers such as Omar the Great remained poor while their people grew rich.

Kandahar had been given by Humayun to the Safavids in Persia, but Akbar took it back, not by war but by diplomacy, seducing Ali Mardan Shah, the Persian governor, with bribes. Ali Mardan gave Kandahar to Akbar, and received as reward, the governorship of Kashmir. But years later, the Shah of Persia took it back. Shah Jahan made several unsuccessful attempts to recover the city; at that time, Kandahar was not important in itself, because trade had shifted substantially to the sea routes, but the repeated failures of the Moguls against the Persians showed that they were no longer the invincible force of Akbar and Jahangir's time. Many years later, Kandahar opened the way for the invincible army of Nader Shah, the Napoleon of the East, to sack Delhi and plunder its fabled treasures.

Shah Jahan busied himself with his fabulous new constructions, the Taj Mahal at Agra, and the new capital, Shahjahanabad, in Delhi. His lifestyle became more relaxed and self-indulgent, with holidays in Kashmir, and the women of his harem. In 1657, the Emperor fell seriously ill. He was now sixty-five years old, his legs swelled up and he was consumed by fever. His doctors advised a change of climate and he moved to Agra. Power was divided between his four sons—Dara, his favourite and heir-apparent, in Delhi; Aurangzeb far south in the Deccan; Shuja, in the east, in Bengal; and Murad in Gujarat.

The sickness of their father presented opportunity and danger—the throne to the victor; death to the rest. Ambition, fear and suspicion poisoned the relationship between the brothers. Dara Shikoh, the favourite, was cultured, charming and the finest scholar of the Mogul dynasty, but he was conceited and thought too highly of himself; his lack of seriousness and ruthlessness left him more at home in a social gathering than on a battlefield. He even inclined to Akbar's free thinking approach to religion. Aurangzeb was an enigma and very religious; at one time, more inclined to life as a fakir than a king. He was very capable, both in politics and in the art of war. He was cunning and devious, but also supremely brave and fearless. Brutally criticized by European travellers and historians but admired almost as a saint by Muslims who studied his life, Aurangzeb spurned personal vanity, luxury and ambition, and saw himself as a champion of Islam. He could be as ruthless as occasion required, and on the road to power, imprisoned his father and killed his brothers. Shuja was an intelligent and capable prince, but a slave to his pleasures, particularly wine and women. His struggle for the crown was motivated by survival rather than ideology. Murad, the youngest, was a good soldier, popular in the barracks, generous and fun loving, but lacking in wisdom, strategy and guile; no match for his brothers. The two girls, Jahanara and Raushanara, also played important parts in the politics of succession—Jahanara, beloved of her father, sided with Dara and then lived with, and looked after, her captive father in Agra; Raushanara sided with Aurangzeb.

Shuja was the first to declare himself a contender for the throne. Murad quickly followed. Aurangzeb played a waiting game, and seemed to be backing Murad, but outplayed all his brothers with strategy, cunning and bravery. Finally, Murad and Aurangzeb locked in battle against Dara. When the battle turned against Aurangzeb, he chained the legs of his elephant to show that he would fight or die, boosting the morale of his hard-pressed troops. Dara, on the other hand, fled, conceding the field to his fearless brother. Dara was defeated, captured and executed; his eldest son, Suleiman, was captured, imprisoned and turned into a zombie by forced opium consumption, till he died. Murad, believing himself the victor, celebrated in a drunken spree and was deposed for his un-Islamic behaviour and killed. Shuja was hunted out of India, robbed by Portuguese pirates and chased into obscurity. The Emperor Shah Jahan was imprisoned in the Agra palace, where he remained his son's captive for seven years till his death. During his captivity he was given every desire except freedom. He was cared for by Jahanara and his concubines; Aurangzeb gave his father respect and even consulted him on matters of policy, but never met him or even entered his presence for as long as he lived.

AURANGZEB

Sayings of Aurangzeb:

'The greatest conquerors are not always the greatest kings.'
'One cannot rule without practicing deception.'
'Sovereignty is the guardianship of the people, not self-indulgence and profligacy.'
'The art of reigning is so delicate, that a king must be jealous of his own shadow.'

Aurangzeb ascended the throne as a mature man of forty years. He took as his title, 'Alamgir,' the Persian word engraved on the sword that his father had gifted him from captivity. He described himself: 'I was sent into the world by providence, to live and labour, not for myself, but for others; it is my duty not to think of my own happiness but of the happiness of my people.' He saw little joy, and lived in suspicion of all around him. He imprisoned his eldest son for life and his second son for six years. He lived simply, worked hard and was universally respected but never loved. His one failing was his inability to win love—perhaps because he did not give love.

Aurangzeb saw himself as a soldier of Islam. He was fervently religious, and prayed, fasted and lived according to the guidelines of The Prophet. His one regret was that he was unable to perform the Hajj due to his being prisoner to the affairs of state. He lived simply, even austerely, and in private, never sat on a throne. In emulation of The Prophet, he 'worked for his living', making prayer caps which he sold. He combined morality with dedication, bravery with intelligence. In the heat of battle, he would dismount to pray, careless of danger or outcome, leading an enemy to exclaim, 'To fight with such a man is self-destruction'.

He had strong views on the upbringing and education of princes. He felt that they were pampered and brought up by women and eunuchs; slaves who understood nothing of kingship. He believed that this system was to blame for the low calibre of princes and their lack of knowledge of the art of war and the principles of government. He was a disciplined man of principle and capable of determined action. Neither time nor trouble could weaken his resolve.

Though Aurangzeb was a staunch Muslim, he was not fanatically anti-Hindu as some historians have presented. At least one of his wives, Udaipuri Mahal, was Hindu; two of his most important generals, Raja Jai Singh of Amber and Raja Jaswant Singh of Jodhpur were Hindu, as was Raja Ajai Singh, whom he made governor of the Deccan. His palace guards were Hindu and the great love of his life, the dancing girl, Hirabai, later known as Zainabadi Begum, was Hindu. He was in his mid-thirties when he met her, and was so smitten that for a while he was distracted from his austerity and prayer. It is said that she once offered him a cup of wine; the besotted prince was about to drink it when she snatched it away, saying, 'My purpose was to test your love and not to embitter your mouth with this wicked and unlucky liquor.' Luckily for Aurangzeb's career, she died early, releasing him from further temptation.

The Emperor was a man of high intellectual powers, a brilliant writer, an astute diplomat, a soldier of immense courage, a skilled administrator, a just and merciful judge, a pious ascetic in his personal habits, and yet a failure. He failed because he attempted to govern a vast empire populated by a Hindu majority on the principles of an ascetic Muslim saint. Where Akbar the Great disrupted the Muslim community by recognizing that India is not an Islamic country, Aurangzeb disrupted India by behaving as though it were.

The first twenty years of his rule were years of peace and prosperity. Then in 1679, the twenty-first year of his rule, Aurangzeb invaded Marwar, a mistake that was to change his life and the destiny of Mogul India. The Rajput rajas provided the foundation of Mogul rule in India, the bridge between the Muslim rulers and their Hindu subjects. The Emperor's handling of the Marwar and Mewar situation alienated him from the Rajputs, who threw their support behind his rebel son, Prince Muhammad Akbar. The combined army of Akbar and the Rajputs was more than a match for the Emperor, and it looked like Aurangzeb's days were numbered; but he was always at his best when under the greatest pressure. Aurangzeb wrote a letter to his son, congratulating him for having brought the Rajputs into the trap; the letter was seized, and the Rajput army deserted the prince. Akbar fled, first to Gujarat, then to the Deccan. He was followed by his father in hot pursuit.

In the autumn of 1681, Aurangzeb moved south to the Deccan with his army in a campaign that was to last twenty-six years. He was never again to return north. For the first twenty-three years of his reign, Aurangzeb ruled as an emperor in the north; for the last twenty-six years of his life, Aurangzeb lived and struggled in the south, like his ancestor Babur, a nomadic general moving his tents from battle to battle.

The Deccan was fabulously rich, and the diamond mines in Golconda produced the greatest and most valuable stones in the world. These were Shia kingdoms, and the Sunni Aurangzeb justified the war as a jihad. But though the Emperor had gone south to fight Shias, it was a Hindu that tied him down in perpetual war in the Deccan. Shivaji, the small, cunning and immensely resourceful Maratha, harassed and stung the massive Mogul army with his lightening raids and retreats and with his guerrilla tactics that made him impossible to defeat. Shivaji's adventures made him a legend, and his leadership created the formidable Maratha nation that was finally to eclipse the Moguls.

The Marathas were very different from the Rajputs. In battle, the Rajputs sought honour; the Marathas sought victory. The Rajputs knew how to die; the Marathas knew how to win. Shivaji was cunning, and fought for plunder, not territory. He was an illiterate, who, through hard experience, became a great leader and died undefeated at the age of fifty-three. He was an excellent judge of people, and like his adversary, Aurangzeb, had a disciplined and austere lifestyle. The British historian Elphinstone writes of him, 'Shivaji persisted in rebellion, plundering caravans and troubling mankind. But he was absolutely guiltless of baser sins, and was scrupulous of the honour of women and children of the Muslims when they fell into his hands.' The Emperor Aurangzeb wrote, 'My armies have been employed against him for nineteen years, and nevertheless his State has always been increasing.'

But even as he fought on, the old emperor understood it had all been for nothing. The Moguls had grown soft with the luxury of the empire, the administration was in shambles and corruption was rampant. Perpetual war in the South had failed in establishing a perpetual peace. The empire was virtually bankrupt as Aurangzeb drew down the reserves accumulated by his ancestors. His unwillingness to punish led to anarchy in government.

As the frail but determined Emperor, now eighty-nine years of age, battled on alone, his seventeen sons prepared for the inevitable war of succession in which one would gain the throne and the others would lose their heads. Frail and sick, he prepared for death, giving orders that a simple grave be prepared for him, to be paid for by the few rupees he had earned from the sale of the caps he had made with his own hands. He wrote,

> I am grown very old and weak, and my limbs are feeble. Many were around me when I was born, but now I am going alone. I know not why I am or wherefore I came into this world. I have not done well by the country or its people. My years have gone by profitless. There is no hope for me in future.

Every plan that he formed came to little good; every enterprise failed. The dying emperor wrote his own epitaph,

> 'Alas, my life has been wasted in vain!
> I have merely consumed a quantity of water and fodder'

After Aurangzeb, it was over. The Moguls ruled India for another 150 years, but it was decadence and decay. Puppet kings held timid sway as their empire crumbled. The Marathas attacked from the south, the authority of Delhi disappeared, and Nader Shah, the great Persian general, swept down with his invincible army, taking Kandahar, Kabul and finally Delhi. Nader was content to take the treasure of the Moguls and depart, but a resistance force killed 900 Persians after the Mogul submitted to the Persian, and even had the effrontery to throw stones at Nader himself. Nader struck back; for one day he ordered slaughter, and by nightfall, 30,000 corpses filled the streets of the sad city. Nader left with such vast treasure that he remitted all the taxes of his country for three years. The wealth accumulated over two centuries, left Delhi—gold, silver, jewels, a thousand elephants, the fabled peacock throne and the Kohinoor diamond.

Nader left, but the predators—the Marathas, the Jats, the Afghans and the Sikhs—continued to rip apart what was left of the Mogul empire. When the marauder Ghulam Qadir took Delhi, he blinded the Emperor Shah Alam II, and made the future emperor, Akbar Shah II, dance for his pleasure. Finally, the new power started to emerge—the British. Slowly but surely, they took control of India. After the three Maratha wars, the army of the East India Company (EIC), a

British trading house, crushed the Marathas. The Maharaja Scindia of Gwalior was dispossessed from Delhi, where he controlled the blind and feeble Emperor, Shah Alam. After Delhi fell to the British in 1803, Shah Alam regained some of his dignity, but little of his power. The grateful Emperor ceded the civil government of Bengal to the British, 'his faithful servants and well-wishers'. At first, the EIC found it convenient to govern in his name, and the Emperor received from his protectors the symbols of an allegiance they did not pay, and affected to dispense an authority he no longer possessed. The effete Muslim elite breathed a sigh of relief as their new Christian protectors released them from Maratha-Hindu domination.

BAHADUR SHAH ZAFAR

Bahadur Shah Zafar, the last of the Mogul dynasty, was crowned King of Delhi at the age of sixty-two. He was a poet who enjoyed cooking, did not drink alcohol but may have been addicted to opium. In matters of religion, he was tolerant, in the tradition of the Moguls, and due to his values inherited from a Sufi father and a Hindu mother. In respect for Hindu tradition, he did not eat beef. His politics was confined to his refined court and the conspiracies of his wives, particularly the young Zinat, who was determined to dominate him and secure succession for her favourite son. She had her rival, Zafar's first wife, imprisoned on the charge of adultery with a nephew of the Emperor. He collected around him poets who would compete to produce the most eloquent turn of phrase. The greatest of these was Ghalib, a gambler who loved adventure, alcohol and mangoes.

At first, the British in India were attracted to the Indian lifestyle and had respect for the local culture. Many 'went native', not just living like the local elite, but even marrying Indian women, often several simultaneously, as was the practice among the Muslim and Hindu elite. These were the 'White Moguls' who represented a blend of cultures and created a new Anglo-Indian elite. But the free thinking spirit of the eighteenth century was overtaken by the racial arrogance and the missionary Christianity of the nineteenth century and the white masters of India grew distant from the brown locals whom they now treated with scorn and disdain.

The mass of Indians had no option but to take it, and to disguise their resentment under the servile smiles of dissimulation; but within the ranks of the large British armies, where five Indian soldiers served each English officer, a deep discontent was smoldering. The sepoys were not happy, mutiny was set to explode; but the isolated British rulers were unaware.

There were many causes of discontent among the Indian soldiers, both Muslim and Hindu, which led to the mutiny. The unabashed system of apartheid that grew in the nineteenth century maintained a cruel racial discrimination with signboards announcing that 'Dogs and Indians not allowed.' Justice was not equal for all in a society where, in the words of George Orwell's *Animal Farm*, 'All animals are equal, but some animals are more equal than others.' The British humiliated the Indians, whose low salaries and slow promotion denied them any chance of a decent career. The total lack of respect for local religions or customs and the growing missionary sense of superiority of the Victorian colonial masters made the Indians fear that 'our religion is in danger; they will force us to become Christian.' The last straw that fired the mutiny was the belief that the new cartridges were greased with pig and cow fat, a combination that incensed both the Muslims and the Hindus.

The mutiny started in Meerut, with the indiscriminate killing of the British, and spread both into the countryside and to other cities. The British panicked as they suddenly realized how weak and exposed they were, surrounded by an ocean of hostile Indians even in the military barracks. Indecision and fear immobilized even the British generals. But if the British were without effective leaders, the mutineers were totally leaderless; it had exploded without planning, without strategy and without a central command.

Three hundred insurgents from Meerut arrived in Delhi, massacred any Christians they could find, and marched into the Red Fort which housed the Emperor, offering their allegiance and demanding that he lead their insurrection. The Mogul Emperor could provide legitimacy and leadership throughout India in their war against the British, a uniting force for Muslims and Hindus. Bahadur Shah Zafar, old and weak, was at a loss. The last thing he wanted was to lead a war in his few remaining years—a war for which he had no army, no arms, no money and no power. He tried to dissuade the insurgents, but they were adamant. And so, unprepared and unwilling, he found himself the leader of the greatest uprising that ever threatened the British Empire.

The rebellion of 1857, whether a Mutiny, as the British call it, or a War of Independence, as the Indians named it, changed the history of India. It ended the rule of the EIC, which had endured for a full century from 1757 to 1857; it imposed the rule of the British government with the new British Raj; it changed forever the relationship between the British and the Indians to rulers and subjects; it almost resulted in the total destruction and razing of Delhi; and it ended forever the dynasty of Timur who had called himself the son-in-law of the legendary Genghis Khan, a family that had ruled the world for as long as people could remember.

The British were enraged by the killing of their comrades and associates, and wanted revenge. In victory over the house of Timur, they were as merciless as the great Timur himself had been, ordering a slaughter of all the inhabitants of Delhi. Most of the Emperor's sons were captured and killed, some being stripped naked and then shot. The citizens were rounded up for execution. One of those captured and brought before the British colonel was the poet, Ghalib. The colonel asked him, 'Are you a Muslim?' Ghalib's reply saved his life as he answered, 'I am half a Muslim.' The colonel retorted, 'What is half a Muslim?' Ghalib countered, 'I drink alcohol, but I don't eat pork.' The colonel, irritated but amused, ordered the poet to get out. When it was all over, Ghalib wrote of Delhi, 'Yes, there was once a city of that name in the realm of India.' In his total despair, he said, 'It is the hope of death that keeps me alive.' Ghalib survived, and is remembered as the greatest Urdu poet of all time.

Amongst the mediocre British leadership, three men stood out. First, the great warrior John Nicholson, whose fearless courage combined with his capacity for extreme brutality made him a legend to British and Indians alike. He was shot in an encounter, and while he lay dying, he sent a warning to his own general, who was vacillating in important decisions, that he still had enough life in him to put a bullet through the general's heart. He died shortly after making this threat. The second was the hustler, William Hodson, who was always looking to grow rich in the turmoil and looting of war. He ran the efficient intelligence service, arrested the royals and was dismissed for embezzlement before being killed at the siege of Lucknow. The third was the administrator, Sir John Lawrence, who history recognizes as one of the greatest of the British rulers of India. Lawrence kept the Punjab safe and secure from mutiny, rescued Delhi, and saved the city from being destroyed by British revenge-mongers led by Lord Palmerston, who demanded that Delhi should be deleted from the map. Later, as Viceroy, Lawrence was to bring about the beneficial reconstruction of the new India.

The eighty-two-year-old Emperor and his wife were taken prisoner, kept in dirt and deprivation and humiliated as animals in a cage. He was tried and convicted a traitor for rebelling against the EIC—he, the Emperor, who had always been the sovereign ruling over the EIC, and who the EIC had always acknowledged as their liege lord. But this was not a time for quibbling over the niceties of law. The absurdity of the EIC's charge against Zafar was ignored. The Emperor was packed off in a bullock cart and exiled to Burma where he spent what little was left of his life. The Emperor and his family were allowed a budget of eleven rupees a day for their food with an extra rupee on Sunday. He was buried in an unmarked grave.

13

The Rise and Fall of the Safavids of Iran

'Religion depends on monarchy, monarchy on the army, the army on suppliers, the suppliers on prosperity and prosperity on justice.'

—Al-Ghazali (In *Advice for Kings*)

'Be careful of the front of a woman, the rear of a mule and all sides of a mulla.'

(Irani proverb)

In the sixteenth century, the world of Islam was dominated by the three 'gunpowder empires'—the Moguls of India, the Ottomans of Turkey and the Safavids of Iran. The Safavids started as a religious order founded by Sheikh Safi al-Din in the early fourteenth century in Azerbaijan in the northwest corner of Iran. Sheikh Safi was a sincere and religious young man, who, in his search for enlightenment, became a disciple of Sheikh Zahid, a revered Sufi mystic, whom he served for twenty-five years, finally marrying his daughter and inheriting the mantle of his authority. Under the leadership of Safi, the order became known as the Safaviyya order.

The Safavid revolution simmered and struggled in the wilderness for 200 years. They enjoyed the protection and suffered from the persecution of kings and emperors, but through it all, they remained constant in their religious purpose. It is said that the great Timur, on his homeward journey after conquering the Ottoman Bayezid, met the Safavid, Sheikh Khwaja Ali, and offered to grant him a wish. Sheikh Ali begged for the liberation of the prisoners, who became his grateful disciples. The Safavid stalwarts adopted the scarlet headgear that earned them the name of 'qizilbash', or redheads.

In 1494, the troops of the Aq Quyunlu king killed Ali, the Safavid leader, whose seven-year-old brother, Ismail, escaped and went into hiding. For five years, Ismail evaded capture and death, and in 1499, the twelve-year-old boy emerged from hiding to make his bid for power. After a hard two-year struggle, in 1501, the fourteen-year-old Ismail was crowned Shah at Tabriz as the first king of the Safavid dynasty.

Ismail was no ordinary boy. He was fired by a belief in his destiny, a conviction that he was special, almost divine. He was 'The Shadow of God on Earth'. He was not just King, but also spiritual leader of the Safavid order, and a true descendent of Ali, the son-in-law of The Prophet. He changed the face of Persian history by declaring that Shia Islam would be the state religion of Iran, despite the fact that Sunnis constituted the majority. He embarked on his campaign of conquest. In 1501, he occupied Tabriz; in 1508, he took Baghdad; and finally in 1510, he conquered Khurasan. In the East, he was faced by the Uzbeks under their great leader, Shaibani Khan, who had driven Babur the Mogul, out of his homeland in Central Asia. At Merv, Ismail defeated Shaibani Khan who was killed and decapitated; his head was mounted in gold and set with jewels to serve as a goblet. Babur breathed a sigh of relief.

In the West, lay the Ottomans, with their formidable sultan, Salim the Grim. Ismail marched to meet Salim with total confidence. He had never seen defeat, but he had never before faced a general of the skill and stature of Salim. Salim was tough and he didn't like Shias! He marched towards Iran with a massive army of 200,000 soldiers. On the way, he killed Shias, about 40,000—more than half of the Shias in his kingdom. Those he spared were branded and exiled to Europe. Not only was the Ottoman army larger and battle-hardened, but, more important, its expertise and experience in the use of artillery and guns was unmatched in the Islamic world. In 1514, they met at Chaldiran where Ismail was totally defeated. Salim took Tabriz, but his army didn't want to spend more time and effort in impoverished Iran when the riches of Europe lay waiting for them; they wanted to get back home. So Persia escaped further annexation by the Ottomans.

Defeat at Chaldiran shattered the myth of Shah Ismail's divinity. The disillusioned Qizilbash barons lost their awe of their Shah, who was now seen to be a mere mortal. Ismail showed himself a bad loser; he lost all interest in government, and withdrew into drunken debauchery. He never again led his troops into war. Ten years after his defeat at Chaldiran, he died at the age of thirty-seven. He had ruled for twenty-three years from his accession at the age of fourteen. He had established a dynasty, created a Shia kingdom, and by the force of his personality, had led his formidable Qizilbash supporters to stabilize a strong state. But destiny had matched him with Sultan Salim. Being great is not enough if your enemies are greater!

Shah Ismail was succeeded by his eldest son, Shah Tamasp, who was ten years old at the time. Real power lay with his regent, an able military commander and an astute politician. Civil war broke out in the struggle for power between rival Qizilbash factions, and Tamasp himself shot his regent and had him killed. For some years, the young Shah was dominated by his guardians, but finally he secured control of the state. He then had to deal with the massive problems that Iran faced at that time—civil war, the fierce Uzbeks on his east, the mighty Ottomans on his west and treachery from his brothers at home. Tamasp survived and reigned for fifty-two years.

Shah Tamasp received two famous political refugees at his court whom he looked after for years. The Mogul emperor Humayun, fleeing from his nemesis Sher Shah Suri in India, was protected and eventually sent with an army to retake his empire. Tamasp exacted two conditions of support. First, Humayun had to convert to the Shia faith; he did, but he reverted to his Sunni belief on returning home to India. And secondly, he had to promise to give Kandahar to Tamasp; he did, but his son Akbar took it back.

The Ottoman prince Bayazid, son of Suleiman the Magnificent, sought refuge with Tamasp from the rage of his father, after his unsuccessful rebellion. Suleiman negotiated for two years to get back his son and finally purchased him for 400,000 pieces of gold. Suleiman offered Tamasp money or war; it was an easy choice. Honour didn't come into it; Tamasp escaped destruction and received a fortune. Bayazid and his four young sons were executed.

Tamasp was brave. For decades, despite a weak state and a small army, he resisted the might of the Ottomans under their greatest sultan, Suleiman. He was David to the Ottoman Goliath. Finally he secured a treaty which gave him peace to rebuild his state. He was also notoriously miserly, offering to pay his creditors with his own discarded clothing, which he would value at ten times the reasonable price.

For over a decade, Tamasp waged war on the Circassians and Armenians, and brought back great numbers of prisoners to Iran. Circassian women were famous for their beauty, the men fierce soldiers, and the Armenians, skilful artisans and shrewd businessmen. These were converted to Islam and lived as privileged ghulams or slaves. The slave contingents became a third force in the Irani politic which till then had been divided between the indigenous Persians and the Turkoman Qizilbash. The ghulam elite in the time of Shah Abbas the Great was to change the balance in the power game of Iran.

In 1574, Tamasp fell ill and the restless Qizilbash started again jockeying for power. Only two of the Shah's sons were suitable candidates to inherit—Khudabanda, the elder, who was practically blind; and Ismail, the younger, who had been imprisoned twenty years before on suspicion of treason and after twenty years in prison, was practically insane. As could be expected, the Qizilbash made the wrong choice, and 30,000 of the Qizilbash demonstrated outside the prison demanding that Ismail be released and enthroned. He hesitated, uncertain whether he was being called to rule or to die, but finally he was installed as Shah and set about murdering or blinding his brothers and other eligible princes. After just a year, the Qizilbash decided to kill him, and took the assistance of the Shah's powerful sister Pari Khan Khanum, who placed poison in his opium flask. Only the blind Khudabanda and his sons had escaped the hand of his murderous brother, Ismail, and he was installed as Shah despite his infirmity.

Khudabanda reigned, but it was his sister Pari Khanum who ruled and through her council of Qizilbash, controlled the government. The blind Shah wanted peace more than power and reconciled himself to her control; but his ambitious wife, Mahd-i Ulya, had Pari murdered, and replaced her as the power behind the throne. She came down hard on the Qizilbash till they could take it no longer and decided to act. A group of Qizilbash confronted the Shah, demanding that his wife be removed from power:

> Your Majesty knows that women are notoriously lacking in intelligence, weak in judgment, and extremely obstinate… Mahd-i Ulya's power and influence in the government of the realm is objectionable to all the Qizilbash tribes, and it is impossible for us to reach a modus vivendi with her. If she is not removed from power, in all probability, revolts will occur which will be to the detriment of both religion and the State.

All attempts at compromise failed and the Queen was strangled, after which the murderers swore their allegiance to the impotent Shah who had no option but to forget the assassination of his wife. With the Shah, blind and feeble, and the Qizilbash totally out of control, anarchy prevailed at court and factions competed for power throughout the land.

While these dramatic events were taking place, the young Abbas, son of Khudabanda, was far away in the East. As a baby, he had been sent to Herat as governor, and had lived with his guardian, Ali Quli Khan Shamlu, and his gentle wife, Jan Aqa Khanum, whom he loved as a mother. Abbas had lived most of his life in Herat and barely knew his real parents. The young prince, like his contemporary the Mogul Emperor Akbar, preferred hunting to studying, and by the time he became King at the age of seventeen, could barely read or write. But his lack of education would not stop him from becoming one of the greatest kings that Iran has known.

A power struggle in Herat removed Ali Quli and replaced him with Murshid Quli, who took control of Abbas as a puppet to establish his legitimacy. The invasion of the Uzbeks convinced Murshid Quli that it would be safer at court. He marched on the capital, Qazvin, and forced the Shah to abdicate in favour of his seventeen-year-old son, Abbas.

SHAH ABBAS THE GREAT

'When this great prince ceased to live, Persia ceased to prosper.'

—Jean Chardin, French resident in
Iran in the 1660s and '70s

In 1587, when Murshid Quli replaced the Shah with his young son, Abbas, Iran was a mess—there was internal anarchy as Qizilbash barons jockeyed for power; the Ottomans invaded from the West, the Uzbeks from the East; and the treasury was bankrupt. In 1629, when Shah Abbas died, Iran was stable and strong, had taken back all her lost territories from the Ottoman, the Uzbeks and the Russians; the treasury was full, the economy prosperous, and the new capital Isfahan, built by Abbas, was the most beautiful city in the world. His achievement enabled the Safavid dynasty to rule for a hundred years, and secured Iran as the home of the Shia sect of Islam thereafter.

In the sixteenth century, the three great Muslim empires—the Ottoman, the Moguls and the Safavids—were ruled by three extraordinary leaders whose reigns overlapped—Suleiman the Magnificent, who ruled from 1520–1566; Akbar the Great Mogul, who ruled from 1556–1605; and last but not least, Shah Abbas the Great, who ruled from 1587–1629. Though not as well-known as Suleiman and Akbar, Abbas is certainly equal to them as a king, and his impact on history, resulting in the Shia Khomeini revolution in the twentieth century, is perhaps the most enduring of the three.

Abbas was a low key, unpretentious and practical man, simple in dress and food, intelligent, full of energy and decisive. He was a kind and considerate man with a sense of humour and an incisive understanding of strategy. He was also totally ruthless in pursuing his objectives. Within eighteen months of becoming Shah, he killed Murshid Quli, the Qizilbash baron who had placed him on the throne, and later he killed his eldest son and blinded the other two. His remaining two sons escaped his wrath by dying before he attended to them. He had a great reverence for justice, and an army of spies to ensure that justice prevailed in his kingdom. He would also go personally, in disguise, to the markets to see for himself. On one occasion, he went dressed as a peasant and purchased some bread and meat for his meal. Back at the palace, he weighed his purchases to discover he had been short-changed; he had the baker thrown into a hot oven and the meat-seller roasted alive. In his kingdom, the merchants were honest and the roads were safe. Trade flourished and the economy grew. It was not about democracy or debate; what the Shah wanted, got done.

Abbas was a devoted Shia with a special regard for Imam Riza. He once made the pilgrimage from Isfahan to Meshed to visit the shrine of the Imam, on foot—a distance of 625 miles covered in sixty-six days. He married all but one of his daughters to clerics. But he was also a man who could hold his liquor, and he enjoyed watching the bawdy and lascivious dances of seductive boys and girls. He would call in comely courtesans to entertain his important guests, but on one occasion, had the girls sent away because they were unsuitable for the aged Spanish ambassador. But first, to the amusement of the company, he had the ambassador admit that his lack of interest was the result of impotence rather than virtue.

On taking the throne, Abbas set about taming the Qizilbash barons who were out of control. A group of disgruntled amirs burst into the palace to kill Murshid Quli, who had organized the coup to oust Abbas's father. Abbas shouted them down, intimidated them and later had them killed to establish his authority. But he had no love lost for Murshid Quli, whom he himself killed a few months later. The chosen assassin was a Circassian Ghulam, Allahverdi Khan, who was amply rewarded and went on to become the greatest general in the land and a governor of Fars, one of Iran's richest provinces. The fabulous Allahverdi Bridge in Isfahan was later built by the Khan and has stood as his monument for 500 years.

To balance the power of the Qizilbash elite who dominated the army, Abbas built a corps of ghulam cavalry troops, a new slave army. He also used these slaves as his administrators to ensure that no threat to his power could emerge from any single group. This new army not only ensured internal security but also enabled Abbas to control his enemies and expand his borders.

Recognizing that he could not take on the Ottomans and the Uzbeks at the same time, Abbas accepted a humiliating treaty with the Ottomans in 1590, allowing the Turks to keep the territories they had wrested from Iran. Abbas agreed to end the persecution of Sunnis and stop the ritual cursing of the first three caliphs in Iran.

Having neutralized the Ottoman threat, he made himself undisputed master of Iran. He crushed rebellions by ambitious provincial governors, he imprisoned and, where necessary, blinded his brothers and he started the practice of consigning rivals from the royal family to the harem, which served as their home and prison, ensuring that they remained totally ignorant of and unequipped to deal with the world outside. He appointed an exceptionally capable grand vizier, Hatem Beg Ordubadi, who ran the administration with clockwork efficiency for twenty years till he died.

Abbas then turned towards east to meet the Uzbek threat. During the last decade of the sixteenth century, the Uzbeks, under their able leader Abdullah Khan, took much of Khurasan and even captured the holy city of Meshed, killing, raping, plundering the shrine and enslaving thousands of captives. Abbas, following the advice of his father that good pay was more important than good fortune as a cause of victory, threw all his gold and silver reserves into the war. Abdullah urged the Ottomans and the Moguls to join him in a jihad against the Shia Safavids. The Ottomans declined because they were comfortable in their peace treaty; Akbar, the Mogul emperor, declined on the grounds that Abbas was a descendant of Ali, the son-in-law of The Prophet himself. The real reason for Akbar abstaining from the Uzbek-Safavid war, was that he was busy retaking Kandahar from Iran, not by force of arms but by bribing the Safavid governor to change sides. In 1598, Abdullah died and Abbas took the opportunity to defeat the Uzbeks and take back his territories. Abbas then had Allahverdi Khan kill the commander of the Safavid troops after which the great ghulam general was appointed commander-in-chief of the armies. For three months, the Shah remained in Meshed, where he performed the tasks of the humblest slave, even sweeping the floors in thanks for the liberation of the shrine. He then returned west to build his new capital of Isfahan.

In 1603, Abbas went to war on the Ottomans. In 1605, at Sufiyan, his 60,000-strong army faced the 100,000-man army of the Turks. Abbas was undecided whether to risk all in a single battle. He consulted his aunt, Zainab Begum, whose advice he respected. She urged him to fight and he joined the battle to win; it was decisively his greatest victory over the Ottomans. The Turks had had enough, and the mother of the Sultan approached Zainab to persuade the Shah to end the war of Muslim against Muslim. Abbas had achieved his objective—the recovery of all Persia's lost territories. He agreed to peace, and made a pilgrimage to Meshed to give thanks for his victory.

The Shah's success in handling the economy was no less than his success on the battlefield. He first created an environment of security, where laws were rigidly enforced with justice for all. He then took simple steps that were required to create confidence in the agriculture and husbandry sectors. The Turks were nomads who lived by pasturing their herds; the Persian peasants were farmers who tilled the fields. A fair crop-sharing system was developed by measuring and compensating the five inputs of agriculture—land, water, plough animals, seed and labour.

Persian roads became famous for their safety, unlike the situation in adjoining countries. A merchant who was robbed could claim and expect compensation from the local governor. Inns, known as caravan serais, were built to offer all travellers free accommodation. An assessment made after the death of Abbas revealed that 1,800 such inns had been built. Much was invested on improving the infrastructure on roads and bazaars.

Persian silk was a most important export, the sixteenth-century equivalent of Iran's twentieth-century oil. Abbas made silk a royal monopoly, making himself Iran's biggest capitalist. He placed his main reliance on the Armenian merchants, who combined skill with financial strength and a wide international network. His policy of religious tolerance allowing freedom of worship, encouraged all to participate in the profitable trade opportunities in Iran. The success of the Armenian merchants and the great wealth they accumulated certainly made the local elite jealous, but Abbas bluntly explained his reasons: 'They are more competent.' Merit overrode religion.

In 1487, the Portuguese had discovered the sea route to India around the Cape of Good Hope. Their great naval general, Albuquerque, had understood the importance of the Red Sea and the straits of Hormuz and Malacca in controlling the sea trade with the East and Far East. To the dismay of Iran, which had no navy, he had conquered the island of Hormuz which controlled access to the Persian Gulf. Shah Abbas used the new emerging strength of England and the EIC to expel the Portuguese, and then, by sharing trading privileges between the Dutch and the English, he retained control and promoted his international trade. Once again, the great strategist had secured his objectives and promoted Iran's interest even where he was weak.

In 1613, the great general, Allahverdi Khan, died. He had led the Shah's armies in the wars on the East and West. Abbas honoured his son, Imam Quli Khan, who succeeded his father as governor, conquered Bahrain for his master and through his performance, earned the love and respect of his shah, going on to become the wealthiest khan in the kingdom.

The years passed and the aging Shah prepared for his death. Like Suleiman the Magnificent of Turkey and Akbar the Great of India, his achievements had been outstanding. He was the greatest Persian king of the last 2,000 years. But where Suleiman and Akbar had both left alcoholic sons to succeed them, Abbas, had no sons left to pass on his throne; all five of his sons were either blinded or dead. After the death of these three titans, the three gunpowder empires of the Muslim world started their slow but irreversible decline.

DECLINE OF THE SAFAVIDS

The story of Shah Abbas showed once again that the rise of an empire was the achievement of a great man; but what followed, showed that the decline of the empire could also be attributed to the acts of the great man. To protect himself from his own family, Shah Abbas started the practice of confining young princes to the harem where they lived among women and eunuchs in a world of frivolity, disconnected from the real world. This kept the Shah safe, but ensured incompetent successors. His policy of converting provinces into crown-territories was continued by his successors till almost all of Iran was governed as crown-lands by administrators who had no commitment to their provinces, but were careerists who needed to show fast results to their patron, the Shah, even if it resulted in long-term deterioration. His blinding and killing of princes, by whom he felt threatened, led to wholesale massacres by the shahs who followed him. This killing was extended to notables, such as Imam Quli, the respected son of Allahverdi Khan, who was murdered along with his four sons in 1633 as his power and wealth had excited the jealousy of the Shah. Five years later, in 1638, the declining Safavids once again lost Baghdad and Kandahar.

Strong provinces were replaced by a strong centre, where power resided in the harem, exercised by eunuchs and concubines. Corruption grew; roads became unsafe and travellers were often robbed by the very officials who were meant to protect them; the military grew weak. Shah Sulayman did not nominate an heir; he told his ministers that if they wanted peace and quiet, they should chose his son Hussain, but if they wanted a strong ruler and an expanding empire, they should choose his son Abbas. They chose Hussain whom they could control more easily. The interests of the empire were not the prime objectives of the selectors. Shah Hussain went on a great pilgrimage to Meshed, accompanied by 60,000 of his retainers at a fabulous expense—a far cry from the austere pilgrimage by Shah Abbas on foot.

THE AFGHAN INTERREGNUM

The leader of the Ghilzai Pathans in Kandahar was an exceptional young man by the name of Mirwais. He was captured and sent as a prisoner to Isfahan, where due to his charm and personality, he became a favourite of the Shah, who gave him leave to proceed to Mecca on pilgrimage. There, he secured a fatwa to the effect that it was meritorious to wage war on the Shias. Mirwais re-established himself in Kandahar by cunning and guile; he declared independence from the Persians; defeated the Persian governor of Khurasan; and then ruled Kandahar till his death. He was the first great leader of the Afghan resurgence.

Mir Abdullah, the brother of Mirwais, seized power and offered the Persians a truce, which disappointed his warlike tribesmen. His nephew, Mahmud, the son of Mirwais, assassinated his uncle and took over as ruler of Kandahar. Mahmud was squat, with a broad face and a neck so short that his head seemed to grow on his shoulders. He was bold to the point of reckless; a fierce disciplinarian who was feared even by his own troops; and altogether an unpleasant character—treacherous, narrow-minded and lacking in generosity. But he could fight.

Mahmud conquered much of Persia including the capital, Isfahan. But when the Shah entered a treaty with Peter the Great of Russia, who offered to expel the Afghans, Mahmud found himself under pressure. Determined not to give in, he invited the Persian nobles to a feast where they were slaughtered, after which he gave the order for indiscriminate killing of the population which carried on for fifteen days. Mahmud then had himself locked in a vault to clean his troubled mind by meditation, but instead of repairing his mind, it drove him crazier. He was replaced and killed.

Iran had been dismembered by the Turks, the Russians and the Afghans, but Shah Tamasp held on, hoping against hope for a saviour. In 1727, the saviour arrived in the form of an obscure army commander with a small but battle-hardened army of 5,000 soldiers. The Shah appointed the new arrival, commander-in-chief. His name was Nader Quli.

NADER SHAH

> *'He is son of Nader Shah, the son of the sword, the grandson of the sword; and so on to seventy instead of seven generations.'*
>
> —Nader Shah (In answer to the demand of the bridegroom's ancestry, during the marriage of his son to the daughter of the Mogul Emperor, after the conquest of Delhi)

Nader Quli was a military genius who has been called the 'Napoleon of the East', but unlike Napoleon, he was never defeated in battle; for Nader, there was no Waterloo. He took back all the lost lands of Persia, defeating the Afghans and the Turks, and forced the Russians to retreat. Baghdad and Baku were taken. He conquered Delhi and brought home the fabulous wealth of the Mogul empire. He was the greatest conqueror of his time.

Nader was born in Khurasan. As a boy, he earned his living making sheepskin coats and looking after a few sheep. When he was eighteen, he and his mother were captured by Uzbeks; they lived as slaves and after four years, his mother died. Nader escaped and entered the service of the Afghan warlord Malik Mahmud, where he grew fast and married his master's daughter. But his ambition led to his downfall. He was beaten and dismissed, lucky to escape with his life.

Nader became a bandit, and was successful in his new career of crime. He built up a small army of desperados and captured Meshed, where he defeated, imprisoned and killed Malik Mahmud, his former master and father-in-law. Shah Tamasp breathed a sigh of relief at the expulsion of the Afghans, and rewarded Nader with the governorship of important territories and gave him the honorary title of Sultan. It seemed that the Shah had found his saviour.

Nader won battle after battle, making it look so easy that the Shah decided to try it for himself. He was defeated by the Turks, losing, in a month, all the territories that Nader had won from the Ottomans and accepting a humiliating treaty. Nader saw his opportunity in this disaster; he rejected the treaty and sent a stern message to the Turks: 'Restore the provinces of Persia or prepare for war.' But before he marched against the Turks, he went to Isfahan, where he arrested the Shah and installed his infant son as the new Shah, with himself as the regent holding the reins of power. The unfortunate Tamasp now saw that Nader was not his saviour but his nemesis.

Having beaten back the Turks, Nader now turned to the territories taken by the Russians. Here luck favoured him with the death of Peter the Great, after which the Russians had no appetite for conflict in their border with Iran. Having defeated all the enemies of Iran, and in control of an unbeatable army, he was now all-powerful. The death of the infant shah in 1736 left the throne vacant and the nobles turned to the only candidate, Nader the Conqueror. Nader went through the drama of refusing the crown daily for a month and then 'reluctantly' accepted the throne.

Nader was finally Shah of Iran—the dream of a lifetime. But it was not enough; he wanted more. The Safavids had used the Shia faith as the foundation for their legitimacy in Iran. But if Nader was to secure legitimacy over the wider territories of the Muslim world, Shia would be a handicap, not a source of strength. Nader changed the official faith of Iran from Shia to Sunni, writing, 'Since the Shia schism has prevailed, this land has been constantly in disorder. Let us all become Sunnis and this will cease.' This forced change did not endear Nader Shah to his Persian–Shia subjects. Nor could a mere edict change the hearts of men and the reality of belief.

Two years after his coronation, in 1738 Nader marched on Delhi, tempted by the tales of wealth and treasure accumulated over centuries by the richest empire on earth. En route, he conquered Ghazni, Kabul, Lahore, Sindh and Kashmir. He was formidable in his prime. The Emperor in Delhi, Muhammad Shah, was a soft and feeble man, reputed to be, 'never without a mistress in his arms and a glass in his hand.' A year before, in 1737, he had been raided by the Marathas who had mauled Delhi. The armies clashed a few miles from Delhi, and Nader won victory in two hours. Nader was magnanimous in victory and received the defeated Emperor as a guest in his tent 'in a manner equal to his great dignity.' They then proceeded into Delhi where Nader was entertained royally and the Emperor formally handed over his treasures including the famous peacock throne studded with emeralds, rubies, and diamonds such as the 186-carat Kohinoor. The plunder was sufficient for Nader to remit all taxes in Persia for three years.

Unfortunately, small resistance groups in Delhi killed some Persian soldiers, and even threw stones at Nader himself. Nader ordered retaliation, and his enraged soldiers massacred, burned and plundered the city. Finally, he ordered them to stop, but the damage was done. The famous Khuni Darwaza or 'Gate of Blood', in Delhi, acts as a reminder of this massacre.

After Delhi, Nader changed. Obsessed by the treasure he brought home from India, he became more bloodthirsty and miserly. In his last years, he constructed pyramids of skulls and indulged in wonton acts of cruelty. He blinded his own son and ordered thousands of executions. Many thought he had become insane. Finally he was killed by two of his tribesmen, whom he had sentenced to death and who were awaiting their own execution. Despite his success as a conqueror who expanded the borders of Iran in every direction, he died, hated by his people, both for his destructive style of government and for his antagonism to the Shia religious leaders and the Shia faith. He lived unloving and died unloved.

14

The Rise of the Ottomans

'Whichever of my sons inherits the throne, it behooves him to kill his brothers in the interests of the world order.'

—Sultan Mehmed the Conqueror

'To control the state requires a large army. To support the troops requires great wealth. To obtain this wealth, the people must be prosperous. For the people to be prosperous, the laws must be just. If anyone of these is neglected, the State will collapse.'

—Kutadgu Bilig (Written in 1069 for a Turkish ruler)

The great city of Istanbul, which straddles the Bosphorus straits linking Asia to Europe, has been the heart of empires for over a thousand years; first as the capital of the Byzantine Empire and known as Constantinople, then for 500 years with its new name of Istanbul, the capital of the Ottoman Empire. Its wonders include the magnificent Haggia Sophia Mosque or the Blue Mosque, the old palace of Topkapi and the new palace of Dolmabace. It's Grand Bazaar with goods from the furthest corners of Europe and Asia was, for centuries, the greatest market in the world.

Constantinople was the gateway to Europe, and it remained firmly closed to the nomadic Turkish tribes that fled west from Central Asia to escape the conquering Mongol hordes of Genghis Khan and his family. One small such tribe was led by a chieftain called Osman. In the power vacuum created by the decline of the Byzantine Empire, Osman and his son Orhan expanded their kingdom.

At first the territory of Osman was small, and gave little indication that he would become the founder of one of the longest-lasting empires and dynasties of history. Under his son Orhan, the kingdom was expanded by war, purchase of territory and marriage. Orhan liked Byzantine princesses, and whether moved by attraction or ambition, married three of them—Nilofer (aka Helen), the mother of his son; then Asporsha and Theodora, both daughters of Byzantine emperors who sought to reinforce their declining power by an alliance with the rough and hardy Turkish warrior chief. Orhan dressed simply, ate with his men, and followed the strange habit of accumulating money and building up a treasury for future needs, an unheard of innovation at that time.

Murad I was a conqueror who took most of the territory of the Balkans and was the first sultan of the Ottoman line. He also took a fifth of the Christian captives, enslaved them and created the janissaries or 'new troops' which were to become the foundation of Ottoman military power. He started the 'devsirme' recruiting system, under which young Christian boys were regularly rounded up, enslaved and prepared to run the empire as elite soldiers and administrators. Under Murad a fiefdom became an empire which would be ruled by thirty-six sultans over 650 years. Until Murad, the Ottoman chiefs were illiterate; his son Bayezid was educated, as were the sultans who followed.

At Kosovo, Murad was assassinated by a Serb. His two sons returned to the camp, and were told of their father's death. Bayezid, later called 'The Thunderbolt', immediately executed his brother and took the crown.

Bayezid was an impatient man and moved with lightening speed.

Short tempered, headstrong and arrogant, he saw himself as a man of destiny. 'I was born to bear arms and to conquer whatever is before me.' He inherited 101,000 square miles from his father Murad, and by the year 1402, had increased it by conquest, to 267,000 square miles. And then his army met Timur at Ankara and it was all over. His valiant but futile resistance was, in the words of the historian Arabshah, 'Like a man who sweeps away dust with a comb or drains the sea with a sieve.'

Arabshah described Timur's ferocity in battle, vividly:

> They shaved heads, amputated necks, crushed arms, cut off shoulder blades, burnt livers, scorched faces, gouged out eyes, split open bellies, blinded the sight, made tongues mute, blocked the hearing, crushed noses to the earth and brought low the lofty noses, lacerated mouths, shattered chests, crushed backs, pounded the ribs, split navels, melted hearts, severed sinews, shed blood, injured private parts, did violence to souls, destroyed men, poured out bodies like molten images, destroyed lives and not a third or fourth part of the subjects of Rum escaped.

Bayezid died in captivity, and Timur returned home to continue his conquests of other lands, leaving Bayezid's heirs to battle each other in civil war for the shattered remnants of the Ottoman Empire.

Murad II consolidated and restored the empire. Like his grandfather, Murad I, he was a capable man. In all, five Murads ruled the empire. Murad III, who followed one and a half centuries later, can only claim one achievement—he fathered twenty-four sons and thirty-two daughters—a record for the family. Murad IV was crazy and violent, and Murad V who ruled for a few months in 1876, was alcoholic and insane.

Murad II was an enlightened ruler, simple and sincere, who believed in honour and justice. He was fair with his enemies, and honoured treaties. Murad had three sons, but when two died, Mehmet, the youngest, was recalled to the capital, to prepare him for rule. Murad was shocked by his son's lack of education and brought in a respected mullah to tutor him with authority, to enforce discipline. When Mehmet refused to study or obey, his tutor gave him the first serious beating of his life after which the young prince became a model student, going on to study philosophy and science, and Islamic, Greek and Latin history and literature.

After his victory over the army of Hungary led by John Hunyadi, Murad, though still a young man in his forties, abdicated in favour of his twelve-year-old son. He wanted to shed the tensions of power and live a peaceful life of retirement. But it was not to be. He was urged to come back, take up once more the reins of government and drive back the enemies of the empire. Again he was victorious, again he retired; but again he was called back to resume the sultanate. This time he ruled for five years before dying of apoplexy after a night of heavy drinking. He was forty-seven and had ruled for thirty years, most of which he had spent at war.

Among those who came to offer obeisance to the new sultan was Halima, the senior wife of his late father; while she was with Mehmed, one of his officers strangled her baby son. Mehmed justified the murder by the Ottoman code of fratricide to prevent wars of succession. He later had the code enacted into law, quoting from the holy *Quran*, 'The execution of a prince is preferable to the loss of a province.'

The last hurdle to absolute power was the corps of the janissaries, the elite standing army of the empire. No sultan could feel secure without their unquestioning loyalty. This professional standing army of slaves recruited from Christian boys captured in war was very different from other armies. No janissary was allowed to learn a trade or work as an artisan. His exclusive occupation was the art of war. He was not allowed to marry. He was the property of, and lived, fought and died for the sultan. The janissaries revolted, demanding higher pay. Even the Sultan could not ignore their demand, and Mehmed, despite his anger, chose rather to be safe than sorry and twice raised their salaries to bring them under control. Later, when time was right, he dismissed the commander and took more direct control of his troops.

Mehmed combined intelligence and energy with a relentless sense of purpose. His one overriding ambition was to conquer Constantinople; if he could not rule an empire which contained Constantinople, he would prefer not to rule an empire at all. As story has it that one night he sent for his grand vizier, Halil, who arrived carrying a dish of gold coins for the Emperor. Asked what they were for, Halil replied it was usual for the Sultan's servants to bring their master a gift when summoned unexpectedly. Mehmed waved the dish aside, saying, 'I only want one thing: Give me Constantinople.'

THE CONQUEST OF CONSTANTINOPLE

Mehmed succeeded his father as Sultan in 1451. In 1453, he conquered Constantinople. Despite the fact that the old empire had long since faded, Constantinople had, for centuries, defied conquest, protected by its massive walls and by a great chain that prevented ships from attacking by sea. Only by a joint land and sea attack could Constantinople be taken. Bad generals lose opportunity; good generals take opportunity; but great generals create opportunity. Mehmed was a great general who took war very seriously. A Hungarian maker of canons by the name of Urban, was looking for a job. Constantinople didn't have the money to hire him; Mehmed did. Urban made some massive canons for Mehmed, which were state of the art for the times. These were a match for even the strongest walls. But it was in organizing his attack by sea that Mehmed showed that he was a true innovator. He built a special road, and moved his fleet overland on oiled timbers, circumventing the protective chain, and surprising the defenders by suddenly appearing behind them on the other side of the water. For three days, his troops plundered the old city, and then Mehmed ordered the looting to stop. The magnificence of Constantinople overwhelmed him with emotion, and at Haggia Sophia, the great cathedral which now became a mosque, he picked up a handful of earth and poured it on his head as a token of humility. Mehmed earned the title of Fatih, the Conqueror, and left his legacy as one of the greatest of the Ottoman sultans.

Having conquered Constantinople, his next task was to rebuild and restore what was left of the city and its inhabitants. The population had sunk to less than 40,000, capital had fled or gone underground and skilled professionals had disappeared. Mehmed made it clear that all nationalities and religions were equally welcome. The last Christian patriarch had fled to Italy so a new religious leader was urgently needed to head the sizeable Christian community. The Sultan's choice fell on the monk Gennadius, a learned and respected scholar, who had been purchased as a slave by a Turkish emir when the city fell. The Sultan persuaded the noble scholar to accept the patriarchal throne and gifted him gold and other support to lead the Christians. The skilled Jews and Armenians were lured back with promises of protection and guaranteed freedom of worship. They would prove indispensible in rebuilding the economy.

Mehmed promoted trade. He constructed the Grand Bazaar which became the greatest centre of commerce in the world. Istanbul was perfectly located to promote East–West trade between Asia and Europe, and as the people flourished, the state treasury was filled by the taxes that were paid. He built a great mosque complex with colleges, hostels and a hospital providing free education, medical treatment and food for travellers. Finally, he built a new palace, Topkapi, which was to be the seat of power for his family for three centuries. Within a century, the population of Istanbul had grown to half a million inhabitants, and the city was recognized as the greatest in the world.

Mehmed ruled for thirty years, much of which was at war. He conquered Serbia, Bosnia, Albania, much of Greece, and finally Hungary, whose great leader Hunyadi, defeated the Ottoman army in battle where Mehmed himself was wounded. But shortly after his victory, Hunyadi died of the plague, leaving the way open for Mehmed. He also subdued Venice and invaded Italy. Europe trembled at his name.

Mehmed was a highly educated man, well versed in the wisdom of both the East and the West. He was fluent in six languages—Turkish,

Greek, Arabic, Latin, Persian and Hebrew. He restructured both the power politics and the administration of the empire, to create a new society and a new type of state. His three most dramatic innovations were the Law of Fratricide, the janissaries and the devsirme.

The Law of Fratricide was cruel but effective. Civil war was avoided and stability ruled. It was justified by misinterpretation of a quote from the holy *Quran*. It shows that Mehmed chose practicality and efficiency over justice and emotion. Power politics overrode Islamic principles. The life span of a prince was short.

The janissaries were a standing army of warriors divorced from every bond other than loyalty and commitment to the Sultan. Without family, roots, or any skills other than war, they were a formidable force that protected their sultan at home and conquered territory for him abroad. Later when the empire declined, they went rogue and frequently became the terror of the Sultan.

The Devsirme was the practice of the imperial army going to the provinces annually to harvest the best of the subordinate Christian youth who were enslaved, converted to Islam and educated in the palace schools to provide for the future administrative, political and military leadership for the state. For these displaced young boys, the Sultan was their only family; his wish, their command. Disciplined through reward and punishment, they developed obedience to a fault and provided dedicated cadres for their master. Their recognition, reward and promotion were determined solely by merit and performance. Many a grand vizier rose from such humble beginnings. They outshone their European counterparts whose power and position stemmed from privilege of birth rather than their own worth.

Except the janissaries who were forbidden other vocational training, all others were encouraged to learn a craft or trade, including the sultans themselves. Salim the Grim and Suleiman the Magnificent were skilled goldsmiths; Abdul Hamid II was a proficient cabinet maker, and Mehmed the Conqueror was himself an expert gardener. Legend has it that he grew a giant cucumber of which he was very proud, but one day it vanished. Suspecting his gardener, Mehmed cut open his belly where he found the remains of the cucumber. Never again were his cucumbers stolen!

As his power grew absolute, the Conqueror became more solitary and withdrawn. After an unpleasant intrusion in the divan, the Sultan stopped attending its sessions, preferring to observe unseen. As his health deteriorated, with his leg swelling hugely with a tumor, he started to eat his meals alone. He survived his enemies; he survived fourteen assassination attempts by the Venetians; and finally sick from excessive eating and drinking, and suffering from gout and colic, he passed away at the age of forty-nine on 4 May 1481. Europe rejoiced as it announced, 'The Great Eagle is dead.'

AFTER THE GREAT EAGLE

Bayezid, the next sultan, was a peaceful scholar, in striking contrast to both his father Mehmed and to his own son who succeeded him as Salim the Grim. He fought the revolt of his brother Jem, who proposed that they share the empire; Bayezid refused with the remark, 'The Empire is a bride that cannot be shared between rivals.' Bayezid was an enlightened ruler who promoted the economy and developed the Ottoman navy. He had eight sons, of whom his favourite was the eldest, Ahmed. By the time the contest for power began in earnest, only three remained alive. Ahmed made the grave mistake of taking the side of the Shias, forcing his father to withdraw his support. Salim marched on his father, whom he now met after twenty-six years and persuaded him to step down in his favour.

Within a year of taking the throne, Salim defeated and killed his two surviving brothers, and executed six of his nephews and three of his own sons, leaving the way clear for his last surviving son, Suleiman. He was a taciturn man who kept his thoughts to himself, ate alone and governed alone. He is remembered in history as Salim the Grim. Like his grandfather Mehmed, Salim was a great conqueror, but his focus was more on his rival Islamic kingdoms than on Christian Europe. He defeated the Persian king, Shah Ismail, and took chunks of Western Persia and then defeated the Mameluks of Egypt, the other great Muslim kingdom of the time, who controlled the holy cities of Mecca and Medina. He brought home from Egypt the holy relics from the time of The Prophet and the Righteous Caliphs, and furthermore brought back the Caliph himself who was living as a puppet in Cairo. In Istanbul, the Caliph is said to have resigned his position in favour of Salim, who thus became the first Ottoman caliph. The Ottomans, who were not even Arabs, let alone from the family of The Prophet, held the caliphate till it was terminated once and for all, by Ataturk in the twentieth century.

Salim ruled for only eight years, but in that short time he doubled the extent of the empire. He inspired fear in both his enemies and those who served him. Failure to perform was punished with death—in his short reign, seven of his grand viziers were executed. He left his son an imperial inheritance without threat or challenge. When Suleiman became Sultan, he was twenty-six-years old and Europe breathed a sigh of relief that the fierce Salim was no more. It was said that, 'a gentle lamb has succeeded a fierce lion... for Suleiman is young, without experience—altogether given to repose.' How wrong they were!

SULEIMAN THE MAGNIFICENT

Suleiman was the tenth and last of the great sultans who ruled the Ottoman Empire. He took the empire to its peak, but also sowed the seeds of its decline. He was quiet and intelligent, a man of both ideas and action. A great administrator, statesman, conqueror and legislator, he was known in Europe as Suleiman the Magnificent, and among the Turks as Suleiman the Lawmaker. He was the greatest and most powerful ruler of his time. Where his father Salim's main conquests had been of Muslim nations, Suleiman turned his attention to Europe, and his main wars were against the Christians. He quickly took Rhodes and Belgrade, and then for a couple of years, remained at Istanbul, to focus on internal affairs. His decision to avoid war for that period almost cost him his life.

The janissaries wanted war with its promise of action and plunder. Prolonged peace kept them at home with nothing to do other than constant military training. They were not allowed either profession or family life; without the chance for loot and plunder, income fell and their pockets were soon empty. The janissaries mutinied in an orgy of killing and even broke into the palace where Suleiman himself killed three of their number before retreating to save his life. Suleiman never made the same mistake again, and himself led thirteen campaigns into Europe and Asia, keeping his janissaries happy and loyal.

Suleiman was a lonely man. Due to his father's murder of brothers and nephews, he had very little family. Instead he was surrounded by his slaves, the converted Christian boys who had grown up in the palace school, or the girls in the harem. Even his mother the Sultana Valida had started life as a Christian slave, as had his wife, Hurrem, 'The Russian Woman', and also his great vizier for thirteen years, Ibrahim the Greek. Three people had the greatest impact on Suleiman's life and reign—Ibrahim, the grand vizier; Hurrem his wife; and Barbarossa, the commander of his navy. Of the three, only Barbarossa started life as a free man as the son of a retired janissary who, after retirement earned his living as a potter; but though Barbarossa was born free, his father, the janissary, had started as a Christian slave.

Ibrahim was the son of a sailor who was captured and enslaved in his youth and educated in the palace school of the Ottomans. He became a close friend of the young prince Suleiman, who after becoming Sultan promoted him to the post of grand vizier, a job he held for thirteen years. Ibrahim was talented, intelligent, capable as both statesman and general and became the most powerful man in the empire after his friend, the Sultan. He accumulated great wealth from his position, and lived in splendour that equaled his master. Suleiman gave Ibrahim every honour and even married Ibrahim to his own sister, making him a close family member.

But all this power and status went to the head of the grand vizier who grew boastful and arrogant, even saying,

> It is true that I govern this vast empire... whatever I do is accomplished. If I wished I could make a stable boy into a pasha. What I wish to give, is given, and cannot be taken away. If the great Sultan gives something and I do not wish it given, then it is taken away. The making of war, the granting of peace, the disposal of treasure—all is in my hands. The Sultan is not better clad than I.

Ibrahim's destruction is a story of pride before the fall. His unmatched power and wealth had excited much jealousy. His credibility was shattered by the statement made by his former mentor, Iskander Celebi, who having been condemned for conspiracy, claimed that Ibrahim had been a partner to his crimes. Most important of all, his backing of the heir-apparent, Mustafa, had earned him a powerful enemy—the Empress who wanted the crown for her own son, Salim. Ibrahim was invited for dinner by the Sultan; the next morning his body was found. No questions were asked; no answers were offered.

Hurrem entered the harem as a slave girl. She was talkative and witty, but no great beauty. Her exceptional qualities were her ambition and her skill in the art of manipulation and conspiracy. She caught the eye of the Sultan, and quickly monopolized his affections. Her first victim was the senior consort, Gulbehar, the mother of the heir-apparent, Mustapha, who moved out and faded from the court. She then persuaded the Sultan to break with tradition and marry her, elevating her to Sultana. Ibrahim was her next victim. Not only had his support of Mustapha convinced the Empress that he had to go, but she also wanted his job for her own son-in-law to further reinforce her power base. After Ibrahim's death, the son-in-law, Rustem Pasha, an Albanian Catholic who converted to Islam, twice held the office of grand vizier for a total of fifteen years till his death; he had a gift for management, never smiled and never spoke unless giving an order. During his time in office, he accumulated massive wealth. Hurrem's final success was in manipulating her husband to murder his heir-apparent, Mustafa, a fine prince loved by the people and by the janissaries. Suleiman summoned his son, who was warned of the danger in going to his father. But the bold prince went alone to Suleiman's tent, saying that if he had to die, it could not be in a better way than by his father's hand. Mustafa was murdered by three deaf and mute people in the tent of his father, and his body was displayed on a carpet for all to see.

By eliminating Mustafa, Hurrem saved the life of her favourite son, Salim, who went on to become Sultan after the death of Suleiman.

THE DEGENERATION OF THE EMPIRE

Salim was short, fat and self-indulgent, and is remembered as Salim the Sot, due to his addiction to wine. With the death of Mustafa, the line of the great Ottomans came to an end; with the crowning of Salim, the degeneration of the empire began. The destructive influence of the harem started with Hurrem and led to the 'Rule of the Favoured Women'. The Ottoman Turks paid a heavy price for the love of Suleiman for Hurrem, the Russian girl who dominated the empire till her death left her bereaved husband broken-hearted to live out his last years.

Khair al-Din Barbarossa was a pirate. The greatest seaman of his time, he was appointed admiral of the Ottoman fleet by the Emperor Suleiman. The power and position of all others in the empire depended on the Emperor; but Suleiman's power in the Mediterranean Sea depended solely on Barbarossa. In the great power struggle between Suleiman the Magnificent and Charles, the Holy Roman Emperor, it was Barbarossa's domination of the Mediterranean that tipped the scale in favour of the Ottoman, and confirmed his position as the greatest ruler of his time.

In fact, there were two Barbarossas—the elder Aruj who took Algiers and dominated the coast of North Africa; and after his death, his younger brother Khair al-Din, who took the Barbarossa legend to new heights. Suleiman's land armies and his famous janissaries were more than a match for the Christian forces, but in the Mediterranean the Sultan's navy was being given a difficult time by the Emperor Charles' fleet led by his great admiral Andrea Doria. The Sultan was always ready to think out of the box and invited Barbarossa to Istanbul where he was appointed admiral of the fleet. For some years, the two great sea captains, Doria and Barbarossa, went at each other. Finally in 1538, at Preveza, the contest was decided. Doria had three times the number of ships, and his ships were much larger than the Ottoman vessels, but Barbarossa was the superior strategist, and skill overcame numbers with total victory for the Turks. The Christian navy was crushed, and Turkish supremacy over the Mediterranean was established. Barbarossa gave to the displaced and exiled Muslims of Spain who had resettled in North Africa, the chance for revenge against their oppressors, the Catholic monarchs of Spain, who had cruelly ended the Muslim civilization of Andalusia. Barbarossa retired with honour and is remembered as the greatest admiral in Muslim history.

After the defeat at Preveza, the Emperor Charles prepared an immense fleet to take revenge for Doria's disaster. They arrived at Algiers to destroy the Barbary corsairs who were once again totally outnumbered. But the great fleet of the Emperor was destroyed, proving again that in warfare it is not numbers that count, but discipline, training and morale. The Emperor and his ruined army limped back to Spain. Algiers was secured for the Muslims. So many were captured and enslaved in Algiers that 1541 is remembered as the time when Christians sold at an onion per head.

In July 1546, Khair al-Din Barbarossa died of a fever in his palace on the Bosphorus. A French historian wrote, 'Never even among the great Greek and Roman conquerors was there another such as he.' He founded the kingdom of Algeria, secured the Mediterranean for the Turks and trained his great lieutenant and successor, Dragut, who became Sultan of Tripoli. His life was violent, his death, peaceful, and his achievements, extraordinary. The Turkish annals for 1546 record simply: 'The King of the Sea is dead.'

Suleiman's greatest rival was Charles Hapsburg, the son of

Philip the Handsome and Joanna the Mad; his titles included Holy Roman Emperor; King of Germany, Italy, Spain, Sicily, Sardinia and Corsica; and Archduke of Austria. Charles, with his brother Ferdinand, King of Bohemia, Hungary and Croatia, fought a losing war for supremacy with the Sultan, and finally accepted a treaty which showed them as the lesser sovereigns. Suleiman drove their ships out of the Mediterranean Sea but they found greener pastures laden with gold and silver across the Atlantic, in the Americas. Finally, Charles, exhausted by a life of struggle, abdicated in favour of his younger brother and retired to a monastery to live a life of peace and contemplation. Francis, the King of France, who had been defeated by Charles, first in the election for the title of Holy Roman Emperor and then in battle, sought the support of the Sultan to 'prevent Charles from becoming the most powerful sovereign of his time' and accepted Suleiman as his protector. Henry VIII of England was far away from the mainstream of European politics, protected by the waters of the English Channel. His main concern was the lack of a successor and the refusal by the Pope to recognize and approve his numerous divorces and marriages. It was a time of great kings, and Suleiman was the greatest.

The great rise of the Ottomans under Suleiman resulted from a combination of factors:

- Salim the Grim's conquests and his stern discipline doubled the empire that Suleiman inherited.
- Salim also made sure that Suleiman's accession was unchallenged and stable.
- Suleiman himself was an exceptional man of unusual capability.
- Suleiman delegated to his chosen lieutenants, and he was an exceptional judge of character.
- The slaves that were brought up in the palace were an extended family based on merit and education. This created a superior quality of generals and administrators. Many believed that the palace school system was the key reason for the success of

the Ottomans.
- The emphasis on justice and law strengthened the empire. Suleiman was a just and fair man, known by his people as Suleiman Qanuni (Law-giver).
- The Ottoman treasury was rich, despite comparatively low taxation. The wars were self-financing and the confiscation of estates of powerful ministers on their death replenished the state coffers.
- The religion of Islam created a common value system, a common code and a common culture that promoted the unity of the community.

But though Suleiman expanded the borders of his empire, rooted out corruption, overhauled the laws, and ruled with tolerance, efficiency and justice over a conglomeration of races and religions, he too had his weaknesses and flaws, which were to end the relentless rise of the Ottomans and pitch the dynasty into a decline that lasted for three centuries till the empire and the caliphate were finally extinguished. He started the lateral entry of favourites into the highest ranks of power. Both Ibrahim and Rustem Pasha were outsiders whom he elevated to the office of grand vizier. Though he chose capable men, the sultans who followed were not such good judges of character. He allowed his grand viziers to amass great fortunes, which set a disastrous precedent. He allowed his grand viziers to sell offices in the administration which later proved most destructive to the efficiency of government. He allowed the influence of the harem to grow like a poison in the government. Hurrem boasted, 'I live with the Sultan and make him do what I wish.' This led to the rule of the favoured women, the sultanas who accumulated fortunes and conspired to elevate favourite and debauched sons to the throne. He killed his sons, Mustafa and Bayezid, and passed succession to the incompetent drunkard, Salim the Sot.

When Bayezid fled, he took refuge with Shah Tamasp of Persia and sent back the message that in the Shah, he had found a new father. Suleiman could not swallow the insult, and declared his son a traitor. The Shah was persuaded with 400,000 gold coins to surrender Bayezid, who was executed. Now only Salim the Sot, an incompetent drunkard, was left.

To make matters worse, the Turkish army failed to take the small island of Malta. In the siege, the great naval commander, Dragut, the successor to Barbarossa, was killed by a fragment of rock that pierced his skull. Suleiman decided that he alone must put things right. First he married Salim's two daughters to his two most important and trustworthy deputies, Sokolli and Piali, to ensure a capable government in the event of his death. Then he announced that he himself would lead his armies into a new war. He was seventy-two years old, his body feeble and racked with pain, and his legs swollen. He could no longer ride, but a litter was prepared. The old Sultan set out with his army. He never returned, but, like the great conqueror Tamerlane, died on the road.

After Suleiman, incompetent and degenerate sultans were not able to control the lawlessness of the janissaries, the fanaticism of the mullas, the corruption of the pashas, the greed and conspiracies of the harem and the rising strength of the Europeans. Most important of all the changes that weakened the empire was the replacement of the Law of Fratricide that ensured the survival of the fittest, by the institution of 'The Cage', the royal prison which produced a series of mad and incompetent sultans totally unfit to rule.

But with his marriage of his trusted Sokolli to Salim's daughter, he postponed the day of the decline of the empire. Salim had no interest in affairs of the state, but left all government in the capable hands of his son-in-law, Sokolli, who ruled as grand vizier throughout the reign of Salim and into the sultanate of his son Murad III.

15

The Decline of the Ottomans

'Never listen to the advice of women; never choose a minister who is too wealthy; keep the treasury filled; and keep the army on the move.'

—Koprolu, the grand vizier
(On his deathbed, his advice to the Sultan)

'Render swift and impartial justice to your subjects, restrain your natural greed for gold and above all keep a close watch on your son Mehmed.'

—Nurbano, the Sultana Valida (On her deathbed, her advice to her son, Sultan Murad)

'Excess of a liberty to which one is unaccustomed is as dangerous as the absence of liberty.'

—Sultan Abdul Hamid

'Revolutions must be founded in blood. A revolution that is not founded in blood will not be permanent.'

—Ataturk

THE DECLINE OF THE OTTOMANS | 231

For over 300 years, ten great sultans had taken the Ottoman Empire to lead the world. Over the next 300 years, fifteen incompetent, degenerate and often insane sultans oversaw the dramatic decline of the empire. True, there were some sultans who were normal, but these few were the only exceptions.

Perhaps the greatest cause of degeneracy of leadership was the replacement of the Law of Fratricide with the institution of The Cage by a sultan who didn't want to kill his brother. A section of the seraglio was constructed as a special prison for brothers of sultans to make sure that they did not create a threat for the ruler. But good intention led to disastrous and cruel results. These wretched royal prisoners lived in The Cage, cut off completely from the world, uneducated, uninformed and unfit to live normal lives. Then suddenly, after an internment of thirty, forty or fifty years, they would be brought out, on the death of the Sultan, to take his place; by this time, many had become totally insane and even those who retained elements of sanity were certainly not normal and definitely not fit to rule.

In the early days of the empire, great sultans such as Mehmed the Conqueror had themselves run the empire, directly controlling both the army and the civil administration. At the peak of the empire, Suleiman the Magnificent had delegated much of day-to-day government to his grand viziers, chosen for their capability; his three famous grand viziers—Ibrahim the Greek;, Rustem Pasha the Croatian; and finally Sokollu Pasha the Serbian—all started their careers as slaves of the Sultan, and finally, to secure their loyalty, were all brought into the family by judicious marriages—Ibrahim to the sister of the Sultan; Rustem, to the daughter; and Sokollu, to the granddaughter. Now power passed to the women of the harem, the Sultana Validas, and mothers of the feeble line of successor sultans. This period, lasting a hundred years and remembered as the period of 'The Rule of the Favoured Women', had disastrous consequences on the empire.

THE RULE OF THE FAVOURED WOMEN

The first of the Ottoman royal women to influence the history of the empire was Hurrem, the wife of Suleiman, who exercised power through her influence over the Sultan and whose conspiracies and manipulation led to the murder of Ibrahim, the powerful grand vizier, and Mustafa, the charismatic heir-apparent. She was instrumental in the passing of succession to the useless Salim the Sot.

Salim was a sweet-natured drunk, who left affairs of state to his son-in-law Sokollu and concentrated on fun, games and alcohol. The only time he overrode Sokollu's policies was when he invaded Cyprus to secure supplies of his favourite wine from the island, where he intended to make his Jewish bootlegger, Nasi, King of Cyprus. Finally, after downing a bottle of his favourite Cyprus wine in a single swig, he slipped in the bath, cracked his skull and died. The second power lady was Nurbano, Salim's wife, who came into her own after the death of her husband. She kept her husband's corpse in an icebox till her son Murad was safely crowned. Murad's first act as Sultan was to execute his five small brothers to eliminate the competition. Murad was totally under the influence of his mother. His interests ran initially from opium, to alcohol, and then to women—first, his Venetian wife, Safiye, and then the endless stream of beautiful girls procured for him by his mother to keep Safiye's influence diluted. Perhaps Murad's only memorable achievement was that he fathered 103 children from his one-night stands; emotionally he remained committed to his wife Safiye.

Nurbano had two obsessions—first to reduce the power of the grand vizier, Sokollu, and second to make sure that she was not eclipsed by Safiye Baffo, the Venetian. She convinced her son, the Sultan, that Sokollu had earned for himself an enormous fortune by selling offices. Murad was greedy and loved money; if anyone was going to benefit from the sale of state offices, it would be him and no other. He had Sokollu assassinated in the divan, and then pardoned the assassin. He then went after the hidden fortune, but to his shock, he discovered there was none. Sokollu had always been an honest man, and died relatively poor. The Sultan lost a valuable deputy, and did not recover any gold or money—a big mistake! With regard to her second concern, to keep her daughter-in-law under control, she was more successful. It was only after her death that Safiye assumed power and importance in affairs of state.

Safiye, who had entered the palace as a captured Christian slave, was now the most powerful person in the empire. Her first act was to persuade her son to kill his nineteen brothers to remove all possible challenges to his rule. The young boys were lined up and told they were to be circumcised; they were, but then they were immediately killed. The Sultan wept, buried them with due decorum, and then went on with his idle life. When the Sultan died, Safiye was moved out and later killed.

The last of the 'Favoured Women' was Kosem, who started life as Anastasia, the daughter of a Greek priest. She became the favourite of Ahmed I, Safiye's grandson, who adored her and could deny her nothing. Kosem's greatest fear was that Ahmed's eldest son was not her son and this would undoubtedly pose a real threat to her children who could be executed in accordance with the Law of Fratricide. Sultan Ahmed had spared the life of his brother Mustafa, who was living in The Cage and was carefully protected by Kosem. She managed to secure succession for Mustafa, the brother of her husband, rather than to her stepson Osman, and this became a precedent for brothers to succeed rather than minor sons when a sultan died.

Kosem used her daughters' marriages with skill and developed a network of alliances that helped her to retain power for half a century. She said to a grand vizier about her wanting to add to her entourage: 'Whenever you're ready, let me know. We'll take care of you right away. I have a princess ready.' Two of Kosem's sons became Sultan, first Murat IV and then the mad Ibrahim.

Kosem played politics for power as she manipulated the government under three mad sultans in turn. Her brother-in-law Mustafa was quite insane, a disability which not only kept him alive in a time when sultans were only too eager to murder their kin, but actually saw him twice enthroned. Between the two reigns of Mustafa, young Usman was made Sultan for four years until he was murdered by the janissaries. Her son Murad IV was a homicidal maniac, and her second son, Ibrahim, who succeeded his brother as Sultan, was a sex-crazy lunatic. Kosem amassed a fortune, which was of no use to her when she was forced to consent to the deposition of her son, the Sultan Ibrahim, after which she managed to install her grandson Mehmed IV, for whom she acted as regent. Three years later, a toothless, hated old woman of sixty-two, she was attacked, stripped naked and shamefully strangled at the gates of the palace.

Murad IV was an exception to the rule at a time when most sultans were ineffectual weaklings. When he became Sultan at the age of ten, his mother first tried to control him by encouraging the young prince towards homosexuality so that he should not fall under the influence of any of his slave girls. But he was not destined to be dominated. He grew into a big, strong man who could outfight, outshoot and outride any of his subjects. He ruled by instilling fear, and in 1637 alone, he executed 25,000 of his subjects. When he conquered Baghdad, he killed 60,000 of its citizens. On one occasion, he drowned a party of women for making too much noise. From his deathbed, he ordered the death of his brother Ibrahim, the last surviving Ottoman, but his mother lied to him that Ibrahim was already dead and saved his life. When Murad passed away and Ibrahim was taken from The Cage to be crowned, he danced around the corpse of his brother screaming, 'The butcher of the Empire is dead at last.'

Kosem now went to work at procuring an endless stream of beautiful virgins for her son. But Ibrahim did not need much encouraging; he was sex-crazy and perverse. One of his little games was to strip all his women naked and have them prance around pretending to be mares while he, acting the part of stallion, would mount them in turn. Once, suspecting infidelity, he murdered all the girls in his harem, tying them in sacks and drowning them in the Bosphorus. He developed a passion for the daughter of the Grand

Mufti, whom he abducted and subjected to the perversions of his harem. This was to be his undoing, for when the Mufti, and his associates engineered a coup and deposed Ibrahim, the question was asked, 'Is it lawful to dethrone and put to death a Padishah who confers all the posts of dignity in the empire not on those who are worthy of them, but on those who have bought them for money?' The Mufti, hungry for revenge for the mistreatment of his daughter, gave his judgement with a single word: 'Yes.'

By this time, the sultans had become non-entities. Dragged from long periods of imprisonment in The Cage, sometimes even fifty years, these sultans were broken men when they ascended the throne. The government was in shambles after the antics of the power-mad and greedy sultanas; the ordinary people of the empire had been reduced to wretched living conditions. While the empire was collapsing, Europe was rising. The control of the seas and the conquest of the Americas had shifted the balance of power. The spice trade from the Far East with its new sea routes, bypassed the empire and gold and silver from the Americas fueled inflation. The Ottoman economy was in a serious decline. Defeat at the battle of Lepanto had shown that even militarily, the Ottomans were no longer invincible.

RISE FROM OBSCURITY

Sometimes hopelessness and despair throw up exceptional saviours. Now, a family rose from obscurity to take the reins of the state, and for fifty years, tried to restore the Ottoman Empire. These were the Koprulus—father, son and brother—who, in turn, ruled the empire as grand viziers of powerless sultans. Mohammed Koprulu was an Albanian who started his career as a kitchen-boy in the palace of the Sultan. He rose, in turn, by favour of the harem, to become governor of Damascus, Tripoli and Jerusalem. At the orders of the Sultana Valida, he was appointed the grand vizier of the empire at the age of seventy. The court nobles criticized and ridiculed the appointment, arguing that he was senile, could not read or write and was totally incompetent. However, the critics were wrong.

Mohammed Koprulu was a just and determined man who hit hard at corruption, crime and incompetence in the administration, judiciary and military. During his five years in office, he executed 35,000 offenders in a rampage of justice that cleaned up the empire. By the end of his short period of rule, the army was disciplined, the judges, honest, and the administration characterized by merit, in place of the mafia of plunder that had grown rampant. He had no love of wealth and lived simply in a modest palace with a small harem.

Mohammed was followed by his son Ahmed, who was no less capable than his father. He was modest, well-educated, and with a natural flair for government. A devout Muslim, he was nevertheless tolerant of other religions. He refused to take bribes, whether for making appointments or for any other official act. He kept the treasury filled. He was a great statesman, and when the Ottoman army was worsted by the Austrians, he negotiated a treaty that actually added to the empire.

After the death of Ahmed, the dynasty of the Koprulus was interrupted by the appointment as grand vizier of Kara (black) Mustafa, the son-in-law of the Sultan. It was a bad choice; Kara Mustafa was bloodthirsty, greedy and corrupt. It was his greed that led to the defeat of the Ottoman army in the second siege of Vienna.

The first siege of Vienna in 1532 by Suleiman had not met with success, but neither could it be called a defeat. The Emperor Charles avoided a battle, and Suleiman had to return home to avoid getting stuck in the winter snows. The second siege of Vienna by Kara Mustafa in 1683 was an unmitigated disaster. The 275,000-man Ottoman army outnumbered the 35,000 soldiers left to defend Vienna. The Turks were also better equipped, better trained and fired by the passion of religion. It was impossible for them to lose.

Kara Mustafa's concern, however, was not to win a victory that he saw as inevitable, it was to maximize his personal gain from the victory. According to the Ottoman traditions of war, if the city was taken in battle, the greater share of the plunder went to the army, but if the city was taken by siege, the greater part of the treasure taken would go to the Sultan and his commander. So Kara Mustafa laid a siege, but the time wasted, enabled an army to come to the rescue of the helpless city. The Turks were defeated, and their reputation as warriors to be feared was forever lost in the fields of Vienna. Kara Mustafa lost not just his dreams of treasure but also his life. The Sultan ordered his execution for his mishandling of the siege. His only words, when the noose was placed around his neck were, 'As God pleases.'

After the demise of Kara Mustafa, it was back to the Koprulus. This time, it was Zade Koprulu, an austere and simple man 'who never committed a crime and never used a superfluous word.' He refilled the treasury, refitted the navy, strengthened the army and replaced incompetent and corrupt governors with honest and reliable men. He was a devout Muslim who practiced toleration for other religions and he adopted a free trade policy which promoted the economy. But in less than two years, he was killed in battle.

The new Sultan, Mustafa II, was well-intentioned and realized that sultans were too frequently the slaves of pleasure. Choosing the army over his harem, he decided to march against the Austrians. At first it looked like a good move, but when he came up against Prince Eugene of Savoy, the most capable general of his time, his luck ran out. The Austrians defeated his army, killed his grand vizier, took immense loot and plunder and destroyed forever the hegemony of the Ottoman military power.

Once more the Sultan turned to the Koprulus, and two more grand viziers were appointed from the family. But it was too late. The glory days of the empire were over. Though it took another two centuries to end the Ottoman Empire, it now limped along, its life extended by the Europeans and Russians rather than by any strength of its own. The days of the two great families were over—the Usmanli sultans who had conquered and carved out an empire; and the Koprulu grand viziers who had, in its declining years, done such a great job in managing it for them. New heroes were to take over the centre stage—Peter the Great and Catherine, in Russia; Mehmed Ali Pasha in Egypt; the English commanders Nelson and Wellington; and towering above them all, a short young soldier from Corsica who was to rewrite history—Napoleon Bonaparte.

After the first ten sultans who created the empire, and after the time of the favoured women, the mad sultans and the Koprulu viziers, a new influence was to be seen during the reign of the next three sultans. This was 'The French Sultana' Aimee Dubucq de Rivery, a convent girl from Martinique who was captured by pirates and gifted to the Sultan. She combined beauty with intelligence and a noble character. The young Aimee won the heart of the old Sultan Abdul Hamid, and bore him a son, Mahmud. Later, she was unusually close to Abdul Hamid's nephew Salim III, who took no interest in his harem, never married and never had children, and finally she became the influential Sultana Valida during the reign of her son, Mahmud the Reformer. She was also a lady with powerful connections—her cousin and dear friend was Josephine, who married the young emperor Napoleon and became Empress of France. During her time, the French influence became predominant at the Ottoman court, and her grandson built the gigantic Dolmabace Palace.

After the death of Abdul Hamid, Salim was crowned and ruled for eighteen years with Aimee by his side to advise him and give him emotional support. The janissaries then mutinied and came after Salim to kill him. Salim saved himself by abdicating and changing places with his cousin Mustafa, the eldest son of the late Sultan Abdul Hamid who was interned in The Cage. Salim abdicated and retired to The Cage and Mustafa became Sultan. But then one of the generals, Bairactar, who was loyal to Salim, marched to the capital to restore him as Sultan. Bairactar intended to save Salim's life but his intervention was to achieve exactly the opposite result; Mustafa, to save his own life, ordered the execution of Salim and Mahmud. Salim was killed, but before Mahmud could be slaughtered by the rampaging janissaries, he hid under a pile of old carpets. Bairactar arrived with his soldiers, dragged Mustafa from the throne, and Mahmud became Sultan.

Mahmud rewarded him by appointing Bairactar as grand vizier.

Aimee, the Sultana Valida, who had started life as a captured Christian slave, supported and encouraged her son's reforms for almost a decade. When she finally lay on her death bed, Mahmud secretly called in a Catholic priest to perform his mother's last rites. As he withdrew the doctor and attendants, he whispered in the dying Sultana's ear, 'Mother, you wished to die in the religion of your fathers; let your wish be fulfilled.'

Mahmud pursued his reforms and prepared his new army on the French model. He could not rely on the janissaries who had killed his beloved cousin, Sultan Salim; had caused the death of his grand vizier; and had almost succeeded in killing him. Though he succeeded in restoring internal order in his empire, its territories were constantly being threatened and reduced, by Russia, by Napoleon, and finally by the remarkable new leader of Egypt, Muhammad Ali Pasha.

Mahmud wanted revenge on the janissaries, but he believed that revenge is a dish that is best served cold. He bided his time as he prepared his counterattack. Finally, in 1826, Mahmud made his move. He provoked the janissaries to revolt, but this time he was ready for the mutinous force that had become masters of government, butchers of their sultans and a source of terror to all save the enemies of their country. The janissaries were slaughtered to the last man; more than 10,000 were killed and this strange army, whose conquests had secured an empire, but then, degenerate and uncontrollable, had become its greatest threat, was eliminated once and for all. The massacre of the janissaries is referred to in Turkish history as 'The Auspicious Event'.

After destroying the janissaries, Mahmud had one more hurdle to cross before he could feel strong enough to push through his important reform program; he had to tame the opposition of the Sheikh-al-Islam, the most powerful official after the grand vizier, and to control the conservative fundamentalist forces that backed him. The Sultan successfully diluted his power and then proceeded with his extensive reform program that was to bring the empire of the Turks into the modern world. The administration, the army and the palace were modernized and westernized. The pattern of education was changed from the traditional madrassah system to a more western model. Offices were furnished in the European style with desks, tables and upright chairs; western clothes started to replace traditional costumes; European architecture replaced Islamic. Mahmud discouraged long beards. A new value system and a new morality in public service was imposed and enforced.

Mahmud was the third great reformer of the Ottoman Empire. Before him, Mehmed the Conqueror and Suleiman the Magnificent had the charisma and authority gained by their conquests. Mahmud's job was far more difficult, because he carried the handicap of being Sultan of a shrinking empire as large territories were lost to external enemies from three sides—in the north, Russia was determined to take the Ottoman territories occupied by Christians; in central Europe, Napoleon schemed and fought to replace old empires with his own new empire; and Mohammad Ali Pasha, who already controlled Egypt, was also dreaming of taking over the Ottoman Empire. All three had their eyes on Istanbul itself. But despite losing wars and territories, and presiding over an empire in decline, Mahmud can be credited for preparing the future of the Turkish nation. The fourth great reformer of the Turks was Ataturk, the Father of Modern Turkey, who exchanged an empire for a nation after the Second World War.

In 1838, Muhammad Ali Pasha declared the independence of Egypt. Mahmud declared war, and sent both an army and a fleet to deal with the Egyptian problem. Both expeditions met with disaster. The major part of his army deserted, bribed by Egyptian gold, and the commander of the Ottoman fleet sailed to Alexandria where he handed over all his ships to Muhammad Ali. This setback destroyed Mahmud, who died the following year. He was followed by the last six sultans of the Ottoman line—his two sons and his four grandsons.

The eldest son, Abdul Mecit, was sixteen years old when he was crowned Sultan. He was well-intentioned but weak; good intentions without strength, lead to nothing. His mother, a conservative lady, made her move; she threw into the Bosphorus, the remaining 50,000 bottles of Mahmud's champagne, brandy and wine! It is remarkable that despite his incompetence, the empire lost no more territory. The five great powers—England, Russia, France, Austria and Prussia—checkmated each other in a balance of power that protected and secured the interest of Turkey. Muhammad Ali was forced to withdraw and confine his ambitions to Egypt, and the Russians were driven back by defeat in the Crimean War.

Abdul Mecit was a big spender. He built the Dolmabace Palace, and a harem to match. His yearly living expenses topped $2 million a year. At this time, America purchased Alaska for $7 million. But though the Sultan spent much time and money on women, they were not a serious influence on affairs of state and neither was the government controlled by the grand viziers. For the first time, the most important influence on the Sultan was a remarkable ambassador from England—Sir Stratford Canning. It was his advice that enabled the Sultan to steer the tricky and dangerous waters of great power politics and to make the decisions that protected what was left of the empire, despite the feebleness of both army and state. The ambassador was a straightforward man with a strong code of honour who loved Turkey. After he retired, he invested his personal savings in Turkish bonds. When the Ottoman state fell into bankruptcy, Lord Stratford received insider information and was advised by a friend to sell his bonds before they crashed. But Stratford felt this was dishonourable, and opted rather to lose his savings. His sense of honour left his daughters impoverished, but they were saved by the support of a friend and admirer of the late ambassador who gave them a pension for as long as they lived.

When Abdul Mecit died, ravaged by tuberculosis and finally pneumonia, he was succeeded by his handsome but stupid younger brother, Abdul Aziz, who promised good government but delivered badly. He promised an economy drive and delivered extravagance on a greater scale than his brother. After clearing out the large harem of his brother, he eventually replaced it with one even larger, running to almost a thousand women and 3,000 eunuchs. With a state tottering under its debt to European financiers, he decided to visit Europe. This was the first time in Ottoman history that a sultan was to enter Europe without an army of conquest. He wasn't able to borrow more money in Europe, but had a good time with the chorus girls of the Folies Bergere; he returned with his exciting purchases—locomotives (though there were no tracks in his empire on which they could run) and naval destroyers (though there were no Turkish sailors who could put them to sea).

Abdul Aziz degenerated from stupid to insane, till finally he was removed in a coup d'etat by the reformist politician Midhat Pasha, who had risen in the administration over the years till he was entrusted with a series of provincial governorships. Abdul Aziz twice appointed him as grand vizier, and also entrusted him with various ministries, but his tenures of office were short-lived due to his commitment to constitutional reform, rather than to the Sultan's person.

THE LAST CHAPTER

1876 was an eventful year in the last chapter of the history of the Ottomans; it saw three sultans come and go and was also the year in which the new constitution was introduced. The deposed Abdul Aziz was removed to The Cage where he was found dead with his wrists slashed by a scissor which he had requested to trim his beard. The four sons of Abdul Mecit were in turn to become sultans. The first was Murad V, who was alcoholic and insane, and was removed within three months because he was obviously unfit to rule. He was followed by his brother Abdul Hamid II.

This strange man was to rule as an autocrat for the next thirty-three years. The West condemned him as 'The Red Sultan', a veritable Satan who was guilty of the Armenian massacres. The Islamists praised him as the greatest sultan after Suleiman the Magnificent. He was a poet, a wrestler and an avid fan of the *Sherlock Holmes* detective novels. He was also a contorted political genius—a statesman and diplomat par excellence. Few rulers in history have had to face the adversities that surrounded him and that he effectively held them at bay throughout his long rule.

He inherited a crumbling and bankrupt empire in which the reformers at home, led by the outstanding politician, Midhat Pasha, had imposed a new constitution to replace the total power of the sultans with constitutional government. These reformers were western in their attitudes and values. Over the centuries, the vast conquests of the Ottomans in Europe had created an empire in which the majority of its subjects were Christian, and the Muslims were reduced to a minority. Midhat Pasha dreamed of an empire which was neither Muslim nor non-Muslim, but only Ottoman, in which a constitution would prevail; a constitution that granted equal rights to all citizens, regardless of religion or race, abolished slavery and enforced a legal code based on civilian, not Sharia law. Abdul Hamid, though forced to go along with this reform program at first, strongly believed that this formula would lead to disaster. He saw Europe as his enemy, a pack of wolves eager to devour what they could snatch from his empire under the guise of protecting the Christians in Ottoman lands. The rise of the nations of Europe who were making inroads into the Ottoman Empire, and even England—posing as friends who were to take Egypt and the Sudan in 1882—made him wary, even paranoid.

Within a year of the promulgation of the new constitution, in 1877, Abdul Hamid moved to rid himself of Midhat Pasha, who was invited to board the royal yacht and promptly banished into exile. The short experiment of parliamentary government was over; all power once again rested in the Sultan. However, in a year, the irrepressible Midhat was back, this time as the governor of Syria. But Abdul Hamid was relentless, and in 1881, Midhat was charged with the murder of the late Sultan Abdul Aziz, the uncle of Abdul Hamid, who, after he was deposed, had been found dead with his wrists slashed. The previous finding of suicide was now replaced by the murder conviction of Midhat Pasha, who was given the death sentence. The Sultan commuted the sentence to banishment and imprisonment in Ta'if in Arabia, where, under the Sultan's orders, the great patriot was assassinated in his cell on 26 April 1883.

Now Abdul Hamid ruled with total control from his secure headquarters at Yildiz with his vast network of spies throughout the country, who could constantly communicate with the Sultan through the new telegraph lines. He was a dictator with Pan-Islamism as his creed. Modernization and improvement of the state moved at a fast pace with the construction of schools, railways, harbours, irrigation works, and improvements in finance, trade and the economy. He was opposed by the Young Turks, a new political party which later changed its name to The Committee of Union and Progress (CUP), but the Sultan remained popular with his people.

Abdul Hamid was approached by Theodor Herzl who was looking for land to establish a state for the Jews and offered 150 million sterling to the Sultan; Abdul Hamid refused the offer and rebuffed Herzl: 'Even if you gave me as much gold as the entire world, let alone £150 million, I would never accept what you ask of me.' The founding of the state of Israel was thus delayed but eventually, with support from Europe, they took their land in the middle of the former Ottoman Empire. Years later, King Faisal of Saudi Arabia was to ask why the Muslim Arabs were forced to sacrifice their territories to compensate the Jews, who had been driven from their homes by the Christian states of Europe. He asked a poignant question, 'if the Christians torture the Jews and take their homes and their businesses, why are the Muslim punished for this crime?'

Extremist groups tried to assassinate the Sultan, first by a bomb attack in 1896, then an assassin with a knife in 1904, and finally a dynamite blast in 1905; but though his attendants were killed or wounded, he survived unscathed. The Armenian Christians, with support from Christian kingdoms of Europe, had rebelled with acts of terrorism and violence against the state and were believed to be behind the assassination attempts. The Turks retaliated hard with the Armenian Massacres, which further alienated them from the powerful European states. Retaliation in conflict has always been cruel, whether by the Turks against the Armenians; by the Americans against the

Japanese at the end of the Second World War; or by President Bush in his attacks on Afghanistan and Iraq after 9/11. But the atrocities of defeated regimes always meet greater condemnation than the atrocities of victorious regimes.

Recognizing that his isolation was increasing, Abdul Hamid opened a new alliance with Germany to counter the powerful but hostile European nations and Kaiser Willhelm II paid a state visit to Istanbul where he was courted by the Sultan. When the German Empress complimented the Sultan on his beautiful gardens, he personally picked and presented her with a bouquet. Nestled amongst the flowers was a massive diamond ring—his gift to the Empress.

In 1908, he ordered a general election, but this was a miscalculation. The CUP won all but one of the 288 seats in parliament. Muslim fundamentalists resisted with street demonstrations, but it was too late. The army moved in, seized Istanbul and took the stamp of approval from the Sheikh al-Islam, on a fatwa that Abdul Hamid was unworthy to rule. The Yildiz palace was stormed, and the lonely old Sultan ate the cold leftovers of the servants' dinner and tried to sleep while his attendant read to him from *The Adventures of Sherlock Holmes*. He was arrested and deported to the villa that was to be his home till he died in 1917 in the arms of the sole wife who remained with him. Her epitaph for her husband was: 'He was the kindest and most understanding of masters, but he never loved anyone, least of all himself.'

In turn, his two brothers were enthroned—old men, broken by half a century of confinement in The Cage. Real power lay with the triumvirate—Enver, Talat and Jemal—the three heroes of the day; soon to become the villains of tomorrow. As Europe moved into the First World War, the triumvirate made the miscalculation of joining the German side. When Germany was defeated, they fled, never to return again to their homeland. Talat was shot dead in Berlin, Jemal was assassinated in Georgia and Enver was killed in action in Turkistan.

ATATURK, THE FATHER OF THE TURKS

Enver was the most charismatic of the triumvirate. He was handsome, dashing and fancied himself as a soldier of destiny. He married an Ottoman princess, lived in a palace and was the darling of the people. He disliked and, in turn, was disliked by the ambitious young soldier Mustapha Kemal, whose career was stalemated by the powerful Enver.

But Mustapha Kemal was a hard man to keep down. Despite the immense difficulties in his early career, Mustafa Kemal was the true man of destiny, the hero who was to succeed against the impossible and was to become the founder of the new nation of Turkey that he was to carve out of the collapsing empire. Mustafa Kemal is remembered as Ataturk—the father of the Turks.

Mustafa was born in a struggling middle class family. His father, like the father of Adolf Hitler, was a minor customs official. His mother, like the mother of Stalin, envisioned a religious career for her son. In school, Mustafa excelled in mathematics and his ambition was to become a soldier. Despite being handicapped by a class background which left him devoid of connections or a network, by the disapproval of his superiors to his revolutionary tendencies and by his blunt and undiplomatic ways in a conservative society, he rose in the army due to one quality above all—he was the greatest soldier of his time, not just of Turkey, but perhaps in the world. He was the only general never to lose a battle—he defeated the Australians, New Zealanders and British at Gallipoli and the Greeks at Smyrna, and forced the victorious allies who had just won the World War to back down rather than start a new war with Turkey. He was a tactician and strategist without equal, totally dedicated to saving and rebuilding his country by withdrawing from the empire and creating the new nation of Turkey.

Gallipoli was the defining moment in Ataturk's early career; victory at Gallipoli made a national hero of the unknown soldier, Mustafa Kemal, and won him recognition and respect, both in the army and in the nation. The entry of the Ottomans into the war in support of Germany blocked the access of Russia, an ally of Britain and France, into the Mediterranean. The Russian ports in the Black Sea were closed by the bottleneck of the Dardanelles and the Bosphorus, straddled by the guns of Istanbul. So Britain decided to take control of the Dardanelles, conquer Istanbul and open the sea route for the Russians. Churchill, the First Lord of the Admiralty, was the key proponent of the Gallipoli campaign, and moved the British navy and the Australian and New Zealand troops into the Dardanelles. It looked like a brilliant and easy victory, and the British mocked the Turkish troops who were more eager to surrender than to engage in battle. But Churchill had not recognized the military genius of Ataturk who, over a nine-month campaign, totally routed the invading army. Defeat at Gallipoli resulted in the demotion of Churchill from his office and was an important factor in the collapse of the Asquith government in Britain, which led to the termination of the military career of Sir Ian Hamilton, the British commander of the Middle East force. Years later, Lloyd George, the prime minister of the UK was to say of Ataturk, his enemy: 'The centuries rarely produce a genius. It was our bad luck that the great genius of our era was granted to the Turkish nation.'

In 1919, the government in Istanbul sent Ataturk to the east to deal with the bandits there who had made a mockery of the rule of the Sultan and his cabinet. They saw a chance to kill two birds with one stone, to get rid of the bandits and to get rid of the troublesome general. Kemal, however, saw in the posting an opportunity, and tricked the government into giving him all the authority and powers that he needed for his plans. Realizing their mistake, the grand vizier ordered Kemal to return immediately but Kemal was no longer in a mood to obey orders from Istanbul. He refused to return, took off his uniform and resigned from the army. But by now his authority needed no uniform. His stature, reputation and political skill won him adherents. His four friends became his principal lieutenants—Rauf, the man of principle; the loyal Kiazim; brave Refet; and the practical Ali Fuad. Even the bandits joined Kemal as he repeatedly offered the only political solution in the face of every crisis.

Between 1919 and 1922, Ataturk led the Nationalist forces to victory in the Turkish War of Independence. He fought the British, the French and their allies and proxies—the Greeks in the west and the Armenians in the east. When the defeated Greek generals were brought before him, he offered words of consolation: 'War is a game of chance. You have done your best. The responsibility rests with Luck. Do not be distressed.' The war ended with the Treaty of Lausanne, the nation of Turkey was born and the Sultan sent into exile; Ataturk had won.

Kemal had already shown that he was a great soldier; he now showed that he was an even greater statesman. When the Sultan and his government in Istanbul refused to recognize his legitimacy, he responded by refusing to recognize their government. When the Istanbul government sought survival by collaborating with the powerful allies who had just defeated their enemies in the World War, he donned the nationalist cloak as the only patriot determined to fight, and if need be, die for his country. When the Sultan called for an election, Ataturk's Nationalists swept the polls.

Kemal was a general who was always ready for war, and who never lost a battle. He was a general who took power through the democratic process but who recognized that great achievements required great men in command, not muddle-headed committees. He told his intimate associates that the only effective form of government was the rule of one man. When questioned what he meant, he replied, 'I mean that I will have everyone do as I wish; carry out what I command.' He had total faith in his convictions and believed that he was always right. Unfortunately for his opponents, he always was; the Sultan, his political rivals, and the Greeks, Armenians and Britain were to recognize this in conflict after conflict. Even the great British politician, Churchill, learnt by bitter experience that it was not safe to attack Ataturk.

In the three years between 1919 and 1922, Ataturk made the following achievements:

- Drove out the Sultan
- Abolished the caliphate
- Fought and won the war against the Greeks
- Bluffed Great Britain to a standstill at Chanak
- Negotiated through his deputy, Ismet Pasha, the Treaty of Lausanne
- Established expanded frontiers for the new state of Turkey
- Wrote a new constitution
- Created a parliament
- Created the new capital of Ankara

But all this was just a preamble to his bigger achievements when in power, which included:

- Modernization of his country
- Emancipation of women and the right to vote
- Westernization of dress and culture
- Replacement of the traditional Arabic script by a new Latin script for reading and writing
- Introduction of widespread modern scientific education in place of the madrassah system
- A new infrastructure of roads, bridges, communication, schools and hospitals
- Replacement of the traditional judicial system with a new secular system
- Replacement of the religious elite with a modern bureaucracy
- The creation of a new opposition party to dilute the monopoly of power of his ruling party

Ataturk is recognized as one of the greatest nation builders of modern times, admired and respected by friend and foe alike. Franklin D. Roosevelt, the American president, described him as 'the most valuable and interesting leader in the world.' His objective was to change Turkey and the Turkish people. He was determined that 'My people are going to learn the principles of democracy, the dictates of truth and the teachings of science.' He demanded sacrifice: 'Men, I am not ordering you to attack. I am ordering you to die.' But his followers knew that what he demanded, he was equally ready to give. He survived two assassination attempts—one, a bomb; the second, poison. He took a defeated people surrounded by determined foes, and left them a strong nation without a single enemy. Ataturk was a modern man and one of the greatest Muslim leaders of the twentieth century. He closed forever, the Ottoman centuries and created the new nation of Turkey, whose name he took for himself.

16

The Birth of Modern Egypt

'I can learn nothing from this man. And as regards cunning, I know far more about it than he.'

—Muhammad Ali Pasha (His comment after reading forty pages of Machiavelli's *The Prince*)

The Egypt, described by the librarian, Ameneman, in the time of the Pharoahs, endured for 3,000 years till it was changed by two great men—Mohammed Ali, the founder of modern Egypt; and Gamal Abdul Nasser, the leader of the Free Officers and their revolution in the twentieth century.

When Salim the Grim conquered Egypt, he left an Ottoman viceroy, or pasha, to govern on his behalf. He had smashed Mamluk power, but he allowed the Mamluks who remained, to govern the twelve provinces which he created, under the Ottoman Pasha. For over 280 years of Ottoman rule in Egypt, a hundred pashas came and went; Mamluk power once again grew, while Ottoman power faded. By the end of the eighteenth century, the Mamluks were again effectively in control of Egypt.

In 1798, Napoleon landed in Egypt with his army. He was

but one more foreign conqueror in the long list of those who had ruled Egypt after the Pharaohs—the Persians in 525 BC, Alexander and his Greeks, Caesar from Rome, the Muslim Arabs under Amr bin al-As, the Shia Fatimids from Tunis, Saladin the Kurd representing the Abbasid caliphate in Baghdad, the Mamluk slave dynasties who ruled Egypt for 600 years, and the great Ottoman conqueror Salim the Grim.

Napoleon announced that he had come to punish the Mamluks because they were not true Muslims, and he would restore the authority of the Ottomans. The true reason was to checkmate the British by cutting off their communication with India, the jewel in the crown of the British Empire. He was determined to create his own world empire, and Egypt was the first stepping stone in Asia. He wrote to his brother, 'Europe is a molehill. There have never been great empires and revolutions except in the East. Egypt is richer than any other country in the world... If all goes well, it will enable me to get to India.' It took Napoleon one day to conquer Egypt, and he immediately set up his administration. In order to win the approval of the Egyptians, Napoleon publically expressed his respect and sympathy for Islam, and some believed that he was close to conversion, but the reality is that Napoleon, like Akbar the Great, recognized the power of religion and used it to manipulate his subjects. Very soon after his army defeated the Egyptians in the Battle of the Pyramids, the British fleet destroyed his navy at the Battle of the Nile. Nelson, Britain's greatest naval commander, attacked the French fleet with speed, genius and daring. He destroyed the French ships, killed the French admiral, and sunk the French flagship together with half a million pounds of gold and diamonds, stolen from the Swiss republic to finance the expedition to Egypt. Napoleon had conquered Egypt, but was now trapped there.

To make matters worse, he received news that in Paris, his wife Josephine was carrying on a love affair with her dancing teacher Hippolyte Charles. Napoleon, who had never yet been unfaithful to Josephine, decided to get even. In Egypt, he would find a trophy mistress, his 'Cleopatra'. Pauline Foures was the wife of a junior French officer, a pretty blonde with a sense of adventure. When Napoleon set eyes on her at an officers' ball, he was smitten. But Napoleon was no Caesar or Mark Antony, and his clumsy efforts at seduction met with little success. Finally, a dramatic seduction was staged over a lunch at the palace, where General Junot spilled coffee over her dress and ushered her into an adjoining room to change. Napoleon left the dining table, where her husband was being entertained by his senior generals, burst into her changing room and threw himself down on his knees, declaring love. Pauline was not interested and burst out crying. But the determined Napoleon persevered, and Pauline finally became his mistress. Her husband returned from the front to discover his wife had moved in with his commander-in-chief and had no wish to meet him.

There was no future for Napoleon in Egypt and he had to get back to Paris; not to confront his unfaithful Josephine, but to take the opportunity presented by the shifting political situation there. Leaving both his army and his mistress, he secretly departed and made his way home. He left General Kleber in command of both his army and the practical Pauline, who, now having acquired a taste for generals, became Kleber's mistress. Kleber was assassinated within a year and was succeeded by General Jacques Menou, who married an Egyptian, converted to Islam and changed his name to Abdullah Jacques Menou.

REIGN OF MOHAMMAD ALI

Napoleon did not have a lasting impact on Egypt, but Mohammed Ali, who followed him, did. Credited as the founder of modern Egypt, he changed the face of the country under his fifty-year rule. Mohammed Ali, an Albanian soldier serving the Ottoman Sultan, was sent to Egypt to deal with the problems created by Napoleon and the Mamluks. In the power vacuum after Napoleon's departure, he took effective power. This brilliant and ruthless man was to secure independence for

Egypt from Ottoman sovereignty and create a dynasty that ruled till it was removed by Nasser's revolution. He was inspired by Napoleon, and carefully studied his life and his writings. He was not, however, impressed by Machiavelli, and after forty pages by the Italian maestro of realpolitik was read out to him, he remarked, 'I can learn nothing from this man. And as regards cunning, I know far more about it than he.' It was not an idle boast, as he showed by success after success through his rule.

Mohammad Ali was orphaned at a young age. He started his working life as a tax collector, became a tobacco trader and then joined the Ottoman army. He came to Egypt with the troops sent to deal with Napoleon. When Napoleon and the British departed, Mohammad Ali remained as the second-in-command of the Ottoman garrison. One morning, the head of the commander was found dead; he had been killed in the night. Mohammad Ali became the commander and Pasha. But two important Mamluk chiefs, Elfi and Bardissy, persuaded the Sultan in Istanbul that Mohammad Ali was not the right man for the job, and an Ottoman admiral arrived from Istanbul with royal orders for the transfer of Mohammad Ali to Greece. The Pasha was not keen to go and bribed the admiral to convince his master, the Sultan, to keep him in Egypt. The Sultan's main concern was money, and the admiral persuaded him that there would be more money coming from Egypt if the Pasha was in charge of the collection. The transfer orders were cancelled and shortly after, the two Mamluks suddenly died. The remaining Mamluks decided that it was better to kiss the hand they could not bite, and committed their support to Mohammad Ali, who, after defeating a British contingent of soldiers, had become a hero of the Egyptians. The unfortunate British soldiers were marched off to the slave market through an avenue of severed British heads.

Mohammad Ali's first concern was to consolidate his position, and this meant dealing with the Mamluks. He invited 500 Mamluks to a banquet where they were all slaughtered. Only one of the invitees failed to show up; perhaps he was a student of history and had read of the Abbasid invitation of the Umayyads to a dinner, centuries before—a trap where they were slaughtered. He alone survived, fleeing from Egypt.

The Pasha then concentrated on building up the economy of Egypt, and conquering the territories around him—the Arabian Peninsula, Sudan, Greece and then Syria. His first overseas expedition at the request of the Sultan in Istanbul was against the Wahhabi uprising in Arabia. The Wahhabis were a new force in Arabia, created by the alliance of the religious reformer Abdul Wahhab, with the Saudi chieftain, Muhammad bin Saud. At this time, led by a grandson, Abdullah bin Saud, they had conquered the holy cities of Mecca and Medina which were under Ottoman suzerainty. The Ottomans wanted their territory back. After seven years of war, the Wahhabis were finally subdued, in 1818, by Ibrahim, the talented son of the Pasha.

Muhammad Ali was lucky to have a son of the calibre of Ibrahim, a daring and fearless soldier with exceptional judgement and intelligence in warfare. He totally lacked the cunning, political guile or suave diplomacy of his father, but he was truthful, disciplined and methodical. He controlled his troops by fear and respect. Ibrahim finally defeated the Wahhabis at Dariyah, their last stronghold. Abdullah bin Saud came to the tent of Ibrahim to concede defeat; he tried to kiss the hand of the victor, but Ibrahim withdrew his hand—he did not want to humiliate a foe whose bravery he respected. When Abdullah said that the war has ended—such are the decrees of fate—Ibrahim offered to supply him guns and ammunition if he wished to fight further! 'No,' said Abdullah. 'God has willed my humiliation.' In Cairo, Muhammad Ali gave the defeated Abdullah full respect, and when he dispatched his prisoner to Istanbul, even pleaded with the Sultan to spare his life. But after three days of being paraded in Istanbul, Abdullah was decapitated. Dariyah was levelled, its date trees cut down, and the inhabitants moved out. But this was not to be the end of the story of Saud and Wahhab. A century later, a descendent of Abdullah, the great Abdul Aziz ibn Saud, was to again conquer this land and create the twentieth-century kingdom of Saudi Arabia.

Though the conquest of Arabia was a success, the invasion of Sudan was not. Conquering was easy, but the conquest proved futile. The purpose of the Sudan expedition was to take the gold, which, according to rumour, was available in abundance, and to capture slaves who could augment the Egyptian army. However, there was no gold, and the slaves had no immunity against the new diseases and germs that they were exposed to; of the 20,000 Sudanese slaves that were taken to fight as soldiers in the Egyptian army, barely 3,000 survived. Ismail, another son of the Pasha, who led the expedition in Sudan, was burned to death in a sneak attack on his tent. Muhammad Ali was torn by grief, and ordered massacre in retaliation, killing 50,000 Sudanese. Half a century later, another would-be conqueror, the British general Gordon, also met his death in Sudan, fighting the Mehdi, a religious reformer who rose in revolt against the British infidels. Gordon was avenged by a small force led by General Kitchener, who mowed down thousands of Sudanese with his new automatic weapon, the Maxim gun, leading Hilaire Beloc to compose his little ditty to explain British invincibility in the era of colonial conquest:

'Whatever happens we have got
The Maxim gun, and they have not.'

Greece still remained under Ottoman control, and now at Morea, revolt took place. The Sultan requested the assistance of Muhammad Ali, and Ibrahim was sent with a fleet and an army to deal with the situation. Once again, Ibrahim proved himself a master of the art of war, and soon Greek slaves were to be seen crowding the slave market of Cairo. But it was not Greece that the Pasha coveted, it was Syria. Success had gone to his head, and now the Pasha overstepped himself.

Ibrahim marched his army into Syria, where cities fell to him and every encounter resulted in one more victory. Three times he faced the Turks in battle; three times he defeated them till his army was within a hundred miles of Istanbul. Was this to be the end of the Ottoman Empire? The army of the Turks was no match for the Egyptian army under Ibrahim Pasha. But the powerful states of Europe were not willing to see Istanbul fall. The delicate balance of power between the Russians, British, Germans, Austrians and French, required the maintenance of the Ottoman Empire. Negotiations were initiated by the British to create a stable balance between the old and impotent Empire and its province, Egypt, which was not yet a state but already an empire. Finally, an agreement was reached. Muhammad Ali would give back the Ottoman fleet that had deserted and come across to join him, and would vacate Syria; in return, the Sultan would confer on him the hereditary right to rule Egypt. Accepting the nominal suzerainty of the Sultan, Muhammad Ali gave up an empire in return for a dynasty.

No less significant than his conquests were the internal changes and reforms that he made to the social structure and economy of Egypt. Napoleon had promised liberty but had only delivered bureaucracy. Muhammad Ali substituted this with an efficient dictatorship and state control, or rather his personal control of national assets. Land, industry and even trade was controlled by the Pasha. He ordered what was to be produced and how it was to be produced. He improved irrigation and increased the acreage under cultivation. He built infrastructure and factories. He introduced long-grain cotton into general cultivation. Muhammad Ali, himself illiterate till the age of forty-seven, attached the highest importance to education; he built schools and also sent promising Egyptian students to colleges in Europe. The only time he was seen angry with his children was when they neglected their studies. He fully understood the importance of skilled and educated manpower, and used trusted European advisors when local talent was not available. Suleiman Pasha trained his army officers and Clot Bey supervised his hospitals and educational facilities—both were French. The top level administrators were Turk, not Egyptian, but he was determined to change that and followed a policy of Egyptianization.

When Muhammad Ali took power over Egypt, justice was a matter of bribes; property, a matter of favour; and life, a matter of luck. Governors did not even pretend that they sought to promote public welfare, but shamelessly pursued their own advantage. The Pasha hated corruption, and his personal life was simple and austere. He loved and pursued fame and power but cared nothing for money except as a means to great ends. His economic policy was simple—raise production and reduce expenditure. His budgets saw more surpluses and fewer deficits, and the treasury grew. He placed much trust in his Armenian finance minister, Boghoz Bey, and kept out of the clutches of the European moneylenders who had started to circle his state. He worked under pressure, saying, 'I am old and what I would have done, must be done quickly.'

But the Pasha was not just growing old, he was also failing in health. When he suffered from dysentery, his doctors prescribed silver nitrate as a cure, but the result was massive brain damage which led to bouts of madness. Muhammad Ali was unfit to rule, and in 1848, the government passed to his son Ibrahim. But Ibrahim, too, had his own health problems; he suffered from tuberculosis and a few months later, he was dead, followed within a year by his father. Abbas, the grandson of Muhammad Ali, succeeded him and immediately stopped work on the Pasha's nation-building projects. Instead, he diverted the funds to building his new palaces. Abbas reversed the policies of his capable grandfather, and quickly set in motion the decline of the emerging empire. Luckily for Egypt, his reign was short; after an uninspiring five years, he was assassinated.

Abbas was succeeded by Said who was weak and lacked self-discipline. As a young boy he was always fat, and Muhammad Ali, the disciplinarian, would order him to run up and down the palace stairs to lose weight; but despite the exercise and the diet, Said just kept growing fatter. In secret, he was being fed plates of spaghetti by his French friend, Ferdinand de Lesseps. Now as ruler, he rewarded his friend with a magnificent contract, to build a canal at Suez. The terms were generous, and despite the legal hurdles, work on the great undertaking started; in fact, the canal was half finished before all formal permissions were finally obtained. The cost was £20 million, and the terms were considered onerous on Egypt, which provided much of the money and all of the backbreaking labour for building the canal; 100,000 Egyptians are said to have died on the job. Opened in 1869, the canal gave Britain its gateway to India; to the Egyptians it gave nothing for the next eighty-eight years.

Said started the canal project; his nephew, Ismail, saw it to its completion. Ismail was the second son of the great general, Ibrahim, and had been sent off to school in France. When his elder brother died in a train accident in an inaugural trip, plunging headlong into a river where the engineers had forgotten to build a bridge, Ismail became the ruler. He had imbibed the lessons of modernization from his grandfather, and he set about transforming Egypt with a vengeance. He built infrastructure, communications, roads, bridges, harbours and industry, and he modernized the administration and also the military. He even built an opera house. He was named Ismail the Magnificent. At first, money was not a problem, since the American Civil War had destroyed the cotton production of the confederate states, resulting in escalating cotton prices around the world, which provided a financial boom to Egypt. His wealth and grandeur attracted moneylenders from Europe. But his grand plans outpaced his money supply and soon Ismail and Egypt were head-over-heels in debt. Ismail had changed the face of Egypt, but at the expense of bankrupting his country.

Ismail wanted the independence of Egypt and tried to bribe the Sultan and his ministers in Istanbul to achieve his objective. The Sultan kept the money but did not give independence; instead, as a compromise, he gave Ismail the title of 'Khedive', with the right of hereditary succession of the eldest son. In his juggling of assets, Ismail bought the title of Khedive but sold Egypt's shares in the Suez Canal Company. The buyer was Britain, the price was £4 million, and the financier was the banker, Lord Rothschild. Ten years after the opening of the canal, in 1879, the British were getting worried about their investments in Egypt. They prevailed on the Sultan in Istanbul to issue a firman deposing Ismail. Ismail listened to the letter of deposition in silence; he then summoned his son Taufiq, kissed his hand and said, 'I salute you, my Khedive.' Ismail sailed to Italy in exile, taking with him whatever cash remained in the treasury.

SEEDS OF REVOLT

Bankruptcy, inflation and the loss of dignity as the infidels from Europe dominated Egypt, led to a rising nationalism. An important instigator of public discontent was the political activist and revolutionary, Jamal al-din Afghani, who had arrived from the east. He was born in Asadabad; there were two towns of that name, one in Iran, one in Afghanistan—and both countries claim him. He was an advocate of Pan-Islamic unity and stressed that western science rather than western culture was the way to meet the western challenge and dominance. He sowed seeds of revolt in a string of countries, including India, Afghanistan, Uzbekistan, Iran, Turkey and Egypt. In each of these countries, he first achieved prominence and respect, and then, falling foul of the establishment, was expelled. In Afghanistan, he was tutor to the son of the King. In Iran, he was involved in judicial reform and then for a while, was made advisor to the King to spearhead his political attack on the ulema, but instead he attacked the King. In Egypt, he was a renowned teacher at the famous Al-Azhar University, till his attacks on the lifestyle of the rich and famous led to his midnight arrest and his deportation in his nightshirt. In Istanbul, he received the patronage and protection of Sultan Abdul Hamid till the latter died from cancer. And in Egypt, he inspired three of his students, who were later to become prominent—Mohammed Abduh, who became the grand mufti; Saad Zagloul, who dominated the politics of Egypt with his Wafd party; and the Medhi, who led an uprising in Sudan and massacred the British force, led by General Gordon.

The weak Khedive vacillated between the rising Islamic nationalism and the demanding British imperial power, till he was confronted by the demands of Colonel Urabi and his fellow officers in the Egyptian army. In an army which was dominated by Turkish pashas, Urabi and his small group of lieutenants were Egyptian—sons of the soil. When the Army High Command arrested Urabi, his regiment mutinied and released him in an effective coup. Urabi negotiated with the Khedive and was appointed minister of war with power to select the new cabinet. The pashas were out; the nationalists were in. The British, fearing a repeat of the mutiny in India, moved to restore a balance of power more to their liking. Bombardment followed by fire in Alexandria, which consumed the European quarter, and looting of shops resulted in a clear-cut rift between the palace and the nationalists. The Khedive, Taufiq, sought the protection of the British.

The final showdown took place at the battle of Tel el Kabir. The night before the battle, Egyptian spies mistook the kilted soldiers of the Black Watch regiment, for women, and a raiding party came out to capture them for an evening of fun. Surprised at the ferocity of the resistance of the 'women', the Egyptians retreated, apprehensive of the 'men' of the British army that they would face in the battle the next day. In a fast and total victory, the British destroyed Urabi's forces. Taufiq heaped honours on the British and disbanded what was left of the Egyptian army, thinking he had won; in fact, he had lost. It was the British who had won by a conquest that would endure till 1954 when Nasser's revolution was to restore power to the Egyptians. After defeat at Tel el Kabir, Egypt was a conquered nation. Under the Veiled Protectorate that followed, the Khedive reigned but the British ruled. All power lay with the new governor-general, the arrogant banker Lord Cromer, who rarely left his residency and lost no opportunity of humiliating the Egyptians as he set about restoring the economy to ensure the repayment of loans to the financiers back in Europe.

In 1907, Cromer resigned as Egyptian nationalism grew. The new governor tried to placate public feeling by appointing Boutros Pasha Ghali, an Egyptian, as prime minister. The new prime minister was certainly an Egyptian, but he was not a Muslim. He was a Copt, and when he moved to promote European interests by extending the concession of the Suez Canal Company, he was assassinated.

THE WARS THAT CHANGED HISTORY

The First World War was the game changer in the history of Egypt and the Middle East. When the Turks joined the Germans, the British declared Egypt a Protectorate under Martial Law and deposed the Khedive, now known as the Sultan, and installed a more suitable puppet. Meanwhile a new political leader, Saad Zagloul, was emerging with his new Wafd Party demanding independence. Riots, strikes and non-cooperation first met a determined resistance from the British who sent Zagloul into exile. But in 1922, the Protectorate was abolished, Martial Law removed and Egypt was declared independent. Elections in 1924 brought the Wafd Party and Zagloul to power. But four areas of policy were reserved for the British:

- The defence of Egypt against foreign aggression
- The security of the Suez Canal
- The protection of foreign interests and minorities
- The Sudan

Zagloul was a hero with mass appeal as compared to King Fuad who was seen as a Turk who could barely speak Arabic. Zagloul seemed invincible, but when the commander-in-chief of the Egyptian army, an Englishman named Sir Lee Stack, was assassinated, blame fell on Zagloul who was forced to resign, forever ending his meteoric career in power politics. Zagloul died in 1927 at the age of seventy, having given Egypt democracy with its new culture of violence, corruption and patronage; a prototype of the new Third World democracies, where personal rivalry and self-advantage take the place of principle in the skirmishes for the struggle for power.

Leadership of the Wafd Party was taken over by Nahas, under whom corruption flourished. His wife soon became notorious as a centre of dirty deals. Whenever there was an election, the Wafd was returned, but immediately the King and the palace elite would conspire with the British to dilute their power. The power of the Wafd lay in the vote and with the street mob; the power of the King lay in the

British soldiers stationed in Egypt.

The Second World War saw the struggle for North Africa between Britain and Germany, with Rommel, the Desert Fox, threatening Egypt with his tanks. Nahas now offered collaboration to the British who demanded that the King reinstate him as prime minister. When the King hesitated, the British troops marched on the palace and burst in on the King with their revolvers drawn and ready to fire. 'I have come for your answer,' asked the British ambassador. King Farouk replied, 'We have already instructed Nahas Pasha to form a government of his choice.' The Wafd Party which had emerged as hero in the struggle for independence had degenerated into collaborators with the British, and had lost the respect of the masses. After the war, the tired British, having created the new state of Israel, wanted to go home; the King, the pashas and the Wafd had all been exposed for the self-seekers that they were.

In 1948, war erupted between the Arab nations and the new state of Israel. The Egyptian army was not equipped for battle and the King sent his handpicked negotiators to Europe to buy armaments. They became millionaires through the hefty commissions they secured by purchasing sub-standard weapons which proved ineffective on the battlefront, and thousands of Egyptian soldiers lost their lives. The Muslim Brotherhood distinguished itself by the heroic martyrdom of many of its soldiers, but were rewarded by victimization and repression by the government of Nuqrashi, the prime minister of the time. Supporters of the Brotherhood assassinated the prime minister, and in retaliation, Hassan al-Banna, the leader of the Brotherhood was himself assassinated.

When British army units attacked a police station, killing a substantial number, riots erupted and the mob set fire to British clubs and businesses around Cairo. The city burned; it was the end of an era. The King, the pashas and the parliamentarians were all discredited. The Egyptian people needed a new hero and a new leadership. They were to find it in an idealistic young colonel—Gamal Abdul Nasser.

17

Saudi Arabia: The Rise of a World Power

'What we want is not a united Arabia, but a weak and disunited Arabia, split into little principalities incapable of coordinated action against us.'

—Lord Crewe (On the British policy on Arabia, after the First World War)

'His Majesty's Government view, with favour, the establishment in Palestine of a national home for the Jewish people and will use their best endeavours to facilitate the achievement of this object.'

—Lord Balfour, the British foreign secretary (His statement in a letter to Lord Rothschild)

Sayings of Abdul Aziz ibn Saud:

'They spin and spin—spin nets for me. What I cede of my rights under force, I will get back when I have sufficient force, Inshallah.'

SAUDI ARABIA: THE RISE OF A WORLD POWER

> *'There are two things that do not mix—running a government and making money. Do not compete with the merchants and they will not compete with you.'*

The glory of Arabia that was created by The Prophet of Islam lasted while the four righteous caliphs ruled the Muslim world from Medina, after which the capital of the Muslim world shifted in turn, to Damascus, Baghdad, Cordoba and Cairo. Leadership of the Muslims passed from the Arabs to the Persians and then to the Turks. For a thousand years, the Arabian Peninsula slumbered.

As the centuries clouded the memory of The Prophet and his message, superstition again ran rife in Arabia. Then in 1703, in the Nejd area of central Arabia, a remarkable man was born by the name of Muhammad ibn Abdul Wahhab, who was to change the destiny of Arabia. He was a pious and committed man of religion, influenced by ibn Taymiyyah who had lived centuries before and was a follower of ibn Hanbal, the founder of the Hanbali School of Islamic Jurisprudence. Both Taymiyyah and Hanbal had been persecuted and imprisoned for their beliefs, and Hanbal had even suffered lashing, but neither could be persuaded to recant. Ibn Taymiyyah issued the controversial fatwa allowing jihad against other Muslims. Muhammad ibn Wahhab was equally committed and determined. It would be his lifelong mission to bring the Muslims of Arabia back to the true path, away from deviation, superstition and idolatry. Wahhab was against the worship of shrines or saints, and even destroyed the dome over the tomb of Zayd, the brother of Hazrat Umar, the second caliph. Wahhab also opposed Shias whose special regard for Hazrat Ali and his family he considered excessive and against the spirit of Islam.

THE DESTINY OF ARABIA

Muhammad ibn Abdul Wahhab was given protection by Muhammad ibn Saud, a tribal chieftain from ad-Diriyah, a small town twenty miles from Riyadh. The alliance that the religious reformer formed with the warrior chieftain was cemented by the marriage of their children, led to the conquest of Arabia, and has endured for 270 years. Wahhab was the founder of the Wahhabi sect of the Muslims. In a community that was basically illiterate, Wahhab was a religious scholar, whose father and grandfather had both been judges. He possessed a small but well-read library, and himself wrote sixteen books. He advocated austerity and imposed hard punishments on those who drank, smoked, stole or committed adultery. He demanded that Muslims strictly follow the Islamic duties of praying and fasting, and that they stay away from luxury and frivolity.

At that time, Riyadh was ruled by Dahham ibn Dawwas, who was notorious for his cruelty. Stories were told of how he had once ordered a woman's mouth to be sown up as a punishment, and of how he had forced one of his prisoners to eat his own flesh. For twenty-five years, ibn Saud and Dawwas waged war. After a bad defeat in 1764, Muhammad ibn Saud died, and his son Abd al-Aziz became Emir. Finally in 1773, Abd al-Aziz conquered Riyadh and a few years later his eldest son, Saud, became heir-apparent and took effective control of the army.

Saud consolidated the Saudi–Wahhabi hold over the Nejd in central Arabia. He then moved westwards and defeated the army of the Sharif of Mecca in 1796 and again in 1798. Saud then went himself to Mecca as a pilgrim. Soon after, in the spring of 1802, a force of 10,000 Wahhabi soldiers attacked Karbala in Iraq, massacred 2,000 men, women and children, plundered the city and demolished tombs including the revered dome over the grave of Imam Husayn. Six months later, they invaded Ta'if in the Hejaz, terrifying the residents there with plunder and slaughter.

Finally, Saud took Mecca and Medina. Now fully confident, he could afford to be softer in his approach. But nevertheless, tombs were destroyed. He even stripped the gold and jewels from the tomb of The Prophet, but did not destroy the dome because ibn Abdul Wahhab had said that though he did not like people to pray at the tomb, he would not want to see the dome destroyed. With the Wahhabis in control of Mecca and Medina, the number of international pilgrims fell substantially. Saud and his Wahhabis now started raiding Iraq, reaching up to the outskirts of Baghdad, and the villages south of Damascus, in what is today, Syria. They justified their raids into Ottoman territory on the grounds that the Ottoman Sultan wore silk, drank alcohol and did not follow the law of Sharia, which made him a fair target for jihad. The Sultan in Istanbul was not amused.

The Sultan asked his viceroy in Cairo to deal with the Wahhabis. Both adversaries—Muhammad Ali in Cairo and Saud al-Kabir in Arabia—were great leaders, though very different in their characters. For the Wahhabis, it was home turf, but the Egyptians were a western-style, disciplined army with modern guns. Religious fervour and bravery were no match against modern technology, and in 1812, Muhammad Ali's army defeated the Wahhabis and took Medina. Mecca surrendered without a fight and the Hejaz was back in the Ottoman fold.

Taking Mecca and Medina was the easy part. Defeating Saud was more difficult, because their base of Riyadh was protected by the vast desert which was home to the Saudis but hell to the foreign invaders. Muhammad Ali called a meeting back in Cairo where he placed an apple in the centre of a large carpet. The carpet was the desert, he said, and the apple was Riyadh; who could find a way to take the apple without stepping on the carpet? His son Ibrahim, already a distinguished general, rolled up the carpet and picked up the apple—he knew how to think outside the box!

Ibrahim found that bribing the Bedouins was much easier than fighting them. Gold and the cancellation of the zakat tax, led to widespread desertions from the Wahhabi cause. By April 1818, he was at the gates of ad-Diriyah, and after a five month siege, Abdullah surrendered, and was sent to Istanbul in chains, where he was executed. Ad-Diriyah was destroyed and remains a ruin till date. It was a bitter lesson, that faith and courage are not enough to defeat a modern army with modern weapons. A century later, this was a lesson that another conqueror of Arabia, the great Abdul Aziz ibn Saud, was to remember.

The Egyptian army killed the males of the al-Saud family, but one young man—Turki ibn Abdallah—escaped and went into hiding. Some years later, he recaptured Riyadh in 1824 and founded the second Saudi kingdom. He ruled for ten years till he was assassinated by a cousin. His son, Faisal, became Emir, but after a few years, was captured by the Egyptians and imprisoned in Cairo. By this time, Muhammad Ali had broken away from the Ottomans, and felt that Faisal would be more useful to him in Riyadh where he could make trouble for the Ottomans, than in an Egyptian prison. Faisal was allowed to escape back to Riyadh where he ruled carefully till he was blinded by an eye disease, and then died. His two sons went to war against each other as they fought for the throne; conflict and disunity weakened their power and Abdullah, the elder son, requested the al-Rashids of Hail to come to his rescue. The al-Rashids came, but rather than giving the small kingdom back to Abdullah, they decided to keep it for themselves. Abdullah's younger brother Abd al-Rahman fled to Kuwait to live in exile. With him went his seventeen-year-old son, Abdul Aziz. The second Saudi kingdom became part of the kingdom of the al-Rashids.

THE LEGEND OF ABDUL AZIZ

In Kuwait, life was hard for the al-Saud family. They lived in three rooms without money and without authority—a life of humiliation. Even the marriage of Abdul Aziz had to be postponed due to lack of money. Abdul Aziz decided to risk all, attack Riyadh and re-establish the small kingdom of his family. Thirty of his friends and relations decided to go with him; among them was his cousin Abdallah ibn Jiluwi, a fierce fighter. Mubarak al-Sabah of Kuwait gave him thirty camels and thirty rifles and he set out.

Against all odds, the small group entered Riyadh by night, scaling walls, and breaking into houses. There they laid in wait for the morning. At daybreak, the governor arrived with his guards, greatly outnumbering the Saudis; but Abdul Aziz was relentless in his attack, and finally the fierce Jiluwi cut down the governor on the steps of the mosque, and victory was secured. Abdul Aziz was master of Riyadh. But being master of Riyadh did not mean much; the al-Rashids were still the lords of the Nejd and dealing with Abdul Aziz was low on their list of priorities.

Abdul Aziz was surrounded by his enemies—al-Rashids in the north; the Sharifs of Mecca in the west; the Turks in Hasa in the east; and the Rub al-Khali, 'the Empty Quarter', a forbidding desert wasteland in the south. Abdul Aziz moved fast. He called back his father from Kuwait, and offered Riyadh to him, but Abdur Rehman declined and abdicated his rights in favour of his son; he would be the advisor—the consiglieri—to Abdul Aziz. Leaving his father to defend Riyadh, he rode out into the desert to deal with the Bedouin, to whom the desert was home. The Bedouin were poor, illiterate herdsmen who roamed the desert seeking water and fodder for their camels and goats. They had their own code, their own values and attitudes, and their own way of life. Simple but independent, they were willing to bow down to no authority. They were slow to give respect and fast to fight. These were the people that accepted the young Abdul Aziz as a leader to respect and follow.

In these years, the legend of Abdul Aziz grew. Young, tall and handsome, he could outrun, outride and outshoot anyone in the desert. Charming, just, compassionate and generous, he became a hero to the people of the desert. His rage was terrible, his smile totally disarming and he carried the conviction that he was on a mission from God. Abdul Aziz was now not just the ruler of Riyadh; he was the lord of the desert.

There are nine key dates in the life of Abdul Aziz ibn Saud:

1876:   Born in the Nejd
1902:   Conquest of Riyadh

1914: Conquest of Hasa
1922: Conquest of Nejd
1925: Conquest of Hejaz (Mecca and Medina)
1932: United his dominions and created the Kingdom of Saudi Arabia
1935: Discovery of petroleum in Saudi Arabia
1945: Historic meeting with Roosevelt
1953: Death

In 1914, Abdul Aziz set out with a couple of hundred men to Hasa. He had decided to evict the Turks who controlled the territory with a garrison of 2,000 soldiers. Suddenly arriving in the capital of Hasa, he bluffed the Turks that he had laid explosives and would blow up the town if they did not surrender. The Turks were happy to surrender, since Hasa seemed a pointless hardship station, and finally they had the opportunity to go back home. With his bold bluff, in one night Abdul Aziz captured what would prove to be 25 per cent of the world's petroleum reserves—a prize that would earn for his kingdom $1 billion a day, and make his family the richest on earth. But this remarkable man who secured for his nation and his family, wealth beyond calculation, lived most of his life in relative poverty and had little personal use for money except to build a nation or give away, due to his overgenerous nature. At heart, he was a man of the desert, who sought to follow the example and lifestyle of The Prophet.

Having conquered the Nejd and central Arabia, having taken Hasa in the east, with its ocean of undiscovered oil under the sands of the desert, Abdul Aziz now looked to the West, to the Hejaz where Hussein Sharif ruled the holy cities of Mecca and Medina and basked in the glory that the British had allowed him after the end of the First World War. The Nejd was an empty wasteland; Hasa, though destined to later become the most expensive real estate in the world, at this time was hardly a prize. But the Hejaz, with its two holy cities, was the centre of pilgrimage for the Muslims of the world, had substantial income from pilgrimage, and was cosmopolitan and international.

Because of Lawrence of Arabia and his Arab revolt against the Turks in the First World War, Hussein Sharif had acquired a fame that was quite undeserved. Due to an accident of history, British policy for the region was divided between their Foreign Office, with its local control in Cairo, and the India Office, whose policy controlled the Persian Gulf with its regional office in Kuwait. These two important control centres operated independently of each other, often with conflicting policies. Cairo, which controlled Lawrence, supported Hussein Sharif; Kuwait, with its focus on the East coast and central Arabia, recognized the importance of Abdul Aziz. Lawrence was to prove wrong, and Cox and his associates from the India Office in Kuwait, were to prove right. But right or wrong could only be understood much later. At this time, Hussein, a small and petty man, preened himself in arrogance, while Abdul Aziz, who was the true giant in the context of history, fumed at being ignored by the British victors of the Great War. When the caliphate was abolished by Ataturk in Istanbul, Hussein declared himself the Caliph of the Muslim world. Thanks to the British, he was King of Hejaz and his sons Abdullah and Faisal had been given kingdoms in Transjordan and Iraq. The Arabs were not willing to accept Hussein as their new caliph, and when Abdul Aziz marched on the Hejaz, many were secretly pleased. Over the years, Abdul Aziz had been persuading the rootless Bedouin to settle down in villages and start simple agriculture. These new settlers were staunch believers in the Wahhabi code, and when the need arose, were fierce fighters. They were called the Ikhwan, and they were to become the awesome fighting force that was to put the fear of God into the Hejazis in Mecca, Medina and Jeddah. The Ikhwan had demonstrated their bloodlust when they had invaded Transjordan and had massacred the inhabitants of a village twenty miles from the capital, Amman. But being totally ignorant of the world outside their desert, they had never seen or understood the technological power of a modern army. The British counter-attacked with aircraft and armoured cars, and of the 1,500 Ikhwan in the raiding party, only a few survived and made it back home.

The Ikhwan now marched on Ta'if, a town in the Hejaz. The town surrendered and the Ikhwan entered unopposed. But once in the town, they started looting and murdering the inhabitants. They slaughtered every man and every boy; even the ulema were not spared. And then they set out for Mecca, their reputation preceding them. Abdul Aziz is said to have wept with dismay and disgust when he heard what had happened at Ta'if. He sent them a clear message forbidding further looting or murder, and forbidding them from fighting within the precincts of the holy city. Mecca panicked. The merchants forced Hussein to abdicate in favour of his son, Ali, and Mecca surrendered without a fight. There was no plunder, no slaughter, but the Ikhwan, fired by their Wahhabi beliefs, destroyed shrines and tombs, musical instruments and pictures of human beings. The Ikhwan imposed their Wahhabi beliefs on the holy cities. Two weeks later, Abdul Aziz himself arrived; he was unarmed and dressed in the simple white clothes of a pilgrim.

After the conquest of the Hejaz, Abdul Aziz ruled a territory as large as Europe; but it was not yet one kingdom. In the Nejd, lived the townspeople and the Bedouin, distinct and separate from each other. In Hasa, the population was Shia, and being a coastal people, they were fisherman and traders. The Hejaz was more cosmopolitan with its exposure to the international world through pilgrimage to the two holy cities. In the beginning, Abdul Aziz did not try to amalgamate them into one state. He placed two of his sons as governors—Saud, the eldest surviving son in Riyadh; and young Faisal in Jeddah. In Hasa, on the East coast, he had, after the conquest, made his cousin Abdullah ibn Jiluwi, governor—a post the Jiluwi family was to retain for seventy-five years. After seven years of slow integration, in 1932, he announced the formation of The Kingdom of Saudi Arabia, a state named after his own family and ruled by himself. In all his major decisions, he was slow and deliberate—never rash, never in a hurry, almost gentle in his method of persuading all to participate in his strategy. But once his mind was made up, he was capable of fast action that retained the initiative and did not give his opponents time or opportunity to counter his plans.

Abdul Aziz now controlled a vast kingdom, but his treasury was small. There was no oil revenue at this time, and the first oil concession was given to the New Zealand prospector Major Frank Holmes for a miniscule annual fee of £2,000, and Holmes had defaulted on even that after a couple of years. Even the revenue from pilgrimage, usually reliable, had diminished due to the great economic depression that had hit the economies of the world. To make matters worse, the British had discontinued his subsidies, which they had been paying during the Great War.

With an empty purse, ibn Saud had to tread a fine line between the Wahhabis and the townsfolk of the Hejaz. To retain the loyalty of the Wahhabis, he had to show that he too followed their beliefs. To the moderate Hejazis, he had to show that he too was a moderate. It was a difficult balancing act. To control so vast a kingdom, he had to use modern means of communication, cars and telegraph. The Wahhabi ulema objected, arguing that the use of such modern technology was against the principles of Islam. Ibn Saud patiently argued that rifles and guns were also modern technology, and they had no qualms in using these. He also made them listen to broadcasts of religious programmes to convince them that an invention that made this possible could surely not be bad. This fine balancing act has maintained stability for the last century in a Saudi Arabia that prohibits women from driving, but has also built the King Abdullah University that, in its territory, operates by a different set of rules and allows boys and girls to study together in a modern international environment. Iran under the Pahlevi Shahs—father and son—tried to impose modern values in a fast track process of change but this resulted in upheaval, revolution and instability. The Irani hare has fallen by the wayside while the Saudi tortoise plods on, slowly but surely.

And then the Ikhwan revolted. They had conquered the peninsula, from the Hejaz in the west to Hasa in the east, but their bloodlust was not sated. They desired to convert or kill more of the unfaithful, and the definition of the unfaithful grew ever wider as their targets became other Muslims who did not accept the Wahhabi faith. But ignorant of the world outside their desert, they did not understand that their camels and muskets were no match for the aircraft and machine guns of a modern army. The rebellion was led by three chiefs, who were all proven commanders of ibn Saud's army—Faisal al Duwaish, sheikh of the Mutair, who had led the attack on Hail; Sultan ibn Humaid, responsible for the massacre of Ta'if, and the conquest of Mecca; and Dhaidan ibn Hithlain, chief of the Ajman tribe.

Whether it was a misguided crusade or just a simple power struggle to take over the important kingdom that ibn Saud now controlled, it was a struggle to the death. Ibn Saud repeatedly offered compromise, but the final showdown took place in the battle of Sibilla in March 1929. The battle lasted fifteen minutes; the victor was ibn Saud. At Sibilla, he destroyed the Ikhwan, which he had created to conquer the deserts of Arabia. With his small armoured brigade of a few Ford and Chevrolet cars, he sped across the desert to consolidate his hold on a new country, which, after the discovery of oil, was to become, within a century, the richest kingdom on earth. In 1931, Faisal al Duwaish died in prison, unrepentant till the end; his dying message to ibn Saud was to offer him forgiveness for his sins.

Having conquered all the territories of the peninsula and having eliminated the Ikhwan threat, ibn Saud created a new unified kingdom, which he named after himself and his family—The Kingdom of Saudi Arabia. But the troubles did not cease. He was broke. The quest for oil began in earnest. But for the first few years, no oil was found. Ibn Saud gave the first important concession to the American company, Socal, but until oil was found, the income was not much more than small change. Six wells came up empty; the seventh proved a bonanza. The oil started to flow, but then the Second World War closed the prospects of the nascent Saudi oil industry. Five long years passed before peace brought the world back to normal.

After the war, ibn Saud had two important meetings—first with

Franklin Roosevelt and then with Winston Churchill. Roosevelt gave ibn Saud consideration and respect, and their meeting was a historic success. Churchill behaved with his usual arrogance and his meeting was a failure. Roosevelt was a chain smoker, but he refrained from smoking in the presence of the King. Himself crippled and wheelchair-dependent, he saw that ibn Saud too had problems and gave his spare wheelchair to the Saudi King. Churchill smoked and drank throughout the meeting and glibly explained that just as ibn Saud's religion forbade both vices, his religion demanded his consumption at all times. Ibn Saud was no fool; he could recognize the essence of a man in a first meeting, and he moved away from a relationship with Britain as he cemented the special bond that exists even today between the Kingdom and America.

During the last seven years of his life, his oil wealth grew and grew. He himself had little interest in money; his main needs were to give it away and to buy weapons for defence. But as he entered his seventies, he was a man of the past rather than a man of the future. He was a great warrior, but there were no more wars to fight; he was a great tribal chieftain, but the tribes had become a nation. He was not a bureaucrat or an accountant, and it was now time for the administrators as the days of building an empire were over. Till the end, he enjoyed his three greatest pleasures—prayer, perfume and women. In 1953, when he died, the oil income of The Kingdom had reached $100 million a year. But the seed that he had laid, continued to grow. By 2008, Saudi Arabia was super-rich, earning $1 billion a day as they pumped out 10 million barrels a day with a price tag of $100 per barrel. The achievement of Abdul Aziz ibn Saud, who started with less than nothing and created the Kingdom of Saudi Arabia, today a world power in terms of oil and money, is unmatched by any Muslim leader in the twentieth century.

18

The Afghans

'I have been struck with the magnitude of your resources, your ships, your arsenals; but what I cannot understand is why the rulers of so vast and flourishing an empire should have gone across the Indus to deprive me of my poor and barren country.'

—Dost Mohammad (On the
British invasion of Afghanistan)

'In Egypt, the veil had been largely discarded, and in Turkey, under the Ghazi, women were galloping towards emancipation. But Turkey is Turkey, and Egypt is Egypt, and Afghanistan is a law unto itself. What changes there are, must come slowly, and with the will of the people.'

—Amir Habibullah (From his autobiography;
About the reforms of King Amanullah
for women's emancipation)

'Unwise mullahs have put religion in chains for you, and have told you falsely about religion, and you have been deceived. The only things you should do are what God ordered and what The Prophet ordered; don't believe what the mullahs say.'

—King Amanullah

Afghanistan was an significant transit zone on the important Silk Road in medieval times. Herat was a glorious city which prospered through trade. The mountains of Afghanistan were the natural barrier which kept the Indians in India and the rest of the world out. But determined invaders made their way through to the riches of the subcontinent, defeating the Afghans en route, but moving on fast since there was little to hold their attention here. Over the centuries, the great conquerors and empire-builders came and went—Cyrus the Great, Alexander, the Omayyad Muslims, Genghis Khan, Tamerlane, Babur the Mogul, Nader Shah of Persia, and finally the British. The Afghans could be called a people but certainly not a nation, since the important centres of Kabul, Balkh, Herat and Kandahar were often controlled by different foreign empires.

In the sixteenth and seventeenth centuries, Kandahar changed hands several times, sometimes falling to the Moguls and sometimes, the Safavids. The Shah in Isfahan sent his best general, Gurghin Khan, a former Christian from Georgia, as his governor to Kandahar. Gurghin ruled as a tyrant, arrested the richest and most influential of the Afghan chiefs, Mirwais, and sent him a prisoner to Isfahan, to be guarded, tortured and if necessary, killed. Mirwais was intelligent, generous and charming; in Isfahan, he saw that the Shah was weak and was surrounded by corrupt ministers. In the court of Shah Hussein, merit was ignored and bribes decided everything. Mirwais purchased the corrupt courtiers, building up a lobby of supporters who had the ear of the Shah. He then asked the Shah to judge whether he was truly guilty of the charges that Gurghin had brought against him. He was acquitted and asked leave to go to Mecca on pilgrimage. In Mecca, he consulted revered ulema and obtained fatwas that sanctioned revolt against a tyrant who was also heretic, creating legitimacy for the rebellion he was secretly planning. On his return to Isfahan, he poisoned the mind of the Shah against Gurghin and convinced him that the governor was planning to revolt with Russian support. The Shah restored to Mirwais all his influence and lands in Kandahar and allowed him to return home.

When Gurghin saw his former prisoner return with honour, he was angry and determined to show who was master. He demanded that Mirwais send him his daughter, the most beautiful girl in Kandahar, not as a wife but as a slave and a concubine. It was an intentional insult, but Mirwais did not let anger cloud his judgement. First, he called a secret meeting of the chiefs, and secured their support; then he disguised a beautiful servant girl as his daughter and sent her to Gurghin, who was deceived and pleased. Now he had convinced the governor that his will was broken, but he still had to get him away from the protection of his strong Georgian contingent of bodyguards. Using cunning and strategy, he persuaded Gurghin to send them to crush some recalcitrant chieftains, after which he invited Gurghin to a feast outside the city limits. The governor and his retinue were wined and dined, and when they fell asleep, were slaughtered to the last man. Mirwais then put on the garments of the dead governor, and his men dressed as the Persians to lay a trap for the returning contingent. The Persians were defeated, and Kandahar—for many years the prize alternatively of the Moguls and Safavids—was now finally, in 1709, ruled by the Afghans. His son, Mahmud, even went on to conquer Isfahan, the Safavid capital, but then the strongman Nader Shah, a Safavid general, took back the lost territories and much more, including the Mogul capital, Delhi. Nader was no less a conqueror than Napoleon, and died undefeated in battle, but at the hand of two assassins.

THE LEGEND OF AHMAD SHAH DURRANI

Nader respected the fighting ability of the Afghan tribesmen, and his personal bodyguard of 4,000 men was led by a young Afghan called Ahmad Khan. Ahmad Khan was also entrusted with the protection of the treasury and Nader's massive collection of gems, including the Kohinoor diamond, plundered from the Mogul Emperor in Delhi. When Nader Shah was assassinated, Ahmad Khan decided that the best way to protect the treasury was to take it, together with his squadron of Nader's 4,000 bodyguards and retreat back to Afghanistan, where he would be safe from the powerful Persians fighting for the pieces of Nader's empire. Back home, the Afghans were trying to decide on a king to lead the unruly tribes, and had called a Great Assembly, a Loya Jirga, to select a king. The young twenty-five year-old Ahmad Khan, though not a candidate, was selected as King. It was a reasonable choice, because he had an unlimited source of funds (Nader's treasure), a small but strong army, and though it was not known at the time, was a natural-born leader who went on to build an empire second only to the Ottomans. He is known in history as Ahmad Shah Durrani. Ahmad Shah ruled over a confederation of tribes and a magnificent empire, but did not rule over a country, for Afghanistan was not really a state or a nation. Acquiring an empire was made easy by the declining power of the Moguls and the Safavids and the legacy of Nader Shah; Ahmad Shah's conquests were wide and fast as he stepped into the vacuum. He first took the cities in Afghanistan (Kabul, Herat and Ghazni); then he entered Persia, conquering Meshed and large tracts of Khurasan; he invaded India seven times and the Punjab three times, taking Peshawar, Kashmir, Lahore, Sindh and Baluchistan; he defeated the Marathas at the Third Battle of Panipat and then took Delhi. He had previously been to Delhi with Nader Shah and on that occasion, after Nader conquered Delhi, a soothsayer pointed out Ahmad Shah and predicted that he would be a great king. The story is told that Nader took out his dagger and clipped the ears of Ahmad Shah, saying, 'When you become King, this will remind you of me.' Ahmad Shah already had the treasure of the Moguls, including the Kohinoor diamond; this time he took a daughter of the Mogul Emperor, as wife for his son. As dowry, she brought with her the provinces of Sind and Punjab.

The Marathas were the rising power in India. Three times they met the Afghans in battle; three times they were defeated. The last battle was at Panipat where a massive army of 70,000 Marathas, after sacking Delhi, faced Ahmad Shah's Afghans. This battle, known in history as the Third Battle of Panipat, changed the history of India.

The Marathas took thirty years to recover from this defeat, giving a small British trading company in Bengal time to recover from their tragedy in the Black Hole of Calcutta (a small prison where the Nazwab of Bengal held British prisoners of war for one night in 1756), and to build a power that was to take all India and create the greatest empire in history. Without Ahmad Shah's defeat of the Marathas, perhaps India may have seen a Maratha Empire instead of the British Empire.

Finally the luck that had followed Ahmed Shah from the time he was a young man, turned sour. Sickness hit him in the form of cancer in his face, which ate away his nose and destroyed his jaw. He covered his deformity with a diamond nose guard, but this could not stop the internal spread of the disease, which finally killed him.

Ahmad Shah was a great general and also a great leader; a man who was mild and compassionate, and persuaded by reason rather than force. His one great failing, like so many other great men of destiny, was his family. Once again, feeble children succeeded a great father and soon the empire was lost as the Mirs of Sindh, the Khans of Baluchistan, the Uzbek Beys and the Amir of Bokhara, broke away. By the time that Dost Mohammad became Amir, only Kabul and Ghazni remained. Ahmad Shah was a great ruler, the founder of an empire who united the Afghans and made a nation of them. His son Timur Shah was intelligent and well-trained by his father, but he was indolent and the growth of empire was at an end.

The great historian Ibn Khaldun described the rise and fall of dynasties as a cycle of four generations. First, The Founder, a self-made man, who, through personal struggle and achievement, creates the dynasty. Having lived roughly for most of his life, he maintains a simple lifestyle, without luxury. He accumulates money but does not like spending it. The second generation is The Inheritor, born to luxury and power, who learns the art of government by watching his father. He likes to spend the money that flows in, on national projects and magnificent buildings. The third generation leader is soft and lacks judgement, a sucker for the flattery of corrupt advisors, he presides over the beginning of the decline of the empire. Last comes The Degenerate, who has none of the skills and all the weaknesses that hastens the collapse, and leads to bankruptcy and the end of the dynasty.

Timur Shah had twenty-three sons, who fought each other for power. Three of them became the king in turn—Shah Zaman, Shah Mahmud and Shah Shuja. When Shah Zaman was defeated and removed from the throne, he was blinded by his brother. When Shah Mahmud was defeated and removed from the throne, Shah Shuja showed mercy and spared his sight; but he was to rue his clemency when Mahmud made a comeback and again took the throne, driving Shuja into exile in British India.

For three generations, two great families ruled Afghanistan—the Sadozai Shahs and the Barakzai Viziers—and any shah who lost the support of the Barakzais did not last long. After the death of Nader Shah of Persia, a Barakzai general, Haji Jamal Khan, was a strong rival to Ahmad Shah, but he accepted a subordinate position and became a powerful army commander and advisor to Ahmad Shah. Haji Jamal's son Payindah was the most powerful of the nobles in the court of Timur Shah. He helped Timur's son, Shah Zaman, rise to power, but they fell out when Payindah joined a conspiracy and Shah Zaman had him executed, starting the blood feud between the Sadozais and the Barakzais. Payindah's eldest son Fathi Khan fled and joined Prince Mahmud, Shah Zaman's brother, and played a key part in winning him the throne, after which he became the vizier in Mahmud's government. The debauched and lascivious amir, Mahmud, left the government in the capable hands of Fathi Khan, but an accident destroyed their partnership. The Amir sent Fathi, together with his younger brother Dost Mohammad, to deal with a rebellious governor in Herat. Having successfully dealt with the governor, they attacked the harem and misbehaved with the governor's wife. The historian Mohan Lal described the incident: 'They seized the jewelled band which fastened the trousers of the wife.' Unfortunately, the wife was the niece of the Amir.

The Sadozais could not ignore the insult to their princess. They had to avenge the honour of their family. Kamran, Amir Mahmud's son, invited Fathi Khan Barakzai for dinner, and when he was drunk and sated with the banquet, his retainers tied Fathi down, blinded him and tortured him, cutting off his ears, his nose, his hands and his feet. Fathi Khan suffered the excruciating torture without a word, but burst into tears when they cut off his beard. Finally, they cut his throat and killed him. Dost Mohammad, Fathi's younger brother, escaped to the hills. This was the end of the partnership between the Sadozais and the Barakzais which had lasted for three generations.

THE GREAT GAME

Civil war between the twenty-three sons of Timur Shah had created chaos of the Sadozai rule; now rivalry between the twenty-two sons of Payindah Khan created disunity and disorder of the dominant Barakzais. Different parts and different cities of Afghanistan fell under different combinations of brothers, while the Barakzais still looked for a suitable Sadozai prince to unite the country in a legitimate leadership. Dost Muhammad saw his opportunity and made his move. At the same time, Shah Shuja, in his exile in India, decided to return and take the crown. The two armies clashed in battle, and Shuja fled with his army in retreat. He had previously shown that he could not govern; he now showed that he could not command an army. Dost Muhammad had taken control of the important cities of Afghanistan and his supporters urged him to become King; but Dost Muhammad was not carried away by his victory and replied, 'I am too poor. It would be absurd for me to call myself a king.' He took the title of Amir. Dost Muhammad was an intelligent and capable ruler, and he quickly started to put right the troubled country that fell into his control. He gave respect to the tribal chiefs, and wanted peaceful relations with the superpowers that pressed in on him—Russia from the north and Britain from the south. He was ready for dialogue with Persia on his west; only with Ranjit Singh and his Sikh nation was he determined to fight, because Ranjit had seized Peshawar, which the Amir could not accept. The Afghans never recovered Peshawar, and when the Muslims of India finally created a nation for themselves, they could thank the Sikh Ranjit Singh that Peshawar fell within Pakistan.

A new governor-general arrived in India, the aristocratic Lord Auckland and his two sisters—a strange family, all unmarried, with no real interest in India and its people. They merely treated India as a 'game'. The governor-general was officially merely the head of the India branch of the EIC, a private citizen in charge of a trading business. In fact, he was the ruler of an empire, and from the time that Britain controlled India until the time when the John Company was replaced by the Raj, he was the de facto ruler of the largest nation in the world. However, Lord Auckland was the wrong man for the job.

British policy for the different parts of their empire in India was hotly debated by two very different types of civil servant—on the one side there were the very experienced India experts in the field, who could speak the local languages, loved the local culture and mingled freely with the natives; on the other hand there were the bookish bureaucrats in the head office who lived in their ivory tower, isolated from the reality of India, but who played power games and held the ear of the governor-general. Sir William Hay Macnaghten was a dry, bookish, pompous bureaucrat, expert at head-office politics but completely wrong in his conclusions and his decisions. He was Lord Auckland's point man for Afghanistan and he wanted to put the exiled Shah Shuja back on the Afghan throne.

The paramount concern of the British was the security of their Indian Empire, and the overriding desire of Russia was to find an all-weather port that would give them access to the warm-water oceans to their south. The interplay of these two superpowers of the time was called 'The Great Game'. It was a war fought not by the clash of armies but by spies and secret agents, and by the bribery and seduction of the khans, princes and tribal chiefs who controlled the people of Afghanistan. The most colourful of the British agents was

Sir Alexander Burnes; the greatest of the Russian agents was Ivan Victorovich Vitkevich.

Burnes was brilliant and charming, and was fluent in Hindi and Persian. He was stationed in Kabul where he lived apart from the British colony, in the town centre, dressing, eating and living as an Afghan. He advised his superiors in India that Dost Mohammad was the man to back because he was not only the best man for the job but also the most popular with the Afghans and a friend to British interests. Frustrated that his advice was ignored by Lord Auckland, he distracted himself with liaisons with local women, a dangerous occupation that was to cost him his reputation and finally his life.

Vitkevich, the Russian agent, was a man of mystery. He was not even a Russian but a Polish nobleman born in Lithuania who, at the tender age of fourteen, was arrested for conspiring against Russia and deported to Kazakhstan to serve out his long sentence. He decided to make the best of his bad situation, and studied the local languages, becoming fluent in Kazakh and Chagatai Turkish. He also learned to recite the *Quran* from memory, and could pass comfortably as a local.

His success won him recognition from the Czar till one day he was found dead in a hotel room. It was never discovered whether his death was the result of suicide or murder.

The Amir asked the British to help him recover Peshawar from Ranjit Singh. Despite Burnes's advice, the British refused. Vitkevich moved fast, offering Russian money, help against the Sikhs and even the recovery of Herat. The Amir would have preferred the British as his ally, but the Russians were better than no ally at all. Lord Auckland would not tolerate an Afghan dialogue with the Russians. He believed, 'You are either with us or against us'—an ultimatum delivered one and a half centuries later by the American president, George Bush.

Lord Auckland, misled by his aide Macnaghten, dispatched an army to replace Dost Mohammad with the deposed king, Shah Shuja, who had been living in exile in India under British protection. The first Anglo-Afghan War had begun. The mighty British army took Kandahar, Ghazni and Kabul, almost without firing a gun.

The Amir and his sons fled to Bokhara. Was victory to be so easy? The Russian–Persian threat had melted away; there remained no hope of stopping the British from putting their puppet Shah Shuja on the throne. The Amir decided to fight and die in battle rather than live a life of shame. But to everyone's surprise, the Amir won the battle; the British lost. And then, the next day, in a move which defies understanding till today, the Amir walked alone into the British camp and surrendered. He proceeded quietly into exile to Ludhiana where he moved into the estate recently vacated by Shuja, to patiently bide his time.

Taking Afghanistan was easier than keeping it. The Afghans fought a guerrilla campaign, avoiding battle but winning skirmish after skirmish and then disappearing into the mountains. The British occupation proved pointless and expensive. It achieved nothing and lingered on without end. The master spy Sir Alexander Burnes, while spending an evening at home with a pretty local girl, was attacked by an enraged mob and killed. The British army was mauled and destroyed, with just one straggler returning back to India. The British returned with another army to take revenge, but all recognized that Lord Auckland's forward policy with its invasion of Afghanistan had been a big mistake.

Shah Shuja was not a great success as a ruler. He looked like, and tried to behave with the dignity of a king but the Afghans considered him a puppet and gave him little respect. In three years, he was assassinated by his godson, a lucky break for the British! Without opposition, Dost Muhammad returned peacefully to Kabul where he once more became the Amir and ruled for the next twenty-one years to the satisfaction of both the Afghans and the British.

Dost Muhammad died, and once more, chaos and disorder spread over Afghanistan. The British agent was again murdered by a mob. The British sent in three armies to reassert their control, and marched confidently into Kabul; in what was a replay of history, the Second Anglo-Afghan War had begun. The King, Yacub, resigned and was taken into exile in India. The British reprisals began, with fines, imprisonments and hanging of miscreants. They burned down villages to intimidate the natives. But it was not working, as one British officer commented, 'We are thoroughly hated and not enough feared.' The Afghans responded with guerrilla warfare. The only achievement of the invaders was to keep spending money till they recognized that their achievement was not worth the cost. The Afghans even won a real battle at Maiwind, but the situation seemed to be bogged down in a stalemate. And then Abdur Rahman arrived from his exile in Bokhara and marched into Kabul. He was the grandson of Dost Mohammad, and held a certain legitimacy; he was ready to negotiate with the British. A deal was quickly made—Abdur Rahman was recognized as the new Amir and the British army withdrew.

THE ASCENT OF THE IRON AMIR

Abdur Rahman was known as the Iron Amir as he was tough. As a teenager, he shot and killed one of his servants for amusement; by the age of seventeen, he was a general. He then went into exile with his father, during which time he supported himself by trading in antiques. Now he was back as Amir. He accepted the borders imposed on him by Mortimer Durand, the British-Indian bureaucrat, and accepted the loss of Peshawar to India. The border, known as the Durand Line, cut through tribes and territory to become a future bone of contention, in turn, with the British, with India and finally with Pakistan. He accepted that Britain would dictate his foreign policy, but within his borders, his authority would not be challenged by them. He then spent the next twenty years in fighting his rivals, consolidating his power and defeating all who opposed him. He centralized control through his agents in the provinces and watched them through his strong spy network.

Everyone was terrified of Abdur Rahman, but the Iron Amir was frightened only of his ferocious wife, Halima. Following the example of the Ottomans, he raised a cadre of privileged slave boys as his loyal administrators; but even with them, the Amir feared hidden conspiracies. Halima once suggested that he kill the boys he did not trust, but the paranoid Amir explained that that wouldn't be practical since he didn't trust any of them! Conspirators—actual or suspected—were caged and left to die of starvation in public view as a warning to others. Abdur Rahman had an enforcer—his interior minister, Mir Sultan—who terrorized and was hated by the Afghans. Finally, when the Amir needed a fall-guy, he accused Mir Sultan of killing 60,000 people without authority and hanged him. But the terror of the Iron Amir tamed the gun-toting Afghans and during Abdur Rahman's time, there was less crime in Afghanistan than in England. He enlisted the support of the mullahs by bribing them and licensing them through a system of exams. He persecuted the Persian-speaking Shia Hazaras of Mongolian descent, and legalized their enslavement. He conquered Kafiristan, converted its heathen people and renamed the territory, Nuristan. He uprooted the Durrani and Ghilzai tribes and scattered their tribesmen in different parts of Afghanistan. By the time he was finished, Afghanistan was one nation with power centralized in its capital, Kabul.

He died in 1901 and was succeeded by his fun-loving son, Habibullah, who was a ladies' man. When Habibullah demanded that one of his officials bring his wife to the palace dinners, the man refused, saying he was at the King's service, but his wife was not. Habibullah was murdered on a hunting expedition. His murderer was never caught. He was succeeded by his son Amanullah, another remarkable figure in the strange story of Afghanistan.

Amanullah's career started well but ended in disaster. Though the Afghan elite liked the British, most ordinary Afghans hated them. The British had suffered through the hardship of the First World War and had lost the will for an empire; Amanullah seized the opportunity by declaring Afghanistan independent. He appointed his father-in-law, Tarzi, as foreign minister. Tarzi had lived in Turkey and was influenced by Ataturk, but Amanullah was even more extreme in his adulation of the great Turkish leader with his modern western ways. Amanullah moved so impetuously with his reforms that even

Tarzi was worried and warned his son-in-law to slow down. But Amanullah was not interested in slowing down; he published his code—*Nizamnama*—which banned torture, slavery and underage marriage; he aggressively pushed for westernization, insisting that his administrators and courtiers shave their beards and wear suits, ties and hats; he discouraged burqa, the chadri that traditional Afghan women wear; and he discouraged polygamy by his own example—he had only one wife, Soraya, the beautiful emancipated daughter of Tarzi.

THE BIRTH OF MODERN AFGHANISTAN

When Amanullah declared his independence from the British, he was so popular that he moved about freely among the people without a bodyguard, saying, 'The nation is my bodyguard.' But his reforms disturbed conventional Afghan Muslims who now whispered that Amanullah was a kafir, an unbeliever. His offer of 'freedom of religion' seemed to conflict with the tenets of Sharia. His grand tour of Europe with his wife, Soraya, thrilled the Europeans who now saw Afghanistan in a new light, but when pictures of Soraya in her elegant western gowns, which left her shoulders bare, were circulated in the mountains back home, the villagers were stunned and shocked. Returning home, she dramatically shed her veil and scandalized Afghans by defying convention.

Amanullah was a reformer, determined to pull his people into the twentieth century, but he lacked wisdom, and his dreams blinded him to the realities of Afghanistan at the time. He was arrogant, impatient and a bad judge of character, surrounded by bad advisors and bad advice. Corruption and nepotism alienated his subjects, and his disregard of Islamic tradition shocked the Afghans.

His cousin, Nadir Khan, felt that Amanullah was treading thin ice and he wisely distanced himself, taking a diplomatic posting in Paris. Discontent grew into rebellion with demands that Amanullah divorce his wife and step back from his westernization program and his so-called emancipation of women. In a desperate attempt to recover acceptance, he recanted, even taking a second wife to re-establish his Islamic credentials, but it was to no avail. Rebellion was rife.

North of Kabul, a Tajik bandit was becoming famous as a local Robin Hood with a strange sense of humour. Habibullah, known as Bachey Saqao, The Water Carrier's Son, was an immensely strong, illiterate opportunist with a natural aptitude for the art of war. Stories of this crude, uncouth man from the most humble background became legend as his popularity grew and that of the sophisticated, refined Amanullah fell. The mullahs rallied behind The Water Carrier's Son whose conventional Islamic beliefs they preferred to Amanullah's modernist western approach. They branded Amanullah, 'kafir', and the King fled with his family in his Rolls Royce car, across the border to Iran and on to Italy, where he lived out his life in exile, making furniture to earn his living. Amanullah passed the crown to his brother who lasted three days till The Water Carrier's Son took the palace.

Bachey Saqao was now King, but totally unfit for the role as he was unlike any other king in history. His story is told in his autobiography, dictated to his aide, titled, *My Life from Brigand to King*. When he entered the palace he was amazed to see bathrooms and other luxuries for the first time in his life. He promoted Malik Mohsin, a hoary old scoundrel of seventy, as governor of Kabul and when the governor saw the billiard table in the palace and asked its purpose, Bachey Saqao mischievously replied that 'it was specially imported from across the seas for generals of renown and of giant frame'. The governor spent a very uncomfortable night on the billiard table and woke up complaining of the terrible cold and the hardness of his bed. The Water Carrier's Son slept on the floor, on a carpet, 'for I too distrusted these Feranghi beds.'

However, beds were a minor problem. The greater problem was finding money to pay the troops so that they could be controlled. The treasury was empty, so twenty of the leading merchants were called to the palace to contribute the required money. But requests produced nothing except excuses. Finally the merchants agreed to lend money, provided there was security. Bachey Saqao first raised his rifle to shoot the leader, but saw that 'even in that tense moment, greed of wealth was greater than his regard for life. I knew that subtler methods must be employed. Moneyed men can hide their gold, and almost invariably do so.' Bachey Saqao's sword swept down, severing the thumb of the merchant. He picked up the thumb and ascended the dais to address the merchants:

> You asked for security and you shall have it. This thumb was formally the property of one of you. It has now been ceded to the Crown. It is security for the left hand of that man. It is also security for your right and left hands. The audience is terminated. Those of you who fail to bring that which is apportioned, will lose their hands. Those who are still contumacious will lose their feet, and noses also. And that need not exhaust the inventory.

He later said, 'These men could see that I meant what I said. I was no Amanullah Khan. Before five o'clock, I had the amount which I had specified.'

But these small sums did not last long in supporting a large army, and other means of raising money had to be found. Bachey Saqao closed the schools, dismissed the teachers, closed the libraries, the laboratories and the Royal Museum and sold off the effects. He printed notes but the new money inspired no confidence. He even issued coins of leather, but the economy collapsed. Bachey Saqao had no fear and moved about openly without a bodyguard despite the frequent assassination attempts. His automatic weapon was more than enough to deal with his assassins. Bachey Saqao enjoyed his time as King, even though the Afghans did not. He married a lady of high birth, a relative of Amanullah, and lived without a worry for tomorrow.

Finally Nadir Khan returned and assembled a force to oppose the brigand-king. Nadir was victorious; Bachey was defeated and gave himself up on the guarantee of safety. But Nadir was unable to make good his promise as the tribes demanded revenge. In defeat there was no despair in Bachey; in captivity, he laughed in the face of death. When he was led to execution, the mullah asked him to pray, but

Bachey declined, saying, 'Why should I raise my hands to Allah? He has given me all that I have desired. I have been King. I have had all my ambitions realized. What more is there for me to ask? How long is this sorry farce to continue? I thought I was coming here to be shot. It seems that I am but an exhibition for the curious!' The death of Bachey and the rise of Nadir closed the chapter on the past and heralded the birth of modern Afghanistan.

19

The Genesis of Modern Iran

'Enemies are of three sorts—enemies, enemies of friends, and friends of enemies.'

(Persian proverb)

'He has created an atmosphere of uncertainty and fear. The cabinet is afraid of the majlis; the majlis is afraid of the army; and all are afraid of the Shah.'

(British ministerial report on Reza Shah Pahlavi)

After the assassination of the great Nader Shah, Persia fell into anarchy as rival contenders fought for power. Nader's nephew, Adil Shah, seized the throne but was defeated and blinded by his brother, who in turn was taken prisoner by his own troops, and both brothers were killed. Shah Rukh, Nader's young grandson, was accepted as ruler but he was challenged by strong rivals and finally replaced by Karim Khan Zand, an able self-made man who then ruled for twenty-nine years, but modestly refused the title of Shah. Karim Khan was shrewd and capable and restored peace and prosperity to

Persia, but on his death, a savage power struggle once again began.

The main contender for power was a vicious eunuch named Agha Mohammed, a Qajar, who had been captured and castrated as a young boy, but after twenty years as a captive, he escaped, and by force of character, emerged as the leader of the Qajar tribe. Agha Mohammed had a horrible and shriveled face, but despite all his handicaps, seized leadership due to his brilliance, perseverance and determination. His three ruling passions were power, avarice and revenge.

Agha Mohammed loved jewels and captured Shah Rukh, torturing him to extract the hidden jewels that he had inherited from his grandfather, Nader Shah. Each day new tortures prized the spectacular jewels from the hiding places of the wretched prince. Finally molten lead was poured onto the forehead of Shah Rukh who disclosed the priceless ruby of the Emperor Aurangzeb, before he expired. Agha Mohammed's greed knew no bounds; once he ordered that the ears be cut off an offender but then overhearing the terrified man offer a bribe to the executioner, to only cut the tips, he made a counter-offer that the man could keep his ears altogether if he paid double the bribe to the Shah himself.

Agha Mohammed defeated what was left of Zand power, at Kerman. He gave the women of Kerman to his soldiers as slaves, to rape or kill as they wished. He then ordered that 20,000 pairs of eyes be presented to him, and after almost the whole male population of the city had been blinded and their eyes heaped in front of the eunuch Shah, he counted them carefully, warning the officer who had been instructed to supervise the atrocity, 'Had one pair been wanting, yours would have been taken.' He slaughtered his prisoners and made a pyramid of the skulls and left Kerman destroyed, a city of blind beggars and raped women. Kerman never fully recovered from his visit.

Agha Mohammed ordered the execution of two offenders, but for inexplicable reasons, not only postponed their execution but left them free to roam in the palace pending their execution. The two criminals, with nothing to lose, assassinated the Shah, and made good their escape. Agha Mohammad died leaving the legacy of a united and peaceful Persia and a new dynasty, the Qajars, which was to last for more than a century.

Agha Mohammed had controlled Persia by terror; his successor, Fath Ali Shah, used marriage to strengthen his power base. He married more than a thousand wives, selected from every tribe and every region. Having forged their links to the powerful tribes and feudal lords, the Qajars ruled through their barons in the provinces and the centre remained weak. Even tax collection was auctioned off to the regional strongmen who had the ability to collect. Much of the tax extracted remained with the collectors, with little reaching the Shah in the capital. A weak treasury meant a weak army, small and poorly-armed.

The Empress Catherine the Great of Russia had many critics and detractors who branded her an adulteress, usurper, murderess, tyrant and nymphomaniac, but European and Asian neighbours alike feared the relentless expansion of her empire. The death of Catherine in the last years of the eighteenth century gave a short respite as the weak and pacifist Paul became Czar, but soon the Russians returned. The two Russo–Persian Wars during the reign of Fath Ali Shah cost Persia large tracts of her Caspian territories—Georgia, Dagestan, Azerbaijan and Armenia passed from Persian to Russian hands and much of the Muslim population emigrated to Persia to escape Christian domination.

The longest reigning shah was Naser al-Din Shah who ruled for almost fifty years (1848–96). He was only seventeen when he was crowned but had a wise and experienced prime minister in Amir Kabir. The Shah trusted Amir Kabir, to whom he gave his sister in marriage, despite Amir's humble background. Amir had travelled and had seen the world; he knew what needed to be done and set about doing it efficiently. He could not fight the modern European armies but protected Persia by an astute foreign policy that successfully maintained the balance between the two superpowers, Britain and Russia; at the same time, he modernized the state, limiting government spending, promoting education, strengthening the army by hiring foreign officers to modernize his troops along European lines and importing armament factories to improve the Persian fighting capability. But the wise and loyal Amir fell victim to court intrigues when the mother of the Shah fanned the suspicions of her son, who exiled him and then had him assassinated.

The Shah was seriously broke. His solution was to borrow more from Russia and to raise money by the granting of concessions to foreign businessmen. His concession to Baron Julius de Reuter granted him the right to a monopoly of building railways, tramways, irrigation, roads, a bank and the exploitation of forests and mines. However, public protest led to a cancellation of almost all the rights granted.

The most notorious concession was the grant to a British businessman, Major Gerald Talbot, the monopoly on the sale, purchase, export and processing of tobacco for fifty years, for which Talbot would pay £15,000 a year and 25 per cent of the profits. The ulema opposed the tobacco concession and the merchants protested against it. The great religious scholar Mirza-ye Shirazi issued a fatwa against smoking, leading to the total boycotting of tobacco. Everyone stopped smoking and the concession was cancelled, but a large compensation was demanded by the company, and under British pressure, was paid, putting Persia under debt for half a million pounds together with interest, for forty years.

The old Shah prepared to celebrate his fifty years of rule. Old and tired, with his sons jockeying for power and his ministers raking in money through corrupt deals, he was finally shot and killed by a convert to the Babi religion, rumoured to be acting under the instigation of the international revolutionary, Sayyid Jamal al-Din Afghani.

Mozaffar Shah, who succeeded his father, was pleasure-loving and weak. He continued borrowing from abroad and sold off more concessions to raise money. The people were not happy and anger turned into protest. The mob went wild and 10,000 protestors took sanctuary in the grounds of the British Embassy. They demanded the reduction of the absolute powers of the Shah, a constitution and the rule of law. The Shah promised a constitution, which he signed on 30 December 1906; but having signed it, he remained reluctant to pass power and died five days later.

His son, Mohammed Ali, continued to deny his people their constitutional rights, and to maintain his hold on absolute power. In June 1908, he bombed the parliament and arrested deputies. He was deposed, sent into exile and died in Italy. The days of all-powerful shahs were over, as after Mohammed Ali, every future shah died in exile—the Qajars, and after them, the Pahlavis.

Ahmad Shah, the last Qajar sovereign, was only twelve when he was crowned. Russia occupied the north and Britain interfered in the government of the south. A regent governed on behalf of the teenage king. Rebellion raged; anarchy ruled. The treasury was empty. An American lawyer, Morgan Shuster, an expert in economic reconstruction, was brought in to put things right, to reform and run the tax system and to control government spending. A Russian army marched on Tehran. The streets were filled with protests. Parliament was closed down. Then in 1914, the world went to war as the European powers attacked each other. Persia tried to stay neutral, but the entry of the Ottomans on the side of Germany, and the Caliph's declaration of jihad turned Muslims against Britain. In 1916, the Russians marched on Tehran, with nothing to stop them. However, Tehran was saved by a miracle—the Bolshevik Revolution that turned Russia inwards, against itself, leaving Persia to its own devices. Britain remained the only great power on the world stage.

The Cossack Brigade was the only disciplined force that survived in Persia. Though it was a small contingent of men, the British recognized that it was the best hope of order, and they provided the money for salaries for its troops. General Ironside, who led the British forces, encouraged the colonel of the Cossack Brigade, Reza Khan, to take power through a coup d'etat. Reza Khan rose fast from colonel to general and then to commander-in-chief and minister of war. The British, who controlled the Imperial Bank as well as oil in Persia, provided the money; Reza Khan and his loyal generals provided the muscle. An election gave an overwhelming victory to Reza Khan, but he needed no electoral legitimacy. At the first opportunity, the Sshah left for Europe; he was never to return.

Reza Khan was a semi-illiterate teenager when he joined the Cossack Brigade. He was known as 'Reza Khan Maxim' after the Maxim machine gun which he adored. When he built his palace after taking power, there was a mosaic of the Maxim machine gun in the entrance hall. Reza took Teheran with a force of 3,000 men and eighteen maxim guns. He spoke less and he was a man of action.

Unlike Ataturk in Turkey, Reza Khan did not replace the Shah with a republic in Persia. The ulema did not want a republic; the example of Ataturk's republic and its effect on religion did not appeal to them. In February 1925, parliament put an end to the Qajar dynasty. In its place, a new dynasty was born—the first Pahlavi shah, Reza Shah Pahlavi, Persia's man on horseback, crowned himself, as Napoleon had done in Paris over a century before.

A NEW DYNASTY IS BORN

The new shah changed Persia drastically, partly for the better, partly for the worse. He streamlined and strengthened the army and the bureaucracy, creating a strong central government and a unified country. He modernized and westernized the nation, building up the infrastructure and education with the money he collected through his improved and efficient tax collection machine and through oil revenues which had started to come in. He improved the status of women, spread the use of the Persian language, imposed military conscription and created the Iran of the twentieth century.

Three men helped Reza Shah install the new regime. This triumvirate—Timurtash, Davar and Firuz Farmanfarma—were the most powerful men in Iran after the Shah. However, Timurtash and Davar were murdered in prison; Farmanfarma was smothered using his own pillow. They were not the only victims of the Shah's paranoia and passion for total control. Terror ruled in Iran.

He was a dictator, violent and oppressive, who made torture and corruption an everyday part of life in Persia, now renamed 'Iran'. Murder and imprisonment created an atmosphere of terror. His rule was described as 'a government of the corrupt, by the corrupt and for the corrupt.' He had an unholy love of land, and soon became the largest landowner in Iran with personal holdings in excess of 3 million acres, acquired through confiscation, fraudulent takeover of state property and forced purchase from landlords at knock-down prices. He wanted paramount wealth and status—the wealth he took from his own people, his own nation; the status he took from Egypt, marrying his son Mohammed Reza, the Crown Prince, to the beautiful princess, Fauzia, the daughter of King Farouk. Like his dynasty, the marriage was not to last. His passion for wealth permeated the court and the cabinet.

Even more than corruption and greed, religion played an important part in eroding the legitimacy of Reza Shah. The people, even women, did not appreciate his forcing them to discard the veil. The wife of one of his governors even committed suicide, preferring death to discarding tradition. The inroads into the powerful Islamic establishment, earned him the opposition of the ulema. His dilution of Sharia law with a European style legal code of justice, disturbed the peasants and the poor. His rigging of elections and refusal to bow down to the rule of law which he so rigidly imposed on others, made him unpopular.

By 1934, the Shah was completely out of control. He signed a new agreement with the AIOC giving it an extension of their concession until 1993, in return for a meager 4 per cent increase in royalties. But his final mistake was his pro-German, pro-Nazi sympathy when the Second World War started in 1939. The British and Soviet armies invaded and deposed the Shah, forcing him to abdicate in favour of his son, and go into exile, where he died in 1944.

20

Jinnah Creates a Muslim Homeland

'The most important man in Asia is sixty-seven, tall, thin and elegant, with a monocle on a grey silk cord, and a stiff white collar which he wears in the hottest weather... The difference between Jinnah and the typical Hindu politician is the difference between a surgeon and a witch doctor.'

—Beverley Nichols, British author
(On Muhammad Ali Jinnah)

'You are free; you are free to go to your temples, you are free to go to your mosques or to any other place in this State of Pakistan. You may belong to any religion, caste or creed—that has nothing to do with the fundamental principle that we are all citizens and equal citizens of one state.'

—Qaid-i-Azam Muhammad Ali Jinnah
(His presidential address to the
Constituent Assembly, on the
foundation of Pakistan)

Jinnah, the founder of Pakistan, dressed English, talked English and thought English; yet this man who was quite unlike any other Pakistani, emerged as the unchallenged leader of the Muslims of India and created the state of Pakistan. Born a Shia Khoja, and throughout his life, tolerant in his religious views, his earliest political mentors were the Parsi, Dadabhai Naoroji and the Hindu, Gopal Krishna Gokhale. Dadabhai became famous as the first Asian to win a seat in parliament in England. When he was contesting the election, Lord Salisbury remarked, 'I doubt that a British constituency would elect a black man'—an inappropriate remark since Dadabhai's skin was a lighter colour than Salisbury's. Gokhale, the professor who went on to become President of the Indian National Congress (INC) was mentor to both Jinnah and Gandhi. Throughout his life, he was an advocate for Hindu–Muslim unity, and his views greatly influenced the young Jinnah.

Jinnah was born in Kharadar, Karachi. His father was a conservative middle-class trader who arranged for Jinnah to be married off at the age of fifteen, after which he sent his son to England to study law at Lincoln's Inn. Jinnah did well, qualified and returned home as the youngest barrister in Asia. But his homecoming was not a happy occasion—his young wife had died and his father had lost a lot of money and was struggling to make ends meet. Jinnah decided to move to Bombay, the big city which could support his ambitions. The first few years were a hard struggle, but soon the brilliant young barrister was recognized as the up-and-coming new star of the Bombay courts.

By 1906, Jinnah was secure in his career and was making enough money to look beyond his personal needs. He decided to join politics. In that year, the Muslim League (ML) was born, but it did not excite Jinnah and he decided to join the INC. Seven years later, in 1913, he travelled to London with his mentor Gokhale, and also joined the ML. Now recognized as the ambassador of Hindu–Muslim unity, he held three political positions, as an important member of both INC and the ML and also a member of the Imperial Legislative Council (ILC). His prospects in politics looked strong and by 1915, he was recognized as an important leader of united India. His hard work and self-discipline had made him financially secure, prominent as a barrister and recognized as a leader to be trusted.

Then Jinnah fell in love. He was forty and had lived alone for more than twenty years. The girl who captured his heart was a seventeen-year-old heiress called Ruttie, the only child of Sir Dinshaw Petit, a Parsi business magnate. Ruttie was beautiful, sophisticated and wilful, and she was captivated by the brilliant and strikingly handsome lawyer who had made such an impact on the political scene of India. Jinnah approached Petit for permission to marry Ruttie. Petit was outraged, and not only refused permission, but took an injunction from court to ensure that the marriage did not take place. In 1918, when Ruttie attained the age of eighteen, she converted to Islam and married Jinnah according to Muslim rites. They had one daughter—Dina—who, when she grew up, fell in love with Neville Wadia, a Parsi who had converted to Christianity. Jinnah was enraged and asked his daughter why she could not have found a Muslim to marry. Dina answered her father with a question, 'Couldn't you have found a Muslim lady to marry instead of my mother?'

Jinnah in love, was a different man; gone was the cold, calculating politician. One night, he and Ruttie attended a formal dinner given by Lord Willingdon, the governor of Bombay. Ruttie was wearing a low-cut dress which did not please Lady Willingdon, who called for a wrap 'in case she felt cold'. Jinnah retorted, 'When Mrs Jinnah feels cold, she will say so, and ask for a wrap herself.' Jinnah left with his wife and never again went to the Government House.

With Britain exhausted by the First World War, the politics of India went into a new phase. Legalistic negotiation gave way to street action, and a push for independence. Gandhi now dominated the politics of India; Jinnah was eclipsed. His new marriage was also disturbing his equilibrium and affecting his judgement. In 1921, Jinnah resigned from the ILC, the Home Rule League and the INC. He was elected to the Legislative Assembly where he still fought for Hindu–Muslim unity and advocated separate electorates to ensure

Muslim representation in the House. But parliament had been replaced by the street, as agitation grew stronger.

His marriage started to fall apart, and in 1928, Ruttie left home and moved to a suite in the Taj Mahal Hotel, from where she proceeded to Europe with her parents. In Paris, she fell seriously ill, and lay in hospital in a coma. Jinnah came to be by her side. She recovered but they again quarreled, and she returned to Bombay.

In 1929, Ruttie passed away, and in the same year, hope for Hindu–Muslim unity also died. It was the lowest period of Jinnah's life as he suffered agony and despair. He left for London to attend the Round Table Conference as one of the fifty-eight delegates of British India; he still hoped for Hindu–Muslim unity. At the conference was another famous delegate, the poet and philosopher, Mohammad Iqbal, who openly rejected Hindu–Muslim unity and argued strongly in favour of the partition of India, with Pakistan as a new homeland for the Muslims. For almost a decade, Jinnah resisted the idea of partition; in political eclipse, he decided to settle in England and give up politics in India. He bought a house in Hampstead, in London, and brought over his sister Fatima to look after Dina, while he resumed his legal practice. At this time, he read, with avid interest, a new biography of Ataturk, titled, *Grey Wolf,* and written by Harold Courtenay Armstrong. He encouraged his daughter, Dina, to read it, and she gave her father the nickname of 'Grey Wolf', saying that they were very similar. Though both men were patriots and nationalists with incisive minds and unbreakable determination, their personalities were very different. Ataturk was a hard-drinking womanizer surrounded by his army commanders; Jinnah lived like a celibate monk, away from wine, women and song. The quiet years spent in London seemed to be the end of Jinnah's political career. He felt defeated, saying, 'I began to feel that neither could I help India, nor change the Hindu mentality. I felt so disappointed and depressed that I decided to settle down in London.' In 1933, Liaquat Ali Khan, who was to become Pakistan's first prime minister after partition, came to London and persuaded Jinnah to return.

At first, things did not look good. The elections held in 1937 gave an overwhelming victory to Congress. Not only were Muslims in a minority, but the ML secured only 5 per cent of the Muslim vote. Nehru proudly announced that there were only two parties in India—the INC and the British. Jinnah replied, 'There is a third party—the Muslims.'

TWO-NATION THEORY AND THE BIRTH OF PAKISTAN

In 1940, Jinnah finally gave up the quest for Hindu–Muslim unity as he came to the sad conclusion that 'Democracy can only mean Hindu Raj all over India.' In Lahore, the Pakistan Resolution was passed, and the two-nation theory was established. Jinnah told the British, who had to decide the fate of India, 'You talk of parliamentary democracy and you fail to realize that the assumptions on which it depends have no application at all to Indian conditions.'

As the Second World War entered its most dangerous years, Gandhi escalated his agitation for independence, but Jinnah worked within the law. Gandhi and his lieutenants were arrested, and Jinnah's organization grew. The personal antipathy between Jinnah and Gandhi grew worse. Sir Stafford Cripps arrived from England to create a new Indian union as soon as the war ended. But the British looked like losers and Gandhi rejected the Cripps proposal which he described as a post-dated cheque on a bank that was about to crash. The World War ended with Britain's victory, and in 1946, a general election was called in India. The ML won seventy-six of the seventy-nine Muslim seats—a vindication for Jinnah. The Hindu Congress won an overwhelming majority, but Jinnah could no longer be denied a place at the table; the Muslims could no longer be ignored. Jinnah was a tired and sick old man who had survived an assassination attempt a few years before when a killer attacked him in his own house; he had a terminal disease which was to kill him within a couple of years—but he had won. Nothing could stop the birth of Pakistan. But long negotiations had to be concluded before the details could be ironed out, the borders decided, the assets apportioned between the two nations that would be born, as the British divided before they quit. While Jinnah fought for clauses, Nehru won the heart of the referee, the Viceroy, Lord Mountbatten, and that of his wife, Edwina, Lady Mountbatten. The affection between the Mountbattens and Nehru tilted the playing field and ensured that Jinnah faced an uphill task and on most issues, Pakistan got the short end of the stick.

Finally Pakistan was born. It was a bloody birth as 14 million people moved across the borders leaving their homes and arriving as refugees to their new countries. The slaughter was terrible as Hindus, Muslims and Sikhs attacked each other with axes, knives or any other weapon they could find. Many wondered if the new state could survive, divided into East and West wings, and separated by a hostile India, without a common language and the treasury empty.

The first to go was Jinnah, who died thirteen months after the creation of the new state. Soon after, Liaquat, the first prime minister, was assassinated. The next casualties were the integrity and moral values that were the essence of Jinnah's character—corruption consumed the power elite and the administration; democracy withered as Martial Law and rule by the generals took Pakistan within ten years of the Quaid's death. Within twenty-five years, the two wings were torn apart, creating the separate states of Pakistan and Bangladesh. The last to go were the Quaid's ideology and beliefs—under Bhutto's leadership, order, discipline and the rule of law disappeared. And finally, Jinnah's Islam—moderate, tolerant and supportive of women's rights—was replaced by General Zia's Islam and the fundamentalist civil strife that followed, leading to violent deaths of Bhutto, Zia, Benazir and many others. Had Jinnah survived, he would have been heartbroken by the Pakistan of today that is so far removed from his dream.

21

Europe Eclipses the Muslim Empires

'British rule may be good for us; but it is neither equally, nor altogether, good for them.'

—Lord Curzon, viceroy of India

*'Whatever happens, we have got
the Maxim gun, and they have not.'*

—Hilaire Belloc, British author

For a thousand years after the death of The Prophet, the Muslims had dominated and led the world. Their armies, their method of government and their higher learning had ensured that the period known as the Dark Ages in Europe were the golden centuries of Islam. Muslim science, culture and their advanced systems of health, education and justice ensured that life in the Muslim world was good, in stark contrast to life in the West which was nasty, brutish and short. Until the end of the seventeenth century, Muslim conquest made inroads into Europe, and Muslim traders won new converts to Islam in Africa and the Far East.

But by the end of the seventeenth century, the balance of power between the East and the West had started to change. The three great Muslim empires of the time—in Istanbul, Iran and India—were past their prime. Luxurious living and resistance to change had led to stagnation and decay. Declining revenues to finance the rising expenditures resulted in empty treasuries. The Ottomans and the Safavids had financed their expenditure through conquest and plunder. The wealth of the Moguls in India came from the Hindu people of India whom they milked to collect the enormous wealth that paid for the extravagant lifestyles of a small elite body of foreign aristocrats.

THE WHITE MAN'S TAKEOVER OF THE WORLD

More important than the internal causes of the relative decline of Muslim power were the changes that had emerged in the West, creating the rise of Europe. Whereas the Muslim empires were land empires controlled by their armies, the Europeans, hemmed in by a smaller landmass where numerous kingdoms competed for space to grow, looked outwards across the oceans. Portugal and Spain, followed by the Dutch and the British, developed naval technology which enabled them to make longer voyages, and armed them to deal with the unknown threats that lay in distant lands across the oceans. What started as private expeditions and piracy, matured into permanent navies owned and backed by the strength of the state. The new heroes of the age were men such as Christopher Columbus, Vasco de Gama, Albuquerque, Drake and Raleigh.

The Moguls, from first to last, were a land power, who made no attempt to conquer the seas. Whereas the Great Mogul had unchallenged power over a fabulous empire, he was as helpless in the ocean as a beached whale on shore. The Persians too, controlled an enormous land empire and saw no need to develop sea power. Their conflicts were with the Moguls on their eastern flank, the Ottomans in the west and the Russians to the north. The landlocked Afghans never even saw the ocean. Only the Ottomans, who had to control the Black Sea and the Mediterranean, developed a navy. Ottoman naval power reached its peak under Suleiman the Magnificent and his Barbary pirates, led by the great warrior of the sea, Barbarossa. After Suleiman, degenerate leadership led to decline of state power and loss of sea power. The one great power that could have controlled the oceans was China with its great Muslim admiral, the eunuch, Zheng He, whose massive ships had already established control of the eastern oceans as far as Africa. But, in an amazing and historic decision, the Chinese Emperor ordered all sea voyages stopped, turning China inwards and putting an end to China as a sea power. The navies of the European states, with their unchallenged monopoly of sea power, were fundamental to the rise of the West.

In economic affairs, the evolution of the West followed different routes from the established economies of the Muslims. The distance between the Muslim economies and the European economies grew greater due to revolution and innovation in finance, commerce and industry. In the world of Islam, the development of banking had, from early days, been restricted by Sharia laws against usury or interest. This was not a problem when money was amply supplied by conquest; but when conquest dried up, the lack of an efficient financial system to manage savings and debt, weakened the state and the rulers. The Jewish bankers in Europe focused on money management, developing strong and effective money markets. Christian banking families also flourished. This gave an important advantage to Europe in financing wars, and as wars grew longer with The Thirty Year War and The Hundred Year War, the need for finance to feed and supply the armies escalated. The European bankers provided their nations with the money to win wars; the Muslim monarchs had no such pool of money. Innovations in commercial law and practice also enabled the take-off of the trading ventures of the West. The Muslims had always been good traders, following the example of The Prophet himself. Sharia law recognized proprietorship and partnership as the vehicles for trading ventures. Trading syndicates had flourished in sponsoring the caravans since the first days of Islam, but they had limited growth beyond a certain point. In sixteenth century Europe, the new corporate vehicle, the joint stock company, resulted in perpetual bodies who were able to plan long-term ventures, and also able to access vast sums of capital both from retention of profits and from the sophisticated money markets which were happy to invest in, or lend to, them. The phenomenal growth of the joint stock companies culminated in the British EIC. It was not just the biggest company ever to exist, but which actually ruled the biggest and richest nation on the planet, India, which, in 1700, was 25 per cent of the economy of the world, while Britain comprised a mere 3 per cent. Banking and the joint stock company boosted Europe and created the domination of the West.

The West now overtook the Muslim world in scientific and technological innovation. Till the fifteenth century, Muslims led the world in science, but after the seventeenth century, Western initiative started to surge ahead. Even where they lagged behind in invention, they were often the first to put invention to practical use. China invented gunpowder, but the armies of the West used it to conquer the world. The Muslims invented the first steam engine, but the only use they could put it to, was in turning a sheep over the fire to get an evenly cooked roast. In the practical hands of the West, the steam engine fired the Industrial Revolution by enabling a machine to do the work of hundreds of men. Mass production by the new machines required mass education to create a workforce capable of working the machines.

For centuries, Islam had led the world in the dispensation of justice; now justice in Muslim countries started to lose its shine, and the West, eager to protect property rights so that commerce could flourish, promoted and refined the rule of law. Where Islam had, for centuries, promoted liberal thought and toleration, now the tables had turned and Muslims became more rigid, while freedom of thought was encouraged in the West. In the matter of women's rights, Islam, which had led the way with property rights for women, now fell behind, earning criticism as a backward community, while the West was praised for the emancipation of women. Even the Muslim armies, feared for centuries as invincible, now grew soft, while the modern armies of the West built up their muscle in the competitive arena of Europe. The system of merit in the Muslim world was replaced by patronage and status, whereas open market competition in the West promoted the survival and rise of the fittest. Last but not least, gold and silver from the new American colonies flooded the economies of Europe, making Portugal and Spain super-rich as the oil-rich countries of the twentieth century became in our own times. But even more important than gold, silver and democracy was the Maxim gun which made resistance to the West, futile. Within a century, the Maxim gun was replaced by the nuclear bomb and other new-age weaponry, which put the West beyond challenge.

The eighteenth and the nineteenth centuries saw the collapse of the three great Muslim empires. The Moguls in India were defeated in turn, by Nader Shah of Persia, by Ahmad Shah Durrani the Afghan conqueror, by the Marathas from South India, and finally the British after the Indian Mutiny of 1857. The Qajars of Persia played at being emperors while their power passed to the British in the southern zone and to the Russians in the north. To pay their bills, they gradually sold off bits of their country to foreigners. The Ottomans, now known as the 'sick man of Europe', survived only because it was not in the interests of the Great Powers to let them be destroyed. Britain protected them against the Russians, the Russians protected them against the British, and both powers protected them against Mohammad Ali Pasha of Egypt.

As the nineteenth century drew to its close, the white man's takeover of the world was complete. The new empires straddled the world, and the wealth of Asia and Africa flowed to Europe. The mightiest empire of all was Britain, which controlled a quarter of the world's territory and a quarter of the world's people. The once proud Muslims were steadily reduced in wealth and power, till they became the serfs of their new white masters, to serve and live off the crumbs that were left to them. The worst fate was reserved for those who were shipped as slaves to America. They were deprived of everything—even their religion—as they were reduced to live as animals if they were lucky enough to survive the Atlantic crossing in the terrible slave ships. The Muslims had sunk into a pit from which it seemed that there was no escape.

In 1914, the great destructive power of the armies of the West now set about destroying itself. For over four years of total war, the great European powers exhausted themselves. In 1917, Russia opted out in response to Lenin's call for peace, bread and land; his revolution eliminated the dynasty of the Czars in Russia and created the world's first socialist state. The Ottomans had made the mistake of siding with Germany, and the victorious British carved up the old empire into a series of new states—Jordan, Iraq, Syria, and Lebanon. The Arabian Peninsula was divided into the new Kingdom of Saudi Arabia, Yemen and the Gulf sheikhdoms. The first generation of nation builders, the secular modernists, emerged—Ataturk, Reza Shah Pahlavi and Amanullah of Afghanistan.

HOPE IS REBORN

In 1939, the Second World War began as Britain and her allies moved to stop Adolf Hitler's drive to conquer Europe. It took five bloody years before Hitler was defeated by the combined forces of Britain, the USSR and America. The wars of the twentieth century killed 100 million people. The cost of Britain's victory was the loss of her empire. The mood of the British people was clearly demonstrated by the defeat of the war hero Winston Churchill in the post-war elections. Britain conceded independence to her colonies—even to the greatest colony of all, India, a continent in itself. The new Muslim homeland was created—Pakistan. In the Far East, Malaysia and Indonesia joined the growing list of new Muslim states. The second generation of secular modernizers—Mohammad Ali Jinnah, Nasser and Sukarno—became world figures. Hope was reborn as Muslims started to believe that the world of Islam was back on the rise, and that they would win back their place in the world. The opportunity of independence was given them by the two World Wars that exhausted their imperial masters; freedom fell into their grasp like a ripe apple falling from a tree. Now there were two problems for the Muslims to address— first their poverty and backwardness, and secondly, the new state of Israel that had been created in Arab lands by the departing British.

22

The Muslims Fight Back

'Persian oil is yours. We share the oil of Kuwait and Iraq. As for the Saudi Arabian oil, it's ours.'

—President Theodore Roosevelt (His statement to Lord Halifax, the British Ambassador)

Out of the debris of the two World Wars, were born the new Muslim nations. As the Europeans withdrew, new Muslim leaders emerged to reconstruct. Among them were the great men who followed Ataturk—Reza Shah and Jinnah, the new heroes of the Muslim world; Nasser of Egypt; King Faisal of Saudi Arabia; Sukarno of Indonesia; Mossadeq and the Ayatollah Khomeini of Iran; the great sheikhs of the oil rich states of the Gulf; Dr Mahathir of Malaysia; Saddam Husain of Iraq; and the enigmatic Gaddafi of Libya, both hero and villain.

In the Middle East, the British entrusted the new countries they created before leaving, to kings and tribal sheikhs. Somehow they felt safer with royalty than with the unpredictable public opinion of democracy; departing, they passed power to the al-Saud family in Arabia, the Shah in Iran, the sons of Hussein Sharif in Jordan and

Iraq, the Gulf Sheikhs, and the kings in North Africa from Morocco to Egypt where the descendants of Mohammad Ali still ruled. But as power passed from Britain, a monarchy, to America, a democratic republic, many of the kings of the Middle East disappeared; some went peacefully, such as the last Ottoman sultan in Turkey and King Farouk of Egypt; some faced bloody revolutions such as in Iraq and Iran; and some survived in Morocco, Jordan and the countries of the Arabian Peninsula.

NASSER: THE MOST POWERFUL SYMBOL OF PAN-ARABISM

> *'The problem with Nasser is that he has no vices. We can neither buy nor blackmail him. We hate this guy's guts, but we can't touch him; he's too clean.'*
>
> —The Central Intelligence Agency [CIA]
> (On Gamal Abdul Nasser)

> *'What's all this nonsense about isolating Nasser or 'neutralizing' him, as you call it? I want him destroyed, can't you understand? I want him murdered... And I don't give a damn if there's anarchy and chaos in Egypt.'*
>
> —Anthony Eden, prime minister of Great Britain

On 1 October 1970, 5 million Egyptians wept as they carried the body of Gamal Abdul Nasser to his grave. All the Arab heads-of-state attended his funeral, with the exception of King Faisal of Saudi Arabia. King Husain and Yasser Arafat cried openly, and Gaddafi of Libya fainted twice from emotional distress. This massive outpouring of grief was for a man who had lost the Six Day War with Israel, tried to resign but was forced to again take up the presidency by the demand of the Egyptian people. Nasser's political story spans the thirty years between 1940 and 1970; he died at the early age of fifty-two.

In the drama that was to unfold in Egypt, the villain was the fat and debauched King Farouk, to whom girls and money were much more important than the problems of his people. The descendants of Mohammad Ali were Albanians, and King Fuad, Farouk's father, had never even bothered to learn proper Arabic, preferring Turkish in private conversations and French in public. Farouk, with his addiction to girls and gambling, and his conspicuous consumption, was an international scandal. With his 240 cars, his two yachts, his fleet of private airplanes and his extensive wardrobe (with a collection of over a thousand neckties), he encouraged corruption and frivolity in an enfeebled nation. In 1942, the British had surrounded the palace with their troops and had forced the King at gunpoint to accept a prime minister of their choice, failing which he would be made to abdicate. The humiliation of their king shamed the Egyptians, and turned the people and the Egyptian army against their colonial masters. The seed of revolution was planted.

Nasser was an unsophisticated boy from a middle-class background, with a passionate sense of patriotism and a strong personal morality. He was determined, from an early age, to lift Egypt from the humiliation of centuries, in which she had been ruled by foreign conquerors, the last of whom were the British. He chose a career in the army as a way to fulfil his mission. His resolve crystallized as a result of the 1942 palace coup by the British and the humiliation of King Farouk, and again in 1948 when a disastrous war against the new state of Israel ended in shameful defeat due to defective arms purchased by corrupt decision-makers at court, who were more concerned by the amount of their kick-backs than about the quality of the weapons they purchased.

For ten long years, Nasser plotted and planned till 300 young officers had joined him in his underground group; they called themselves 'The Free Officers'. The most senior of The Free Officers was their leader, Nasser, and he was merely a colonel. His two closest deputies were Amer al-Hakim and Anwar Sadat. They needed a general—a figurehead—who would give them credibility. Their first choice was the honest General Fouad Sadek, but even as they were discussing his role, a message arrived that the King had appointed him commander-in-chief. Their second choice was General Naguib, a respected war hero.

Corruption and incompetence at court fired the resentment of the people. The first to move was the well-organized Muslim Brotherhood. They assassinated the prime minister Nokrashy. The secret police responded with the murder of Sheikh Hassan al-Banna, the leader of the Brotherhood. The mood in Cairo was dangerous.

Terrorist movements started against the British and Egyptian commandos attacked British garrisons. Skirmishes with British troops resulted in Egyptians casualties. When the news reached Cairo, demonstrations and riots began. The day is remembered as Black Saturday. The Badia cabaret and Rivoli cinema were set ablaze. Next, other places frequented by foreigners were set on fire—Metro cinema, Turf club, the Jewish department stores and the British department stores, and the Ford Motor car showroom. These were followed by attacks on the Trans World Airlines office, the French Art Gallery, Barclays Bank, and prominent cafes and restaurants. Flames and smoke were everywhere. The firing and destruction of the famous Shepherd's Hotel with its ivory-inlaid furniture, was the grand finale, after which, the looting began. As dusk fell, Martial Law and curfew was declared.

Nasser sensed that it was now time to move. He passed the word to ninety of his most trusted officers. The opportunity created by Black Saturday caused Nasser to move the date of the revolution forward; originally planned for 1955, the new date was now in 1952. The small band of revolutionaries could only hope to prevail, if the main army could be cut off and isolated in their barracks outside Cairo. The crucial job of cutting the communications to the army had been given to the firebrand, Sadat, but he was nowhere to be found; he had gone to the cinema with his wife!

Sadat's disappearance was the first of several setbacks that night. As he prepared to set out with Amer, Nasser was stopped by the arrival of a young soldier who warned him to give up his plans—news of the coup had leaked; it was now too dangerous. Nasser still decided to proceed. With the news out, there was no going back. A short way from his home, his small car was stopped by a traffic policeman for lack of a functioning tail-light. The policeman wanted to take him to the police station, but Nasser talked him out of it. Then as he rounded the corner, he ran into a blaze of headlights—a convoy of soldiers. This time Nasser was arrested by the lieutenant. Was it all over in so few minutes, after so many years of planning? The lieutenant called his superior officer who drove up in his jeep and, seeing Nasser, exclaimed, 'What are you doing here?' It was no enemy; the officer was one of his own most loyal supporters. Nasser ordered the officer to follow him to the military general headquarters (GHQ); the coup was on.

At the GHQ, the generals were engrossed in a meeting on how to tackle the situation. Nasser's troops stormed the building. A ten-minute shootout ended the ten years of preparation. Two guards were killed, two wounded and then twenty generals were captured and marched out as prisoners with their hands above their heads. Shouting and commotion announced that another officer had been arrested; it was Sadat who had finally arrived. Nasser, happy to see his friend, ordered his release.

The phone rang; it was General Naguib wanting to know what was going on. Nasser took the call: 'General, this is Gamal Abdel Nasser. Our boys have occupied GHQ. Wouldn't you like to come and join us?' The general said he had a newspaperman with him, Heikal; Nasser replied, 'Bring him with you'. Having made his revolution, Nasser now announced its leader, General Naguib.

Naguib was a good choice. He was honest and respected as a war hero. He had been wounded three times, the last of which almost proved fatal when he crawled 500 yards under fire to save one of his wounded officers. At the age of fifteen, he had run away from home to join the army, and had travelled 1,000 miles disguised as a servant to reach the recruiting office. Once there, he faced a hard disappointment when he was refused because of his height—five foot two inches, against the required minimum five foot three. He did stretching exercises but this only gave him an additional half an inch. In tears, he pleaded with the British recruiting office, 'I promise I will grow, sir.' He was accepted and later grew as promised! He constantly puffed at his pipe while Nasser chain-smoked his cigarettes. Naguib came from a line of distinguished officers; he was regularly top of his class and spoke English, Arabic, French, Italian, German and even some Hebrew. Like Nasser, he was an ardent admirer of Ataturk, but as a boy, his hero was Napoleon. He would sleep on the floor because Napoleon liked to sleep on the floor.

As Naguib basked in the limelight of public adoration as the hero of the revolution, Nasser remained hidden in the shadows. He took no office and no ministry. His name was unknown except to the 300 Free Officers who constituted the core power base of the new regime; it wasn't even mentioned in the newspapers and foreign governments were unaware of his existence. Censorship had taken over as Nasser wanted anonymity. Naguib did not seem to want real power; Nasser did not want recognition. But slowly, fame went to Naguib's head and he started to believe that he was the real leader.

All decisions were taken by the committee of the Free Officers but the first clash came after the removal of the King. Some were unhappy that his life had been spared. They now wanted to make up for lost time by executing the cronies of Farouk. A vote was taken and seven were voted for death; the only dissent came from Nasser. Nasser resigned as head of the committee and from the Free Officers and announced that he would also resign from the army. The committee was shattered; they could not do without Nasser. Hence, they capitulated—they would accept his every decision, but he must come back.

After eight months, Nasser made some important changes. He appointed Amer, commander-in-chief, and himself took the job of deputy prime minister, reducing Naguib's authority but leaving him at the top. This uneasy balance endured as Naguib grew frustrated at being dictated to by Nasser, and Nasser grew irritated by Naguib's resistance to his policies. The final clash came over the issue of democracy or revolution. Naguib wanted a return to democracy; Nasser wanted to continue with the revolution. He had already passed land reforms, but there was much more to be done. Suspicion and jealousy was already spoiling the relationship of the two men at the top.

This time it was Naguib who resigned. He was no longer prepared to be a mere figurehead; he wanted power. The Revolutionary Command Council (RCC) accepted his resignation, and Nasser was designated prime minister. The breech was now out in the open. Khalid Mohieddin, the young communist, sided with Naguib. But then, Naguib was abducted by Nasser's security men and driven out into the desert. After a few hours, he was returned to his house without an explanation. Was there a move to murder him followed by a sudden change of mind? No one knew the answer. Naguib was restored as President, with Nasser as his prime minister. Crowds came out on the streets shouting 'Long live Naguib,' and behind them were the hard core members of the Brotherhood.

At a massive public meeting, Naguib offered to forgive and forget, and then without agreement from his associates, announced that he was going to call an election of a parliament. Naguib had made his move and war began between the two leaders. It looked like Naguib would be the winner. He was restored as prime minister and chairman of the RCC. He called a press conference where he claimed that officers supporting Nasser had threatened his life. Nasser responded with cunning, offering to restore political parties and to return the soldiers to the barracks. Naguib was thrilled that parliament was to be restored and said he would not be a candidate in any election because he was a revolutionary, not a politician. Then Nasser counterattacked, bringing into the streets the powerful labour union, the Federation of Cairo Transport Workers, with their chanting, 'We want the revolution'.

Naguib had tied his star to the Brotherhood which provided him the strength of the street that he needed to counter Nasser. However, the Brotherhood was also to provide the justification of his downfall. Nasser had already started his war on the Brotherhood, when Naguib released 500 of their hard-line workers who had been arrested in the crackdown. In the confrontation that was unavoidable, he relied on his popularity, his stand on democracy and the support of the Brotherhood. Nasser controlled the Free Officers, represented change and most important of all, was ready to risk everything to reach his objectives.

Naguib went to the airport to say farewell to King Saud, who had been in Egypt on a state visit. As the King entered his aircraft, Naguib was escorted by security guards and the RCC made a formal decision postponing elections indefinitely. Naguib was replaced as prime minister by Nasser for the second time. Nasser called a massive public meeting in Tahrir Square. As he started to speak, an assassin in the eighth row fired several shots at him. By a miracle, Nasser was not hit; undeterred, he continued speaking and in that moment, won forever the heart of Egypt. The assassin, Mahmoud Abdul Latif, was a member of the Brotherhood. Arrests led to confessions and a massive conspiracy was revealed to kill over a hundred of the Free Officers; only Naguib was to be spared. Naguib was placed under house arrest, sentenced to ten years' imprisonment and moved to permanent isolation on an estate in the suburbs of Cairo. Nasser was now the undisputed leader of the revolution and of Egypt—he had successfully executed the Second Revolution.

In 1952, Nasser had led the Revolution of the Free Officers and then stepped aside and given leadership to General Naguib. By 1954, he had disposed of Naguib and had emerged the undisputed leader of Egypt. Within two years, by 1956, he had changed the history of Egypt and was recognized as an important leader of the Third World. In these two years, he first crushed the Muslim Brotherhood and the Egyptian communists, creating a one-party state; he then joined the unaligned states of the Third World with Nehru, Zhou Enlai, Tito and Sukarno, after which he signed an arms deal with the Communist bloc. Nasser then announced that he would build the High Dam at Aswan which would be his legacy to Egypt, and it would be seventeen times larger than the greatest pyramid built by the pharaohs. However, there was no money for this great scheme. Nasser adroitly played East against West, and hinted that Russia had offered over $1 billion to finance the project. America made a counter-offer, but the issue was clouded in uncertainty.

In 1956, Nasser ordered elections. He was the only candidate for President and he secured 99.9 per cent of the votes. But then his luck seemed to run out as America withdrew support for the dam when Nasser recognized Communist China. Nasser did not like being told what to do and reacted by calling an important public meeting in Alexandria where he spoke for three hours and twice repeated the name of the Frenchman who had built the Suez Canal, 'Mr Lesseps'. This was the signal that governor Riad had been waiting for; he marched into the headquarters of the Suez Canal Company and took possession. In Alexandria, Nasser announced the nationalization of the Canal Company, and that it would be run by Egyptians from now on. The crowd went wild with joy, Britain protested, France favoured military occupation, America criticized his move and Russia gave Nasser its unqualified support. Martial Law was declared in the Canal zone.

Britain froze the Egyptian bank accounts in England, imposed sanctions and fermented counter-revolution in Egypt. Their radio propaganda stated, 'The salvation of Egypt depends on ousting the mad tyrant, Gamal Abdul Nasser.' The Canal Company offered large incentives to employees to induce them to resign so that Nasser would lack the technical capability to run the canal. Nasser responded, 'Give them exit visas at once. Tell the airlines to give them priority reservations'.

Britain, France and Israel met secretly and planned war. On 29 October 1956, when Nasser was celebrating the birthday of his five-year-old son, he received the news that Israel had invaded Egypt. Britain and France called for Egyptian troops to withdraw from the canal. Nasser broke off diplomatic relations with Britain and France and ordered the seizure of all their property in Egypt. His security advised him to move his family to safety, but Nasser refused, saying that it would set a bad example. He spoke to the people of Egypt,

'We will fight from village to village, from house to house... We shall fight, fight, fight and never surrender.'

With Britain, France and Israel aligned against him, analysts around the world predicted the end of Nasser. But fortune favours the brave. From China, Mao Zedong announced that he would send 300,000 Chinese to defend Egypt. From Moscow, Premier Bulganin sent letters to the prime ministers of Britain, France and Israel that Russia was prepared to use force to 'crush the aggressors and restore peace'. Bulganin hinted that unless Britain and France halted their attack, it could result in full-fledged nuclear war. Under pressure from the USA, the British prime minister, Eden, who had demanded the murder of Nasser, was forced to withdraw unconditionally. The crisis was over; Nasser had won. In January 1957, Anthony Eden resigned as prime minister of Britain.

Nasser's Suez Canal victory made him a Third World hero. Success followed success. Russia provided money to start work on his cherished scheme to construct the Aswan Dam, which had been a dream for Egyptian rulers for a thousand years from the time when al-Haytham had offered to build it for the Caliph al-Hakim. The dam, 3.5-kilometres-long and 111-metres-high created the 500-kilometre long Lake Nasser and was the greatest new project undertaken in any of the countries of the Third World.

Nasser united Egypt and Syria and the new country of the United Arab Republic (UAR) was born. But the new union floundered and when Arif was removed from power by Qasim, Egypt and Syria reverted to their former status as two separate countries. Despite the failure of the UAR, Nasser remained the most powerful symbol of Pan-Arabism throughout the Middle East.

Nasser's attempt to modernize Egypt was frustrated by the lack of foreign investment. After his takeover of the canal, the West did not like Nasser and kept away from Egypt. Nasser responded by taking the economy to the left, and the market economy of Egypt was converted to a mixed economy with the state playing a growing part in the ownership of business. In 1961, the Socialist Decrees ushered in extensive state nationalization of banks and other industries. But starved of foreign exchange, the economy had started to flounder.

THE SIX DAY WAR

On 5 June 1967, the Israeli army attacked. The Six Day War, from 5–10 June, saw the greatest defeat and humiliation of the Arabs. The Israelis simultaneously attacked Egypt, Syria and Jordan.

In the first seventy-two hours, Israeli aircraft destroyed the Egyptian air force on the ground. In six days, the Israelis captured the West Bank, the Gaza Strip and the Sinai Peninsula up to the Suez Canal. The new territories conquered contained 600,000 Palestinians who formed a resistance force under the Palestine Liberation Organisation (PLO). The Six Day War changed the history of the Middle East.

The War was a shattering blow to Nasser. On 9 June, he made a speech which was broadcast throughout Egypt, taking full responsibility for the defeat and resigning from his every office. He would fight on as a simple citizen and soldier. But history has strange and unexpected twists. Where Churchill had been rejected by his people after winning the World War, Nasser was acclaimed and endorsed by the Egyptian masses after his defeat. Over 2 million people crowded the streets of Cairo demanding back as leader, the man who had overthrown the King, ended the British occupation, taken the Suez Canal, started the High Dam at Aswan, carried out land reforms, built factories and schools and brought clean water and electricity to the villages. His integrity and the example of his simple middle-class life, as a man who loved his family but did not want either wealth or dynasty, had won the heart of Egypt. The next day Nasser withdrew his resignation.

Nasser's closest friend, Amer, the commander-in-chief of the army, took the fall for the humiliating defeat. Dismissed and arrested, he allegedly committed suicide. After his death, a vilification campaign publicized lurid revelations of his womanizing and drug-taking. Nasser also attacked 'The New Class' of privileged officers with conspicuous lifestyles. Broken by the humiliation of the Six Day War, on 28 September 1970, he died of a heart attack.

Nasser was succeeded by his friend and fellow revolutionary, Anwar Sadat. In 1973, Sadat avenged the defeat of the Six Day War with a joint Egyptian–Syrian attack on Israel. Four years later, in 1977, Sadat made his news-breaking visit to Jerusalem and in 1979 signed a peace treaty at Camp David. As reward for the peace treaty, Egypt received large financial support from America; as punishment for his friendship with Israel, Sadat was assassinated. In eleven years, Sadat had reversed the Nasser revolution in Egypt and Nasser's romanticism was replaced by Sadat's practical approach. Nasser's leftist economic policies were also replaced by Sadat's capitalism and his alliance with the USA. Nasser's puritan government was replaced by the free wheeling and dealing of the Sadat regime. Nasser's hostility to the Brotherhood was replaced by Sadat's disastrous attempt to befriend them. One era died, but a new era was born.

KING FAISAL

'I only wish I had three Faisals.'

—King Abdul Aziz, Faisal's father

'Is there one verse in the Quran that forbids teaching women to read?'

—King Faisal

'If you want to be generous, be generous out of what you possess.'

—King Faisal (His statement during his UN speech against the partitioning of Palestine to create the state of Israel)

Nasser was a great man fired by his belief in Islamic socialism and Pan-Arabism. King Faisal of Saudi Arabia, different in every way from Nasser, had an even greater impact on history with his promotion of

Islamism and his handling of oil politics to make Saudi Arabia into a super-rich world power. Both men, the commoner and the King, who were destined to become adversaries, were honest men who believed in simple living. Nasser rejected the presidential palace, preferring to live in his modest middle-class home. Faisal, on being shown his royal palace, refused to occupy its magnificent bedroom, preferring to sleep in a small room with a single bed. Nasser's integrity was legendary; Faisal discouraged corruption. In fact, when the latter heard that Raytheon had appointed his son, Abdullah, as their agent, with a $75-million commission, he gave the billion-dollar contract to their competitor, Vinnell Corporation. Both men were shy of power—Nasser sat patiently in the shadows for two years while Naguib ruled, and Faisal patiently endured his frustration with his brother, Saud's style of government for eleven years. Both men took and withdrew from power several times before finally and irrevocably taking the reins of government.

Faisal's mother was a descendant of ibn Abdul Wahhab. She died when Faisal was only seven and he grew up in the house of her father, a strict religious teacher. At the age of fourteen, he was sent by his father, King Abdul Aziz, to England on his first official visit, and was eased into the role of foreign minister, a role he held till his death. Faisal was married to the younger sister of Hassa al Sudairi, the wife of ibn Saud, whose seven sons became the most powerful princes in the realm. His official travels as his father's representative also took him to Russia, where he met Stalin. In Istanbul, he met a sophisticated and well-read Saudi lady, Effat al-Thunayan, and it was love at first sight. They married, and for the rest of his life, Faisal remained devoted only to her, never marrying again. She encouraged her sons to pursue high-level education at top international universities, and promoted the education of girls in the kingdom. Faisal's personal character and accomplishments under his father won him the respect of the family and of the kingdom.

King Abdul Aziz, on his deathbed, called Saud and Faisal and made them promise to work together—Saud as King and Faisal as

Crown Prince. It was a promise Faisal worked hard to keep. Saud inherited a country with a reasonably strong cash flow from its oil revenues. But he lacked intelligence, was over-generous and excessively spendthrift. He spent more on his palaces than on national education or health budgets. Ignoring his brothers, he gave key ministries such as the Defence and the National Guard to his sons. His lifestyle damaged his health, necessitating frequent trips to medical institutions in the West and leaving him unfit to rule. Saud had numerous wives and 107 children, many of whose names he could not even remember. He was a bad judge of people and appointed his chauffeur, who was an accomplice in his vices, as controller of the royal budget.

Within the first five years of his reign, Saud had shown that he was incapable of running the affairs of the kingdom. In 1957, the relationship with Nasser's Egypt took a turn for the worse. The Saudi security police made arrests when they unearthed an assassination plot which they claimed was sponsored by Egypt. Saud countered with a plot to blow up Nasser's airplane and promised £20 million for the job. An advance payment of £1.9 million was made by three checks, which were shown to the press by the recipient and beneficiary, Syria's Chief of Intelligence. By 1958, the government was broke. The princes asked Faisal to step in and repair the damage. Faisal imposed an austerity program, reduced spending, reigned in inflation and balanced the budget. Within a short time, government finances were restored to health. But Faisal's economic policies tightened the belt for both princes and merchants, the latter of whose profits were reduced. Faisal's last act in this two-year period of controlling the government was to have Saudi Arabia join with the other major producers of oil—Iran, Iraq, Kuwait, Libya and Venezuela—in creating the new body called Organization of the Petroleum Exporting Countries (OPEC).

In 1960, Saud was back and again demanded power. Faisal bowed out and allowed his elder brother to take back control. But within a year, Saud collapsed, vomiting blood, and was hospitalized. He flew to America for treatment leaving Faisal once more in charge. Faisal moved fast to sack the Nasserites in the Saudi government, including the passionate and brilliant oil minister Abdullah Tariki, who had played an important part in creating OPEC and clawing back a balance of power from the Western oil companies. Faisal replaced Tariki with Ahmed Zaki Yamani, a quiet and intelligent Harvard-educated lawyer, who was to dominate world oil for the coming decades.

Faisal was surrounded by problems when he again took control in 1962. Nasserism was on the ascendency throughout the Middle East. Radical regimes ruled in Egypt, Yemen, Iraq and Syria. Talal and two other liberal princes, admirers of Nasser, were in Cairo. Thus, many predicted the end of the Saudi monarchy. Faisal moved fast in purging the pro-Nasser elements in the Saudi government. He also sacked Saud's sons from their key military commands. He announced a ten-point program of reform, which included improved education of women. When demonstrators resisted, he asked them, 'Is there one verse in the *Quran* that forbids teaching women to read?' He invested heavily in improving the infrastructure and building airports, roads, electricity, desalinization plants for drinking water and all the other requirements of a modern country. He passed a law abolishing slavery to placate America even though slavery in the world of Islam was not the cruel and harsh institution that it had been in the USA. In 1943, Faisal had visited America with his black slaves, and had shocked the management of the famous Waldorf Astoria Hotel in New York when he had insisted that they eat with him in the 'whites-only' Wedgewood dining room. Most of the freed slaves in The Kingdom continued to serve their masters as domestic servants in the establishments that they considered home. In 1963, Saud returned, demanding that Faisal pass power back; after all, he was still King. Faisal was deferential as ever to his elder brother, kissing his hand, sitting at his feet and even kneeling to put Saud's slippers on his feet, but it was time for the showdown. Saud locked himself into his palace and deployed the Royal Guard around its walls. Prince Abdullah surrounded the Royal Guard with his National Guard, and Faisal ordered the arrest of Sultan, the son of Saud. Saud, not ready to be a figurehead, retorted, 'I am not Queen Elizabeth.'

The following year, two important meetings took place—the clerics and the princes both decided that Saud had to go. Sixty-eight princes and twelve senior clerics signed the declaration that Saud was out and Faisal was the new king. Still, Saud refused to abdicate. Muhammad, the third oldest brother, known for his temper, went to Saud with an ultimatum—resign, or lose your property and your freedom. Saud, recognizing that there was no other option, signed the document of abdication. After eleven years it was finally over; Faisal was King.

Faisal was a great king. To observers in the West, he seemed to be an excessively conservative rightist, but to many in his own country, he was too modern and not conservative enough. His attitudes towards women's education and emancipation of slavery did not please the fundamentalist clerics. He promoted television and allowed famous singers such as Umm Kalthoum to reach mass audiences. Demonstrators protested, and one of his nephews, Khalid ibn Musaid, led a crowd to destroy the TV station. Faisal responded hard, and told the chief of Police, 'None of us is above the law. If the prince fires at you, you must fire back.' The prince was killed in the shootout. This sad death of the prince was later to boomerang on Faisal.

Faisal's problems were not restricted to the economy—there had been a power struggle with his elder brother, the King; the growth of Nasser's influence and Nasserite sympathies even amongst the princes; and the resistance of the clergy to his reform policies. He also had to deal with a proxy war on his doorstep in Yemen where 60,000 Egyptian soldiers—three times the number of his own army—threatened the peninsula. Patiently, he dealt with every difficulty, quietly and calmly responding to his opponents' moves. His own initiatives were on three fronts:

- Creating an international community of Islamic countries, which would be united against Zionism, communism and Western imperialism
- Reforms in the kingdom
- The intricate game of oil politics

Shattered by his defeat in the Six Day War, and having failed in Yemen, Nasser died in 1970. Faisal had a warm relationship with Anwar Sadat, more Islamist and less socialist than his predecessor. When Sadat prepared his revenge on Israel through the Yom Kippur War, Faisal backed him, first with money and then in 1973, by stopping all oil sales to America. The oil embargo was the culmination of a decade of strategic oil politics by Faisal and Yamani that changed the economic balance of the world.

In the 1960s, America was almost self-sufficient in oil; by the 1970s, oil demand in the USA, Europe and Japan had grown very substantially, and all were now dependent on the Middle East oil supply. When the Trans-Arabian Pipeline was blown up by terrorists, Gaddafi raised his demands and increased taxation and royalties on the oil companies. Others followed Gaddafi's lead and in 1971, the new balance of power was recognized in the Tehran Agreement. The day of the Seven Sisters was over; OPEC was now in control. The next demand of the oil producers was for shareholding in the oil companies working in their countries.

In 1972, Sadat purchased Soviet arms and prepared for war with Israel. King Faisal sent Yamani together with his son Saud, the deputy petroleum minister, to Washington to urge America to take a more balanced approach to the Middle East situation. Washington did not take the Saudi warnings seriously, Kissinger refused to meet them, and the CIA told Nixon, 'Faisal is bluffing.' King Faisal made a statement that 'America's complete support for Zionism makes it extremely difficult for us to supply its petroleum needs.' Gaddafi, ever the hawk, announced the nationalization of 51 per cent of the shares of oil companies operating in Libya. The USA threatened Libya with boycott and litigation. Nixon warned Gaddafi that oil without a market would not do a country much good. But Nixon was out of touch with reality, as the *New York Times* commented, 'President Nixon has not yet grasped that today the problem is not whether oil will find markets, but whether markets will find oil.' Twenty years earlier, Mossadeq had tried the nationalization of oil companies in

Iran; he failed because supply was greater than demand. Now Gaddafi succeeded because his action was timely, with demand much greater than supply.

1973 was the year in which the scales tipped in the world oil market. Over the eight preceding years, world demand had doubled; raising the price from $1.80 to $5.12, and The Kingdom—with 23 per cent of world exports—was the swing producer. The Yom Kippur War started with the Egyptian army's advance into the Sinai territories, which had been occupied by the Israelis in the Six Day War. Nixon responded fast and hard, immediately sending $2.2 billion worth of advanced weapons, three times as much as the Israelis had requested. He commented, 'If we are going to do it, let's do it big.' Faisal announced a total halt in oil exports to the USA. Other Arab producers joined the embargo. Tensions mounted as the USA threatened countermeasures; Yamani warned that if America imposed sanctions, Saudi Arabia would cut production by 80 per cent.

Japan, with only fifty-nine days of oil reserves, was the first to break ranks. Europe imposed emergency measures, with petrol rationing, and harsh cutbacks on all consumption. In America, gas stations shut down as stocks ran out, the lights in Times Square were switched off and weekend driving stopped. The international price of oil rose above $11 with auction prices topping $17 a barrel. Consumers wept, while profits of the Western oil companies, Exxon, Texaco, Gulf and Shell, soared to record highs.

Faisal's oil embargo and the consequent price rise of oil led to the greatest transfer of wealth in history, which soon exceeded $100 million a day and forty years later, even topped $1 billion a day. The Arab oil producing nations with their massive incomes and small populations became the super-rich of the world. This was Faisal's legacy. *Time* magazine named Faisal its 'Man of the Year.'

On 25 March 1975, Faisal went to his office at 10.25 am. Seven minutes later, his twenty-seven-year-old nephew, Prince Faisal ibn Musaid, the brother of Khalid ibn Musaid, who had been killed in a police shootout years before, walked in and shot the King in revenge for his brother; three bullets hit Faisal, killing him. Within three months, Prince Faisal was executed for the assassination.

MOHAMMAD MOSSADEQ

'Iran is not in a revolutionary or even a pre-revolutionary situation.'

—The CIA (in 1978)

'Who is this Khomeini?'

—Empress Fara Diba (in 1978)

When Reza Shah abdicated and departed in exile, his son, Mohammad Reza became King. Timid, unsure of himself and dominated by his aggressive twin sister Princess Ashraf, he relied on the experienced French-speaking Qajar aristocrats to run his government. He kept himself busy, chasing pretty young starlets around Europe, and enjoying the lifestyle of a royal jetsetter. He married the beautiful Princess Fawzia of Egypt, but soon, bored of life in Iran, she returned to her cosmopolitan Cairo, where she sought a divorce. He then married the even more beautiful Soraya, but shed her when she failed to give him a son and heir. Finally, he married the glamorous young Fara Diba, who became his empress and the mother to his children. But despite this series of beautiful wives, he kept himself very busy with his extra-curricular activities; the Shah was a serious womanizer.

In February 1949, a lone assassin fired five shots at point blank range at the young Shah. Three bullets hit the Shah's cap, one bullet tore through his right cheek, and the fifth bullet hit his shoulder. The Shah faced his assassin who raised his gun to fire the sixth shot. However, a miracle saved him from certain death as the gun jammed and the security guards killed the assassin. This incident changed the Shah, who now saw himself as the instrument of God with an important destiny. The Shah used the assassination attempt to justify a crackdown on the strong Communist party, The Tudeh. But regardless of divine destiny, the Shah was not ready to confront British interests in Iran. The British control of Irani oil had kept her position as a world power, and her governments recognized that without Irani oil there would be no hope of maintaining the British standard of living.

The AIOC was the greatest British corporate asset in the world, comprising of massive oil reserves, tankers, a trading and distribution network and the world's largest oil refinery at Abadan. The British were obsessively jealous of their control of Irani oil, and were prepared to go to any lengths to protect it. The Iranis accused them of cheating and falsified accounts, and maintained that Iran was short-changed while the Company kept the lion's share of the profits. They also kept the thousands of Irani labour who worked for the company, in sub-human conditions, which were an embarrassment to the civilized world.

In 1933, Reza Shah had signed the agreement that formed the basis of British control of Irani oil. Now, in 1949, the Company came forward with a Supplementary Agreement to bring the terms up to date. The young Shah was not in a mood to take risks; he had his cabinet accept the Supplementary Agreement. But the Majlis, or Parliament, was not ready to approve the deal. The opposition to the Supplementary Agreement was led by a sixty-seven-year-old aristocrat, Mohammad Mossadeq.

Mossadeq was born to power; his mother was a Qajar princess and his first government office was at the age of fifteen. Educated in France and Switzerland, he was a democrat, a nationalist and an incorruptible idealist. Throughout his long life, he regularly refused career opportunities, and even when he accepted, was always ready to resign on point of principal. When Reza Shah took the crown, Mossadeq boldly opposed the move and went into retirement during his long rule.

The AIOC was defended by the recently re-elected Winston Churchill who called Mossadeq, 'an elderly lunatic bent on wrecking his country and handing it over to the Communists.' *Time* magazine chose him as its Man of the Year (1951), preferring him over Churchill, Truman and Eisenhower. The results of this epic struggle changed the history of the region for the next half-century.

Lunatic or not, and despite his eccentric behaviour and his public appearances in his famous pink pajamas, Mossadeq rose on his unswerving opposition to the AIOC to become the most popular man in Persia—the people's hero. The Shah tried to contain him by raising General Razmara, the able and ambitious commander-in-chief to prime minister. But Razmara ruled for less than a year before he was assassinated by the Fedayeen-e-Islam, an extremist religious group with links to the Ayatollah Kashani, the most politically prominent religious leader of the time. Within three months of the general's death, Mossadeq was prime minister. His time had come. Offered the primeministership, he agreed on the condition that nationalization of the AIOC be ratified that very day.

The Shah controlled the army, and through the army, controlled Iran. The War Ministry was by tradition, his right. Mossadeq informed the Shah that he would keep the War Ministry for himself, and by doing so, earned the enmity of his ruler. The Shah went hostile; so in response Mossadeq resigned. But Mossadeq was already more than just a prime minister, he was a symbol of nationalization of the AIOC and its replacement by the National Iranian Oil Company (NIOC). The mobs took the streets and Mossadeq's National Front was beyond challenge as it was joined by Kashani's rightists and the Tudeh leftists. Iran was united by Mossadeq; the British were determined to destroy him.

When the British tried to resist Mossadeq's nationalization, he took over the AIOC wells, pipelines, refinery and offices. The British responded by evacuating all British personnel, blocking the export of oil and lodging a complaint with the UN. They planned to remove Mossadeq by force, but before they could move, the wily prime minister severed diplomatic relations and closed down the British embassy. The British, in reply, seized Irani assets in British banks and moved their battleships into the Gulf. Mossadeq consolidated his power at the Shah's expense; he transferred the vast 'royal estates' back to the state, cut the palace budget and exiled the Shah's politically-active twin sister, Ashraf.

The British were determined to fight. Their AIOC had the world's biggest refinery and was the second largest exporter of crude oil with the third largest oil reserves in the world. If Mossadeq succeeded, it would set an example to others in Iraq, Indonesia and Venezuela. British confidential memos stated, 'The security of the free world is dependent on large quantities of oil from Middle-Eastern sources. If the attitude in Iran spreads to Saudi Arabia or Iraq, the whole structure may break down along with our ability to defend ourselves... The United Kingdom has to keep control of the real resources involved.'

The British turned to America for help. Churchill was a strategist and rather than admit to Eisenhower that it was all about British oil interests, he argued that it was about Communism that was determined to take over the world, and that the contest for Iran oil was the battlefield that the Free World could not afford to lose. Eisenhower was assisted by two brothers—John Foster Dulles, the secretary of state; and Allen Dulles, the director of the CIA. They sent in one man to deal with it—the soft spoken super-spy, Kermit Roosevelt.

Kermit prepared his ground. Misinformation, street action, rent-a-mob, subversion in the army and buying parliamentarians whose loyalties were for sale, were his weapons. He prepared his coup d'état. The candidate to replace Mossadeq as prime minister was General Fazlollah Zahedi, a strange choice. Some years earlier, when the war was being fought against the Germans, the British had decided that General Fazlollah needed to be removed. He was kidnapped by a small team, flown to Palestine and imprisoned for the remainder of the war. A search of his private quarters revealed a collection of German weapons, an assortment of silk underwear and a photo collection of Tehran's call-girls. The general was a ladies' man, addicted to gambling and beautiful women; but he was also a professional soldier connected to every officer in the army. Now that they needed a compliant general as prime minister to play ball, he was resurrected, and prepared for his part.

The last requirement that Roosevelt needed before he could start was two firmans signed by the Shah—the first sacking Mossadeq; the second appointing General Zahedi, prime minister in his place. The Shah was frightened to sign, because, as he correctly pointed out, these orders would not be legal; it would require the Majlis to remove a prime minister. First, the Americans tried to get Princess Ashraf to persuade her brother. Ashraf, in exile, was living it up in Monte Carlo, where she was persuaded by the gift of a fur coat and a wad of cash to go back to persuade her brother. She tried, but it didn't work. The next attempt was made by General Norman Schwarzkopf, the father of the general, who was to become famous in a later Gulf War against Saddam Hussein. This too failed. Finally, Kermit Roosevelt himself met the Shah at midnight in secrecy, and persuaded him to sign the sensitive document.

The coup was ready to go and was given the code name 'Operation Ajax'. Roosevelt gave the signal, and the street mob was activated by the Rashidian Brothers, wealthy businessmen who worked as agents of the British. Ayatollah Kashani and his agitators escalated the street action, together with street toughs such as Shaban the Brainless and bodybuilders from the wrestling school. Colonel Nassiri proceeded with a brigade to Mossadeq's house. On the way, he was to arrest the army commander-in-chief. The chief's house was deserted, so Nassiri moved on to arrest Mossadeq. But he was in for a surprise; Mossadeq had been forewarned, and was protected by the chief and his troops, who in turn, arrested Nassiri. General Zahedi went into hiding. The coup had misfired; all was lost. Roosevelt was ordered by his command to get out before he was killed. The Shah flew his own aircraft to Baghdad, and then on to Rome. He wryly commented that he would need to find work soon since he did not have the funds for a long stay.

Ordinarily, that should have been the end of the story. Nothing is as dead as a failed coup. But Kermit Roosevelt was not your normal bureaucrat; he decided he would have one more try. Over the next few days, once more he rented his mob, once more he created chaos in the streets, once more he persuaded and bought army generals, once more he activated Kashani and his religious supporters, and once more, he paid Shaban the Brainless and his toughs to take over the streets. The countercoup was successful. Zahedi was installed and Mossadeq put to flight. The Shah had won; Mossadeq had lost. The Shah was having dinner in the Excelsior Hotel in Rome with his lovely wife Soraya when he received the news. He jumped up exclaiming, 'I knew it. They love me!' Soraya steadied her husband's arm, murmuring, 'How exciting!'

Mossadeq surrendered to Zahedi at the officer's club where the general was headquartered. They met and greeted each other with mutual respect, and Zahedi housed his foe in a comfortable suite in the club. But once the Shah was back, the tone changed; it was a time for punishment and it was a time for reward. Mossadeq was sentenced to three years' imprisonment, followed by house arrest till his death. Hussein Fatemi, the former foreign minister was executed. Six hundred army officers who had remained loyal to Mossadeq were arrested, and of these, sixty were shot. Roosevelt was invited to the palace where the Shah thanked and toasted him: 'I owe my throne to God, my people, my army—and to you.' Colonel Nassiri was promoted to General and was made head of Sāzemān-e Ettelā'āt va Amniyat-e Keshvar (SAVAK), or the Organization of National Intelligence and Security. General Fazlollah Zahedi became prime minister. His son Ardeshir, was married to Shahnaz, the daughter of the Shah, and was rewarded with the ambassadorships of the UK and the USA. Captain Khatami, who piloted the Shah to Baghdad and Rome when he fled, was made commander of the Air Force. Shaban the Brainless was given a yellow Cadillac which he proudly drove around town with his band of toughs. And last but not least, America gained entry as a partner in the NIOC operations to share the prize with the British for years to come, till the wheel of history turned full circle again.

The next twenty-five years were the Shah's golden years. He was the prime beneficiary, first of Mossadeq's oil nationalization and then of OPEC's victory over Western oil. Over the twenty years between 1955 and 1975, Iran's oil revenues rose from $34 million to $20 billion. The rate of growth of the Irani economy surpassed even the massive Chinese growth under Deng. The Shah boasted that the standard of living in Iran would soon surpass that of Europe; within a generation he would make Iran the fifth most powerful country in the world, after the USA, the Soviet Union, China and Japan. By 1975, the Shah had the largest navy in the Persian Gulf, the largest air force in Western Asia, and the fifth largest army in the world.

In the Shah's White Revolution, education, infrastructure and industry grew; and with it grew massive income inequality, as the rich grew richer and the poor grew poorer. Land reforms cut down the power of the great estates, but did little to increase agricultural production. It was all about oil, and who got a piece of the action. The elite who prospered the most were the army, the bureaucrats and those close to court, who harvested the business opportunities, which were plenty. His Pahlavi Foundation dispensed charity, patronage and promoted the immense wealth of the Shah and his family, estimated in excess of $20 billion.

The Shah's growing arrogance created a court of sycophants who feared him but recognized that he could give them wealth or power on a mood or a whim. His SAVAK used imprisonment, terror and torture to cow down his people. His one-party state, under his Rastakhiz Party, dominated political activity. If he meant well, he was nevertheless too impatient, too intolerant, and with his Western education and values, was too far removed from the reality of the Irani people. His reforms ignored traditional values and overrode the Sharia, which set the rule for the day-to-day lives of the masses. Women's emancipation was followed by Western fashions and the décolleté, which exposed too much skin, and it was not well received. His crushing of the clerics and his exiling of Khomeini, led to a simmering resentment. He was America's darling, but was hated by his own people. And as the years passed, he grew sick, remained hidden from his people, as cancer spread through his body.

RUHOLLAH KHOMEINI

His nemesis was the iron-willed ayatollah, Ruhollah Khomeini, who resisted the Shah, struggled against his regime, overthrew him and created the revolutionary Islamic Republic of Iran. As a boy, Khomeini was happy and energetic, and his favourite games were wrestling and leapfrog. His family was well-off and he was able to focus on religious studies. In the sixties, the Shah launched his White Revolution and backed it with the strength of the state. His Westernization program disturbed the clergy, but their leadership, cowed by the threats and the danger in taking the path of resistance, backed down. The most senior ayatollahs advised keeping a distance from political opposition and did not resist. Khomeini feared nothing and spoke out defiantly against the Shah and his White Revolution: 'We neither care about the constitution nor want anything to do with it. Our constitution is the law of Islam.' He saw that the senior ayatollahs, Shariatmadari and Golpaygani, were not ready to fight and that they were not the men for the battlefield. Thus, he decided to struggle alone. As the clashes grew between the police and the demonstrators who protested against the Shah, Khomeini's stature grew in recognition of his fearlessness and his readiness for personal risk. After his most insulting speech against the Shah, Khomeini was arrested. Riots started in Qum and the establishment troops responded hard; twenty-eight of the demonstrators were killed by automatic fire. General Nassiri, the head of SAVAK, and the hawks, wanted Khomeini tried and executed. The Ayatollahs wanted his release, so they declared Khomeini an Ayatollah, since an ayatollah could not be tried, let alone executed. Khomeini himself was dismissive of his interrogators: 'You have no right to question me. Take your paper and pen and leave this place. I do not want you to sit here.' The cultured and gentle General Pakravan was sent to talk to Khomeini; he suggested that Khomeini's speech had been too strong, and his insulting language to a head of state was excessive. Khomeini replied, 'I may have used strong language, but the intention was to advise.' The general laughed and said that Khomeini was free to go, but advised him against participating in politics, which is a world of lies, deceit, hypocrisy and cheating. Khomeini replied that he had never been involved in this type of politics. Ten months after his arrest, Khomeini returned home. The battle had been lost but his leadership had been established.

The Shah owed his crown to the CIA countercoup which had removed Mossadeq and brought the Shah back from his exile in Rome. He was also indebted to US aid and American support. In 1964, his government passed the law giving diplomatic immunity to American military personnel in Iran. This gave Khomeini an opportunity to renew his attack. In a historic and hard-hitting speech, he proclaimed:

> They have reduced the Irani people to a level lower than an American dog. If someone runs over a dog belonging to an American, he will be prosecuted. Even if the Shah himself were to run over a dog belonging to an American, he would be prosecuted. But if an American cook runs over the Shah, the head of state, no one will have the right to interfere with him. Why? Because they wanted a loan and America demanded this in return.

Khomeini was arrested, driven to the airport and sent in exile to Turkey.

Ataturk's secular Turkey was a culture shock to Khomeini. He was lodged with a colonel from Turkish Intelligence, where he lived with the family. At first, he was uncomfortable with the colonel's wife, but when she understood the Ayatollah and started to wear long dresses and a headscarf, family life grew more relaxed. The family became attached to Khomeini, who they addressed as father, and there were tears in the eyes of Khomeini and his hosts when they finally said goodbye. Despite their friction in the beginning, his hostess described him as a 'nice old man and very polite.' When Khomeini first came to them, he was penniless, but soon visitors and money started reaching him; by the time he left, he was a millionaire with a large fortune gifted by his admirers.

In October 1965, Khomeini was allowed to move to Najaf in Iraq. Najaf was a major centre of Shia Islam, and Khomeini was moving back into his own world. He arrived at Baghdad airport where there was no one to meet him, so he took a taxi after haggling over the price. He may have had millions, but he was always frugal with money, which he considered as a trust. He then checked in to a cheap hotel. As news spread of the Ayatollah's arrival, visitors started to arrive to greet him. By the time he reached Karbala, a large welcoming committee received him and his celebrity status was restored. The students and religious public welcomed him with affection and respect, but would the grand ayatollahs see him as a friend or as a problematic rival?

The senior clergy were wary of Khomeini, and it was remarked, 'This Seyyed has created havoc in Qum. We must be careful not to let him do the same in Najaf.' Khomeini wanted the politicization of religion; the ayatollahs of Iraq believed this course of action was rash, foolhardy and dangerous. In Iran, Shiaism was the state religion; in Iraq, under the Baath Party, repression was the order of the day. The grand ayatollahs, Hakim and Kho'i, opposed him, arguing that there was no point in sending people to certain death. Khomeini replied that The Prophet was also political.

Unable to fight, Khomeini concentrated on writing. He formulated his theory of velayat e faqih, the guardianship of the jurist, which was to later form the basis of his revolution and the Islamic government that followed in Iran. Khomeini's velayat e faqih was, in every way, a revolutionary doctrine and was opposed by the senior ayatollahs both in Iraq and in Iran, but he was determined that this was the way, and like Lenin in Russia, he developed, over many years, a cadre committed to his philosophy, a network that was to prove crucial when the time to strike finally arrived. Khomeini lived, for thirteen years, as an exile in Iraq, before he was asked to leave by Saddam Hussein in 1978. He then moved to Paris, where, at first, he was the guest of Bani Sadr in his fourth floor apartment but soon he moved into his own villa in the suburb of Neauphle-le-Chateau, where he held court till his return to Iran. His schedule ran like clockwork, but one day before mid-day prayers, Khomeini took a long time to emerge from the toilet. Finally, he came out and when his concerned wife asked him why he had taken so long, he replied, 'The people who come to use the lavatory are my guests. It is my duty to help you keep this place clean.'

By 1978, the Shah was in an advanced stage of cancer. Demonstrators demanding the end of the Shah had established that the strength of the street was more than a match for the strength of the state. The uprising was orchestrated by Khomeini from Paris, through tapes, pamphlets and a military level precision in strategizing and mobilizing his network in Iran. The Shah vacillated between concessions and crack-downs, with a purge of the hawks in his team, which further demoralized his supporters. In August, a fire in the cinema in Abadan resulted in the deaths of 477 people and finally in September, the Shah declared Martial Law. But it was too little too late; the bloodshed continued and the final confrontation came to a head on 'Black Friday.' Ayatollah Kho'i commented with sarcasm, 'It shows they are donkeys. Human beings do not stand in the street facing machine guns.' The Shah prepared his exit and appointed his last prime minister, Shahpour Bakhtiar.

Crowds of millions flooded the streets, shouting 'Death to the Shah. Long live Khomeini.' On 16 January 1979, The Shah left Iran with his family, never to return. On 1 February, Khomeini returned to Iran in a chartered Boeing jet. He was seventy-seven years old.

All the opposition activist parties had accepted Khomeini as their leader, their flag. These included not just the religious establishment but also the Tudeh Communist Party, the nationalists from Mossadeq's National Front, the liberals and democrats. Towering above politics and parties was Khomeini, unchallengeable and accepted by the Irani people as practically divine. To hold together his coalition, Khomeini decided that his prime minister would not be from the clergy, so he chose Mehdi Bazargan as his first prime minister. Bazargan was a respected politician who had studied engineering in France, had served as a professor at Tehran University, had been a minister in Mossadeq's National Front, and had been the first Irani chairman of the NIOC. Subsequently he had been imprisoned by the Shah, had remained a democratic activist and had supported Khomeini.

Bazargan was independent-minded, and tried to govern according to his principles; but in so doing, he confronted the power centres around Khomeini. Finding himself powerless, he resigned. At first Khomeini did not accept his resignation, but after the capture of the American embassy and the taking of the hostages, the prime minister went public with his criticism and again resigned after writing to Rafsanjani,

> The government has created an atmosphere of terror, fear, revenge and national disintegration... What has the ruling elite done in nearly four years, besides bringing death and destruction, packing the prisons and cemeteries in every city, creating long queues, shortages, high prices, unemployment, poverty, homeless people, repetitious slogans and a dark future.

This time his resignation was accepted.

In the election that followed, Bani Sadr was elected as the first President of the Islamic Republic. He was supported by Khomeini who still did not want a cleric as President. Though Bani Sadr was not a cleric, his father had been an Ayatollah and a trusted friend of Khomeini, and he had offered Khomeini his home in Paris. After the revolution he had served as finance minister and then foreign minister. With Khomeini's support, he was elected with 78.9 per cent of the vote in January 1980. Bani Sadr lasted sixteen months before he was impeached. He accused the establishment of terror tactics and amassing of wealth. The clerics had had enough of his independent style; only Montazeri supported him. Bani Sadr went into hiding and managed to escape back to France.

While Bazargan and Bani Sadr struggled for their principles, Ali Khamenei had his own massive troubles. He was determined to consolidate his Islamic Republic, but first he had to deal with the series of crises that hit Iran. In November 1979 the US Embassy was seized by students and the staff taken hostage for 444 days. The Iranis had not forgotten the CIA countercoup that toppled Mossadeq and reinstated the Shah in the fifties, and apprehended that repeat action by the Americans could bring the Shah back for the second time. Then in September 1980 Saddam Hussein invaded Iran, starting a war that would last for eight years. Internally, Khamenei was facing a violent challenge from rival groups such as the Mujahedeen e Khalq and the Fedayeen which escalated after Bani Sadr's impeachment. In May Ayatollah Motahari had been assassinated. Within a week of Bani Sadr's removal, there was an assassination attempt on Ali Khameini, followed by the Hafte Tir bombing which resulted in the deaths of seventy-four Islamic Republic Party leaders including Ayatollah Beheshti, the most powerful cleric after Khomeini; besides him, the list of the dead included four cabinet ministers, ten deputy ministers and twenty-seven Majlis deputies. Two months later President Rajai was assassinated. But Khomeini with his remarkable sense of strategy, turned each problem into an opportunity as he relentlessly moved forward towards his objectives, undeterred by the war with Iraq, civil war at home, division amongst the ayatollahs over Khomeinei's velayat e faqih, and international isolation.

The Iran Iraq War lasted eight years (1980–88), claimed half a million lives, cost over $1 trillion and left Iraq in debt of $130 billion—a debt-to-GDP ratio of over 1000 per cent—making it the most indebted country in the world. It has never been conclusively established what made Saddam invade Iran, starting the war; some say he wanted to revise the Algiers agreement over the border between the two countries, others say that he was secretly incited by America, who wanted revenge for her humiliation in the hostage crisis. At first Iraq had the upper hand as it took important Irani territory at the border, but then Iran pushed Iraq back, taking the advantage and causing international anxiety that Iran might win; finally, with increased international support Iraq restored her position till the UN brokered a ceasefire which nullified the territorial impact on both sides and demonstrated that the war had been an exercise in futility at a heavy cost.

The revolution had left the Shah's army in shambles, and the US embargo on the sale of spare parts left the Irani military vulnerable. But what the Iranis lacked in conventional strength they more than made up for by the intensity of their passion, as they countered

Iraq's money and equipment with human waves of young teenagers who, armed merely with 'plastic keys to heaven' marched through minefields offering themselves as martyrs. The conventional army was reinforced by the Revolutionary Guards and the Basij which became a power in Iran. When it looked like the Iranis might actually win, the Arabs escalated their monetary support to Iraq, and the US not only supported Iraq, but even on occasion, joined as a combatant. When the USS Stark was attacked by Iraqi missiles, it was quietly ignored, but the USS Vincennes was shot down an Irani commercial flight, killing all 290 passengers on board. When asked to explain, the Americans falsely claimed that the incident took place in international waters, that they had mistaken the commercial aircraft for an F-14 Tomcat fighter, and finally justified their slaughter saying they feared they had come under attack. The US supplied Iraq with chemical weapons and provided CIA reconnaissance to facilitate chemical attacks on Iran. The principal reason why the American navy helped destroy the Irani navy was the fear that if Iran won the war, it could destabilize the whole oil-producing region by forging Shia unity. The war saw extensive use of ballistic missiles, chemical weapons and finally attacks on oil shipments, known as the Tanker War, which gave windfall profits to the massive dry docks in Dubai, constructed by the astute Sheikh Rashid.

Khomeini used the war to consolidate his revolution as the national fervour united behind him. The communists and the nationalists were eliminated and liberal clerics were disempowered. When a plot to assassinate Khomeini was exposed, Ayatollah Shariatmadari was implicated, forced to confess on television and defrocked. Montazeri, who had earlier been designated Khomeini's successor, came under attack for his independent attitude and his criticism of the injustices and corruption of the regime. Matters came to a head at the end of the war when several thousand political prisoners were executed; Montazeri spoke out that it was against the principles of Islam to execute those who were one's captives. His famous remark that the people of the world were being led to believe that 'our only task here in Iran is to kill' took him beyond the pale as he was sidelined, discarded, removed from the political arena and placed under house arrest till his death.

On 18 July 1988, Iran announced a ceasefire. It broke Khomeini who could only beat his chest and moan. He could no longer walk; he was eighty-six and was suffering from cancer in addition to heart problems. He never again went to speak at the mosque, and was taken to hospital. On 3 June 1989, he said farewell to his family, 'I have nothing more to add. Those who want to stay may do so; those who don't, may go. Put the light out. I want to sleep.' Power passed to the partnership of Ali Khamenei and Rafsanjani.

SADDAM HUSSEIN

> 'You Americans, you treat the Third World in the way that an Iraqi peasant treats his new bride. Three days of honeymoon and then it's back to the fields.'
>
> —Saddam Hussein

In its long history Iraq had never been a country. Its territory had made up three provinces in the Ottoman Empire. The country was created after the break-up of the Ottoman Empire by the British after the First World War. Winston Churchill, who was responsible for the creation of the new state, was completely ignorant of the area or its people and asked his aide,

> Let me have a note in about three lines, as to King Faisal's religious character. Is he a Sunni with Shia sympathies, or a Shia with Sunni sympathies, or how does he square it? What is his father, Hussein? Which is the aristocratic high church and which is the low church? What are the religious people at Karbala? I always get mixed up between these two.

Despite, or perhaps because of his ignorance, the British decided to make Faisal, King; Faisal was not from Iraq, nor was he known in

Iraq, but beside being a misfit, he was imported for the job, as were Ahmad Chalabi and Iyad al-Allawi whom the Americans imported to run Iraq eighty-three years later. Not one of these transplanted rulers was a great success. Iraq was an artificial creation which attempted to merge three distinct groups, the Sunnis, the Shias and the Kurds. Till today this is a problem that has not been solved.

In 1958, the Iraqi royal family was massacred in a violent and bloody coup. The powerful Anglophile Nuri Said, fourteen times prime minister, was caught trying to escape dressed as a woman, and killed. The generals led by Qasim and Arif took control, but their partnership soon disintegrated, mainly over the issue of Nasser in Egypt whose Pan-Arabism was changing the face of the Arab world. Arif was a great fan of Nasser; Qasim was not. In 1959 Qasim conducted a purge of the Baathists, who reacted by attempting to assassinate him. An amateur four-man hit team, led by Abdul Karim Shaikhally, attacked Qasim's car, killing the driver and wounding Qasim who survived. One of the wouldbe assassins who fled to Cairo, was a young tough by the name of Saddam Hussein.

Saddam was born in the village of al-Ouja, eight miles from the town of Tikrit, which had been the birthplace of the medieval hero of Islam, Saladin. Al-Ouja was backward without electricity, running water, paved roads or schools, and Saddam grew up, without money or education, a street urchin under his poor but strong-willed mother, Subha. His father disappeared and his mother remarried; her new husband was a no-good idler, known in the village as 'Hasan the Liar' for his false claim of the title of Haji which he used to enhance his status. The young Saddam moved to Tikrit to live with his uncle Khairallah, a schoolteacher with a strong interest in politics. Saddam admired and befriended his cousin Adnan, and later married Adnan's sister, Sajida. Khairallah married his son, Adnan, to the daughter of his friend, Ahmad Hassan al-Bakr, a fellow Tikriti army officer; in addition, he also married his daughter, the sister of Sajida, to al-Bakr's son. Later, when al-Bakr became President of Iraq, this happy family ruled Iraq and changed the history of the Middle East. Al-Bakr followed the advice of his friend from Tikrit: 'Saddam is your son. Depend on him. You need the family to protect you, not an army or a party. Armies and parties change direction in this country.' Khairallah became mayor of Baghdad, Adnan commander in chief of the army, Hassan the Liar's sons became the chiefs of the powerful security agencies, and Saddam became the dictator of Iraq who imposed a harsh and violent terror on his people as he led his country into three disastrous wars, against Iran, Kuwait and finally America.

In Cairo, Saddam used his time to educate himself. He was an avid reader, whose principal subject of interest was Stalin. Saddam was a most devoted fan of the Russian dictator, and built up a complete library of books on Stalin, which he studied very carefully, to fully understand the personality and methods of his role model. Other than Stalin, his favourite book was *The Godfather*, the famous novel of Mafia life. His favourite movie was *The Day of the Jackal*. The lessons of Stalin's terror and violence, Don Vito Corleone's philosophy on family and life, and the elimination of political enemies through the use of professional assassins such as The Jackal, were lessons never to be forgotten by Saddam. In Cairo his best friend was his co-assassin Shaikhally, who was so close to Saddam that he was called 'Saddam's twin brother'.

In 1963, another coup saw the removal and execution of Qasim, and the return to power of Abdus Salam Arif, whose new prime minister was none other than al-Bakr, who moved fast in placing many of his fellow Tikritis in important positions. Qasim had committed the unforgivable sin of getting too close to the USSR, and his leftist principles threatened the clerics, the international oil companies and America. Qasim was a nationalist who hosted the first OPEC meeting, and took back from the Iraq Petroleum Company consortium 99.5 per cent of the land they had obtained rights to but were not utilizing. He paid for his mistake with his life. Following a familiar pattern, the new government went after the communists with hundreds of executions and the widespread use of torture. Their interrogator was the vicious Nadim Kazzar who would stub out his cigarettes in the eyeballs of his victims and developed terrible machines such as chairs with iron spikes on which the prisoners were made to sit, and machines which chopped off fingers. Kazzar was later to become Saddam's head of national security. At this stage of his career Saddam was involved in security, intelligence and even acted as a bodyguard to al-Bakr. He was a hawk who expressed his attitude without qualms: 'We must kill those who conspire against us.' America had effectively dealt with the communist threat in Iraq.

Arif fell out with the Baathists, removed al-Bakr and installed a military cabinet. The Baathists, in turn, tried to remove Arif's government and Saddam was arrested. After two years in prison he managed to escape with a few of his associates including his friend, Shaikhally. Arif's policies threatened US commercial interests in Iraqi natural resources, particularly oil; so once again a coup was hatched with Washington pulling the strings from behind the screen. Abdur Rahman Arif had taken over from his brother who died in a helicopter crash, and he was now persuaded to resign and depart to London in exile. The new government was led by the RCC with al-Bakr back as its chairman.

Saddam was not considered important enough to be included in the RCC, but his power grew in the shadowy world of security and intelligence. He set about removing those that stood in his way:

- Nayyef, the prime minister was arrested by Saddam while he was having lunch with the President al-Bakr. At gunpoint, Saddam drove him to the airport and exiled him as ambassador to Morocco.
- Al-Rikabi, the former secretary-general of the Baath party, was imprisoned and stabbed to death in his cell.
- Ammash, the Vice President and interior minister, was stripped of his posts but his life was initially spared on the intervention of al-Bakr. Demoted to ambassador, he died mysteriously in Finland.
- Shaikhally, Saddam's 'twin', the foreign minister, was demoted

to ambassador to the UN. After his return from New York, he was shot and killed while visiting the post office to pay his electricity bill.

Saddam was a firm believer in Stalin's theory that problems came with people; if the people disappeared, the problem disappeared. But Saddam was more than just a killer; he was a brilliant and hardworking executive whose photographic memory enabled him to retain facts and deal with his growing responsibilities most efficiently. He was also determined to improve the lives of the Iraqi people and to build Iraq into a power in the region. He was the man to get things done. More and more the President grew to rely on Saddam who came to be known as 'Mr. Deputy'. Saddam was invariably polite and respectful to his president as he quietly and without friction, took over executive power. People in the power game, politicians, bureaucrats and generals soon realized that it was best not to irritate the ruthless Saddam, and fell into line accepting his authority.

By 1970 Saddam was fully in control. Luck was with him as the boom in oil prices raised Iraq's oil income from $575 million in 1972 to $5.7 billion in 1974, ten times in two years. Saddam set about creating one of the largest economic development programmes ever undertaken by a Third World country. At this time Saddam was determined not to allow corruption, and executed two deputy ministers who were caught taking bribes. Saddam streamlined the oil income, and implemented a crash programme of electricity, water, roads, hospitals and particularly schools. UNESCO gave Saddam an award for his campaign to eradicate illiteracy.

There were two faces to Saddam. On the one side he was the determined nation-builder who would work till late at night and sleep in a small military cot in his office; who could intervene to save a Jewish businessman from execution when he recognized the man who had been kind to him with tips when he was a street urchin selling cigarettes. On the other side he was the ruthless conspirator, murderer and inhuman torturer rumoured to have personally thrown one of his victims into a tub of acid and watched the body decompose. The oil boom gave Saddam more power than he ever imagined, but absolute power corrupts absolutely and Saddam lost his balance as he started to believe that there were no limits to what he, the man of destiny, could achieve.

Saddam used hard action to crush the communists. But the Kurds and the Shias presented a more complicated problem. The Kurds sat on huge oil deposits; the Shias constituted a majority of the population of Iraq. Saddam's constituency comprised of lower middle class Sunnis, with the leadership mainly from Tikrit, with his family at the apex. Using a combination of bribes and repression Saddam imposed his will on Iraq. In 1979 Saddam removed al-Bakr from presidency, and formally took over the power that was in fact already his.

For Saddam formal power was not enough; he wanted total power. Using the pretext of a conspiracy, Saddam started a purge of the Baath party with the dismissal of the secretary-general of the RCC, Abdel Hussein Mashhadi. He then summoned a meeting of 400 of the RCC and other top party officials which became a witch-hunt. In this massive purge of anti-Saddam elements, twenty-two leaders were executed, forty were imprisoned. Saddam locked himself in his bedroom for two days. When he emerged his eyes were red from weeping. He then went to see the widow of Adnan Hamdani, his friend and one of the victims, to condole. He explained that he had loved Hamdani as a brother but had no choice but to sacrifice him for the cause. He gave the widow a beautiful house as a gift and promised her that she would want for nothing as long as he lived.

In 1980, Saddam invaded Iran. The futility, cost and consequences of the Iran–Iraq War have been covered earlier in this chapter in the section on Iran, and also in my earlier book *Saints and Sinners*. The war years saw the worst of Saddam's family rule, with his uncontrollable son Uday running wild. Sajida, Saddam's wife, would use the presidential jet on her shopping trips to her favourite haunts in London and New York—Hermes and Bloomingdales. Her brother, Adnan, the defence minister, accumulated a fortune through shady land deals and commissions on military purchases and built up a personal collection of 500 cars. Saddam's sons were totally out of control, setting a trend that was continued by other Mid-East dictators, Assad of Syria, Mubarak of Egypt and Gaddafi of Libya.

Saddam started an affair with the tall and sophisticated blonde Samira, the wife of the director-general of Iraqi Airways. Saddam liked blondes, but this time it was serious. His wife, Sajida was jealous and tried to compete by dying her own hair blonde. She made the mistake of complaining to her crazy son, Uday, who reacted by bursting into a formal dinner for the wife of the Egyptian President and beating to death Georgo, his father's bodyguard, food taster and facilitator of Saddam's love life. Saddam was enraged; he denounced his son on TV, stripped him of his responsibilities and put him on trial for murder. Uday took sleeping pills, was jailed and then sent to Geneva in exile. When the Swiss authorities demanded that he leave, he returned home where he was reconciled with his father. Sajida argued with Saddam in defence of her son, saying, 'Why arrest him? After all it's not the first time he has killed. Nor is he the only one in his family who has killed.'

As his marriage with Sajida soured, Saddam grew disenchanted with her brother, Adnan, the powerful and able army chief, who was popular with his officers. Saddam decided he had to go, and shortly after, Adnan's helicopter exploded, killing him as he took off. Later, when Hussein Kamel, Saddam's son-in-law defected with his family, he confessed to the CIA that he had placed the explosives on board on Saddam's orders. Hussein and his brother, both sons-in-law of the President, were persuaded to return; trusting Saddam's promise of amnesty, they returned to Iraq where they were killed.

The war with Iran had left Iraq broke and so heavily in debt to her Arab allies that there was no way to repay. Kuwait pressed for repayment and simultaneously increased her oil production ensuring that the price of oil would stay depressed. Saddam resorted to the old claim that Kuwait was a part of Iraq, and had been unjustly separated by the British. He also insisted that Kuwait was stealing Iraqi oil by slant drilling into the Iraqi part of the massive Rumaila oil field. When threats proved ineffective Saddam had his historic meeting with the US ambassador, April Glaspie; when he raised the issue, her enigmatic reply to him was, 'We have no opinion on Arab–Arab conflicts, like your border disagreement with Kuwait.' Saddam took this as a green light and invaded Kuwait within the week. The world was shocked and Saddam's popularity soared in Iraq. The Emir of Kuwait escaped with his family to the Kingdom of Saudi Arabia where he set up a government in exile. The brother of the Emir remained in Kuwait and Saddam offered him the crown to give some legitimacy to the invasion; the brother refused and was killed resisting the Iraqi army. Finally, Saddam announced the annexure of Kuwait as the nineteenth province of Iraq, and appointed as governor, his vicious cousin, 'Chemical Ali' who had earned his title by chemical warfare against the Kurds. The short time that Saddam controlled Kuwait was filled by looting, murder and rape.

The USA decided to liberate the conquered oil state. It took months of planning and assembling an alliance of nations to show that America was not alone in her endeavour. For all the countries that joined there was a pay-off—in all, the inducements used to persuade the allied nations constituted the greatest bribe in history. On 16 January, the bombing of Iraq began; it lasted forty days as 110,000 sorties dropped 85,000 tons of explosives that destroyed Iraq and its people. On 20 February, the US troops invaded and within 100 hours the 'Mother of All Battles' was over.

It looked like the end of Saddam. The Kurds and the Shias, victimized for so many years, were induced to rebel against what was left of Saddam's government. The think tanks in Washington reconsidered the consequences of removing Saddam, and the likelihood of the Iranis filling the vacuum and dominating Iraq. They concluded that bad as Saddam was, Irani control would be worse! The US walked away, sacrificing the Kurd and Shia rebellions to their fate. Saddam survived.

Twelve years later in 2003, the United States used the excuse of weapons of mass destruction to again invade Iraq. The real reason was of course oil. In 2003, Uday and Qusay were killed by American troops in a shootout and Saddam was captured; but the war did not end. Chaos and civil war ravaged Iraq, aggravated by American mismanagement and corruption. Billions of dollars were flown across in plastic wrapped 'cashpacks', which disappeared. The US army ended their formal occupation eight years later in 2011, leaving a destroyed country and a shattered people in their wake. The financial cost of the war has been estimated in trillions of dollars; deaths caused directly or indirectly by the war have been estimated between 500,000 to 1,000,000 people.

Saddam's three wars destroyed Iraq. But his reputation among the Muslims of the Middle East survived. His missile attack on Israel, followed by his offer to withdraw from Kuwait if the Israelis would also withdraw from occupied Arab territories endeared him to the large anti-Zionist majority in the region. His behaviour at his trial and his fearlessness and dignity as he was hanged, was watched the world over on YouTube and other social media, made him a hero to many who had despised him before. The chaos, corruption and instability that followed Saddam's removal made many wish him back. But the reality of his treatment of Shias and Kurds could not be erased. Without a doubt Saddam was a cruel dictator, but could democracy or any other alternative have done more for Iraq?

Saddam's trial did not inspire credibility. Three judges in turn presided over the trial; one resigned under pressure, another was considered too sympathetic to Saddam and was removed, and the judge who passed judgement was a Kurd from Halabja who was hostile to the defence for personal reasons. Three of the defence lawyers were assassinated. It came as no surprise when Saddam was convicted and sentenced to face the hangman. He died, defiant and fearless to the end. In 2014 the judge who sentenced him was captured by ISIS and executed.

GADDAFI

'I shall die a martyr in the end.'

—Muammar Gaddafi (February 2011)

On 20 October 2011 Muammar Gaddafi was beaten, sodomized and killed by a rebel mob after his convoy was hit by a NATO missile strike that destroyed his car, injured his legs and forced him to hide in a drain pipe where he was discovered. He had taken power in a coup d'état forty-two years earlier on 1 September 1969. Who was this man?

President Reagan named him 'The mad dog of the Middle East.' Nelson Mandela called him 'One of the great revolutionary icons of our time.' After his death the question was asked, 'Was Gaddafi a good or a bad person?'; the question contained a list of the 'good that Gaddafi did for the Libyan people':

- Electricity was supplied free for all Libyans.
- Zero per cent interest was charged on loans as banks were state-owned.
- Homes were considered a human right in Libya. Gaddafi vowed that his parents would not get a house till everyone in Libya had a home.
- All newlyweds were given a gift of $50,000 to help them start their life together.
- Medical treatment and education were free in Libya.
- The government subsidized the purchase of a first car by providing 50 per cent of the cost.
- Petrol price was $0.14 per litre.
- Libya had no external debt, and its frozen foreign reserves were $150 billion.
- The Libyan government paid a salary to all graduates who were jobless.
- A part of oil revenues received by the government was paid

directly into the personal accounts of citizens.
- A new mother received a payment of $5,000 on the birth of her baby.
- Forty loaves of bread cost fifteen cents.
- 25 per cent of Libyans had a university degree.

Gaddafi came from a poor tribal background. He joined the army as a way to fulfil his political ambitions. His hero was Colonel Nasser, and like his hero he set about preparing his small group of young military revolutionaries. Always austere and religious, Gaddafi imposed criteria for selection—the recruits should not drink alcohol or chase girls.

Finally, the date for the coup was fixed for 12 March 1969, but had to be postponed because it clashed with a concert of the famous singer Umm Kalthoum, an Arab icon. The coup was rescheduled for the 24th but again aborted when news leaked out and King Idris was moved to safety. The would-be revolutionaries were accident-prone and on two occasions, were almost caught; the first time his car crashed as a result of a puncture; the second time Gaddafi's driver and fellow revolutionary was so busy reciting verses from the *Quran* that he hit a large cow, which damaged the car but fortunately not the cow. When the coup finally did take place on 1 September, the comedy of errors did not end; the group that was to take over the radio station in Tripoli lost their way and could not find the station; and Gaddafi himself, on his way to take over the Benghazi radio station got separated from his troop when he took the left turn at a fork but his men, in the heat of the moment, mistakenly took the right. When Gaddafi's men went to the house of the army chief to arrest him, he jumped into the swimming pool in his pyjamas and hid. At the palace the Crown Prince had the brilliant idea to turn off all the lights which misled the invading force into assuming that the palace was empty. But despite all, the revolutionaries took over in a bloodless coup with minimum resistance and in the early morning Gaddafi announced that they had overthrown 'the reactionary and corrupt regime.'

The handsome new leader had always been eccentric, with a strong hatred of the colonial powers. In school he was rude to his English schoolteacher, Mr Johnson. Once, when ordered by Johnson to leave the room, the young Gaddafi replied, 'You are the one who should leave for good; not this room but the whole country.' Fired by his socialist, nationalist and anti-imperialist beliefs, Gaddafi was determined to change his people and his country. Nasser, his hero and guide, sent his confidante Heikal to Libya. Gaddafi told him, 'We have carried out this revolution. Now it is for Nasser to tell us what to do.' Heikal wrote to Nasser that Libya's new leaders were 'shockingly innocent and scandalously pure.'

The young revolutionary was bursting with idealism. But the road to hell is paved with good intentions. He was impatient, arrogant, mercurial and childish. If he was crossed, he would threaten to resign or disappear into the desert; sometimes he would refuse to talk to his fellow revolutionaries if they didn't agree with him. His 'universal truths' did not always excite others as much as they excited him; as for example his simplistic definition of women in his *Green Book*, 'It is an undisputed fact that both man and woman are human beings.' He moved fast to close down British and American military bases in Libya, and also casinos and nightclubs; he banned alcohol.

He would 'save' Libya even if he had to do so by force. His regime became repressive, with new laws that punished party politics with death, banned trade unions and imposed heavy censorship on the press. He wanted his fellow revolutionaries to follow his own austere lifestyle; he did not even have a personal chauffeur; he took no benefits or facilities from the state. He was often insulting in public which evoked harsh response from even his allies and associates, one of whom threatened him with a machine gun. On one occasion, carried away by his own oratory, he even threatened his mentor Nasser, who slammed his fist on the table in rage and told his impassioned host to shut up.

Students protested his policies, demanding change. They were shocked by Gaddafi's response. He hanged the protestors on the campus. He also hanged others who were branded as traitors in the main square of Benghazi and twenty-two military officers convicted for involvement in a coup attempt. He wanted perpetual revolution and those who resisted would be crushed. He created revolutionary committees that rooted out opposition, even arresting the ninety-year-old Grand Mufti, and killing the popular Imam of Tripoli. He gave up formal government office, becoming 'Brother Leader', but he did not give up control; his personality cult dominated Libya. The revolution was becoming a nightmare.

Gaddafi was dissatisfied with his Libyans, complaining that 'Nobody is doing anything except for the sake of remuneration; nothing is performed save in exchange for some reward.' Gaddafi's solution was a cultural revolution with new laws, an administrative revolution, an armed people's militia and a new way of thinking. Like Mao's Cultural Revolution in China, the result was chaos, but in Libya, Gaddafi had at his disposal the massive wealth created by the boom in oil prices in the seventies. He was able to promote not just domestic chaos but also a degree of international chaos. He first went on a massive buying spree to build up his military capability. Soon he had more fighter aircraft than fighter pilots. His development projects were wasteful and frequently failed to deliver the intended result. He provided funds to support revolution around the world. In his own region he tried a series of abortive mergers of Libya with Egypt, Tunisia, Syria, Sudan, Morocco, Algeria and Chad. The temptation of sharing Libya's oil wealth was overcome by the nightmare of political marriage with the Colonel.

Within Libya his experiments at social restructuring created a reign of confusion and terror. On the international scene the Colonel's support of revolution earned him the enmity of rulers the world over. His World Revolutionary Headquarters provided training to a generation of leaders who were to become the bane of Africa— Charles Taylor of Liberia, Foday Sankoh of Sierra Leone, Laurent Kabila of Zaire, Blaise Compaore of Burkina Faso and Kukoi Sanyang of Gambia. He funded revolutionary groups which included the Irish

Republican Army, the Red Brigades of Japan and Italy, the Basque Separatist Movement, the Moro Liberation Front, the Sandinistas of Nicaragua and several Palestine guerrilla movements; he provided support to the world famous terrorists, Carlos the Jackal and Abu Nidal; he befriended dictators such as Idi Amin and Bokassa; he financed Scargill, leader of the British National Union of Miners and Louis Farrakhan's Nation of Islam in America.

Gaddafi encouraged Emperor Bokassa to convert to Islam and gifted him $1 million at his conversion ceremony, but three months later Bokassa renounced his new religion and converted back to Christianity. When Gaddafi warned him that the punishment for apostasy in Islam is death, the emperor who had been circumcised on his becoming a Muslim, complained, 'What kind of religion is it that has the end of your penis cut off when you join it, and your head cut off when you leave it.' But in Africa it was not only the tyrants that the Colonel supported, it was also the saints. He was one of the most generous financiers of Nelson Mandela and his African National Congress, earning the undying gratitude and appreciation of Mandela who replied to an aggressive reporter in America, saying, 'Those who feel irritated by our friendship with President Gaddafi can go and jump in the pool.'

The Colonel's greatest crime in the eyes of America and Europe was his nationalist oil policy:

- In 1970 he raised the price of oil and the tax on western oil companies.
- In 1971 he nationalized British Petroleum's oil interests in Libya.
- In 1973 he took over 51 per cent of the equity of foreign oil companies working in Libya.

Twenty years earlier, Mossadeq had tried but failed in his oil struggle with the West. Now, due to the changed realities of supply-demand, Gaddafi succeeded and became a leader in OPEC starting the unprecedented transfer of wealth from the oil-consuming West to the oil-producing nations of the Middle East.

Gaddafi created enemies at home, in the Middle East and in the West, many of whom tried repeatedly to assassinate him. He, in turn, had no hesitation in assassinating his enemies, wherever they may flee. In April 1986 a bomb exploded in a disco in Germany killing two American servicemen. Ten days later eighteen US bombers dropped sixty tonnes of explosives on Libya, destroying Gaddafi's home and killing his four-year-old adopted daughter. On 21 December 1988, Pan Am flight 103 was destroyed when an explosion killed all 259 people on board at Lockerbie. Though less destructive than the American missile attack five months earlier which shot down Iran Air flight 655 killing 290 passengers, the fact that this time the victims were mainly American created a far greater international impact. America led the UN to impose sanctions on Libya and freeze her international assets, resulting in great economic hardship for the Libyans.

By the nineties, with the USSR disintegrated and socialism discredited, Gaddafi was out of touch with the times. Political Islam was growing in power throughout the Muslim world. Though a devout Muslim himself, the Colonel did not see 'Islam as the solution' and resisted the Islamists. Armed Islamist groups tried agitation, coup attempts and assassination, but the Colonel was more than a match for them as he clamped down hard. The Libyan Islamic Fighting Group (LIFG) veterans of the Afghanistan struggle against the Russians, led the fight to bring down the 'Pharaoh' Gaddafi. Gaddafi rounded up the most militant of the Islamists and locked them up in Abu Salim prison. When the prisoners rioted, 1,286 of them were massacred. After Abu Salim, the Islamists knew they were beaten.

In his relationship with the West, Gaddafi was in a corner from which it seemed there was no way out. On 11 September, the airborne attack by terrorists on the World Trade Centre in New York gave the Colonel the opportunity that he needed. He was among the first to condemn the attack and by his sympathetic diplomacy, he rebuilt bridges to America and created the grounds for his rehabilitation. In return for peace, he offered oil, economic opportunities for western companies and compensation for the Lockerbie victims. Gaddafi always protested his innocence in the air disaster, but agreed to pay each family the $10 million demanded by the USA as the price for buying peace. In a remarkable U-turn the West accepted the Colonel back in return for oil, money and business.

The new Libya changed from socialist to capitalist in order to attract foreign investment and revitalize the economy. The Colonel's heart could not change and remained committed to his socialist Jamahiriya; so he withdrew, passing more authority to his capitalist sons, particularly Saif al Islam, the flamboyant artist who had taken his pet tigers to Vienna to keep him company while he studied for his MBA far from home. Saif represented the soft face of the family, the reformer and the negotiator with the West; Mutassim represented the iron fist and the security services of the regime. Saif sponsored his friend Shukri Ghanim, an economist, as effective head of the administration to revive the economy through the application of free-market economics. The Colonel backed these moves publically, but frequently his emotions would burst out, countering Ghanim's attempts with decisions that totally contradicted the reformist efforts. He bowed down to necessity, but was frustrated in doing so.

He was also frustrated by the behaviour and the values of his sons. All his life he had advocated simple living, Islamic beliefs and an anti-Western lifestyle. His sons went to the other extreme. They went about the business of making money with a frenzy and every major deal or business had a family member sponsoring or owning it. They also lived the high life, western style—yachts, private jets, parties with hired stars such as Beyonce, model girlfriends and the champagne overflowing. For a revolutionary who had required his associates to abstain from wine, women and song, the wild and unrestrained behaviour of his children was the final blow. But he was helpless; the man of the desert was no longer the man he had been; the handsome young idealist had been changed by life's harsh realities into a strange-looking botoxed relic of the past, with his Michael-Jackson-type outfits and his outmoded conclusions.

At the start of 2011 when the Arab Spring exploded, removing the established rulers of Tunisia, Yemen and Egypt, Gaddafi was no longer the man he was when he first took power, but he was still strong enough to deal with the rebellion that started in the eastern province. He secured his hold over the capital, Tripoli, and marched on Benghazi, the centre of rebel operations. He was close to taking the city when the western powers, Britain, France and the USA intervened and under the UN umbrella, bombed Gaddafi's forces; with their support the rebels were able to drive Gaddafi back. Even the Arab League backed the West against the Colonel. Seeing the game was over, government figures defected, the most important of whom were Moussa Koussa, the security chief and Gaddafi's second in command Abdul Salam Jalloud. Gaddafi retreated to Sirte and to his village, announcing that he would not flee but would die in Libya. Gaddafi was killed; three of his sons were killed (Khamis, Mutassim and Saif al Arab); two of his sons were captured (Saif al Islam and Saadi); his wife escaped with two of his sons, Hannibal and Mohammad and with his beautiful daughter Aisha, known as the Claudia Schiffer of Africa. They fled first to Algeria and then to Oman. Gaddafi's body was put on display and finally he was buried in an unmarked grave.

Gaddafi had many detractors; Sadat described him as, 'He is 100 per cent mad.' The Italian journalist Oriana Fallaci said, 'He's stupid. He's clinically stupid.' But the Colonel also had many admirers who praised him on his death:

- 'He died in honour, fighting for the Libya that he believed in.' (Louis Farrakhan)
- 'Liberator of Libya... He will always be remembered as a great fighter, a revolutionary and a martyr.' (Hugo Chavez)
- 'In the darkest moments of our struggle, when our backs were to the wall, Muammar Gaddafi stood with us.' (Nelson Mandela)

Is Libya better off without the Colonel? Many in Libya think not. Libya is a fractured country without a central government. The internationally-recognized government is resisted by a government in Tripoli. Three cities, including Sirte, are in the control of IS. Benghazi is almost completely destroyed. War rages between the government and Islamist groups. On Sunday 16 March 2014, *The Independent* newspaper published an article by Patrick Cockburn titled 'Three years after Gaddafi, Libya is imploding into chaos and violence.' The article emphasizes that political murders have grown, over 8000 political prisoners are incarcerated by militia groups which are growing stronger, schools remain closed, and prices are skyrocketing in a shattered economy where oil exports have fallen from 1.4 million barrels in 2011 when Gaddafi was killed, to 235,000 barrels three years later. Gaddafi was demonized by the West who proclaimed they had saved Libya from him. Today Libya is no longer cited as an example of successful foreign intervention and many Libyans complain that life under Gaddafi was much better than it is now.

In March 2014, *Al Jazeera* news wrote the final chapter of the Lockerbie air crash, for which the Colonel had been condemned, made to apologize and compensate the families of the victims, and for which the Libyan people had been made to suffer much for very long. Abolghasem Mesbani, an Iranian intelligence officer who defected to the West, confirmed what the US defence Intelligence agency had long known, that Megrahi, the Libyan convicted for the disaster, was innocent and the bombing had been organized by Iran in retaliation for the downing of their passenger flight by the USS Vincennes.

On his death, the renowned author and journalist Patrick Cockburn wrote,

> The NATO powers that overthrew him—and by some accounts gave the order to kill him—did not do so because he was a tyrannical ruler. It was rather because he pursued a quirkily nationalist policy backed by a great deal of money which was at odds with western policies in the Middle East. It is absurd to imagine that the real objective was to replace Gaddafi with a secular democracy.

23

Pakistan and the War on Terror

'We don't understand the definition of terrorism. Those who are fighting with small rifles are terrorists, and those who are dropping bombs are not?'

—Fazalur Rehman Khalil, a fighter of Harkat-ul-Mujahideen

Over the last half century, Pakistan has been ruled by the Bhuttos, the Sharifs and by four army generals. Over this period the Pakistan created by Jinnah became the Pakistan of today. General Ayub Khan presided over the rise of Pakistan as an example of good governance in the Third World, recommended by the World Bank as a model to countries such as South Korea who were learning how to get it right. General Yahya presided over the breakup of Pakistan with the secession of half the country and the creation of Bangladesh.

THE NATION'S LEADERS

The brilliant but mercurial Zulfiqar Ali Bhutto replaced traditional values with his brand of Islamic Socialism which in the end, was disowned by both Islamists and Socialists alike, and created the most famous political dynasty of Pakistan. He destroyed the economic foundation that General Ayub had created, by his nationalization program and erratic policies, created a sense of participation for the masses and most important of all, started Pakistan's long journey to the creation of the Islamic Bomb. He was overthrown in an army coup led by General Zia ul-Haq, imprisoned and after a long and dramatic trial was hanged. Three of his four children were assassinated over thirty years—Shahnawaz and Benazir by their enemies, and Murtaza during the rule of his sister, was assassinated (according to rumour), by forces closer to home. A huge Taj-Mahal-type shrine has been built to house their graves in Sindh which has emerged as a place of pilgrimage.

General Zia was selected by Bhutto as his army chief more for his weaknesses than his strength. But the self-effacing and seemingly dull Zia once installed, showed his true colours as a shrewd and competent strategist, who seized the opportunity of the conflict in Afghanistan between America and the USSR; a pious and devout Muslim, he changed the ideology of Pakistan from Bhutto's Islamic Socialism to impassioned Islamist politics, in step with the transition from Socialism to Islamism throughout the Muslim world. Bhutto's banning of alcohol and redefining of the minority Ahmadi sect as non-Muslims was mere strategy; Zia's encouragement of prayer and Islamic values was missionary.

Zia negotiated a new deal with America in which Saudi and American money channeled through the Inter-Services Intelligence (ISI) funded the Mujahideen freedom fighters who defeated the Russian Army in Afghanistan in an Islamic jihad. The blowback of this jihad has changed the region which even today, twenty-five years later is still afflicted by lawlessness, crime, heroin empires and a residue of trained fighters with weapons left over from the war. When the Russian war ended, the Mujahideen were replaced first by the warlords and then by the Taliban, students of Islam trained at the thousands of madrassas which had sprung up in Pakistan and Afghanistan.

The leader of the Taliban was the one-eyed Mullah Omar, intense, idealistic and primitive, whose passion for justice catapulted him to fame when he executed a Mujahideen commander who had raped two village girls and left his body hanging on a tank as a warning to others; his Pashtunwali code committed him to support Osama bin Laden, his guest in Afghanistan, even when it was not practical to do so in the face of American hostility. The USA, after 9/11, wanted revenge against bin Laden and his al-Qaeda. They named this revenge 'The War on Terror'.

The charismatic and politically astute Benazir Bhutto, scarred by the painful end of her father led the Pakistan Peoples Party (PPP) her father's party to victory, becoming prime minister twice. She proved good at capturing, but bad at retaining power and was removed for corruption first by Ghulam Ishaq, the éminence grise, who had taken over as President when Zia was assassinated in a plane crash, and then by her own appointee President Farooq Leghari.

Nawaz Sharif has ruled Pakistan longer than any other leader, and is now in his third term as prime minister. Lacking the charisma of the Bhuttos—father and daughter—he has nevertheless created a political legacy and a dynasty which is second to none in Pakistan. The Bhuttos are feudal Sindhis; the Sharifs are Punjabi businessmen. Benazir was assisted by her husband, the controversial Asif Zardari, who took control of the PPP after her death and became President of Pakistan. Nawaz is not highly educated but is very shrewd, practical, determined and bold. He has been assisted by his brother Shahbaz, whose exceptional work in the Punjab has created a legend for efficiency, and who has made Lahore the finest city in the country. Shahbaz has built up a reputation for hard work, efficiency and honesty, but is also capable of ruthlessness to achieve his objectives.

Nawaz is a fighter whose tenacity, boldness and ability to take punches have carried him through a roller coaster of ups and downs that would have floored any ordinary man. The immense fortune created by his father was snatched away by Bhutto's nationalization of the steel industry. When President Ghulam Ishaq decided to topple his government, Nawaz went down fighting and brought the President down with him. He survived through power struggles with the judiciary and the mighty Pakistani generals. But after he secured the resignation of the army chief Jehangir Karamat, he made his biggest mistake which almost cost him his life. Bhutto believed that General Zia was the least dangerous of the generals and appointed him army chief; a mistake that cost Bhutto his crown and his life. Nawaz promoted Pervez Musharraf as Chief of Army Staff (COAS), considering him to be no threat, but he misread his man and when Nawaz tried to remove Musharraf after the Kargil debacle, Musharraf, in a commando style countercoup, removed Nawaz, imprisoned him, had him convicted of kidnapping and treason, but under pressure from the Saudi King sent him into exile to the Kingdom.

Pervez Musharraf is a pleasant and sociable man, liberal and western in his values, a secular modernizer who grew up an admirer of Ataturk. At heart, he was a commando ready for any adventure with an ability to attract the loyalty of his friends and fellow officers. When appointed COAS, he embarked on the Kargil misadventure without sanction or authority. The prime minister Nawaz Sharif, was kept in the dark, and even the powerful core commanders were informed late in the day. Musharraf's objective in 'capturing' a few extra miles of useless territory in the frozen mountain heights of the Line of Control between the Indian and the Pakistani forces still defies understanding. He succeeded in derailing the normalization of relations between the two countries, and taking the sub-continent to the brink of nuclear war.

Nawaz flew to Washington to enlist the support of President Clinton to diffuse the situation and nuclear disaster was averted. Nawaz decided that Musharraf had to go. When Musharraf left on a trip to Sri Lanka, General Ziauddin, the head of the ISI, was appointed as the new army chief and Musharraf's return flight was not allowed to land at Karachi airport. But the commando general had secretly developed a contingency action plan. Within hours of his dismissal, Musharraf's men moved. His loyal Brigadier Satti, head of the crucial 111 brigade, surrounded and sealed the prime minister house where the new COAS General Ziauddin was trying to sack the key Musharraf loyalist generals, Aziz and Mahmood, who had to break up their tennis match to take control of their prepared counter-coup. Major-General Iftikhar spoke to Musharraf, still confused on the aircraft, 'Sir, the situation is all right. We have taken over.' The takeover was reconfirmed to Musharraf by General Usmani the local core commander.

Nawaz was imprisoned in Attock Fort, convicted of hijacking and terrorism and sentenced to life imprisonment. It is the only time in history that a person has been convicted of hijacking without having set foot on the aircraft and without any agent, bomb or threatening device on the aircraft. The defence lawyer was killed during the trial, and the judges trying the case had recently sworn a controversial oath of allegiance to General Musharraf; all senior court judges who refused to sign were removed from the bench. Media the world over announced that Nawaz's political career was over. Nawaz was a prisoner for life in a dank and dismal cell in a notorious medieval fort converted into a special prison, without any hope for the future. But then, in the dark on the night of 10 December 2000, he was ordered out of his cell and bundled into a black Mercedes limo. Musharraf had been persuaded by the Saudi King to send Nawaz into exile in Saudi Arabia. Property owned by the Sharif family valued at over $8 million was confiscated and he was banned from politics for the next twenty-one years.

Just as the war in Afghanistan gave General Zia a new lease of life, 9/11 and the destruction of the World Trade Centre in New York was a universal game changer. President Bush required General Musharraf, or 'The CEO' as he now called himself, to stand up and be counted with the stern warning, 'You are either with us or against us.' Musharraf assured the US that he was with them in the War against Terror. But reality was more complicated than Musharraf's promises to Bush. The Taliban who now ruled Afghanistan were more than Pakistan's allies, they had been brought to power by the ISI in their quest for strategic depth in their constant manoeuvres with a hostile India. The ISI, together with many religious groups in Pakistan, were not prepared to treat the Taliban as a mere enemy. Musharraf walked a fine tightrope as he tried to balance the often conflicting interests of America and Pakistan. He needed American money but he also needed the Taliban's contribution of strategic depth.

In an attempt to satisfy both adversaries, he succeeded in making them both angry. The US wanted Pakistan to make inroads into Afghanistan in their war against the Taliban; instead, the newly formed Tehrik i Taliban Pakistan (TTP) attacked, making inroads into Pakistan. From their secure bases in Waziristan, they destabilized north Pakistan through their guerrilla attacks and suicide bombings. Soon they had succeeded in terrorizing the people, disrupting the local economies and threatening the lives of Pakistani leaders; the prime minister Shaukat Aziz, the Citibank banker come to resuscitate the economy, survived an attack on his car, and Musharraf himself survived two attacks on his car. The TTP attacked military targets and came within sixty miles of the capital, Islamabad. When the American establishment accused the Pakistani government of double-dealing and hypocrisy, Pakistanis resented the accusation when Pakistani deaths, Pakistani economic dislocation and destruction in Pakistan far outweighed America's sacrifice in what was perceived as purely an American war.

Musharraf's weak political skills led him from bad to really disastrous decisions. Having ensured that the leaders of all the mainstream parties (Nawaz, Benazir and Altaf Hussain) were out of Pakistan and living in exile, he cobbled together his own king's party comprising of corrupt and vulnerable politicians whom he bribed to leave their leaders and join him. Seen at first as a white knight he quickly disappointed expectations by his criteria of selection, according to which, corruption became a qualification instead of a disqualification. His referendum to legitimize his government was rejected as fraudulent by public opinion. His rough methods in Baluchistan resulted in the scandals of 'missing persons' and culminated in the killing of Sardar

Akbar Bugti, the octogenarian chief of the Bugti tribe. His attempts to dominate the Supreme Court led to his twice dismissing the popular chief justice, Iftikhar Chaudhry, which triggered the protest of the Lawyers' Movement and the Democracy Movement and finally led Musharraf to declare 'an emergency.' He then did a deal with Benazir Bhutto under which the state condoned and forgave all the corruption charges against her, against her husband, Asif Zardari, and also against all the supporting cast of corrupt politicians; Musharraf's deal was named the 'National Reconciliation Ordinance' but it should not be confused with Nelson Mandela's Truth and Reconciliation Commission; Mandela's Reconciliation was a noble nation building measure whereas Musharraf's Reconciliation was a cynical condoning of corruption in Pakistan's new politics in which 'Anything Goes.' When Benazir was assassinated in a bomb blast, Zardari produced a will to legitimize his takeover of the party and after securing a massive sympathy vote, quickly reneged on the deal with Musharraf, sacked him and appointed himself as President in his place.

Zardari's only objective as President of Pakistan was to earn as much money as he could by any means possible. He was uninterested in the political issues, and when the country was inundated by massive floods that dislocated the nation, Zardari was in Europe to enjoy a luxury chateau mysteriously purchased in France. He was highly successful in earning an illegal fortune, but in the process, eroded the PPP's significance on the national scene, suffered a humiliating defeat in the elections, and reduced the PPP to a Sindhi party.

After fourteen years in the wilderness, Nawaz secured a resounding victory in the elections, becoming prime minister for his third term. Once again he secured his base in the Punjab by selecting his brother Shahbaz as chief minister. His new army chief Raheel Sharif set about combating insurgency by the TTP with determination. Stability seemed to prevail in Pakistan. America's withdrawal of support was more than compensated for by the new Pak–China initiatives of the Sharif administration. But through it all, the opposition leader Imran Khan relentlessly pursued his crusade against corruption, targeting the leaders of the two major parties, the Pakistan Muslim League [Nawaz] (PML[N]) and the PPP.

Some great leaders make history; other leaders are made great by history. Nawaz Sharif will be remembered for two historic events that changed the fate of Pakistan. First and foremost he made Pakistan a nuclear power; Bhutto may have initiated the Islamic Bomb project, General Zia may have kept it going by securing President Regan's annual certificate of confirmation that Pakistan was not developing a bomb, but it was Nawaz who took the historic decision to go ahead with the tests in response to India's nuclear tests. Bhutto had said that Pakistanis would have the bomb, even if they were reduced to eating grass; when Nawaz ordered the tests, US sanctions bankrupted Pakistan and almost reduced Pakistanis to 'eating grass'. Pakistan became the eighth nuclear state following the US, Russia, France, UK, China, Israel and India and now has between 100 to 150 nuclear bombs together with an effective delivery system. The hero of the Pakistani bomb was Dr A.Q. Khan who became notorious first for stealing the blueprints that enabled the realization of Pakistan's nuclear ambitions and then again when he took the rap for trying to sell nuclear secrets to Iran, Libya and North Korea through his Khan Network. It was the possession of the bomb that saved Pakistan from war after the Mumbai bombing, a dramatic terrorist attack that left 164 dead and 308 wounded.

The second historic contribution of the Sharif government is the China-Pakistan Economic Corridor (CPEC), a collection of projects with a total value around $50 billion which will rapidly expand and upgrade Pakistan's infrastructure through China's twenty-first-century Silk Road initiative. The CPEC is greater than all foreign investment into Pakistan since 1970, is equal to 17 per cent of the GDP, will create 700,000 jobs for Pakistanis between the years 2015–30, and will add 2.5 per cent to the country's growth rate. The Indian news organization *Firstpost* commented that 'The CPEC will be a strategic game changer in the region which will go a long way in making Pakistan a richer and stronger entity than ever before.' This massive project will add railways, roads, oil and gas pipelines, and over 10,000 MW of new electric power generation. The CPEC is the silver lining in Pakistan's gloomy political scenario. The fast track 'Early Harvest Projects' will establish that Pak–China friendship is, 'Higher than the mountains, deeper than the oceans, sweeter than honey, stronger than steel.'

The Sharif brothers have two constituencies that have provided the foundation of their power base. They are the first Punjabi leaders and have focused their development programs on the Punjab, where government under their rule, has outperformed the other three provinces; and in a country traditionally ruled by generals and feudal lords, they are the first industrialists to dominate the Pakistani political scene. Their pro-business policies have been appreciated by the business community in Pakistan.

Another recent welcome development is the serious effort initiated by the COAS Raheel Sharif and Nawaz to contain terrorism and take on the insurgents who have created instability by misusing the name of Islam. After a long period of capitulation and foolish attempts at compromise, finally the establishment has taken a stand that could restore some semblance of law and order, expose and eliminate these insurgents, many of whom are motivated by economic self-interest which they disguise as religious jihad.

The seeds of terror laid by the US war in Afghanistan and the Mujahideen gave birth to many terror groups, the most prominent of which are:

- Al-Qaeda, the anti-American Osama bin Laden organization whose objective is a global caliphate won by a global jihad.
- The Taliban whose objective is to govern Afghanistan as an Islamic state.
- The TTP whose objective is to turn Pakistan into an Islamic state.
- The Lashkar i Jhangvi and the Sipah e Sahaba Pakistan whose objective is to turn Pakistan into a Sunni Islamic state by the assassination of Shias.

- The Haqqani Network whose objective is the purification of Afghanistan.
- The Jaish e Muhammad and the Lashkar e Taiba whose objective is to liberate Kashmir from Indian oppression.

These groups have destabilized Afghanistan, Kashmir, Pakistan and India, and have deserted the vision of the founder of Pakistan, the westernized Shia, Jinnah, in their struggle for a fanatical fundamentalist Islamic state, or even a Sunni fundamentalist Islamic state.

On the night of the 1 May 2011, twenty-three US SEALs, the most deadly commando units of the US army, took off from the Jalalabad base in Afghanistan for the sleepy Pakistani provincial town, Abbottabad, named after a British colonial administrator James Abbott. Accompanying them were a Pakistani–American interpreter and a dog named Cairo. Their mission was to end the most expensive manhunt in American history and to honour President Obama's promise, 'We will kill bin Laden. We will wipe out al-Qaeda. This is our biggest national security priority.' In a fast and finely practiced raid, the SEALs killed Abu Ahmed al-Kuwaiti, Osama's trusted courier; Abrar an Osama soldier who came out with an AK 47; and then Khalid, Osama's twenty-three-year old son. They killed Osama with two shots, one in the chest and one in the head. Leaving the women and children, they took Osama's body with them in a body bag. Needing to confirm that the body was that of the six-feet four-inch Osama, they looked for a tape measure, but when none could be found, one of the SEALs who was six-feet tall lay beside Osama's corpse. Once confirmation was complete, the body was prepared according to Muslim rites and buried at sea. The SEALs were taken to President Obama to give him a private debriefing. When the President learned that a dog had accompanied them on their mission, he said, 'I want to meet that dog.' He never asked who fired the fatal shot, and the SEALs never volunteered to tell him.

The combination of Islamic militant groups and the expanding nuclear armoury in Pakistan has created a serious security problem and a fear that terrorists could actually get hold of a nuclear device. This danger makes Pakistani politics an important concern to both the region and to world powers who maintain a close watch on developments in the country.

As Nawaz reached the pinnacle of his power, Imran Khan stepped up what seemed like a futile attempt to expose his corruption. Then in 2015, 11 million documents were leaked from the Panama-based law firm, Mossack Fonseca; these documents exposed 214,488 offshore companies and hinted fraud, corruption and money laundering. Amongst these were three companies belonging to the family of Nawaz Sharif—Nescoll Ltd, Nielsen Enterprises Ltd and Hangon Property Holdings Ltd.

The Supreme Court of Pakistan ordered an investigation, while Nawaz and family denied wrongdoing. After a year of speculation, on Friday, 28 July, at 11.30 am, the court announced its decision; Nawaz and his finance minister, Ishaq Dar, were disqualified from holding public office, and cases are to be filed with the National Accountability Bureau against Nawaz, his three children and his son-in-law.

For the third time, Nawaz has been unable to complete his term in a Pakistan in which no civilian prime minister has ever completed a five year term. With the elections scheduled for 2018, excitement and uncertainty prevails. What will be the shape of the next government? And will other leaders also have to answer for their misdeeds?

—◆—

24

The Periphery

INDONESIA

'The rhythm of a revolution is destruction and construction.'

—Sukarno

'If we lose a chicken, they will take a cow.'

(Popular saying as to why Indonesians
don't go to the police)

Indonesia, home to 250 million people, has the largest Muslim population of any country in the world. It is an archipelago of 14,000 islands with a high concentration of natural resources and wealth in the form of oil, gas, rubber, tin, copper, gold, nickel, timber and palm oil. It has also been the scene of one of the largest massacres in modern history, led the world in brutality and corruption and lived through the thirty-two year dictatorship of the most corrupt tyrant of modern times, who looted up to $20 billion from the poor and wretched people of his country. The history of Indonesia reads like an unbelievable novel with two larger-than-life characters—Sukarno and Suharto; hero and villain—which is the hero and which the villain, is still a controversy with two very opposed points of view.

For 350 years, the Dutch brutally ruled their Indonesian colonies. The twentieth century saw the birth of a nationalist independence movement led by the charismatic Sukarno. Rising from a poor and humble background, he was, from childhood, passionately anti-imperialist and determined to achieve freedom for his people, or to die trying. Much as he disliked the Dutch, the young Sukarno did like white Dutch girls. He fell hopelessly and madly in love with Mien Hessels, his 'yellow-haired pink-cheeked tulip', and had the temerity to go to her father to ask her hand in marriage, only to be thrown out and unceremoniously rejected. It hurt, but the young lover picked himself up and proceeded with his life. Twenty-three years later, a fat old matron, ugly and unkempt, accosted him in the street: 'Sukarno, can you guess who I am?'

'No madam, I cannot.'

'Mien Hessels', she giggled.

He thought, 'My beautiful fairy princess had turned into a witch. I thanked God for having saved me.'

It was naïve for Sukarno to have believed that his proposal for the girl had a chance, in a time when the attitude of the Dutch was expressed in the sentence of a colonial official, 'May not a man in Europe do as he likes with his cattle?' The young Sukarno immersed himself in the liberation struggle against the Dutch. He founded the Partai Nasional Indonesia in 1927 and was soon recognized as the leader of the struggle for independence. He earned the enmity of his Dutch colonial masters and spent a decade as their prisoner, exiled to the most primitive and remote islands. He was saved by the arrival of the conquering army of Japan in the Second World War. The Japanese summoned Sukarno and told him that they wanted his help to ensure minimum resistance of the Indonesians to Japanese rule. Sukarno made a historic and strategic decision to work with the Japanese, on agreed terms, provided they recognized that he was a nationalist leader and would never work against the interest of his nation. Despite international criticism that he was a collaborator, he increased his power, influence and respect amongst his people, and finally, defeated by the Allied armies the Japanese withdrew.

Sukarno's careful strategy in moving towards independence and his repeated compromises with Japan as they withdrew under pressure of the Allied advance earned him many enemies particularly among the hot-headed youth wing of the movement. On one occasion he was kidnapped along with his wife, but when his kidnappers saw that the revolution did not move any faster with Sukarno off the scene, he was returned to leadership unharmed. On 17 August 1945, Sukarno declared independence of the state of Indonesia. During the meeting one of the notables said that a state needs a President, and suggested the name of Sukarno, who casually agreed with one word: 'Okay.' Sukarno then walked home stopping on the way to pick up some satay chicken from a street vendor for his family. Even as President, he never thought of mundane things like money, saying, 'Liberty was the food I lived on. Ideology... Idealism... The nourishment of the soul... That's what I fed on. I myself lived in rags, but what did it matter? Pulling together my party and my people, that's all I lived for.' His lack of concern for money or wealth is illustrated by the story of his friend, Dasaad,

> The morning I walked out of prison a free man, a gentleman whom I never saw before thrust 400 guilders into my hand for no reason other than he knew that I was without funds. Today this man Dasaad, is the richest capitalistic Socialist in the country and my dear friend. When he gave me the money he never thought he'd get it back. Come to think of it, he never did get it back. I'm still borrowing from him.

Sukarno ruled for twenty-two years, first by a system of Parliamentary Democracy, then by his Guided Democracy and for the last two years, as a powerless figurehead as Suharto consolidated his hold on power. The great achievements of his life include winning independence; the unification of the 14,000 islands of the Indonesian archipelago into one nation with one language; and the creation of the unaligned block of Third World countries with 130 countries and 80 per cent of the world's people. In this, he worked alongside Nasser and Nehru.

Always independent-minded, he was not willing to accept the hegemony of America regardless of practical considerations. America saw him as an enemy; he would have preferred America as a friend, as he exclaimed, 'Oh, America, what is the matter with you? Why couldn't you have been my friend? I would love to have been yours.' He was described by the US ambassador of the time as a cross between Franklin Delano Roosevelt and Clark Gable, when he went on an official tour of America. There, journalists asked him what he thought was the biggest difference between their two countries, he replied, 'The way politicians are elected to office, your American way of shaking hands with mothers and kissing babies is where we differ sharply. The Sukarno way is to shake hands with the babies and kiss the mothers.'

It was a time of turmoil, and the temperament of the Indonesians was ill-fitted to European Parliamentary Democracy so Sukarno replaced it with his new system which he called Guided Democracy. In the new system he made a coalition of the strongest forces in the country, the army, religion and the communists under the banner NASAKOM, with himself on top as the uniting factor. Guided Democracy involved more guiding and less democracy than traditional democracy, but did away with the petty selfishness and vote-catching that led to constant argument without results.

Colonel Nasution tried an army coup, which failed. Sukarno dismissed Nasution but later, forgiving as ever, reinstated him and promoted him to defence minister. Rebellion in the outer islands was stoked by the USA, with demands to hang Sukarno. American bombing of Indonesia in support of the rebels led to an embarrassing incident of the shooting down of an American pilot by the name of Allen Pope, who was tried and convicted. Pope's wife, a former Pan Am air hostess, came to Sukarno to plead clemency for her husband. As he recounted in his autobiography, 'When it comes to women, I am weak. I cannot stand a woman's tears.' He pardoned Pope with the advice, 'Go. Lose yourself in the USA secretly. Don't show yourself publicly. Don't issue statements. Just go home, hide yourself, get lost and we'll forget the whole thing.'

Others were not as forgiving as Sukarno. There were at least six assassination attempts; grenades were thrown at him wounding forty-eight children, aircraft dropped small bombs on his home, gunshots were fired at him but it was not his fate to die at the hands of assassins. Nor was he intimidated. When his well-wishers suggested that he retire, he replied, 'Retire? I could not. I could not live out my last years in peace and freed from fear of assassination—no I must work for my nation with whatever breath I have left. Besides where would I go? I have no home of my own. No land. No savings.'

Sukarno never seemed to understand that superpowers do matter. He was not willing to kowtow before the American government; his policies followed his conscience. His nonalignment was unacceptable to the US secretary of state, Mr Dulles, who told him, 'You must be on one side or the other. Neutralism is immoral.' Finally, the US government threatened him with a withdrawal of aid. Sukarno replied in a mass rally in Jakarta, 'The hell with your aid.'

He was also critical of the UN and its refusal to recognize China, the country with the highest population in the world. Finally, Indonesia, under Sukarno, left the fold of this revered international association; Peking applauded, Moscow disapproved. These policies, together with his inclusion of the communists of Indonesia in his power platform made America decide to bring him down. Much as he insisted that Sukarno is not, and can never be a communist, US state officials were not prepared to listen. Accusing the World Bank and the IMF of conspiring with multinationals, he forced them to leave Indonesia. And all the while the Communist Party of Indonesia grew; it became the third biggest in the world, after Russia and China, with a membership of 3 million people.

On the night of 30 September 1965, six generals were brutally murdered. Later stories alleged that they were tortured and castrated before being killed. The anti-Sukarno forces in the army and the Muslim extremists, manipulated by the CIA, said the communists did it. The pro-Sukarno forces and the communists said the Suharto group in the army did it. Whoever killed the generals, the reaction was terrible—the inhuman slaughter of a million people, communists, Chinese and supporters of Sukarno. Nor was the killing just random rage; the CIA distributed lists of those to be killed to the Suharto forces who hunted their targets mercilessly. The victims were brutally tortured, raped and mutilated before being killed. The leading Indonesian novelist, who himself was imprisoned at the time, wrote of the events:

> It was a coup. Suharto's supporters used one faction in the military to kill six generals—an act that triggered mass slaughter. The victims were communists, Chinese, and all supporters of Sukarno. The military and Suharto staged the coup and then accused others of staging it, eventually killing two million people. Do you understand? They killed two million people as 'revenge' for something they had done themselves.

Abdurrahman Wahid, later the President of Indonesia and former leader of Nadhlatul Ulama, the largest Muslim organization in the world, was embarrassed by the part played by the Islamists in the 1965 massacres and announced, 'I apologize to the communists. I offer this apology because I don't want Islam to go down in history as a bigoted religion. And I am a Muslim.'

Time magazine described it as 'The West's best news for years in Asia.' The CIA officer in the US embassy in Jakarta, who provided lists of communists to the Indonesian military, for extermination, explained, 'It really was a big help to the army. They probably killed lots of people and I probably have a lot of blood on my hands, but that's not all bad. There's a time when you have to strike hard at a decisive moment.' Another CIA officer said, 'No one cared as long as they were communists, that they were being butchered.' One of the very few prominent Americans to condemn the massacres was

Robert F. Kennedy. The UN avoided commenting on the killings. Within Indonesia there was an ominous silence caused by the fear of the people and the coverup by the Suharto establishment. The best book on the massacres, *Pretext for Mass Murder* by John Roosa was banned. The international film, *The Year of Living Dangerously,* was banned, as was the film, *The Look of Silence,* in which the killers boast on camera how they dismembered, eviscerated, castrated and beheaded alleged communists. In the words of Adi Zulkadry, a death squad leader in the massacres,

> We shoved wood in their anus till they died. We crushed their necks with wood. We hung them. We strangled them with wire. We cut off their heads. We ran them over with cars. We were allowed to do it. And the proof is we murdered people and were never punished.

The new man was General Suharto, who had served under Sukarno. Under his bland expression he hid his hunger for money and power. When Sukarno appointed him to clamp down on smuggling, he partnered with the smugglers and soon became the biggest of them all. Now, over a two-year interim period he totally neutralized Sukarno before removing him from his post as President. Sukarno was to die a few years later, a broken man. The US welcomed Suharto as 'Our kind of guy.'

Suharto ruled for thirty-one years from 1967 to 1998. From the time of his takeover, American aid, loans and economic support flowed in. In the three years from 1966 to 1969 inflation fell from 660 per cent to 19 per cent. His economic team, dubbed 'The Berkeley Mafia', led the restructuring of the economy. Investment in infrastructure was significant. Tax-free opportunity to invest in Indonesia's huge natural resources, lured in foreign companies, who with strategic partnerships with the Suharto family were able to secure sweetheart concessions—The Freeport Corporation for the copper mountain in West Papua, the Alcoa Company for Indonesian bauxite, and other western companies for timber, nickel and last but not the least

Indonesian oil and gas. With the richest hoard of natural resources, Indonesia was the greatest prize in East Asia. Local industry was dominated by Suharto's crony capitalists and given monopolies in return for partnerships with The Family; these businessmen were Chinese–Indonesians, who could pose no political threat. Foreign businessmen landed at an airport owned by one of Suharto's sons, took a taxi owned by his daughter, paid the road tax to another son and checked into a hotel owned by another member of The Family.

Suharto's New Order was hailed as the economic miracle of Southeast Asia. He was heralded in Western press as The Benign Dictator. But corruption and mismanagement soon exposed the economic miracle as a house of cards. In 1975 Pertamina, the state oil company, defaulted on its foreign debt; the government bailout doubled the national debt. Many questioned the 'benign' qualities of the dictator as the 1965 historic massacres were followed by the East Timor massacre of 1975 in which 30 per cent of the population was eliminated, and the Papua massacres in which over 100,000 people were killed. In 1997, hit by the Asian Financial Crisis, the house of cards collapsed. Indonesia was the worst hit of the countries in the region, as its rupiah fell from 2,600 to 17,000 to the dollar. The economy shrank by 13 per cent, bankruptcies, unemployment and poverty increased, riots destabilized the nation. The army, resentful of the family and their cronies, withdrew support and Suharto was forced to resign. Though this was the end of Suharto, it was not the end of his 'system'. The generals rallied around him, protecting the deposed President and the billions of dollars he and his family had stolen. Charges against him were not followed up on the excuse that he was too ill to stand trial. On 27 January 2008 Suharto died peacefully in his sleep.

Born poor, rumour has it that he was convicted for stealing clothes and given the choice of prison or the army. He chose the army. He died, according to *The Economist*, the sixth richest man in the world. *The Telegraph*, in his obituary, claimed, 'He was hailed in the West for having saved Indonesia from desperation, penury and communism.' President Nixon called him, 'The man of the hour, as Abraham Lincoln was the man of the hour for America hundred years ago.' President Yudhoyono declared a week of mourning in respect for the deceased dictator.

Suharto's legacy was an Indonesia where bad roads and traffic jams caused millions to arrive late for meetings daily, ferries sank due to overcrowding and bad maintenance, airplanes crashed so frequently that in 2007 the European Union banned Indonesian airlines from landing at their airports, trains crashed on an average of once every six days, less than half of Indonesians had access to clean water and sanitation and despite the fact that Indonesia was the world's largest exporter of coal and the third largest exporter of liquefied natural gas, one-third of Indonesians had no electricity.

CENTRAL ASIAN REPUBLICS

> 'Under our system only the guilty are accused. You must allow us our own traditions.'
>
> —Uzbek foreign minister (His statement explaining why there are no acquittals in Uzbek courts where cases invariably end in convictions)

On 31 December 1991, the Muslim Republics of Central Asia seceded from the USSR and declared independence. Their birth as nations resulted from the collapse of the USSR which followed the Russian withdrawal from Afghanistan and Gorbachev's glasnost and perestroika. The defining milestones in this region's history were:

- The early Muslim conquests and the defeat of the Chinese at the battle of Talas
- The conquests of Genghis Khan
- The conquests of Tamerlane
- Tsarist expansion under Peter the Great and Catherine the Great

- Lenin's Bolshevik Revolution
- Stalin and the Great Patriotic War
- The collapse of the USSR

These milestones resulted in a Muslim people living in a vast area ruled by the communists in Moscow, cut off from the outside world. Today almost 70 million people live in the Central Asian Republics; half of these live in Uzbekistan. The major part of the Central Asia land mass falls within the territory of Kazakhstan, the ninth largest country in the world, which, with its 2.7 million square kilometres of territory is bigger than the whole of Europe.

The founding fathers of the new Central Asian states were all hard self-made men who had risen through the ranks of the Communist Party of the USSR. They were also all engineers:

- Islam Karimov of Uzbekistan was born poor, graduated as an engineer but later studied economics which led to his joining the finance ministry where after seventeen years, he finally became finance minister.
- Saparmurat Niyazov of Turkmenistan grew up in an orphanage after the death of his father in the Great Patriotic War and the death of his mother and two brothers in the earthquake of 1948. He survived by digging himself out of the rubble, a feat that is reputed to have taken him over a week. He joined the Communist Party, graduated as a power engineer and like Karimov, married an ethnic Russian girl.
- Nursultan Nazarbayev of Kazakhstan graduated from the Karaganda Polytechnic Institute and worked in harsh conditions in the blast furnace of a steel plant, where the heat made him drink half a bucket of water to replace the sweat he lost in a shift. He took a correspondence course in economics and rose through the ranks of the Communist Party.
- Askar Akayev of Kirghizstan was the most liberal of the new presidents, which led to his downfall and ouster in the Tulip Revolution. The son of a farm worker, he graduated as an award-

winning nuclear physicist from the St. Petersburg Institute of Exact Mechanics and Optics. He was close to Gorbachev who offered him the post of Vice President of the USSR. He refused, preferring to stay home. After his ouster he was given refuge by Putin and resumed his teaching career as a professor in Moscow State University.

- Imamali Rahmanov of Tajikistan followed the standard career path of Central Asian independence leaders—through the Communist Party, working as an electrician in a factory and studying economics as he rose to the top of the political ladder in Tajikistan.

KARIMOV'S UZBEKISTAN

In Uzbekistan, Timur has replaced Lenin as the father of the nation. He is revered in this role despite the fact that he wasn't an Uzbek, didn't speak Uzbek and massacred a huge number of Uzbeks on his trails of conquest. He was a hard man, and perhaps Karimov sees himself as a new version in Timur's mould.

Karimov's Uzbekistan has two claims to fame; firstly, as one of the world's leading practitioners of torture, and secondly, as America's ally in the War against Terror. World revulsion against his methods peaked when two dissenters, Avazov and Alimov, were boiled to death in a massive cauldron. The corpse of Avazov, a thirty-four-year-old father of four, was delivered in a sealed casket to his mother who opened it and photographed the body with its missing fingernails and horrible burn marks from the boiling water in which Avazov had been immersed. Torture was routine in Uzbekistan and was used to extract confessions. In a survey on state brutality, a tall Russian student with long ash blonde hair was asked what independence of Uzbekistan had meant to her; she replied that it had resulted in her being arrested and raped three times by the police. The system believed in confessions followed by convictions, but routine rape of pretty girls was a fringe benefit of the job even when no confessions were being sought. Uzbekistan became notorious for its appalling human rights violations. Karimov was recognized as the friend and ally of America when he leased a large air base to the USA and joined them in their War against Terrorism in Afghanistan. Threatened by Islamists in Uzbekistan, he was only too ready to see the Taliban as his enemy as he battled the Islamic Movement of Uzbekistan and the Hizb ul Tahrir at home.

Karimov inherited corruption from his predecessor, Rashidov, who successfully frustrated investigation into his crimes till after his death in 1983. The exposures released in 1986 led to the arrest of more than 2600 officials in Moscow and Uzbekistan, the sacking of ten out of the twelve members of the CPU Politburo, the replacement of 143 of the 177 members of the central committee and the death sentence for Yuri Churbanov, Brezhnev's son-in-law. Rashidov and his mafia embezzled $2 billion from the treasury by immense fraud in the state-controlled cotton sector of Uzbekistan. Uzbekistan is the fourth biggest exporter of cotton in the world, but has become notorious for the use of slave labour of over a million Uzbeks and manipulation of pricing and forced procurement to ensure that benefit goes only to a small elite.

Corruption, under Karimov, was the major growth industry in Uzbekistan. The President grew immensely rich from the state gold mining venture, and from everything else that he could get his hands on. By 2014, he ruled over one of the world's most corrupt governments, (166th out of 174 according to Transparency International's Corruption Perception Index) and was described as a 'Dictator with Mafioso tendencies.' His daughter Gulnara worked hard to outdo her father, and built a fortune which led to international investigation after a Swedish telecom company admitted to a payment of $320 million. The Swiss government seized $912 million of assets suspected to be hers. Finally, her father put his loving daughter under house arrest, where her associates complained she was 'living in conditions worse than dogs.' She is, according to WikiLeaks, the most hated person in the country.

This land had produced Avicenna, the father of medicine;

al Khwarizmi, the father of algebra; and Ulugh Beg, whose famous observatory was centuries in advance of its time. Its capital, Tashkent, which had been the fourth city of the USSR, was reduced to a city without a single bookshop, and import of Russian literature was made illegal, despite the fact that 99 per cent of all Uzbeks are literate in Russian. The total number of Uzbek books printed was 140, six of which were by Karimov.

On 13 May 2005, demonstrators took twenty officials hostage and called on Karimov to resign. Karimov ordered his troops to shoot to kill and over 500 of the crowd was murdered. This brutal event, known as the Andijan Massacre, was the turning point in his relations with the West. Europe imposed sanctions and even America was openly critical. Angered by the condemnation of his action, he ordered the US to quit the Karshi Khanabad air base which had won him the warm friendship of America. He moved back into Moscow's camp. But despite the withdrawal of US support, despite the simmering war with the Islamic opposition in Uzbekistan, and despite the wretched condition of his people aggravated by inflation, joblessness, and bad governance, he ruled secure.

NIYAZOV'S TURKMENISTAN

Niyazov has been described as 'one of the wealthiest and most powerful lunatics on earth.' He personifies the outcome when absolute power, money and mental illness are combined. A heavy drinker, bully and wearer of bling, this President-for-Life renamed the months of the year—January after himself, April after his mother and so on. He wrote the *Ruhnama* and announced, 'If you read my book three times you will go to heaven. I asked Allah to arrange it.' It became compulsory reading; studied at all schools, it was essential for getting a good job. Over a million copies were printed in Zulu, Japanese and Braille. He ordered dogs to be banished from Ashgabat, his capital, banned smoking, and outlawed ballet, opera, beards and long hair.

Turkmenistan has one of the world's largest deposits of natural gas, its Galkynysh gas field with 21 trillion cubic metres of reserves, is the second largest field in the world. Niyazov used the wealth from his country's gas to give his countrymen free gas and electricity, to build a white marble capital with gold statues of himself, and to ensure that his family would never be short of funds. He died of a heart attack, leaving his political empire to Gurbanguly Berdimuhamedov, a former dentist, who has carried on a long relationship with his former assistant, a dental nurse. His wife lives in London.

New pipelines take Turkmenistan's gas to China and Iran but attempts by America to promote the Unocal TAPI pipeline through Afghanistan and Pakistan to India did not meet with success. Many believe that the pipeline was the real reason for the US–Afghan war.

NAZARBAYEV'S KAZAKHSTAN

Kazakhstan is the ninth largest country in the world, with a territory bigger than Europe. The Kazakhs lived for centuries as nomads moving with their sheep and horses across the steppes. This land was absorbed into the expanding Russian empire, and Russian settlers arrived. Stalin moved other nationalities into the area with his large-scale colonization schemes, and decimated the Kazakh population with his collectivization programme which led to crop failure; as a result of the famine of 1932-33 the Kazakh population declined by almost 40 per cent and Kazakhs were reduced to a minority in their own land. Today the massive territory of Kazakhstan is home to only 18 million people.

In the days of the Cold War, Kazakhstan became the centre of USSR nuclear testing and space launches; the Russian Sputnik was launched from the Baikanor Cosmodrome in Kazakhstan. The high level of nuclear testing in Kazakhstan led to radioactive contamination of an area over 115,000 square miles inhabited by 2 million people, resulting in birth defects and mental illness. Nursultan Nazarbayev demanded a stop to nuclear testing as an important part of his platform on his rise to power. In 1992, after the declaration of independence,

Nazarbayev negotiated the disbanding of most of his massive nuclear armoury in return for aid from America. The disbanding of Kazakhstan's nuclear industry rendered jobless a high number of young women who had chosen the promising career previously open to them as nuclear scientists.

Kazakhstan was rich in land, minerals, and most of all, significant oil and gas reserves waiting to be exploited. Oil that was produced could only be moved through the established pipelines which ran to Russia, making oil extraction totally dependent on Russia, which was not desperate to increase Kazakh production, preferring to prioritize its own Siberian reserves. Independence enabled the Kazakh oil industry to grow, and with foreign capital and know-how, more than 200 fields have been proven, the largest of which are the giant Kashagen, Tenghis and Karachaganak deposits.

The birth of the new country, saw the Communist party elite move fast to capture the assets and opportunities that the new state provided. President Nazarbayev discarded his former communist credentials and emphasized his Kazakh nationalism, building the Kazakh power base at the expense of the large Russian minority population. All the best jobs and all the most profitable business opportunities now went to Kazakhs.

But despite the huge natural wealth and the very small population, the birth of the nation was accompanied by terrible misery. Having discarded communism, they had no idea or experience of capitalism. The rape of the USSR economies by the West and the local elite, when combined with the worst economic decisions and mismanagement, led not only to widespread poverty and contraction of the economy but also to the total collapse of the ruble, which remained at first the currency for all the breakaway countries. Within a few years the ruble which had started with a value of $2, fell to an exchange rate of 7,000 rubles to $1. Government ministers drawing a salary equivalent of $30 a month were docile prey to the invading foreign businessmen who arrived with pockets full of dollars to buy the assets and deals that were there to be taken. The locals were lost and confused in this new and unknown system of capitalism. At the time I had a business in Kazakhstan and one day my interpreter, a young girl called Irena, approached me with tears in her eyes because the government had decided to privatize state housing and had asked her to pay $20 for her apartment; the concept of ownership of property was beyond her understanding. To stop her tears, I took $20 from my pocket and told her, 'Go buy yourself an apartment.'

The politics of Kazakhstan has been as exciting as any mafia movie. Gorbachev promoted the rise of Nazarbayev, who flew the flag of Kazakh nationalism and anti-nuclear tests. Shortly after independence, Nazarbayev called an election to legitimize his presidency. The rules required candidates to produce 100,000 supporting signatures to qualify, which Hasan Kojahmedov, a rival candidate, managed to do. But two days before the deadline, government thugs attacked him in the street and stole his signatures, resulting in his disqualification. Nazarbayev was elected with an overwhelming mandate.

The next threat to Nazarbayev came from Akezhan Kazhegeldin, a former prime minister, who led a movement for honest elections. He was forced into exile where he continued his crusade against the corruption of the ruling family, while he was prosecuted for tax evasion by Rakhat Aliyev, the powerful son-in-law of the President. Aliyev started life as a surgeon, but after marrying Dariga, graduated into a full-fledged don having made his fortune in sugar racketeering before taking control of a bank, an airline, media interests and several other businesses. He allegedly kidnapped the chairman of Nurbank, the seventh largest bank in Kazakhstan, and forcibly took his shares. The bodies of two senior executives of the bank were found dumped in trash bins. Aliyev was getting out of hand, but it was when he declared his presidential ambitions that Nazarbayev decided it was time to act. Aliyev was first moved out as ambassador to Austria, but was then sacked. He was arrested in Vienna on charges of kidnapping, money laundering and organized crime, and died in his cell. The authorities claimed suicide, but Aliyev's lawyers maintained foul play. Before he died, Aliyev divulged the secrets of power politics in Kazakhstan—

rigged elections, the murder of opposition leaders and corruption.

Before being booted out, Aliyev scored a serious own goal when he instituted an international enquiry to discover the hidden wealth of the exiled Kazhegeldin. The Swiss authorities unearthed secret bank accounts with billion-dollar deposits; the only problem was that the accounts belonged not to Kazhegeldin but to Nazarbayev himself, flaring up into the scandal dubbed 'Kazakhgate'. High level corruption had been exposed in the James Giffen affair. Giffen, an American facilitator of big government deals, when arrested for bribery, claimed he was acting with full knowledge and consent of the US authorities, and was America's link to the ruling family in Kazakhstan. In 2002 Bermuda was, after Russia, the second largest trading partner of Kazakhstan, not because of the physical flow of goods to the island, but because clandestine transactions were booked in the offshore haven. In 2005 the World Bank showed Kazakhstan to be as corrupt as Angola, Bolivia, Kenya and Pakistan. When the *Respublica* newspaper published stories of the corruption, a dog's head was placed outside their offices with the note, 'There will be no next time'—a warning in the style of the head of the racehorse in Mario Puzo's *The Godfather*.

Despite all, Nazarbayev's hold on power remained stable and secure. His foreign policy and economic measures were constructive and led to growth of the oil sector, growth of foreign investment, and growth of the economy. He built the magnificent new capital of Astana where statues of the President were conspicuously absent. To sycophants who urged him to create monuments to himself, he replied, 'Astana is my memento'. Succession remains a problem; the President has no sons and his three daughters seem to have disqualified themselves through their inappropriate marriages.

TAJIKISTAN AND KYRGYZSTAN

Both the two smallest of the Commonwealth of Independent States' republics border China. Tajikistan has a population of 8 million and

Kyrgyzstan, 5 million people. They are poor and both are substantially dependent on remittances from overseas expatriate workers— 40 per cent of GDP in the case of Kyrgyzstan and almost 50 per cent in the case of Tajikistan. Corruption and human rights abuse plague both countries.

The first two presidents of Kyrgyzstan, Akayev and Bakiyev, were both removed by opposition protests, and the current head of state is Akmazbek Atambayev. An important opposition figure to Akayev was the retired general Felix Kulov who had served as interior minister and mayor of Bishkek. Generally respected, he was nevertheless arrested from his hospital bed on trumped up charges of forgery and abuse of power. A military court acquitted him but when he became a candidate for president, he was disqualified for failing his language test. The new president, Bakiyev, appointed him prime minister. Corruption, including the sale of government jobs, keeps one-third of the population below the poverty line and the foreign debt higher than the GDP. The Tulip Revolution has changed the government but has not affected the US airbase or the rampant drug smuggling and organized crime.

The mountain republic of Tajikistan has since 1994, been ruled by Emonali Sharipovich Rakmonov, who has dominated the political scene through elections that are neither free nor fair. In 2013 Zayd Saidov, a businessman who set up a political party to oppose Rakmonov in the elections, was arrested and sentenced for twenty-six years for fraud, corruption and having sex with a minor. A year later his lawyer was jailed for nine years for alleged fraud and bribery. The white economy is based on aluminium, cotton and hydroelectric power with a planned 1000 MW export to Pakistan. The black economy is fed by drug smuggling and the transit route from Afghanistan to Russia

MUSLIMS IN CHINA

Islam reached China in the seventh century when Sad Ibn abi Waqqas, under instructions from the third Caliph, Usman, led Arab and Persian traders to go east. The Muslims came both by land, via the Silk Road, and by sea. Centuries later the Mongols under the family of Genghis Khan, conquered China; Genghis himself was no Muslim, and described himself as a punishment on Muslims sent by God, but he was tolerant of all religions, and many of the soldiers of the Mongol army were of Arab, Persian and Turk descent. The Muslims traders brought perfume, medicine and pearls and in exchange took silk, porcelain and tea. They also brought to China, medicine, mathematics and astronomy, and took home Chinese inventions, the compass, gunpowder and paper.

Under the Song dynasty Muslims dominated foreign trade in China. Under the Yuan emperors, Muslims flourished. Under Kublai Khan, Genghis's grandson, eight of his twelve governors were Muslim and Muslim culture and learning became a recognized alternative to the Confucian system. Many outstanding Muslims served the Ming emperors—the generals Chang Yuchan and Hu Dahai; Hai Rui, the administrator famed for his justice; and the great admiral Zhang He whose seven voyages took the Chinese fleet to the furthest corners of Asia and Africa. But when the Qing attacked the Ming, Muslim loyalists resisted, leading to the slaughter of 100,000 Muslims.

By the twentieth century, there were over 20 million Muslims in China, with the biggest concentration in Mongolia and Xinjiang. The Japanese invaders destroyed 220 mosques and killed large numbers of Muslims; the rape of Nanking saw many mosques filled with the dead bodies of those massacred. The Communist government under Mao followed a policy of discouraging religion, which climaxed in the Cultural Revolution, but Deng was more tolerant and Muslims were allowed to follow their religion; even to go on Hajj to Mecca. However, a fine line was drawn between Hui Muslims, and the Uyghurs who lived in the far western province of Xinjiang and in the Central Asian republics of the former USSR. The Hui had over centuries assimilated Han ways and culture—even Chinese names—and lived content in China which they saw as home. The Uyghurs, in the northwest, though

Muslim, were seen as separatists wanting to form their own state, and even had a terrorist element which created instability in their territories. Xinjiang with its capital, Urumchi, is very different from the rest of China, with its shop boards in Arabic script, its Muslim citizens looking middle-eastern rather than Chinese, its restaurants serving Halal food, and its mosques with the call for prayer, wafting over the city. The Han Chinese government in Beijing has countered with a strategy of increasing the Han population to reduce the Muslims to a minority, but the situation is far from stable.

Of the 20 million Muslims in China, just over half are Hui and just under half are Uyghur. There is no repression of the Hui who carry on their religious practices without obstruction, but the Uyghur are treated more harshly—religious pilgrimage to Mecca is restricted, hijab in public is discouraged Muslim religious practices are repressed. Their majority in Xinjiang has been erased by internal immigration of the Han Chinese, who now constitute a majority in this formerly Muslim province. The Chinese authorities argue that they are not clamping down on Muslims but on Uyghur separationists and terrorists who happen to be Muslim. They show as an example of their tolerance, the 34,928 mosques in China, and the 5,000 hajjis a year who make the pilgrimage to Mecca. In contrast, violence against Muslims in Tibet in 2008 resulted in Tibetans burning down the main mosque; Kashgar the most anti-China city in the far northwest, has seen terrorist activity sponsored by the East Turkestan Islamic Movement.

MUSLIMS IN EUROPE

About 50 million Muslims live in Europe and the UK. This is the legacy of the empire. After the British withdrew from India, Indians, Pakistanis and Bengalis followed them back to England. Many of them knew some English and they moved to where jobs were available. French-speaking Muslims from the French colonies of North Africa, moved to France, the Turks moved to Germany and Denmark, Iraqis and Iranis chose Sweden, Moroccans preferred Belgium and Spain, and Pakistanis also felt comfortable in Norway. Albania and Bosnia were majority Muslim nations with 70 per cent of the population following Islam. The 9 million Turks were the largest Muslim ethnic group, but in Russia there were more than 15 million believers. In cities such as Burlington, Blackburn, Bradford and Brussels, more than a quarter of the local population were Muslims, who seemed to like cities whose names started with the letter 'B'. Muslim population was young whereas the Europeans grew older, and Muslims had more children than the Europeans. The combination of immigration and more children resulted in Islam becoming the fastest growing religion in Europe.

When the European empires withdrew from Asia, they welcomed Asian immigrants to take the menial jobs that they didn't want. These early immigrants had grown up under a dominant Western culture. They understood and aspired to Western values and attitudes. Their Islam was gentle and peaceful, inspired by The Prophet in his early days in Mecca. They integrated despite being regarded as second class citizens. Soon the immigrants outnumbered the jobs available. Europe tried to shut the gates, but an unending stream of new arrivals found new tricks to breech the borders. Political asylum, refugees, marriage, health problems, education were just some of the excuses that flooded the immigration authorities. The new arrivals were also experts at milking the welfare system.

The eighties created the massive oil wealth of Saudi Arabia and the Gulf states; Saudi money together with Wahhabi missionary zeal gave a boost to the madrassa system of education with its more aggressive interpretation of religion. After the training and experience gained from participation in the Afghan war against the USSR, militant Islam with its emphasis on jihad, transformed the attitudes of the new arrivals. This led not only to terror attacks and deadly suicide missions, but also resulted in an arrogance and belief that their own culture was superior to that of the Europeans. They refused to integrate, and lived in community ghettos without learning the language or the conventions of their host countries. Some countries, such as Sweden encouraged segregation, alienation and welfare with the result that the Muslim immigrants were denied jobs and happily lived on welfare. Muslim activists argued, 'We will eventually be a majority; then we take over.'

The attitude of the new Muslim arrivals created a backlash of resentment. France banned the hijab in schools. Rightist anti-immigration parties encouraged racism, and tolerance was replaced by the clash of civilizations. Acts of terrorism became more frequent and escalated after 9/11. The Madrid train bombings, the attack on the London transport system, the murder of British soldier Lee Rigby and the Charlie Hebdo killings in France, were but a few incidents that disrupted life and security in Europe. New books such as *Londonistan* and *While Europe Slept* provided a wake-up call to white Europeans. A new breed of Islamist terrorist, born, brought up and educated in the West, emerged, and young jihadis made their way first to Afghanistan, then Iraq and finally to Syria to join ISIS and participate in brutal and dramatic acts of terrorism. The response of the West resulted in many changes in day-to-day living. Airport security demanded that passengers reach airports at least two hours before take-off to enable security vetting. Liquid was removed from hand luggage after a terrorist attempt to smuggle deadly chemicals in water bottles to blow up a plane. Cameras proliferated to ensure that 'Big Brother is watching you.' Both the pattern of day-to-day life and the attitudes of Europeans and Muslims changed.

Arab oil wealth has made central London property an enclave for the super-rich from the Gulf. The al-Nahayan royal family are now the largest landowner in Mayfair after the Duke of Westminster, and it is estimated that 50 per cent of all homes over £10 million in value are owned by Arab high net-worth individuals. By far the greatest investment in central London property has come from Qatar, which includes in its London portfolio, Harrods, The Shard, Canary Wharf, the US Embassy in Grosvenor Square, and the luxury hotels, Claridges, The Berkeley and The Connaught. After their One Hyde

Park, the most expensive apartment building in London, they are now developing The Chelsea Barracks, a massive residential enclave for the super-rich. Qatari holdings in London are larger than the Crown Estate which manages the Queen's property portfolio. Mayfair, Knightsbridge and Marble Arch are now populated more by Arabs and rich Asians than by the British who have moved out to the suburbs, though young Englishmen can be seen on summer evenings driving the cycle rickshaws that have moved from Delhi to London.

The immense wealth of the Muslim oil states in the Middle East had made them important buyers of the exports of European countries. These export markets for Europe's industrial goods and armaments made the Muslim oil states a key economic partner. This further complicated the East–West relationship. Though the white majority in Europe had grown more hostile to the Asian and black immigrant community, big business and government had grown dependent on Muslim oil and Muslim oil wealth. Europe's search for release from dependence on the Middle East led to development of North Sea oil, and integration with gas supplied by the Russian giant, Gasprom. Russian power re-emerged under Putin as the world's largest petro state.

ISLAM IN AMERICA

The first impact of Islam on American life was the conversion of black Americans by Elijah Muhammad and his Nation of Islam. Elijah Muhammad led the Nation from 1934 till his death in 1975. He was mentor to Malcolm X, Louis Farrakhan and Muhammad Ali, the greatest heavyweight champion of all time.

Elijah Muhammad used explosive language to change the mentality of the black community of America, who had been brought over from Africa in the eighteenth and nineteenth centuries as slaves. Without fear of the white brutality and segregation of the time, he proclaimed, 'Whites lynched us, raped us, castrated us, tarred and feathered us. The white man of America is a blue-eyed, blond haired Devil.' In his

Nation of Islam his followers practiced economic solidarity, respect for women, proper diet, and abstinence from alcohol, crime, juvenile delinquency and adultery.

The most influential leader of the Black Muslim movement in America was Malcolm X, born Malcolm Little. His father and three uncles were murdered by a Klu-Klux-Klan-type white racist group called The Black Legion. His father's death was officially written down as 'run over by a tram.' His mother was locked up in a mental hospital, and Malcolm grew up first in foster homes and then on the streets. He dropped out of law school when a white teacher told him that 'Law is no realistic goal for a nigger.' He then indulged in a career of petty crime, pimping, drugs and theft till he was sentenced to eight to ten years. In prison he discovered Islam through the teachings of Elijah Muhammad and through extensive reading. He emerged from prison a preacher and a dynamic orator and multiplied the following of The Nation of Islam by more than fifty times, making it a force in the USA. Malcolm was a fighter with unlimited courage. He split from Elijah Muhammad's Nation, disillusioned by Elijah's womanizing and the luxurious lifestyle of senior ministers. He went on Hajj and converted to Sunni Islam. Meeting white Muslims on his tours, he modified his Black dogma, and became a famous international figure with recognition from Nasser and Castro. Initially refused entry to Mecca by the Saudi authorities, he was then admitted as the guest of Prince Faisal, later to become King Faisal.

He received many threats on his life and moved with bodyguards for his protection. Malcolm was assassinated while making a speech; gunmen fired twenty-one bullets into his body. Streets and schools in many US cities were named after him. The US Post brought out a commemorative stamp in his honour, and his autobiography is recognized as one of the most influential books of the century.

Malcolm met the young Cassius Clay who became Islam's most famous convert in the twentieth century and changed his name to Muhammad Ali. Ali was not just the greatest heavyweight champion of all time, but was a determined and idealistic leader of the Black

Muslim movement in America. He lost his title and the right to fight when he refused to go to Vietnam as a conscript. As he emerged from the court he was thronged by the press asking why he refused to fight for the US army in Vietnam; he replied, 'Ain't no Vietcong ever called me nigger!' When Malcolm X converted to Sunni Islam, rejecting Elijah Muhammad, Ali severed his relationship with Malcolm; but later, Ali too converted to the Sunni mainstream, commenting that 'turning away from Malcolm was one of the mistakes that I regret most in my life.'

Much later, after 9/11, Ali was asked by a reporter, 'How do you feel about the hijackers of 9/11 sharing your faith?' Ali replied, 'How do you feel about Hitler sharing yours?' This one sentence is still today the most powerful rebuttal to those who would condemn Islam for the acts of a few misguided terrorists.

But it was not only the Islamization of the Afro-American black community that affected life in America. The militant response of jihadis to US aggression and domination of the Islamic world, particularly the control of the oil industry in Muslim countries and the unbalanced support of Israel at the expense of the Arabs was to have a far greater effect in changing day-to-day life in the USA. US military might was beyond challenge, but the jihadi response with its new style of guerrilla warfare and the deployment of suicide bombers—a tactic which had been used with devastating effect centuries ago by the Ismail Assassins—evened out the playing field. The Beirut bombing and the attacks on US embassies in Kenya and Tanzania were but some of the examples of the new warfare; but it was the 9/11 attacks on the World Trade Centre and the Pentagon that changed not just the rules of the game, but changed the game itself. America responded in rage with the war on Afghanistan, an expensive decision which achieved little, and the war on Saddam in Iraq, which was successful in removing Saddam but created such disastrous havoc that in retrospect Saddam looks like a knight in shining armour. America lost the respect of the world as it adjusted its technique of war with destruction from the skies but no boots on the ground.

The destruction of Libya was the cost of removing and killing Gaddafi. Once again the tragedy that followed the regime-change was a step back, not a step forward. Now the attempt to remove Bashar al-Assad in Syria has morphed into the horror of ISIS. Bashar retains government, but a brutal war has destroyed the life of millions of Syrians. Once again a monster has been created which has come back to haunt its original sponsors.

Fortress America has introduced the Patriot Act and other measures to promote domestic security, which restrict personal freedoms in the manner of Martial Law in Third World countries. Discrimination and demonization of Muslims has forced many to return to their home countries. Humiliation at airport immigration has angered visitors to America. And finally Donald Trump, the US President, has threatened to send Muslims home. Is Trump the face of tomorrow's America?

Unlike in Europe and the UK, the Muslim immigrants in America have integrated with the mainstream community. They have learned English, adopted American values, and tried to become real Americans. But now they are insecure in their new land. They watch the demonization of Islam, the hatred being created and the resurgence of racism, with anxiety. They watched the presidential campaign and asked themselves if they should prepare to return to their countries of origin.

ISLAM IN AFRICA

In 614 AD, twenty-three Muslims fled persecution in Mecca and received the protection of the King of Abyssinia, they were led by Amr bin al-As who later conquered Egypt. Within a hundred years after the death of The Prophet, the Muslims had conquered the whole of Mediterranean Africa and set up a dynasty in Spain. Scholars followed the conquerors and conversion of black Africa began. There was no racism or colour prejudice in Islam; in fact the first muezzin had been a black man, Bilal.

Africa gave birth to great Muslim dynasties, the Fatimid and Almoravid; Muslim empires grew in Mali, Ghana, Songhay, Kanem and Bornu. The great traveller, Ibn Battuta, who visited these territories in the fourteenth century, commented that belief in Islam was so strong and mosques so crowded on Fridays that unless one went very early, it was impossible to find a place to sit. He was impressed with the wealth and culture that he found and described the people as law abiding with much gold jewellery, who ate off Chinese porcelain. He wrote that the exalted Sultan of Kilwa 'is a man of great humility who sits with poor people, eats with them and respects the ulema.'

The first Muslim university of Africa was established in Timbuktu. Education flourished, with famous scholars such as the historian Ibn Khaldun and Leo Africanus, who moved to Morocco after his family was expelled from Spain by Ferdinand and Isabella. Leo visited Timbuktu and was later captured by pirates and gifted to Pope Leo X, who freed him in recognition of his learning and commissioned him to write a survey of the continent; this survey was the base of Europe's knowledge of Africa for the next few centuries.

The Muslim civilizations of Africa were not without their setbacks. The Black Death was followed by the rise of Portuguese naval power; in 1505 they occupied Kilwa, destroyed all 300 mosques and slaughtered the population. The Sultan of Oman came to their rescue and moved his capital from Muscat to Kilwa, but Europe could not be contained. In the seventeenth century the Dutch replaced the Portuguese as the dominant power. The Dutch were followed by the British, Germans, Portuguese and Italians who carved up East Africa between themselves. Recognizing that resistance was futile, the Sultan of Zanzibar sold his important cities, Dar es Salam, Kilwa and Lundi to the Germans for 4 million marks. If he could not make a virtue of necessity, at least he could make a profit out of necessity. Some tried to fight, such as the Mahdi of Sudan and Omar Mukhtar of Libya, becoming folk heroes and creating legend; but it was futile. The Muslim civilizations of North, West and East Africa were all absorbed by the new European empires.

The slave trade took a 100 million Africans and sent them either to their death on the treacherous sea journey to America, or to a brutal enslavement when they arrived in their new land. The missionaries followed the conquerors, and missionary schools reshaped the thinking, the values and the attitudes of African Muslims to better serve their new colonial masters. It was a hard time till the Great Wars of the twentieth century ended the age of empire and Africa gained independence. But through it all, Islam survived and grew. Today Africa is home to one-third of the world's Muslims.

25

The Muslim World Today

'The oil in this region is the single biggest prize in history.'
—Everette Lee DeGolyer (In 1944)

The war in Syria has destroyed homes and cities, resulted in the death of over 100,000 people and the displacement of almost 5 million. While we are all aware of this brutal war, we don't really know why it started and why it continues. Newspaper headlines laud the West for taking on the brutal dictator Bashar al-Assad, but we have already seen the destruction of two other 'dictators', Saddam and Gaddafi, both of whom were replaced by such chaos that many wish they were back. Allegations of chemical weapon use by Assad don't carry credibility, particularly after the bogus 'Weapons of Mass Destruction' allegations against Saddam. Why then does this inhuman war continue?

On Friday, 30 August 2013, the respected *Guardian* newspaper published an article with the headline, 'Syria intervention plan fueled by oil interests, not chemical weapon concern'. Syria holds the largest oil discoveries in the Eastern Mediterranean, which Western oil companies would love to get their hands on. But more important than oil in the ground is the geography which makes Syria the crossroads for any pipeline from the Middle East to Europe. Russia holds practically the monopoly of supply of gas to Europe. America would very much like to break that monopoly and weaken Russia's influence in Europe. The American plan was to pipe gas from Qatar through Syria to Europe. Assad would not agree. Instead, he joined Iran and Iraq in an alternate pipeline for Irani gas to reach Europe. America was not ready to allow this, and decided to knock out the Assad regime. Their think tanks advised, 'We don't know what to do about terrorists, but we can take down a government.'

Taking down Assad proved more difficult than expected. The Russians were not going to let that happen. The Americans, the Israelis and the Saudis lined up against the Russians, Chinese and the Iranis in a proxy war with Syria as the battlefield. The struggle for the control of oil was presented as a Sunni–Shia conflict but what it will really decide is which pipeline will feed gas through to Europe.

THE CONTROL FOR OIL

The nineteenth century saw the entry of oil into big business. The first oil tycoons fought to dominate their markets—Rockefeller in America and the Rothschilds and Nobels in Europe. The Middle East entered the world of oil in the early nineteenth century with discoveries in Iran and Iraq, and the first Eastern oil tycoon to take his share from the Western oil companies was the astute Calouste Gulbenkian, Mr Five Percent. Gulbenkian had a passion for hard work, a capacity for vision and unmatchable skill as a negotiator. At heart he was a bazaari, a master of trading, intrigue and the acquisition of useful information.

The Western oil companies that entered the Middle East were rich; the nations where oil was to be found were poor, and only too grateful if their countries were selected for prospecting. The negotiating table was not an even playing field. Desperate for money, Muzaffar al Din Shah of Iran gave away concession rights over

75 per cent of his country for sixty years for £20,000 in cash, an equal amount in shares and 16 per cent of annual profits. For many years, Saudi Arabia was unable to interest drillers, as Western companies wrote it off as unlikely to hold oil in significant quantities. For decades, as oil discoveries grew, the lion's share of the profits were taken by the Western companies and their governments who took more in taxes than the total return to the oil-producing countries. In May 1933, the concession agreement was signed between Socal and the Kingdom of Saudi Arabia; it provided for £35,000 upfront payment in gold—£5,000 as the first year's payment and the rest as a loan. Further loans would be extended on the discovery of oil. The term was sixty years and the area of the concession about 360,000 square miles. In 1938, oil was struck in both Kuwait and in the Kingdom, where Well Number 7 in the Dammam Zone opened the gates to Saudi fortune.

Resentment against the unbalanced sharing of profits started to spread through the Middle East; the first to move was the Irani strongman Shah Reza Khan. In 1932, he unilaterally cancelled the Anglo-Persian concession. Negotiation led to compromise; the Iranis got more money, the company got an extension of a further thirty-two years. But this earned him the enmity of the British and when he sided with Hitler in the Second World War, he was forced to abdicate in a deal that gave the throne to his son.

The war established the importance of oil. The great general Rommel found himself helpless in his Africa campaign without fuel, and spoke from experience when he said, 'The bravest men can do nothing without guns, the guns nothing without plenty of ammunition, and neither guns nor ammunition are of much use in mobile warfare unless there are vehicles with sufficient petrol to haul them around.'

Germany had the steel but Britain had the oil. The great German fleet of aircraft sat grounded due to lack of aviation fuel.

Though Middle Eastern oil production was less than 10 per cent of US production, the future was clear and lay in the desert sands.

The two world powers—one on the rise; the other, fading—negotiated hard for their share. Roosevelt told the British, 'Persian oil is yours. We share the oil of Iraq and Kuwait. As for Saudi oil, it's ours.' Churchill didn't like it and replied, 'We are being hustled.'

Mossadeq in Iran was the next to attack Western domination of Middle Eastern oil. He nationalized the AIOC. The West fought back, reinstated the deposed Mohammad Reza Shah and had Mossadeq put away for life. But even this hard lesson was not enough to stop the producing countries from demanding more. The next milestone was the 50:50 sharing agreement. Strong as they were, The Seven Sisters, who dominated oil (actually there were eight—Exxon, Mobil, Chevron, Texaco, Shell, BP, Gulf and CFP of France) capitulated. 50:50 was better than nationalization.

But soon even the 50:50 barrier was to be smashed. In 1957 Enrico Mattei, the maverick Italian newcomer, wanted in and was ready to pay more. He offered two shares to Iran, as landlord and partner, which together gave the Iranis 75 per cent to Mattei's 25 per cent. Japan followed suit, and it was soon common knowledge that the 50:50 rule was as dead as a dodo. But the oil majors simply raised production and dropped prices, ensuring that their profits continued to rise despite the steady onslaught of the producing nations.

In 1971, negotiations in Tehran and Libya established the 55 per cent principle, OPEC developed muscles and the balance of power shifted from the oil companies to the oil countries. Gaddafi nationalized BP in Libya and also Hunt Petroleum holdings. He made it clear that those who wanted a future in Libya must concede greater rights and greater shares. Iraq followed with the nationalization of holdings of Exxon, Royal Dutch and Mobil. A few years later Kuwait, Qatar and Saudi Arabia followed.

In response to US, massive support to Israel when the Yom Kippur War started in 1973, Gaddafi announced an embargo on the shipment of oil to America. On 20 October 1973, Saudi Arabia and the other Arab producers joined the embargo. The effect was dramatic and immediate. By 1974, the price of oil had jumped from $3 to

$12 per barrel and Kissinger was sent to negotiate the end of the embargo with King Faisal. He later commented, 'The King always spoke in a gentle voice, even when making strong points. He loved elliptical comments capable of many interpretations.' Faisal insisted that a fundamental condition for him was that Jerusalem becomes an Arab–Islamic city. Kissinger inquired about The Wailing Wall. Another wall, Faisal replied, could be built somewhere else for the Jews to wail against.

After the embargo, the producers had won; they were in control. The age of colonial power was ended. The last to move was Saudi Arabia; they took over the giant Aramco, but did not sign till fourteen years later. The $700 billion transaction was concluded with a 'Gentleman's agreement.'

The post-embargo years established the Muslim oil-producing countries as the super-rich of the world. No longer would concessions over vast territories be given for a pittance. Now newspaper headlines talked of $100,000,000 a day. A popular joke in the seventies described the birthday of Sheikh Zayed's son. He called his ambassador in Washington and asked him to buy a nice little Mickey Mouse outfit; the ambassador put his advisors to work and bought the Chase Manhattan bank! By 2008, Saudi Arabia alone was pulling revenues of $1 billion a day. But then oil prices fell. By the end of 2014, prices which had hovered above $100 fell below $50. The price war reflected Saudi determination to drive shale oil drilling out of the market. (The low price hurt the Saudis, but ravaged the US shale oil industry.)

This amazing inflow of money changed the region and the lives of its people; it also gave opportunity to poor Muslim nations whose people found employment in the Gulf. Remittances became a major part of foreign exchange earnings. But even after the massive spending, surpluses continued to rise, resulting in huge sovereign wealth funds to be managed.

The first to take the new financial opportunity in the seventies was Agha Hasan Abedi, the brilliant Pakistani banker who made a close relationship with Sheikh Zayed of Abu Dhabi and created the controversial the Bank of Credit and Commerce International whose dramatic rise and fall over a decade was one of the most amazing stories of twentieth-century finance. To the West, Abedi was a villain; to the Third World, Abedi was a hero. To Pakistanis, Abedi was the man who made Pakistani bankers elite and sought after by international banks the world over. After his death, his Chief Financial Officer was to comment, 'I remember looking into his eyes and seeing God and the Devil balanced equally between them.' The trail of Abedi's power covered President Carter and Clark Clifford, the powerful former defence secretary who acted as advisor to four presidents, General Noriega of Panama, and a host of other heads of state. The BCCI under Abedi had a strong presence in seventy-two countries with 16,000 employees when it was destroyed by the governments and central banks of America and Britain for money laundering. By that time Abedi, who had survived a heart transplant, had retired and moved back to Pakistan. Western governments tried to extradite him to answer charges but the Pakistan government who saw him as a philanthropist and hero, refused to give him up. He died a broken man in 1995.

The West could stop the BCCI but it could not stop the massive mountain of money accumulating in the petro states. These surplus petrodollars needed to be recycled back into the Western economic system. So, under 'advice' from Western experts, a policy was put into place to direct the surplus into areas where the West had the greatest need of it—treasury bills and bonds, fixed income securities. Direct purchase of significant American companies was discouraged, as in the case of Dubai's attempt to purchase six US ports and China's bid for the US oil company Unocal. Managers of the new sovereign wealth funds (SWF) were wary of investing in the less developed countries (LDCs) whose shortcomings were only too obvious—mismanagement, corruption, a lack of skilled labour and infrastructure.

In the eighties, Kuwait tried to develop its own financial institutions as an alternate to the West, but this came to an abrupt stop with the collapse of the Souk al Manakh, the wildly speculative alternative financial market. The Souk at its peak, had the third highest capitalization in the world, behind only the US and Japan. Speculation had replaced trading and real estate in Kuwait as the principal investment activity. When I made my first trip to Kuwait, KPMG, my financial advisors in the UAE, told me about two Kuwaiti businessmen who had been my friends in school. One, they told me, was an old established and successful trading house with important international agencies, a workforce in the thousands and a profit in the tens of millions. The other had a staff of three—a market trader, a bookkeeper and a peon; he had earned a profit well in excess of $1 billion in a few years trading. Speculation was the name of the game. But it all came to an end in the massive crash. The lesson learned was that you should not confuse brains with a bull market.

The problem with this strategy was that it was prone to being hit by a double whammy in times of recession; falling oil prices meant falling revenue and recession in the international economy resulted in erosion of asset values. In addition, inflation was endless with a constant erosion of the value of money in real terms. This terrifying scenario hit in 1978, 1985 and 2008. On 19 January, 2009 Muhammad al Sabah, the finance minister of Kuwait, stated that rough estimates showed that Gulf Cooperation Council (GCC) countries lost in less than four months of the crisis, more than $2.5 trillion (including $600 billion of SWF assets) as oil collapsed from $147 to less than $35, Saudi stocks lost 60 per cent of their value and more than 60 per cent of all new projects were put on hold. The other inherent danger of investing in Western economies was a nightmare that was never mentioned; the US had a bad habit of seizing or 'freezing' assets of countries which were stepping out of line.

Defence expenditure placed another heavy demand on budgets. First, purchase of armaments and aircraft from the West cost hundreds of billions of dollars; in addition GCC countries were expected to join in financing the wars that America waged or incited in the region. In the Afghan wars, Saudi Arabia had to match US support to the Mujahideen dollar for dollar. Kuwait gave billions to Saddam to fight the Iranis, and was taken over by Saddam when they raised a demand for repayment. The Saudis contributed $65 billion in the Gulf War. In Africa they financed the Safari Club, created to counter communism in African nations.

All stakeholders in The Kingdom wanted a piece of the action. The public enjoyed the fast improving infrastructure, the free medical and educational support; the princes and merchants wanted the business opportunities that offered wealth; the Wahhabi religious establishment, a long term partner of the Saudi dynasty, wanted funds to promote their version of Islam. A huge missionary program was initiated with funding for education and the promotion of religion. The number of madrassas multiplied throughout the Muslim world.

New mosques, support in education and other works of charity won over millions of Muslims to this interpretation of Islam. The millions of expatriate Muslims working in the GCC came under the influence of this teaching. This doctrine, born in the desert, advocated a back-to-basics approach to the time of The Prophet.

But the religious establishment was not content to just receive handouts. They wanted involvement and even partial control of the entire financial system. They demanded that banking and finance follow the principles of Sharia; they wanted Islamic Banking. Islam condemns and forbids riba which has resulted in a debate over the meaning of the word: Is riba interest or usury? But Islamic finance is concerned with much more than just interest on loans. It requires that capital be a partner in enterprise, sharing the risk. This is very different from the western system where financiers take a defined and risk-free amount, called interest. Furthermore, Islamic finance forbids investment or lending for purposes that don't conform to Islamic principles. This means that not only is it forbidden to invest in businesses dealing in pork, alcohol or vice, but even conventional banking that deals in interest, bills and bonds and speculates in futures and derivatives is off limits. Anything involving gambling or speculation is forbidden. Lending should be linked to real economic activity, agriculture, production and trade. This led to the birth of the modern Islamic Banking system which has grown significantly as a by-product of the new oil wealth of Muslim countries.

UNDERSTANDING JIHAD

The war in Afghanistan gave a new role to passionate Muslims who believed that jihad in the sense of actual participation in battle for their religion was an essential duty. They believed that the greater or inner jihad was not enough. In Afghanistan, would-be warriors became hardened and experienced soldiers. Their inspiration came from Hassan al Banna, Syed Qutb and the Muslim Brotherhood in Egypt. When the war in Afghanistan ended with the withdrawal and breakup of the USSR, the flow of jihadis did not dry up. The Mujahideen were followed by the Taliban, al Qaeda and the TTP. The most recent evolution of this phenomenon has been ISIS.

Syed Qutb is the founding father of modern jihad. He was sent to America to study education; he returned with strong views on the Americans and on life, which he expressed in no uncertain terms: 'Nowhere on earth could I find people that excel in education, knowledge, technology, business and civilization like the Americans. However, the American values, ethics and beliefs are below the standard of a human being.' Qutb followed the teachings of Ibn Taymiyyah and inspired revolt and assassination. He inspired two attempts to assassinate Nasser, was imprisoned and executed. His legacy lives on in his book, *Milestones*. Qutb taught, 'The order in which Allah gave Islam to Muhammad was gradual and progressive to maximize positive results towards Islam. Many Muslims take the early verses of this progression of teaching out of context as if they are Allah's final and complete instructions.'

This referred to the debate created by the contradictions in the *Quran*. The early verses, which were received by The Prophet while in Mecca, did not talk of war; they were more accommodating and peaceful. Examples are:

- 'Let there be no compulsion in religion' (2:256)
- 'If it had been the Lord's will, all those who are on earth would have believed.' (10:99)

But the Medina verses were much harder:

'Fight and slay the Pagans wherever you can find them, and seize them, beleaguer them, and lie in wait for them in every stratagem (of war)' (9:5)

In Mecca The Prophet was a spiritual leader and religious guide. In Medina, he was also a political leader and the commander-in-chief of the Muslim army, who led his troops into twenty-seven battles and ordered his generals to engage in several other military engagements. The Muslims were instructed to fight those who persecuted them and to conquer those who rejected Islam in their region. Mawlana Mawdudi, the Pakistani scholar of Islam, went further: 'Muslim nations are special because they have a command from Allah to rule the entire world.'

These contradictions led to two different streams of opinion; the majority of Muslims who believed that Islam was a religion of peace, and the minority of radical Muslims who believed that Islam was a religion of war with the world divided into two territories, Dar al Islam and Dar al Harb. The radicals insisted that the earlier verses had been abrogated by the latter verses. The peaceful Muslims pointed to the Muslim greeting as 'salamu alaykum' (may peace be on you) and argued that Islam was a religion for all times and that interpretations should be flexible to suit the requirements of both time and circumstance. They believed that war can be fought to repel aggression and lift oppression; not wantonly against all. They quoted the sentence, 'Leave the Abyssinians in peace so long as they leave you in peace.' They did not believe that Islam ordered random killing of all non-Muslims. Extreme radicals even argued for killing those Muslims that were lax in following the Islamic duties of prayer, fasting and Hajj whereas the moderates were firm that a Muslim could only be killed if he was inciting rebellion and refusing to obey the law.

The jihadis were used by the US to fight proxy wars. But the Frankenstein they had created grew totally out of their control. Those who would use this passion for jihad were sitting on a tiger and couldn't get off. Terrorist attacks on America and Europe followed, which changed life the world over. The temptation to use fighters, who in the words of Khalid bin Walid centuries ago, 'Love death even as (they) love life' was too good to let go. After Afghanistan the jihadis believed that with God on their side, they were invincible.

ISIS has become a very serious problem and their sponsors have realized that if they win in Syria, they will, for sure, not stop there. But ISIS is only the most recent of radical groups that started in the seventh century with the Kharijites and which included the Assassins of Hasan al Sabah, both of whom created havoc with their terrorist tactics. All of these extreme groups have killed more Muslims than non-Muslims and bad as the impact has been on the Christian countries of the West, the damage and destruction has been much greater at home in the Muslim states.

A CLASH OF VIEWS

But jihad has not been the only serious issue or difference between radical Salafists and the moderates of the Islamic world. The status and role of women is an issue which affects every Muslim home. When The Prophet and his group arrived in Medina they noted the different behaviour of the Medina women. Umar, the champion of male privilege, commented, 'We men of Quraysh dominate our women. When we arrived in Medina, we saw that the Ansar let themselves be dominated by theirs. Then our women began to copy their habits.' One day when he was railing at his wife, she answered him in the same tone of voice. When he expressed his shock and disappointment, she replied, 'You reproach me for answering you! Well, by God, the wives of The Prophet answer him.' It did not help that the two most influential leaders of early Islam, The Prophet and his most powerful and admired lieutenant, Umar, had very different views on women and how they should be treated.

After the wedding feast on the marriage of The Prophet and Zainab, the guests stayed too long and didn't leave. This led to the Quranic verses instituting seclusion,

> O ye who believe, enter not the houses of The Prophet, unless you are invited to a meal, and then not in anticipation of its getting ready. But enter when you are called, and when you have eaten, disperse, linger not in eagerness for talk. This was a cause of embarrassment for The Prophet…When you ask any of the wives of The Prophet for something, ask from behind a curtain. That is purer for your hearts and for their hearts. (54:33)

In Medina, rowdy hooligans were harassing even decent women on the streets. Men would make advances and try to pick up women they came across. When challenged, they gave the excuse that they had believed the women they accosted to be slave girls. In this context Allah revealed verse 59 of Sura 33 in which He advised the wives of The Prophet to make themselves easy to recognize by pulling their jilbab over themselves, 'O Prophet! Tell thy wives and thy daughters and the women of the believers to draw their cloaks close around them (when they go abroad). That will be better, so that they may be recognized and not annoyed.' In this way the hijab descended on Medina. Throughout Muhammad's lifetime, veiling, like seclusion, was observed only by his wives so that the phrase, 'she took the veil' is used in the hadith to mean that a woman became the wife of The Prophet.

Of all the wives of The Prophet, Um Salama was the most demanding for the rights of women. She asked The Prophet why women did not receive equal mention in the *Quran*; she also asked about the *Quran*'s position on inheritance rights of women. Till then a woman could not claim an inheritance, but she herself could be inherited by her stepson on the death of her husband. Um Salama's questions were satisfied by Sura 4 An-Nisa (Women). But even so, the debate continued with Umar in the corner of men's rights and The Prophet protecting the rights of women. Umar did not condemn violence against women; The Prophet never raised a hand against anyone, let alone his wives. This debate still carries on today.

After the Battle of the Camel, al Bakra claimed to have heard The Prophet say, 'Those who entrust their affairs to a woman will never know prosperity.' This hadith has been frequently quoted as a saying of The Prophet. But was it? Al Bakra was not highly respected and had a history of coming up with opportune hadith. Once he was whipped by Umar for giving false evidence in an adultery case. Hadith were always suspected unless there were very good grounds for acceptance. Al Bukhari studied over 600,000 hadith before concluding that there were 596,725 false hadith in circulation, and only 7,275 were reliable. Muslims have certainly not given too much importance to this hadith, because from the middle ages Muslim queens took power—Razia Sultan, daughter of Iltutmish in India; Shajar al Durr, who started the Mamluk dynasty; and Sitt el-Mulk, sister of the Fatimid caliph, al Hakim. In modern times Benazir Bhutto of Pakistan, Megawati Sukarnoputri of Indonesia, Tansu Ciller of Turkey and the two Bangladeshi leaders, Khaleda Zia and Shaikh Hasina, are well known names. Senegal, Mali, Kosovo and Mauritius have all known female heads of state, and even Iran has had a woman as Vice President.

Once Umar tried to instruct Um Salama on how to behave; she was offended. In front of the other wives she told him off, 'Why are you interfering in the private life of The Prophet? If he wanted to give us such advice, he could do so himself.' After the death of The Prophet when Umar became Caliph, Aisha's sister, Um Kulthum, refused to marry him because he was very harsh and rough with women.

In the Abbasid times, the position of women became worse. Conquest and wealth resulted in a multitude of slaves and concubines. This trend continued under the Ottomans, whose caliphs, for several generations, gave up marrying altogether, preferring to live with concubines and slave girls, until Hurrem captured the heart of Suleiman the Great and he made her his queen. In the nineteenth century, Britain and the other colonial powers became master of most of the Muslim world. They imposed their values and frowned on Eastern habits such as polygamy and the veil. Many of the Muslim elite followed the British example, hoping to win the favour of their colonial masters. The veil started to disappear in high society. Lord Cromer, in Egypt, condemned the veil as contrary to the rights of women, but back home in England he was founder and President of the Men's League for Opposing Women's Suffrage. In Egypt his crusade against women's rights led him to discourage the education of Muslim girls and the training of female doctors!

Despite the desire of The Prophet to protect and promote the rights of women, it has been a hard struggle throughout the 1,400 years of Muslim history. Today, there is still a clash of views. On the one hand, modernists and reformers follow a lifestyle closer to the West (though without the total focus on women as sex symbols), and on the other, traditionalists believe firmly in the veil and that a woman's place is in the home. This clash became international drama on 9 October 2012, when subsequent to the Taliban banning girls, attendance at schools, a gunman boarded a school bus in Swat, in Pakistan, asked for Malala Yusafzai by name and then fired three bullets at her, one of which entered her head and exited her shoulder. Malala recovered, determined not to be cowed. She was awarded the Nobel Peace Prize, becoming the youngest ever to receive this prestigious award and was named by *Time* magazine as one of the hundred most influential people in the world in 2013.

Today there is no stereotype Muslim. There are jihadis and heart surgeons; there are glamorous young women and there are veiled girls covered even to the tips of their fingers, with gloves which hide their hands from male eyes. In the oil-rich countries there are the international tycoons with their private jets, and in the highly populated poverty-stricken nations of Asia and Africa, there are uneducated villagers living hand-to-mouth. There are the Sunnis and the Shias. There are those that look back at the past, and those who see change and the future as their hope.

There are some glaring differences between the world of the Muslims during their golden years and the Muslims of today. Whereas education, justice and the concern for right and wrong were exceptional in the Islamic world during its rise, they are conspicuous in their absence today. Perhaps it was education, justice and the concern for right and wrong that in turn, was the real cause of the rise and fall of the Muslims. An enlightened Muslim traveller who visited Europe a century ago commented on his return, that in Europe he had seen Islam everywhere but Muslims nowhere, whereas back home he saw Muslims everywhere but Islam nowhere.

We have not reached the end of the story; only the crossroads. Where does the future lie? The philosopher, George Santayana, commented that those who cannot remember the past are condemned to repeat it. But this was not his only brilliant saying. Another Santayana quote, much less known, is very appropriate to the Muslim world of today: 'Fanaticism consists of redoubling your efforts when you have forgotten your aim.'

Epilogue

'They're not coming to this country if I'm President.'

—Donald Trump (On Muslims)

Donald Trump was not bluffing in his election speeches. One of his first acts as President was to ban the entry of Muslims from seven countries into America. The courts blocked his attempt, but the matter is still in play. It is clear that Trump does not like Muslims, just as Hitler did not love Jews.

Trump appointed James 'Mad Dog' Mattis as the new defence secretary; Mattis had called Iran 'The single biggest state sponsor of terrorism in the world.' He selected as national security adviser, another anti-Iran hardliner, Michael Flynn, who put Iran on notice. His new CIA chief was Mike Pompeo who had earlier advocated bombing Iran's military facilities. The respected newspaper *The Independent* warned in its headline, 'Donald Trump will spark a war with Iran' and commented that the administration is heavily loaded with crackpots, fanatics and amateurs with contempt for the truth, legality or democracy.

America has long had a fondness for Israel, but under Trump, their relationship gets even closer. Israel now has over 400 nuclear warheads, enough to wipe out every capital in the Muslim Middle East. Israel does not subject its nuclear warheads to International

Atomic Energy Agency's approval. If Trump decides to wage war on Iran, he can either do so directly or move through his proxy, Israel.

The Nuclear Proliferation Treaty (NPT) gives all non-nuclear states the inalienable right to uranium enrichment on their own soil, so long as it is not for weapons manufacture. Brazil, Germany and Japan are but a few of the countries that have these facilities without problem, but the US refuses to recognize Iran's right to do the same. Trump's America has grave suspicions of Iran's peaceful intent, despite the fact that Iran hasn't attacked another country for 200 years, doesn't occupy the land of any other country, and played no part in the 9/11 destruction of the twin towers.

After the break-up of the USSR, America was the world's only superpower, but the last twenty-five years have seen the emergence of China. Today, China's vast reserves contrast with America's massive debts and deficits. Today China offers a viable alternative to America, and more Asian countries are turning to China for economic support. In Pakistan, the CPEC has resulted in China replacing America as 'Big Brother'; and Pakistan is not alone in exploring this route.

When Nixon went to meet Mao in Beijing, he managed to drive a wedge between the USSR and China. Today, Russia and China are again able to work together to promote their common interests. How would they react to an attack on Iran by Israel or the USA working together?

For almost half a century, since Muslim countries became the dominant players in the energy politics of the world, the US has played a contorted and cunning strategy to promote its interests. The result has been the escalation of violence in the Middle East. Is this to be the closing chapter in this strange story, with America now openly declaring against the Muslims as she prepares for her next war? Will America manage to keep the fires of Sunni–Shia hostility alive and succeed in a policy of divide and rule, as she attacks first one and then the other? Will the millions of Muslims who have made their home in Europe and the USA, now reassess their future? The coming years may prove to be the most exciting chapter in the long story of the Muslims.

Acknowledgements

I want to thank those who have played an important part in helping me complete this book.

Over five years, the research necessary for this book required me to buy hundreds of books from the UK and the USA. Since most sellers in the West don't deliver to Pakistan, I relied on a friend of mine, Anila Tanna, to accept delivery after delivery and store them till I could transfer them to Dubai—the first leg of their journey home. Without complaint, Anila received these consignments, month after month, and year after year. The books were carried to Dubai by my brother Zia, my old friend Ali Afdhal, and my grandchildren, Sophia and Daniel. Without this logistic chain, I don't know how I could have collected the essential research material.

The organization and office support, without which I could not have hoped to manage this endeavour, was provided by Babar Khurshid, who managed to fit in my requirements while simultaneously carrying out his very onerous duties of managing cost control and supervising credit and recoveries

Zaigham Hidayatullah was a brilliant editor (not his normal job) and amazed me with the speed of his work and the depth of his observations. Khurshid Hadi was both editor and advisor. Amann Omar Mahmood was my IT expert, who covered for my lack of computer knowledge and understanding. Arsalan Ahmad provided important logistic support in getting the book ready for publication.

When the writing is finished, the hard work of bringing out the book begins. Hamid Haroon, my cousin, who has produced many beautiful books, showed me the way, and his advice made the difference between an amateur and a professional product.

Nusi Jamil handled the public relations that exposed the book to its audience, and her help has been invaluable in the post-publication work that she has done selflessly for the book.

A new friend who has promoted the book to an international diplomatic audience, is Shaukat Fareed, the Permanent Observer of Parliamentary Assembly of Mediterranean to the United Nations. I am grateful for his support.

Publishing my book in India was made possible by Natwar Singh who introduced me to Rupa Publications. Over forty years, I have admired Natwar's scholarship, mastery of diplomacy and political astuteness, and I am grateful for his support.

Finally, I am grateful to the team at Rupa, which, under the leadership of Mr Kapish Mehra, has worked with impressive speed in bringing out the book faster than I could have hoped for.

Bibliography

1. Abrahamian, Ervand. *A History of Modern Iran.* Cambridge University Press, 2008.
2. Abrahamian, Ervand. *The Coup: 1953, The CIA, And The Roots Of Modern US-Iranian Relations.* The New Press, 2013.
3. Aburish, Said K. *Nasser: The Last Arab.* Macmillan, 2004.
4. Aburish, Said K. *Saddam Hussein: The Politics of Revenge.* Bloomsbury Publishing USA, 2000.
5. Adams, Cindy Heller. *Sukarno: An autobiography.* Bobbs-Merrill, 1965.
6. Ahmed, Leila. *Women and Gender in Islam: Historical Roots of a Modern Debate.* Yale University Press, 1992.
7. Alexander, Anne. *Nasser.* Haus Publishing, 2005.
8. Ali, Ayaan Hirsi. *Heretic: Why Islam Needs a Reformation Now.* Knopf Canada, 2015.
9. Ali, Muhammad, and Hana Yasmeen Ali. *The Soul of a Butterfly: Reflections on Life's Journey.* Simon and Schuster, 2004.
10. Alkhateeb, Firas. *Lost Islamic History: Reclaiming Muslim Civilisation from the Past.* Oxford University Press, 2017.
11. Allawi, Ali A. "The Occupation of Iraq: Winning the War." *Losing the Peace.* 2007.
12. Al Tabari. *The Early Abbasid Empire.* 900 AD.
13. Ansari, Ali M. *Confronting Iran: The Failure of American Foreign Policy and the Roots of Mistrust.* 2006.
14. Ansary, Tamim. *Destiny Disrupted: A History of the World through Islamic Eyes.* Public Affairs, 2009.
15. Ansary, Tamim. *Games Without Rules: The Often-interrupted History of Afghanistan.* Public Affairs, 2014.
16. Armstrong, Harold Courtenay. *Grey Wolf: Mustafa Kemal.* Minton, Balch, 1933.
17. Armstrong, Harold Courtenay. *Lord of Arabia: Ibn Saud.* 1934.
18. Aslan, Reza. *No god but God: The Origins, Evolution, and Future of Islam.* Random House, 2011.

19. Axworthy, Michael. *Empire of the Mind: A History of Iran*. C. Hurst & Co. Publishers, 2007.
20. Axworthy, Michael. *The Sword of Persia: Nader Shah, from Tribal Warrior to Conquering Tyrant*. IB Tauris, 2010.
21. Barber, Noel. *Lords of the Golden Horn*. Macmillan, 1973.
22. Barfield, Thomas. *Afghanistan: A Cultural and Political History*. Princeton University Press, 2010.
23. Bawker, Bruce. *While Europe Slept: How Radical Islam is Destroying the West from Within*. Doubleday. 2006.
24. Bennison, Amira K. *The Great Caliphs: The Golden Age of the Abbasid Empire*. Yale University Press, 2014.
25. Bergen, Peter L. *The Osama bin Laden I Know: An Oral History of al Qaeda's Leader*. Simon and Schuster, 2006.
26. Bhutto, Benazir. *Daughter of the East: An Autobiography*. Simon and Schuster, 2014.
27. Bhutto, Benazir. *Reconciliation: Her Final Words on Islam, Democracy and the West*. 2008.
28. Bhutto, Benazir. *Whither Pakistan: Dictatorship or Democracy?* Vani Prakashan, 2007.
29. Bianco, Mirella. *Gadafi: Voice from the Desert*. Longman Publishing Group, 1975.
30. Bird, Tim, and Alex Marshall. *Afghanistan: How the West Lost Its Way*. Yale University Press, 2011.
31. Blanch, Lesley. *The Wilder Shores of Love*. Simon and Schuster, 2010.
32. Blandford, Linda. *Super-Wealth: The Secret Lives of the Oil Sheikhs*. William Morrow & Co. 1997.
33. Blow, David. *Shah Abbas: The Ruthless King Who Became an Iranian Legend*. IB Tauris, 2014.
34. Blum, William. *Rogue State: A Guide to the World's Only Superpower*. 2000.
35. Bolitho, Hector. *Jinnah: Creator of Pakistan*. John Murray, 1954.
36. Boyle, J.A. *Genghis Khan: the History of the World Conqueror* by Ala-ad-Din Ata-Malik Juvaini. 1260 AD.
37. Bradford, Ernle Dusgate Selby. *The Sultan's Admiral: Barbarossa, Pirate and Empire-builder*. Tauris Parke Paperbacks, 1968.
38. Bradley, John R. *After the Arab Spring: How Islamists Hijacked the Middle East Revolts*. St. Martin's Press, 2012.
39. Bradley, John R. *Inside Egypt: The Land of the Pharaohs on the Brink of a Revolution*. 2008.
40. Bridge, Antony. *Suleiman the Magnificent: Scourge of Heaven*. Granada, 1983.
41. Buchan, James. *Days of God: The Revolution in Iran and its Consequences*. Simon and Schuster, 2013.
42. Burke, Jason. *The New Threat: The Past, Present, and Future of Islamic Militancy*. The New Press, 2017.

43. Carr, Matthew. *Blood and Faith: The Purging of Muslim Spain*. The New Press, 2009.
44. Catrou, François. *Manucci: Memoirs of the Mogul Court*. 18th century.
45. Chomsky, Noam. *How the World Works*. Soft Skull Press, 2011.
46. Cockburn, Patrick. "Who are ISIS? The Rise of the Islamic State in Iraq and the Levant." *The Independent*. https://www.independent.co.uk/news/world/middle-east/who-are-isis-the-rise-of-the-islamic-state-in-iraq-and-the-levant-9541421.html. 2014.
47. Cole, Juan. *Engaging the Muslim World*. St. Martin's Press, 2009.
48. Cooley, John K. *Libyan Sandstorm*. Holt McDougal, 1982.
49. Coughlin, Con. *Khomeini's Ghost: The Iranian Revolution and the Rise of Militant Islam*. Ecco, 2009.
50. Coughlin, Con. *Saddam: The Secret Life*. 2002.
51. Dalrymple, William. *The Last Mughal: The Eclipse of a Dynasty, Delhi 1857*. London: Bloomsbury. 2006.
52. Dalrymple, William. *The Return of a King: The Battle for Afghanistan, 1939-42*. 2013.
53. Darussalam. *The Honourable Wives of The Prophet*. 2004.
54. Dashti, Ali. *Twenty Three Years: A Study of the Prophetic Career of Mohammed*. 1985.
55. De Bellaigue, Christopher. *Patriot of Persia: Muhammad Mossadegh and a Tragic Anglo-American Coup*. Harper, 2012.
56. Dempsey, Amy. *The Life and Times of Saddam Hussein*. Parragon Book Service. 1996.
57. Dreyfuss, Robert. *Devil's Game: How the United States Helped Unleash Fundamentalist Islam*. Macmillan, 2006.
58. Eddé, Anne Marie. *Saladin*. Belknap Press. 2008.
59. El Fadl, Khaled Abou, and L. Carl Brown. *The Great Theft: Wrestling Islam from the Extremists*. New York (2005).
60. Elphinstone, Mountstuart. *The History of India*. 1843.
61. Engdahl, F. William. *Full Spectrum Dominance: Totalitarian Democracy in the New World Order* (2009).
62. Eraly, Abraham. *The Age of Wrath: A History of the Delhi Sultanate*. Penguin Books Limited. 2014.
63. Eraly, Abraham. *The Mughal Throne*. Phoenix. 1997.
64. Eraly, Abraham. *The Mughal World: India's Tainted Paradise*. Orion Publishing Company, 2007.
65. Erskine, William. *A History of India Under the Two First Sovereigns of the House of Taimur, Baber and Humayun*. Vol. 2. Cambridge University Press, 2012.
66. Esposito, John L. *The future of Islam*. Oxford University Press, 2010.
67. Esposito, John L. *Unholy War: Terror in the Name of Islam*. 2010.
68. Evans, Martin. *Afghanistan*. 2001.
69. Eversley, George Shaw-Lefevre, and Valentine Chirol. *The Turkish Empire from*

1288 to 1913. T. Fisher Unwin ltd., 1924.
70. Fardust, General Hussein. *The Rise and Fall of the Pahlavi Dynasty*. 1999.
71. Feldman, Noah. *The Rise and Fall of the Islamic state*. 2008.
72. Felton, Greg. *Enemies by Design: Inventing the War on Terrorism*. Tree of Life Books, 2005.
73. Ferguson, Niall. *Civilization: The West and the Rest*. 2011.
74. Festing, Gabrielle. *When Kings Rode to Delhi*. Lancer Publishers, 2008.
75. Fletcher, Richard. *Moorish Spain*. Berkeley. 1992.
76. Flower, Raymond. *Napoleon to Nasser: The Story of Modern Egypt*. London: Tom Stacey. 1972.
77. Filiu, Jean-Pierre. *The Arab Revolution: Ten Lessons from The Democratic Uprising*. Oxford University Press, 2011.
78. Freely, John. *The Grand Turk: Sultan Mehmet II: Conqueror of Constantinople, Master of an Empire and Lord of Two Seas*. IB Tauris, 2009.
79. Freely, John. *Inside the Seraglio: Private Lives of the Sultans in Istanbul*. IB Tauris, 2016.
80. Gabriel, Mark A. *Islam and Terrorism*. Charisma Media, 2002.
81. Gaddafi, Muammar, and Henry M. Christman. *Qaddafi's Green Book*. Buffalo, NY: Prometheus Books, 1988.
82. Galbraith, Peter W. *The End of Iraq: How American Incompetence Created a War Without End*. Simon and Schuster, 2007.
83. Glass, Charles. *Syria Burning: ISIS and the Death of the Arab Spring*. OR Books, 2015.
84. Goodwin, Jason. *Lords of the Horizons: A History of the Ottoman Empire*. Random House, 2011.
85. Habibullah, Amir. *My Life: From Brigand to King*. Octagon Press, 1990.
86. Haider, Khwaja Razi. *Ruttie Jinnah*. Oxford University Press. 2010.
87. Hamid, Tawfik. *Inside Jihad: How Radical Islam Works; Why It Should Terrify Us; How to Defeat It*. Mountain Lake Press, 2015.
88. Hazleton, Lesley. *After the Prophet: The Epic Story of the Shia-Sunni Split in Islam*. Anchor, 2010.
89. Hazleton, Lesley. *The First Muslim: The Story of Muhammad*. Penguin, 2014.
90. Haykal, Muhammad Hasanayn. *Autumn of Fury: The Assassination of Sadat*. New York, NY: Random House, 1983.
91. Hilsum, Lindsey. *Sandstorm: Libya in the Time of Revolution*. Penguin, 2013.
92. Hindley, Geoffrey. *Saladin*. Barnes & Noble Books, 1976.
93. Hiro, Dilip. *After Empire*. (2010).
94. Hiro, Dilip. *Apocalyptic Realm: Jihadists in South Asia*. Yale University Press, 2012.
95. Hiro, Dilip. *Inside Central Asia: A Political and Cultural History of Uzbekistan, Turkmenistan, Kazakhstan, Kyrgyzstan, Tajikistan, Turkey and Iran*. New York: Overlook Duckworth. 2009.
96. Hiro, Dilip. *Iran today*. Politico's, 2006.

97. Hiro, Dilip. *Iran under the Ayatollahs.* 1985.
98. Hitti, Philip K. *History of the Arabs.* Palgrave Macmillan, 2002.
99. Hitti, Philip Khuri, and Francis Clark Murgotten. *The Origins of the Islamic State.* Columbia University, 1916.
100. Hourani, Albert Habib, Albert Hourani and Malise Ruthven. *A History of the Arab Peoples.* 1991.
101. Howarth, David Armine. *The Desert King: Ibn Saud and his Arabia.* McGraw-Hill, 1964.
102. Hughes, John. *The End of Sukarno: A Coup that Misfired; A Purge that Ran Wild.* Angus & Robertson Publishers, 1968.
103. Hussain, Zahid. *Frontline Pakistan: The Struggle with Militant Islam.* IB Tauris, 2006.
104. Hussain, Zahid. *The Scorpion's Tail: The Relentless Rise of Islamic Militants in Pakistan and How it Threatens America.* Simon and Schuster, 2010.
105. Ibn Ishaq. *The Life of Muhammad.* 8th century.
106. John, Robert St, and Gamal Abdel Nasser. *The Boss: The Story of Gamal Abdel Nasser.* McGraw-Hill, 1960.
107. Johnson, Chalmers. *Nemesis: The Last Days of the American Republic.* Macmillan, 2006.
108. Karanjia, R. K. *The Mind of a Monarch.* 1977.
109. Karsh, Efraim, and Inari Rautsi. *Why Saddam Hussein Invaded Kuwait.* 1991.
110. Kawczynski, Daniel. *Seeking Gaddafi: Libya, the West and the Arab Spring.* Biteback Publishing, 2011.
111. Kennedy, Hugh. *The Court of the Caliphs: The Rise and Fall of Islam's Greatest Dynasty.* Weidenfeld and Nicolson, 2004.
112. Kennedy, Hugh. *The Great Arab Conquests: How the Spread of Islam Changed the World We Live In.* Da Capo Press, 2007.
113. Khan, Mohammad Ayub. *Friends Not Masters: A Political Autobiography.* 1970
114. King, Stephen D. *Losing Control: The Emerging Threats to Western Prosperity.* New Haven and London: Yale University Press, 2010.
115. Kinross, Lord. "Atatürk and his Achievement." *Journal of the Royal Central Asian Society.* 51.1 (1964): 15-22.
116. Kinross, Lord. *The Ottoman Centuries: The Rise and Fall of the Ottoman Empire.* 1977.
117. Khan, Mahomed, ed. *The Life of Abdur Rahman: Amir of Afghanistan.* Vol. 1. J. Murray, 1900.
118. Klare, Michael. *Blood and oil: How America's Thirst for Petrol Is Killing Us.* London: Hamish Hamilton. 2004.
119. Krane, Jim. *City of Gold: Dubai and the Dream of Capitalism.* St. Martin's Press, 2009.
120. Lacey, Robert. *The Kingdom.* Harcourt Brace Jovanovich, 1981.
121. Lacey, Robert. *Inside the Kingdom: Kings, Clerics, Modernists, Terrorists, and the Struggle for Saudi Arabia.* England: Viking Penguin Group. 2009.

122. Lal, Mohan. *Life of the Amir Dost Mohammed Khan of Kabul.* Vol. 2. Longman, 1846.
123. Lamb, Harold. *The Crusades: Iron Men and Saints.* 1931.
124. Lamb, Harold. *Genghis Khan: The Emperor of All Men.* 1927.
125. Lamb, Harold. *Omar Khayyam.* 1934.
126. Lamb, Harold. *Suleiman the Magnificent: Sultan of the East.* 1951.
127. Lamb, Harold. *Tamerlane: the Earth Shaker.* 1928.
128. Lamb, Harold. *The March of the Barbarians.* Doubleday, Doran, Incorporated, 1940.
129. Lane-Poole, Stanley. *Medieval India Under Mohammedan Rule (AD 712-1764).* Vol. 59. Fischer Unwin, 1917.
130. Lane-Poole, Stanley. *The Moors in Spain.* 1887.
131. Lane-Poole, Stanley. *Saladin: All-Powerful Sultan and the Uniter of Islam.* Cooper Square Pub, 2002.
132. Lane-Poole, Stanley, and James Douglas Jerrold Kelley. *The Barbary Corsairs.* Putnam, 1901.
133. Levy, Adrian, and Catherine Scott-Clark. *Deception: Pakistan, the United States, and the Secret Trade in Nuclear Weapons.* Bloomsbury Publishing USA, 2007.
134. Lewis, Bernard. *The Middle East: A Brief History of the Last 2,000 Years.* Simon and Schuster, 1995.
135. Lewis, Bernard. *A Middle East mosaic: Fragments of Life, Letters and History.* Modern Library, 2007.
136. Lewis, Bernard. "The Assassins: An Historical Essay." *Encounter.* 1967.
137. Lister, Richard Percival. *The Secret History of Genghis Khan.* Peter Davies, 1969.
138. Lowney, Chris. *A Vanished World: Muslims, Christians, and Jews in Medieval Spain.* Oxford University Press, USA, 2006.
139. Loyn, David. *Butcher and Bolt: Two Hundred Years of Foreign Engagement in Afghanistan.* London: Hutchinson. 2008.
140. Maalouf, Amin. *Samarkand.* Hachette UK, 2012.
141. Malleson, Col. *History of Afghanistan.* 1878.
142. Man, John. *Genghis Khan: Life, Death and Resurrection.* Bantam Pres, New York. 2004.
143. Mansel, Philip. *Sultans in Splendour.* 2000.
144. Manucci, Nicolao. *Memoirs of the Mogul.* 1709.
145. Marcovitz, Hal. *Islam in Africa.* Simon and Schuster, 2014.
146. Marozzi, Justin. *Tamerlane: Return of the Sword of Islam.* 2004.
147. Marshall, Robert. *Storm from the East: From Ghengis Khan to Khubilai Khan.* Univ of California Press, 1993.
148. McCabe, Joseph. *The Splendour of Moorish Spain.* Watts & co., 1935.
149. Merriman, Roger Bigelow. *Suleiman the Magnificent, 1520-66.* 1944.
150. Milam, William B. "Bangladesh and Pakistan: flirting with failure in South Asia." *Survival.* 51.5 (2009): 215-216.
151. Moin, Baqer. *Khomeini: Life of the Ayatollah.* IB Tauris, 1999.

152. Moorcraft, Paul. *The Jihadist Threat: The Re-conquest of the West?* Pen and Sword, 2015.
153. Morris, Chris. *The New Turkey*. 2005.
154. Muir, William. *The Caliphate*. 1892.
155. Muir, William. *The Mameluke; or, Slave Dynasty of Egypt, 1260-1517, AD*. Smith, Elder, 1896.
156. Naji, Kasra. *Ahmadinejad*. London: IB Tauris. 2008.
157. Nasser, Gamal Abdel. *Egypt's Liberation the Philosophy of the Revolution*. 1955.
158. Nasser, Tahia Gamal Abdel. *Nasser: My Husband*. Oxford University Press, 2013.
159. Nasr, Vali. *Meccanomics*. Oneworld Publications, 2010.
160. Nasr, Vali. "The Shia Revival." *Military Review*. 87.3 (2007): 9.
161. Nicolle, David. *The Mongol Warlords: Genghis Khan, Kublai Khan. Hulegu, Tamerlane*. Firebird, New York: Military Service. 1990.
162. Nicolle, David. *The Ottomans: Empire of Faith*. Thalamus, 2008.
163. Numani, Shibli, Muhammad Shibli Numani, and Jamil A. Qureshi. *Umar: Makers of Islamic Civilization*. IB Tauris, 2004.
164. Onon, Urgunge, ed. *The History and the Life of Chinggis Khan: The Secret History of the Mongols*. Brill Archive, 1990.
165. Osman, Tarek. *Egypt on the Brink: From Nasser to Mubarak*. Yale University Press, 2010.
166. Pargeter, Alison. *Libya: The Rise and Fall of Qaddafi*. Yale University Press, 2012.
167. Paton, Andrew Archibald. *A History of the Egyptian Revolution, from the Period of the Mamelukes to the Death of Mohammed Ali: From Arab and European Memoirs, Oral Tradition, and Local Research*. Vol. 2. Trübner & Company, 1870.
168. Peterson, Scott. *Let the Swords Encircle Me: Iran--A Journey Behind the Headlines*. Simon and Schuster, 2010.
169. Phillips, Eustace Dockray. *The Mongols*. No. 951.7 P4. 1969.
170. Phillips, Melanie. *Londonistan*. Encounter Books, 2007.
171. Polk, William R. *Understanding Iran: Everything You Need To Know, From Persia to the Islamic Republic*. 2009.
172. Polk, William R. *Understanding Iraq: The Whole Seep of Iraqi History from Genghis Khan's Mongols to the Ottoman Turks to the British Mandate to the American Occupation*. 2005.
173. Pope, Nicole, and Hugh Pope. *Turkey Unveiled: A History of Modern Turkey*. Woodstock: Overlook Press, 1997.
174. Rashid, Ahmed, and Ahmed Rashid. *Descent into Chaos*. Penguin, 2008.
175. Rashid, Ahmed. *Pakistan on the Brink*. Viking, NY. 2012.
176. Rashid, Ahmed. *Taliban*. 2009.
177. Rawlinson, George. *Ancient Egypt*. 1887.
178. Raymond, André. *Cairo*. Harvard University Press, 2000.
179. Robinson, Francis. *Knowledge, its Transmission and the Making of Muslim Societies: The Cambridge Illustrated History of the Islamic World*. 1996.
180. Robinson, Francis. *The Mughal Emperors: And the Islamic Dynasties of India,*

Iran and Central Asia, 1206-1925. Thames & Hudson, 2007.
181. Rogers, Paul. *Iraq and the War on Terror: Twelve Months of Insurgency 2004/2005*. IB Tauris, 2006.
182. Rogerson, Barnaby. *The Prophet Muhammad: A Biography*. Hachette UK, 2010.
183. Rogerson, Barnaby. *The Heirs of the Prophet Muhammad: And the Roots Of the Sunni-Shia Schism*. Hachette UK, 2010.
184. Roosevelt, Kermit. *Countercoup, the Struggle for the Control of Iran*. McGraw-Hill Companies, 1979.
185. Sadat, Anwar. *In Search of Identity: An Autobiography*. New York: Harper & Row, 1978.
186. Sadat, Anwar. *Those I Have Known*. Continuum Publishing. 1985.
187. Sanders, John Herne. *Tamerlane, or Timur: The Great Amir*. Luzac, 1936.
188. Sicker, Martin. *The Islamic World in Ascendancy: From the Arab Conquests to the Siege of Vienna*. Greenwood Publishing Group, 2000.
189. Streusand, Douglas. *Islamic Gunpowder Empires: Ottomans, Safavids, and Mughals (Essays in World History*. 2011.
190. Sykes, Percy Molesworth. *A History of Persia*. 1915.
191. Taheri, Amir. *The Persian Night: Iran under the Khomeinist Revolution*. 2009.
192. Timur. *Institutes Political and Military*. 1783.
193. Truell, Peter, and Larry Gurwin. *False Profits: The Inside Story of BCCI, the World's Most Corrupt Financial Empire*. Houghton Mifflin Harcourt (HMH), 1992.
194. Von Tunzelmann, Alex. *Indian Summer: The Secret History of the End of an Empire*. Macmillan, 2007.
195. Waterson, James. *The Ismaili Assassins: A History of Medieval Murder*. Frontline Books, 2008.
196. Weston, Mark. *Prophets and Princes: Saudi Arabia from Muhammad to the Present*. John Wiley & Sons, 2008.
197. Wright, Robin. *The Last Great Revolution: Turmoil and Transformation in Iran*. Vintage, 2010.
198. Wright, Robin. *Rock the Casbah*. 2011.
199. Yergin, Daniel. *The Prize: The Epic Quest for Oil, Money, and Power*. Minnesota: Simon and Schuster (1991): 912.
200. Yergin, Daniel. *The Quest: Energy, Security, and the Remaking of the Modern World*. Penguin, 2011.

Index

Abadan, Persian city 331, 340
Abbasa, sister of Harun al Rashid, 63–64
Abbas, grandson of Muhammad Ali Pasha 258
Abbas ibn Firnas, Muslim inventor in Spain, 72
Abbasid, 20, 41, 56–59, 62, 65, 72, 75–81, 83–85, 87, 92, 95, 112, 130, 252, 254, 413
Abbas, Shah of Persia, *See* Shah Abbas
Abbas s/o Mamun 77
Abbas, Uncle of The Prophet 2, 7, 10–11, 39, 57–58
Abbottabad, 371
Abd al Aziz bin Marwan, b/o Umayyad caliph, 51
Abd al Aziz ibn Saud, founder of Saudi Arabia, 255
Abd Allah bin Zubayr, 46, 48
Abdallah ibn Yasin, 116
Abd al Malik, Umayyad ruler, 39–40, 47–48, 53–55
Abd al Mumin, Almohad caliph 117–18
Abd al-Mutalib, grandfather of The Prophet, 2
Abd al-Rahman, founder of the Umayyad dynasty in Spain, 106–08, 110–11, 268
Abd al-Rahman II, 109

Abd al-Rahman III, 110–11, 118
Abd al-Rahman V, 114
Abd al Rehman, Muslim general killed at the Battle of Tours, 53, 58
Abdel Hussein Mashhadi, Sec. Gen. RCC Iraq, 349
Abdel Malik, 106
Abd Manaf, 38
Abdollah bin Abi Sarh, 12
Abd Shams, 38Abdul Aziz ibn Saud, founder of Saudi Arabia 255, 264–65, 269–70, 275
Abdul Hamid II, 34th Ottomon Sultan, 220
Abdul Hamid, 27th Ottomon sultan, 230, 238, 242–45, 260
Abdul Karim Shaikhally, leader of the Iraqi assassination attempt on Qasim, 345
Abdullah bin Saud, 255
Abdullah ibn Jiluwi, Saudi governor and loyal associate of King Abdul Aziz 272
Abdullah ibn-Ubayy, opponent of The Prophet, 7
Abdullah Jacques Menou, general of Napoleon in Egypt, 253
Abdullah Khan, Uzbek leader, 206
Abdullah Tariki, Saudi oil minister, 325
Abdul Mecit, 31st sultan of the Ottomon Empire, 240–42

Abdul Salam Jalloud, prime minister of Libya under Gaddafi, 360
Abdul Wahhab, Saudi religious reformer, 255, 265–66, 324
Abdur Rahim, 177
Abdur Rahman, 78, 286–87, 347
Abdurrahman Wahid, Indonesian President 378
Abdur Rehman, 41, 269
Abedi, Agha Hasan, founder of BCCI Bank, 405–6
Abolghasem Mesbani, Libyan security official and defector, 361
Abrar, bodyguard of Osama bin Laden 371
Abu Abdullah, 85, 119
Abu Ahmed al-Kuwaiti, 371
Abu al Hasan, King of Granada, 118–19
Abu Bakr ibn Umar, 116
Abu Dhabi, 405
Abu Hanifa, founder of the Hanifi School of Jurisprudence, 75
Abu Jahl, Meccan leader, 6–7
Abul Fazl, Grand vizier of Akbar, author of Akbarnama, 179
Abu Lulu, Persian slave, assassin of Caliph Umar, 29
Abu Musa, Caliph Ali's arbitrator in dispute with Muawiya, 36–37
Abu Muslim, Abbasid general, 56–57, 59, 85, 112
Abu Nidal, founder of Fatah: The Revolutionary Council, 357
Abu Nuwais, Persian poet, 65
Abu Salama of Kufa who supported Abbasid takeover, 58
Abu Salim, prison and massacre in Libya, 358
Abu Sufyan, 7–8, 10–11, 24, 39–40, 43–44
Abu Talib, father of Caliph Ali, 2–3, 46
Abu Ubaydah, ibn al-Jarrar, companion of The Prophet, 22, 24
Abyssinia, 398

Abyssinian Yacut, favourite of Razia Sultan, 151
Achilles, 17, 22, 26
ad-Diriyah, 65, 67, 265, 267
Adham Khan, son of Maham Anaga, 177
Adil Khan, son of Sher Shah Suri, 174
Adil Shah, nephew of Nader Shah, 292
Adi Zulkadry, leader of death squad in Indonesian massacres, 379
Adnan, brother-in-law of Saddam Hussein, 350
Adnan Hamdani, friend and victim of Saddam, 349
Adolf Hitler, 246, 310
Adudal Dawla, an emir of the Buyid dynasty, 81
Afghan, 161, 168, 172, 177, 209, 211, 277–78, 283–84, 287–88, 309, 386, 393, 407
Afghanistan, 45, 49, 57, 130, 135, 145, 149, 245, 260, 276–77, 279, 281–83, 285, 287–88, 291, 310, 358, 363–64, 366–67, 370–71, 381, 384, 386, 390, 394, 397, 409, 411
Africa, 12, 27, 40, 45, 51–52, 58, 80, 85, 100, 105, 107, 111, 113, 115, 117, 119, 225–26, 262, 306–7, 309, 313, 356–57, 360, 391–92, 395, 398–400, 403, 408, 414
Agha Hasan Abedi, 405
Agha Mohammed, eunuch, founder of the Qajar Dynasty in Iran, 293–94
Aghlabids, 85
Agra, 72, 167–69, 171–72, 174–76, 178, 181, 188–89
Ahmad Chalabi, Iraqi politician, founder of the Iraqi National Congress, 345
Ahmad Hassan al-Bakr, 4th President of Iraq, 345
Ahmad ibn Hanbal, scholar of Islam, 75–6
Ahmad ibn Tulun, Abbasid slave

general who founded the Tulanid dynasty in Egypt, 84
Ahmad Shah Durrani, Afghan Emperor, 278–82, 309
Ahmed I, Ottomon sultan, 233
Aimee Dubucq de Rivery, Ottoman Sultana Valida, 238
AIOC, Anglo-Iranian Oil Company, 298, 331-33
Aisha, 3, 9–10, 13, 15–16, 20, 27, 29, 34–35, 118, 360, 413
Ajman tribe, of Saudi Arabia, 274
aka al-Mansur, second Abbasid caliph, 75
Akayev, President of Kyrgyzstan, 382, 390
Akbar Shah II, Mogul Ruler in Delhi, 193
Akbar the Great, Mogul Emperor, 163, 169, 175–81, 187, 191, 204, 208, 252
Akezhan Kazhegeldin, second prime minister of Kazakhstan, 388
Akmazbek, Atambayev, President of Kyrgyzstan, 390
Al-Adid, 14th and last Fatimid caliph, 92
Alamgir, aka Aurangzeb, Mogul Emperor, 189
Alamut, Ismaili mountain fortress in Persia, 94–95
al Andalus, 51, 123
Alaska, 241
Alauddin Khalji, second ruler of Khilji dynasty in India, 147
al Azhar University, 112
al-Aziz, 5th Fatimid caliph in Egypt, 86, 266
al-Bakr, Ahmad Hassan, President of Iraq, 345-7, 349
Albania, 219, 393
Albanian, 224, 235, 253
Alboacen, aka Abu al-Hasan Ali, Nassirid ruler in Spain, 119
Al Bukhari, 3, 413

Albuquerque, Portuguese naval commander, 207, 306
Al Capone, Chicago gangster, 154
Aleppo, 125
Alexander the Great, 51
Alexandria, 26, 102, 240, 261, 320
Algebra, 67, 70, 385
Algeria, 51, 117, 226, 356, 360
Algiers, 225–26, 342
Algorithms 96
al Hajjaj ibn Yusuf, Umayyad governor in Iraq, 40, 47
al Hakim, second caliph of Cordoba, 111
al-Hakim, 6th Fatimid caliph, 98, 314, 321
Alhambra, Muslim palace and fort in Granada, 119
al-Haytham, Arab scientist and mathematician, 70, 321
Ali bin Isa, 65
Alids, 43, 55, 57, 59, 61, 77
Ali Fuad, 247
Ali Khamenei, Supreme Leader of Iran, 341, 344
Ali Mardan Shah, Persian governor of Kandahar in time of Emperor Akbar, 187
Alimov, Uzbek dissenter, boiled to death by Karimov, 383
Ali Quli Khan Shamlu, Qizilbash commander in chief of Shah Abbas, 203
Aliyev, President of Azerbaijan, 388–89
Aljai, w/o Timur, 138
Al Jazeera, 361
al-Karaouine, Morocco, oldest continually operating university in the world, 112
al-Khwarizmi, Persian philosopher, 70
al-Kindi, aka 'The Philosopher of Arabs', 78
Allahabad, 181
Allahverdi Khan, Irani general and

statesman under Shah Abbas, 205–8
Allen Dulles, Director CIA, 333
Allen Pope, CIA aviator, shot down and captured in Indonesia, 376
al-Mamun, 72, 84, See also Mamun
Almanon, moon crater named after al-Mamun, 72
Almohads, Moroccan, Berber, Muslim dynasty in Spain, 118
Almoravid, Muslim dynasty that ruled over the Magreb and Spain, 115–16, 399
al Muizz, 4th Fatimid caliph, 85
al Muntasir, Abbasid caliph, 87
Al Murtada, 17th Abbasid caliph, 78
al-Mushafi, Jafar, Umayyad vizier in Cordoba, 112
al-Mutamid, 15th Abbasid caliph, 115–17
al-Nahayan, ruling family of Abu Dhabi, 394
al-Nasir, Almohad caliph in Spain, 101, 118
al-Ouja, village in Iraq, birthplace of Saddam, 345
Alp Arslan, Second Sultan of the Seljuk dynasty, 82
al Qaeda, Miltant Sunni Islamist organization, 364, 370–71, 409
al Qahira, Cairo, 855
al Qanun fi al Tibb, encyclopedia of medicine compiled by Ibn Sina, 69
al Rashid, tribal chief enemy of Abdul Aziz ibn Saud, 60, 62, 64, 67
al-Razi, pioneer of medicine, 69
Al-Rikabi, secretary general of Baath Party in Iraq, 347
Al Saffah, first Abbasid Caliph, 62
al-Salih Ayyub, Kurdish, Ayyubid ruler of Egypt, 97
al-Saud, ruling royal family of Saudi Arabia, 268, 312
al-Tabari, early Muslim scholar and historian, 3

Altaf Hussain, Pakistani politician, 367
Aly Rida, aka Ali Reza, 8th Shia Imam, 74–75
Amalric, King of Jerusalem, 92
Amanullah, King Afghanistan, 276, 287–90, 310
Amer, 179, 314–15, 317, 322
Amer al-Hakim, Egyptian general, Nasser's deputy, 314
America, 98, 119, 154, 241, 275, 310, 313, 320, 323, 325–26, 328–29, 333, 335–36, 338, 342, 346–47, 351, 357–58, 363, 367–68, 376–77, 381, 383–87, 389, 395–98, 400, 402, 404, 406–7, 409, 411, 417–18
American, 2, 72, 249, 259, 274, 284, 296, 309, 338, 341, 343, 352, 355, 358, 363–64, 367, 370–71, 376–77, 379, 389, 395, 397–98, 402, 406, 409
American Civil War, 259
American Empire, 2
Americas, 120, 123, 227, 235
Amina, Mother of The Prophet, 1
Amin, 6th Abbasid Caliph, s/o Harun al Rashid, 62–63, 65–66, 76, 357
Amir Abdur Rahman Khan of Afghanistan (Iron Amir), 286–88
Amir Hussayn, brother-in-law of Timur, 139
Amir Kabir, Qajar prime minister in Persia, 294
Amir Mahmud, Afghan ruler, 282
Amir of Bokhara, 280
Amman, capital of Jordan, 271
Ammash, interior minister in Iraq under Saddam, 347
Amr ibn al-As, 17, 26
Anastasia, aka Kosem, Ottoman Sultana Valida, 233
ANC, African National Congress 357
Andalusia, 106–8, 110–11, 117, 119, 226
Andijan, city in Uzbekistan, 165
Andijan Massacre in 2005 in

INDEX | 433

Uzbekistan, 385
Andrea Doria, Italian admiral, 226
Anglo-Afghan War, 284–85
Anglo-Indian, 195
Angola, 389
Animal Farm, English novel, 195
Ankara, 143–44, 216, 249
Ansar, inhabitants of Medina, 411
April Glaspie, US ambassador in Iraq, 351
Aq Quyunlu, aka the White Sheep Turkomans, 199
Arab, 12, 21, 27, 53–55, 57, 61, 68, 80, 106–8, 111, 147, 161, 263, 271, 311, 313, 321, 329, 345, 350–52, 354, 359–60, 391, 394, 404–5
Arabia, 16–17, 21, 26, 103, 243–44, 255, 264–67, 270–75, 310, 312–13, 323–25, 329, 333, 351, 366, 393, 403–5, 407
Arabian Peninsula, 255, 265, 310, 313
Arabic, 39, 47, 68, 102, 220, 249, 262, 314, 317, 392
Arabshah, historian, 125, 140, 216
Arab Spring, 359
Aramco, Saudi oil company, 405
Ardeshir Zahedi, Irani diplomat, son-in-law of the Shah, 335
Arif, President of Iraq, 321, 345–7
Arik Buka, Mongol prince, youngest son of Tolui, 136
Aristotle, 68–69
Arjumand, 183, 186
Armen Firman, stuntman in Cordoba who attempted flight, 72
Armenia, 125, 294
Armenian Massacres, 242, 244
Armenians, 201, 219, 244, 248
Army of the Peacocks, 48
Aruj Barbarossa, Ottoman admiral, 225
Asadabad, 260
Asaf Khan, notable at the Mogul court, 183–86
Ashgabat, 385

Ashraf, twin sister of the Shah of Iran, 330, 332, 334
Asia, 17, 40, 45, 49–50, 57, 64, 68, 70, 76–77, 79, 84, 88, 99, 103, 130, 132, 135, 137, 165, 167–68, 179, 199, 214–15, 219, 223, 252, 299–300, 309, 336, 378, 380–82, 391, 393, 414
Asian, 294, 300, 380, 382–83, 391, 393, 395, 418
Askar Akayev, former president of Kyrgyzstan, 382
Askari, b/o Mogul Emperor Humayun, 169–70
Asma, d/o Abu Bakr, m/o Abdullah bin Zubayr, 10, 48
Asporsha, w/o Ottoman Sultan Orhan Gazi, 215
Asquith, Herbert Henry, British PM, 247
Assad, Bashar, 398, 401
Assassins, 71, 80, 83–84, 93–95, 136, 397, 411
Assassins of Hasan al Sabah, 411
Astana, 389
Astrolabe, 72
Astronomy, 64, 67, 94, 391
Aswan Dam in Egypt, 88, 91, 190, 319, 321–2
Ataturk, 222, 230, 240, 246–50, 271, 287, 297, 302, 310, 312, 317, 338, 365
Athens, 133
Atlantic, 39, 51, 227, 310
Atlantic Ocean, 2, 40, 77
Atlas Mountains, 116
Attock Fort, in Pakistan, 366
Aurangzeb, aka Alamgir, Mogul Emperor, 117, 164, 182–83, 186, 189–94, 293
Australian, 247
Austria, 120, 227, 241, 388
Austrians, 236–37, 257
Avazov, Uzbek torture victim, 383
Avicenna, 69, 385, *See also* Ibn Sina
Ayatollah Beheshti, 342

Ayatollah Kashani, 332, 334
Ayatollah Kho'i, 340
Ayatollah Khomeini, 312
Ayatollah, Khomeini, 312
Ayatollah Montazeri, 341, 343
Ayatollah Motahari, 342
Ayatollah Shariatmadari, 343
Ayaz, Malik slave and king of Lahore, 82
Aybak, husband of Shajar al-Durr, first Mamluk sultan, 98-99
Ayn Jalut, Battle of, 84, 100
Ayubid, 84, 98
Azerbaijan, 135, 198, 294

Baathists, 345, 347
Baath Party, 339
Babur, Moghul Emperor, 77, 146, 148, 160, 162-63, 165-69, 172-73, 176, 182, 191, 199, 277
Babylon, 26, 125
Bachey Saqao, Habibulla Kalakani, The Water Carrier's son, King of Afghanistan, 289-90
Badr, Battle of, 16, 24
Baghdad, 60-62, 65-66, 68, 70, 72, 74-77, 79-80, 83-87, 101, 107, 109, 111-12, 125, 130, 135-36, 139, 143, 149, 199, 208, 210, 234, 252, 265, 267, 334-35, 338, 346
Bahadur Shah Zafar, last Mogul Emperor, 194-203
Bahrain, 85, 208
Bahri Mamluks, 99
Baibars, 4th Mameluk Sultan in Egypt, 100
Baikanor Cosmodrome, 386
Bairactar, Ottoman general and grand vizier, 238-39
Bairam Khan, general and vizier of Akbar, Mogul Emperor, 171, 175-76
Bakiyev, Kurmanbek, second President of Kyrgyzstan, 390
Baku, 210

Balban, Ghiyas ud din, 9th Sultan of the Slave Dynasty of Delhi, 151-2
Balian, of Ibelin, Crusader in Jerusalem, 83, 95-96
Balkans, 215
Balkh, 30, 277
Baluchistan, 50, 279-80, 367
Bangladesh, 304, 362
Bani Sadr, Abolhassan, President of Iraq, 339, 341-42
Banu'n-Nadir, Jewish tribe in Medina, 8
Barakzai of Afghanistan, 281-82
Barani, Ziauddin, historian of the Delhi Sultanate, 155-58
Barbarossa, 122, 223, 225-26, 229, 307
Barbary, 226, 307
Bardissy, Mameluk chief in Egypt, 254
Barmakids, 62-64, 183
Barnaby Rogerson, British historian, 3
Baron Julius de Reuter, British-Jewish banker and businessman, 295
Barquq, first Sultan of the Mamluk Burji dynasty in Egypt, 102
Barsbay, 9th Mamluk Burji Sultan in Egypt, 102
Bashar al-Assad, President of Syria, 398, 401
Basij, Army of the Guardians of the Islamic Revolution in Iran, 343
Basque Separatist Movement, 357
Basra, 25, 31-32, 35, 43-44, 58
Battle of Badr, 16, 24
Battle of the Camel, 35, 413
Battle of the Nile, 252
Battle of the Pyramids, 252
Battle of the Trench, 8
Battle of Yarmuk, 17
Batu, Mongol ruler and founder of the Golden Horde, 132, 134-36
Bayazid, Ottoman sultan, 143-44
Bayezid, Prince, s/o Suleiman the Magnificent, 201
Bayt al Hikma, aka House of Wisdom in Abbasid Baghdad, 66-68

INDEX | 435

Bazargan, Mehdi, first prime minister after the Irani Revolution of 1979, 340–41
BCCI, Bank of Credit and Commerce International, 405–6
Bedouin, 2, 7, 269, 271–72
Bedr el-Gemali, Fatimid general in Egypt, 90
Begum Isan Daulat, grandmother of Mogul Emperor Babur, 164
Beijing, 392, 418
Beirut, 397
Belgium, 393
Belgrade, 222
Benazir Bhutto, 364, 368, 413
Bengal, 149, 179, 188, 194, 280
Bengalis, 392
Benghazi, 354, 356, 360
Beni Umayya, 31
Berber, 51–53, 87, 105, 113–14
Berke Khan, Mongol leader of the Golden Horde, 136
The Berkeley, hotel in London, 379, 394
Berlin, 245
Bermuda, 389
Bernier, Franois, Physician, traveller and writer in the Mogul Court, 186
Beyonce, American singer, 359
Bhagwan Das, Hindju notable in court of Mogul Emperor Akbar, 179
Bhatinda, Governor of, jailor and then husband of Razia Sultan, 151
Bhutto, See Zulfiqar Ali Bhutto
Bihar Khan, ruler of Bihar, employer of Sher Shah Suri, 172
Bikaner, 179
Birbal, friend of Mogul Emperor Akbar, 179
Bishkek, 390
Black Death, 399
Black Muslim in USA, 396
Black Sea, 247, 307
Blaise Compaore of Burkina Faso, 356
Blue mosque in Istanbul, 214

Boabdil, aka Muhammad XII last Muslim ruler of Granada, 104, 119
Boghoz Bey, Minister of Muhammad Ali Pasha in Egypt, 258
Bohemia, 227
Bokassa, President of the central African Republic, 357
Bokhara, 45, 49, 136, 280, 284, 286
Bolivia, 389
Bolshevik Revolution, 296, 381
Bombay, 300–2
Book of Government or *Rules for Kings*, 44
Bo'orchu, one of the Four Coursers of Genghis Khan, 128
Bornu, Muslim empire in Africa, 399
Bosnia, 219, 393
Bosphorus, 214, 226, 234, 240, 247
Boutros Pasha Ghali, Egyptian prime minister, 261
Braille, 385
Brazil, 418
Brigadier Satti, 366
Britain, 247–49, 252, 259, 262, 275, 282–83, 286, 294, 296, 301, 303, 308–10, 313, 320–21, 360, 403, 406, 413
British, 2, 162, 168, 192, 194–97, 246–48, 252, 254, 256–57, 259–64, 270–71, 273, 276–77, 280–81, 283–88, 292, 295–96, 298–300, 302–6, 308–12, 314–15, 317, 321–22, 331–35, 344, 351, 355, 357, 371, 392, 394–95, 399, 403–4, 414
British Empire, 2, 196, 252, 280
British India, 281, 302
British Petroleum, 357
Buddhism, 49
Buffles, 178
Bugti tribe of Balochistan, 368
Buhlul, 161
Bulganin, Nikolai, Soviet politician, 321
Burji Mamluks, 99, 102
Burma, 197

Burnes, 283–5, *See also* Sir Alexander
Buyid Dynasty in Persia, 81, 83, 85
Byzantine Empire, 20, 23, 214–15
Byzantines, 1–2, 21

Cadillac, 335
Caesar, 1, 17, 32, 98, 112, 252–53
Cairo, 27, 68, 70, 72, 80, 85, 87–89, 94, 97, 99, 111–12, 222, 255–56, 263, 265, 267–68, 271, 315, 318–19, 322, 326, 330, 345–46, 371
Calcutta, 280
Caliph, 17–24, 26, 28–36, 40–49, 51–52, 54, 56, 58–60, 62–66, 68, 70, 72, 74–79, 81, 84, 86–92, 98, 101, 106–7, 109, 111–12, 117, 136, 145, 222, 271, 296, 321, 391, 413
Camp David, 323
Canary Wharf, 394
The Canon, 69
Cape of Good Hope, 102, 207
Captain Khatami, 335
Carlos the Jackal, 357
Caspian, 294
Cassius Clay, aka Muhammad Ali, world champion boxer, 396
Castile, 115, 118, 120, 125
Castro Fidel, Leader of the revolution in Cuba, 396
Catherine of Aragon, 122
Catherine the Great, Empress of Russia, 120, 122, 238, 294, 381
Catholic, 118, 224, 226, 239
Catholic Monarchs, 226
Cays, Egypt representative of Caliph Ali, 35
Central Arabia, 265–66, 270–71
Central Asia, 40, 45, 49–50, 57, 68, 70, 76–77, 79, 84, 88, 99, 103, 130, 132, 135, 165, 167, 179, 199, 215, 381–83, 391
Central Asian Republics, 381–83
Chad, 356
Chagatai, s/o Genghis Khan, 132–34, 139
Chagatai Turkish, 284
Chaldiran, Battle of, Ottomans victory over Safavids, 200
Chalkis, Greek town, 22
Chang Yuchan, Muslim general in China, 391
Charlemagne, 67, 108
Charles Hapsburg, 226
Charles Martel, aka The Hammer, 53, 106
Charles Taylor of Liberia, 356
Charles V, 122
Chase Manhattan Bank, 405
Chemical Ali, cousin and minister of Saddam Hussein, 351
Chevron, oil company, 404
Chila'un Bahadur, one of the Four Coursers of Genghis Khan, 128
Chileidu, previous husband of Hoelun, m/o Genghis Khan, 126
China, 2, 39–40, 43, 50, 67–69, 77, 93, 124, 129–30, 133, 135–37, 145–46, 160, 307–8, 320–21, 336, 356, 368–70, 377, 386, 389–92, 406, 418
Chinese, 53, 126, 133, 136, 139, 145, 307, 321, 335, 378, 380–81, 391–92, 399, 402
Chosroes, 24
Christian, 26–27, 30, 43, 53, 70, 81, 83, 88, 92, 95–98, 104, 106, 109–13, 115–19, 121–22, 136, 194–95, 215, 217, 219–21, 223, 225–26, 233, 239, 243–44, 277, 294, 307, 411
Christianity, 6, 122, 180, 195, 301, 357
Christian Louboutin, 88
Christians, 23, 43, 75, 83, 87, 95–97, 106, 109–11, 113, 115–17, 119–22, 196, 219, 222, 226, 240, 243–44
Christopher Columbus, 119, 306
Churchill, Sir Winston, British prime minister, 247–48, 274–75, 310, 322, 331, 333–44, 404
CIA, US Central Intelligence agency,

INDEX | 437

313, 328, 330, 333, 338, 341, 343, 350, 378, 417
Clark Clifford, US Democratic Party, 406
Clark Gable, American actor, 376
Claudia Schiffer, international model, 360
Clavijo, ambassador to court of Timur, writer, 125
Cleopatra, 97, 252
Clot Bey, French doctor, Chief surgeon to Muhammad Ali Pasha, 257
COAS, General Ziauddin, Pakistan, 366
COAS Raheel Sharif, Pakistan, 370
Cold War, 386
Colonel Nassiri, commander of the Shah's Imperial Guard in Iran, 334-35
Colonel Nasution, 376, See also Nasution
Colonel Urabi, Ahmed, Egyptian nationalist army officer, 260
Communism, 333
Communist Party, 340, 377, 382-83
Confucian, 391
The Connaught, hotel in London, 394
Conquest of Syria, 22-24
Constantinople, 81, 214-15, 218-19
Control for Oil, 402-9
Copt, 10-11, 261
Cordoba, 58, 68, 72-73, 105, 108-11, 113-16, 118, 265
Corsica, 227, 238
Cossack Brigade, Iran, 296-97
Count Julian of Spain, 52, 105
Covenant of Umar, 23
CPEC, China Pak Economic Corridor, 369-70, 418
Crassus, 112
Crete, 109
Crimea, 132
Crimean War, 241
Cripps, Sir Stafford, British politician, 303

Croatia, 227
Croatian, 231
Cromer, 261, 414
Crusaders, 23, 92-93, 95, 100
Cultural Revolution, 356, 391
CUP, Committee of Union and Progress, Turkey, 244-45
Cyprus, 232
Cyrus the Great, 277
Czar, 284, 294
Czar Alexander II, 145

Dadabhai, Naoroji, Indian Politician, 300
Dagestan, Russian Republic, 294
Dahham ibn Dawwas, cruel ruler of Riyadh, 266
Damascus, 22, 24, 34-35, 37, 40, 46, 50, 52, 55-57, 85, 97, 125, 235, 265, 267
Dammam Zone, 403
Daniel Bartoli, priest and historian in Mogul India, 178
Daniyal, s/o Akbar the Great, 180, 182, 186
Dar al Harb, abode of Islam, 410
Dar al Ilm, House of Knowledge in Cairo, 87
Dar al Islam, 410
Dar al Muratabin, madrassa in Morocco, 116
Dara Shikoh, eldest son of Emperor Shah Jahan, 186
Dardanelles, 247
Dar es Salam, 399
Dariga, d/o of Nazarbayev, President of Kazakhstan, 388
Dariyah, 255
Dark Ages, 72, 305
Darya, love of Omar Khayyam, 71
Dasaad, Irani notable of Reza Shah Pahlavi, 375
Da Vinci, Leonardo, 72
Dawwas, 266, See also Dahham

Deccan, 168, 188, 190–92
Delhi, 72, 142–43, 147–53, 155–62, 167–68, 171, 175–76, 187–88, 193–94, 196–97, 210, 212, 278–79, 395
Delhi Sultanate, 147–48, 160, 162
Democracy Movement, 368
Deng Xiaoping, Leader of China, 335, 391
Denmark, 392
Desert Fox, 262
Despina, w/o Sultan Bayezid, 145
Dhaidan ibn Hithlain, tribal chief who rebelled against King Abdul Aziz ibn Saud, 274
Dina d/o Jinnah, Pakistan, 301–2
Din-i-Ilahi, religion formulated by Mogul Emperor Akbar, 180
Dogs of War, 128
Dokuz Khatun, w/o Hulagu Khan, 136
Dolmabace Palace, 238, 241
Dome of the Rock, 47
Doria, Admiral, 226
Dost Mohammad Khan, Amir of Afghanistan, 276, 280–2, 284, 286
Dragut, Ottoman admiral, 226, 229
Drake, Sir Francis, English sea captain, 306
Dr A.Q. Khan, Pakistani nuclear scientist, 369
Druze, 87, 89
Dubai, 20, 343, 406
Duke of Westminster, 394
Durand Line, 286
Dutch, 207, 306, 374, 399, 404

East India Company 360, 194
East Turkestan Islamic Movement, 392
Edwina Mountbatten, w/o viceroy of India, 304
Effat al-Thunayan, 324
Egypt, 12, 26–28, 31–32, 35, 37, 43, 51, 56, 66, 78, 80–81, 83–87, 89–93, 97, 99, 101–2, 109, 111, 117, 128, 136, 139, 149, 222, 238–41, 243, 251–62, 276, 298, 309, 312–14, 319–23, 325–26, 330, 345, 350, 356, 360, 398, 409, 414
Egyptian, 85, 90, 98, 100, 240, 253, 256–57, 260–63, 268, 313–15, 319–23, 327, 329, 350
Egyptians, 27, 84, 252, 254, 259, 261, 267–68, 313–15, 320
Einstein, 70
Eisenhower President, 331, 333
Elijah Muhammad, leader of Black Americans, 395–97
Elphinstone, Mountstuart, Scottish statesman and historian in India, 192
Emonali Sharipovich Rakmonov, 390
Emperor Aurangzeb, 192, 293
Emperor Bokassa, 357
Emperor Charles, Holy Roman Emperor, 226, 236
Emperor Heraclius, 12
Emperor of Tartary, 137
Empress Fara Diba of Iran, 330
Empty Quarter, Saudi desert, 269
England, 96–97, 118, 120, 122, 168, 207, 227, 241, 243, 287, 300, 302–3, 320, 324, 392, 414
English, 178, 195, 207, 227, 238, 300, 317, 355, 392, 398
Enrico Mattei, Italian oil businessman, 404
Enver Pasha, Young Turk revolutionary leader, 245–6
Erzerum, Turkish city, 125
Ethiopian, 8, 11–12, 18
Europe, 17, 53, 64, 67–68, 72, 77, 82, 93, 106, 109, 120–22, 129, 135, 140, 143, 145, 200, 214–15, 219, 221–23, 235, 240, 242–45, 252, 256–57, 259–61, 263, 272, 288, 297, 302, 305–10, 328–30, 336, 357, 368, 374, 382, 385–86, 392–95, 398–99, 402, 411, 415, 418
European Parliamentary Democracy, 376

Europeans, 69, 229, 237, 288, 306, 312, 393–94
Exxon, oil company, 329, 404
Ez Zaghal, aka Muhammad XII, King of Granada, 119

Fadhl, Barmakid vizier, 74
Fadl ibn Sahl, Abbasid vizier, 66
Faisal al Duwaish, rebel Sheikh against Kin Abdul Aziz, 274
Fakhita, d/o Abu Talib, 3
Fara Diba, *See* Empress Fara Diba of Iran
Far East, 49, 86, 126, 135, 207, 235, 306, 310
Farewell Pilgrimage, 11–13
Farghana Valley, 84
Farid, aka Sher Shah Suri, 171–72
Farmanfarma, Firuz, Irani politician, 297
Farouk, King of Egypt, 263, 298, 313
Fars, 50, 205
Fatepore, aka Fatehpur Sikri, 178
Fath Ali Shah, Qajar ruler in Persia, 294
The Father of Kings, Abd al Malik, Umayyad Caliph, 47
Fathi Khan Barakzai, 282
Fatima daughter of The Prophet, 16, 34, 66, 83, 302
Fatimid, 78, 84–87, 92–93, 98, 399, 413
Fauzia, Egyptian princess, w/o Shah of Iran, 298
Fedayeen-e-Islam, Irani terrorist group, 332
Ferdinand de Lesseps, French diplomat and developer of the Suez Canal, 258
Ferdinand, King of Aragon, 118–19, 120, 227, 258, 399
Fergana Valley, 49, 165–6
Fez, 119
Fidayeen, Ismaili Assassins, 93, 95
Finland, 347
Firoz Shah, Tughluk king, 159

First World War, 245, 261, 264, 270–71, 287, 301, 344
Firuz Farmanfarma, influential Persian politician, 297
Flora, Christian martyr in Cordoba, 109
Florinda, d/o Count Julian in Spain, 52, 105
Foday Sankoh of Sierra Leone, 356
Folies Bergere, Paris night club, 242
Four Dogs, Generals of Genghis Khan, 125, 127
France, 5, 53, 106, 122, 135, 227, 238, 241, 247, 259, 320–21, 331, 340–41, 360, 368–69, 392, 394, 404
Francis, King of France, contemporary of Suleiman, 227
Franklin Delano Roosevelt, US President, 376
Fratricide, Ottoman Law of, 220, 229, 231, 233
Free Officers, Nasser's rebel army cadres, 251, 314, 317, 319
French, 53, 97, 186, 226, 238–39, 248, 252, 257–58, 314–15, 317, 330, 392
F-14 Tomcat, American fighter aircraft, 343
Fustat, 26–27, 31–32, 37

Gaddafi, Muammar, 312–13, 328–29, 350, 353–62, 398, 401, 404
Galen, 68–69
Gallipoli, Battle of, 246–47
Gandhi, Mahatma, 300–1, 303
Gang of Four, Chinese political faction led by wife of Mao Zedong, 43
Gasprom, Russian gas company, 395
Gaza Strip, 322
GCC, Gulf Cooperation Council, 407–8
General Ayub Khan of Pakistan, 362
General Fazlollah Zahedi of Iran, 333, 335
General Fouad Sadek of Egypt, 314
General Gordon of Khartoum, 260

General Ironside, British general in Persia, 296
General Jacques Menou, Napoleon's general in Egypt, 253
General Junot, French general, 253
General Kitchener of Sudan, 256
General Kleber, Napoleonic general in Egypt, 253
General Noriega of Panama, 406
General Norman Schwarzkopf, 334
General Pakravan of Iran, 337
General Razmara of Iran, 332
General Rustam, 24
General Suharto, 379
General Yahya of Pakistan, 362
General Ziauddin of Pakistan, 366
General Zia ul-Haq of Pakistan, 363
Geneva, 350
Genghis Khan, 17, 76, 79, 84, 99–100, 124, 126, 128–29, 131–32, 136–37, 139, 143, 150, 152, 164, 196, 215, 277, 381, 391
Gennadius, Patriarch of Constantinople, 219
George Orwell, British writer, 195
George Santayana, Spanish philosopher, 415
Georgia, 245, 277, 294
Georgo, bodyguard to Saddam, 350
Germans, 257, 262, 333, 399
Germany, 121, 227, 245, 247, 262, 296, 310, 358, 392, 403, 418
Ghalib, Indian poet, 112, 194, 196–97
Ghana, 86, 399
Ghanim, *See* Shukri Ghanim
Ghazan, descendent of Hulagu, 136
Ghazi Malik, aka Ghiasuddin Tughluq, 158
Ghaznavids, Persianate Muslim Dynasty, 79
Ghazni, city in Afghanistan, 69, 81, 148, 150, 212, 279–80, 284
Ghiasuddin Tughluq, founder of the Tughluk Dynasty in India, 158

Ghilzai, famous Afghan tribe, 209, 287
GHQ, General Headquarter of the Egyptian army, 316
Ghulam Qadir, Chieftain who conquered Delhi, 193
Gibbon, Edward, historian, 19
Gibraltar, Jebal Tarik, The Rock of Tariq, 52, 165
Giffen, James, American businessman in Kazakhstan, 389
The Godfather, 346, 389
Goharara, d/o Mogul Emperor Shah Jahan, 186
Gokhale, Gopal Krishna, 300
Golconda, 192
Golden Age, 86, 123
Golden Horde, Mongol kharate, 100, 132, 134, 141–42
Golpaygani, Mohammad Reza, Grand Ayatollah, 337
Gorbachev, Russian leader, 381, 383, 388
Gordon, 256
Great Patriotic War, 382
Great War, 271, 273, 400
Greece, 137, 219, 254–56
Greeks, 68, 246, 248–49, 252
Green Book, 355
Guadalquivir, 107
Guardian newspaper, 401
Guided Democracy, 375–376
Gujarat, 179, 188, 191
Gulbehar, senior consort of Suleiman the Magnificient, 224
Gulf War, 334, 408
Gurbanguly Berdimuhamedov, 386
Gurghin Khan, 277
Gwalior, 194

Habibullah, s/o Abdur Rahman (The Iron Amir) of Afghanistan, 276, 287, 289
Hadi b/o Harun al Rashid, 61–62
Hafiz, Persian poet, 140

Hafsa, d/o Umar, w/o The Prophet, 9
Hafte Tir suicide bombing attack in Tehran, 342
Haggia Sophia, Mosque in Istanbul, 214, 218
Hail, city in Saudi Arabia, 268, 274
Hai Rui, Muslim official of the Ming Dynasty, 391
Haji Jamal Khan of Afghanistan, 281
Halima w/o Ottoman Sultan Murad, 217, 286
Hamida Begum, m/o Akbar the Great, 170
Hamid Khan, noble in the Delhi Sultanate, 161
Hampstead, London suburb, 302
Hamza uncle of The Prophet, 2, 7-8, 10-12, 18, 39
Hanafi School of Islamic Jurisprudence, 75
Hanbali School of Islamic Jurisprudence, 75-76, 265
Han Chinese, 392
Hannibal, General of Carthage, enemy of Rome, 360
Haqqani Network, 371
Hasa, Eastern Province of Saudi Arabia, 269-70, 272-73
Hasan bin Ali, 59
Hasan Kojahmedov, Kazakh Presidential candidate, 388
Hasday ben-Shaprut, Jewish physician in Cordoba, 70
Hashemite, 38, 58
Hassa al Sudairi, w/o King Abdul Aziz of Saudi Arabia, 324
Hassan al-Banna, founder of the Muslim Brotherhood, 263, 315
Hatem Beg Ordubadi, grand vizier of Shah Abbas, 205
Hazrat Ali, 75, 184, 265
Hazrat Umar, 19, 265
Hebrew, 220, 317
Heikal, prominent Egyptian journalist, 316, 355
Hejazis, people of the Hejaz, 271, 273
Hejaz, Western region of Saudi Arabia, 85, 266-67, 270-73
Hejra, journey from Mecca to Medina, 2
Helen, aka Nilofer, w/o Orhan, 215
Hemu, Hindu general of Sher Shah Suri, 175-76
Henry III of Castile, 125
Henry VIII of England, 227
Heraclius, Byzantine Emperor, 12, 17, 22-23, 96
Herat, 30, 139-40, 166, 203, 277, 279, 281, 284
Hermes, international fashion store, 349
Herzl, Theodor, father of modern political Zionism, 244
High Dam, Egypt, 319, 322
Hijab, 114, 392, 394, 412
Hilaire Beloc, British writer, 256
Hims, Battle of, 101
Hindal, s/o Mogul Emperor Babur, 169-70
Hindu, 70, 148-49, 154, 156-58, 159, 161, 171, 174-75, 179-80, 190-92, 194-95, 299-303, 306
Hindu Queen Padmini, 154
Hindu Rajput, 179
Hindustan, 160, 163, 167, 171
Hippocrates, Greek pioneer of medicine, 68
Hippolyte Charles, lover of Empress Josephine Bonaparte, 252
Hirabai, Hindu dancing girl, love of Emperor Aurangzeb, 190
Hisham III, last caliph of Cordoba, 114
Hitler, 121, 246, 310, 397, 403, 417
Hittin, Battle of, 95
Hizb ul Tahrir, Islamist militant organization, 384
Hoelun m/o Genghis Khan, 126, 128-29
Holmes, Major Frank, first Saudi oil

concessionaire, 273
Holocaust, 121
Holy Roman Emperor, 120, 225, 227
Holy Sepulchre, 23
Home Rule League, 301
Hormuz, 207
House of Wisdom, 66
Hubble telescopes, 71
Hu Dahai, Muslim Chinese general, 391
Hudaibiyyah, Truce of, 11
Hui Muslims of China, 391
Hulagu, grandson of Genghis Khan, 76–77, 79, 99–101, 133, 135–36, 152
Hulan, w/o Genghis Khan, 126
Humayun, second Mogul Emperor 67, 168–71, 173, 175, 182, 184, 187, 201
Hunayn ibn Ishaq, medieval Iraqi scholar, 68
The Hundred Year War, 307
Hungarian, 218
Hungary, 129, 217, 219, 227
Hunt Petroleum, 404
Hunyadi, John, Hungarian military leader, 217
Hurrem Sultan, aka Roxelana, w/o Suleiman the Magnificent, 223–25, 228, 232, 413
Husayn, *See* Amir Hussayn
Hussein Fatemi, Irani foreign minister, 335
Hussein Kamel, son-in-law of Saddam, 350
Hussein Sharif, Emir of Mecca, 270–71
Hussein Sharif in Jordan, 312

IAEA, International Atomic Energy Agency, 417–18
ibn Aamir, kinsman of Caliph Uthman, 31
Ibn Abbas, cousin of Ali ibn abi Talib, 34
ibn Abdul Wahhab, Saudi religious leader, 265–66, 324
ibn Abdus, Umayyad vizier, 114
Ibn abi Dinar, 17th-century historian, 52
Ibn al Abbar, historian, 117
ibn al-Haytham, Muslim scientist, 70
Ibn Battuta, medieval Moroccan traveller, 399
Ibn Firnas, medieval Andalusian inventor, 72–73
Ibn Ishaq, early Arab Muslim historian, 3
Ibn Khaldun, Arab African historian, 280, 399
ibn Saud, Abdul Aziz, Founder of Saudi Arabia, 255, 264–66, 269, 273–75, 324
ibn Sina, aka Avicenna, 69
ibn Taymiyyah, medieval theologian, major influence on contemporary Wahhabism, Salafism and Jihadism, 265, 409
Ibn Tumart, Berber religious scholar in Morocco, spiritual leader of the Almohads, 117
Ibrahim Lodi, Afghan Sultan in India, 167–8
Ibrahim Pasha, general, s/o Mohammad Ali Pasha of Egypt, 256
Idi Amin, Uganda President, 357
Ifriqiya, Northern Africa, 52
Ikhwan, Saudi army of King Abdul Aziz Ibn Saud, 271–74
Il-Khan, dynasty in Persia founded by the Mongols, 79, 100, 136
Iltumish, third ruler of Delhi Sultanate, 149–51
Imam Abu Hanifa, *See* Abu Hanifa
Imam Ahmad ibn Hanbal, *See* ibn Hanbal
Imamali Rahmanov, President of Tajikistan, 383
Imam al Shafii, founder of the Shafi School of jurisprudence, 75
Imam Malik ibn Anas, founder of the

Maliki School of jurisprudence, 76
Imam Mowaffak, famous teacher of Omar Khayyam, 70
Imam Quli, s/o Allahverdi Khan, 208
IMF, 377
Imperial Bank, 296
Imperial Legislative Council, 300
Imran Khan, Pakistani politician and former cricketer, 372
The Independent, 361, 417
India, 21, 40, 50, 68–70, 72, 77, 81, 86, 93, 102, 117, 125, 139, 142, 147–50, 154, 159–63, 167–76, 180, 189, 191, 193–98, 201, 207–8, 212, 252, 259–61, 271, 277, 279–86, 300–10, 367, 369, 371, 386, 392, 413
Indian, 148, 158, 168, 179, 194–95, 283, 286, 300, 303, 309, 365, 369, 371
Indian Mutiny, 148, 309
Indian National Congress, INC, 300
India Office, 271
Indonesia, 310, 312, 333, 373–81, 413
Indonesia, 373–81
Indus, 149, 152, 276
Iran, 57, 70, 139, 143, 198–203, 205–8, 210–13, 260, 273, 289, 292, 297–98, 306, 312–13, 325, 329–33, 335–36, 338–44, 346, 349–50, 358, 361, 369, 386, 402, 404, 413, 417–18
Iran Air flight, 358
Irani, 198, 201, 273, 331–32, 335–36, 338, 340, 342–43, 351, 402–3
Iran-Iraq War, 342, 349
Iraq, 31, 46–47, 51, 65–66, 91, 123, 135, 245, 266–67, 271, 310, 312–13, 325–26, 333, 338–39, 342–52, 394, 397, 402, 404
Iraqi, 48, 93, 343–45, 347–48, 350–51
Isabel de Solis, concubine and consort of Sultan of Granada, 118
Isabella, Queen of Castile, 118–22, 399
Isa bin Musa, Abbasid prince, 62
Isfahan, 72, 140, 203–6, 209–11, 277–78
ISI, Pakistani Military Intelligence agency, 363, 365, 367
ISIS, Islamic State of Iraq and Syria, militant jihadist group, 352, 394, 398, 409, 411
Iskander Celebi, long serving finance minister of Suleiman the Magnificent, 224
Islam, 1–2, 4–7, 11–12, 15–19, 21, 25, 28–29, 32, 34, 36, 39, 41–43, 45, 48–49, 51–55, 57, 69, 80, 83–84, 94, 96, 99, 101, 103–4, 111, 115, 117–18, 136–37, 139, 148–49, 159, 161, 168, 180, 187–88, 190, 198–99, 201, 203, 220, 224, 228, 239, 245, 252–53, 265, 273, 301, 304–8, 311, 326, 332, 337–38, 343, 345, 357–60, 363, 370, 378, 382, 390, 393, 395–400, 408–11, 415
Islamic, 6, 16, 26, 37, 39, 53, 61, 67, 70–71, 75, 87, 135, 180, 189, 191, 200, 217, 220–21, 240, 260, 265–66, 288–89, 298, 323, 327, 337, 339, 341–42, 358–59, 363, 369–71, 384–85, 392, 397, 405, 408, 410–11, 415
Islamic Banking, 408
Islamic Bomb, 363, 369
Islamic Empire, 61, 135
Islamic Jihad, 363
Islamic Republic of Iran, 337
Islamic Socialism, 363
Islamic world, 53, 70, 87, 200, 397, 411, 415
Islam in Africa, 306
Islam in America, 357
Islamist, 328, 358, 361, 363, 394
Islam Karimov, 382
Ismaili, 71, 80, 83, 87, 93–95, 136
Ismaili Assassins, 71, 80, 93, 136
Ismaili Fatimid, 80, 93
Ismaili Imam, 87
Ismaili Shia, 83, 95
Israel, 244, 263, 311, 313–14, 320–21, 323, 328, 352, 369, 397, 404, 417–18
Israeli, 322

Istanbul, 72, 214, 219, 222, 226, 240, 245, 247–48, 254–56, 259–60, 267, 271, 306, 324
Italian, 78, 254, 317, 360, 404
Italian Renaissance, 78
Italy, 219, 227, 259, 289, 296, 357
Itimad-ud-Daula, aka Mirza Ghiyas ud-Din Beg, 183
Itimad, w/o al-Mutamid, Muslim king in Spain, 116–17, 183
Ivan Victorovich Vitkevich, Russian spy in Afghanistan, 283–84
Iyad al-Allawi, Iraqi politician, 345

Ja'da w/o Hasan bin Ali, 42
Jafar, 58, 60, 62–64, 112
Jahanara, d/o Emperor Shah Jahan, 186–89
Jahangir, Mogul Emperor, 179–87
Jaipur, 179
Jakarta, 377–78
Jalalabad, 371
Jalaluddin Khalji, 153
Jamahiriya, Libya, 359
Jamal al-din Afghani, 260
James Abbott, British administrator in India, 371
James Giffen, 389
James 'Mad Dog' Mattis, 417
Japan, 328–29, 336, 357, 374–75, 404, 407, 418
Japanese, 245, 374–75, 385, 391
Jats, 193
Jawhar, Sicilian general in Egypt, 85
Jebel Tarik, Gibraltar, 105–6
Jeddah, 271–72
Jehangir Karamat, Pakistani general, 365
Jelme, general of Genghis Khan, 125, 128–29
Jemal, member of the Young Turk triumvirate, 245
Jem, b/o Salim the Grim, Ottoman Sultan, 221

JeM (Jaish e Muhammad), militant Islamist group, 371
Jerusalem, 5, 12, 23, 47, 83–84, 93, 95–97, 235, 323, 405
Jewish, 5, 7–10, 33, 70, 89, 121, 232, 264, 307, 315, 348
Jews, 7, 23, 26, 75, 87, 105, 117, 119–21, 219, 244, 405, 417
Jihad 6, 49, 51, 79, 81, 168, 192, 206, 265, 267, 296, 363, 370, 393, 409–11
Jiluwi, cousin of Abdul Aziz ibn Saud, 268–69, 272
Jin dynasty of China, 130
Jinnah, Founder of Pakistan, 299–304, 310, 312, 362, 371
Jizya, tax on non-Muslims, 19
Joanna, 'The Mad', d/o Ferdinand & Isabella, 120, 227
Joanne, Sister of King Richard of England, 97
Jochi, eldest son of Genghis Khan, 139
Jodhpur 216, 228
John Foster Dulles, US secretary of state, 333
John Hunyadi, 217
John Roosa, author, 379
Josephine, w/o Napoleon, 238, 252–53
Juan, s/o Ferdinand and Isabella, 120
Julian, Count, Spanish general, 52, 105
Julius Caesar, 98
Juzjani, historian, 150

Kaaba, 2, 12, 45–46, 49, 63, 66, 85
Kabul, 30, 166–70, 175, 180, 183, 193, 212, 277, 279–280, 284–87, 289
Kafiristan, 287
Kafur, Abu al-Misk, powerful Egyptian eunuch, 84–85, 156–57
Kaikobad, ruler of the Slave Dynasty of India, 153
Kaiser Willhelm II, 245
Kalinjar, fortress in India, 175
Kamran, b/o Mogul emperor Humayun, 169–70, 282

Kanauj, Battle of, 173
Kandahar, 170, 183-84, 187, 193, 201, 206, 209, 277-78, 284
Kara, 236-37
Karachaganak
Karachaganak, oil deposits in Kazakhstan, 387
Karachi, 300, 365
Karakorum, 136
Kara Mustafa, Ottoman grand vizier, 236-37
Karbala, 39, 45-46, 49, 58, 266, 339, 344
Kargil, 365
Karim Khan Zand, Persian ruler, 292
Karimov, President of Uzbekistan, 382-85
Karshi Khanabad Air Base in Uzbekistan, 385
Kashagen, oil deposits in Kazakhstan, 387
Kashani, 332, 334
Kashgar, 392
Kashmir, 179, 187-88, 212, 279, 371
Kazakh, 284, 386-88
Kazakhgate, 389
Kazakhs, 386-87
Kazakhstan, 76, 135, 284, 382, 386-89
Kazgan, patron of young Timur, 138
Kazhegeldin, Kazakhstan opposition politician, 388-89
Kemal, 18, 246-48
Kennedy, Robert F., 378
Kenya, 389, 397
Kerman, 50, 293
Kermit Roosevelt, CIA agent in Iran, 333-34
Khadija w/o The Prophet, 3, 7, 9
Khair al-Din Barbarossa, Ottoman admiral, 225-26
Khairallah, uncle of Saddam, 345-46
Khakhan, Khan of Khans, 134-36
Khaleda Zia, Begum, Bangladeshi President, 413

Khalid bin Waleed, 8, 10
Khalid ibn Musaid, Saudi prince, 327, 329
Khalid Mohieddin, Egyptian Free Officer, 318
Khalid the Barmakid, 60
Khan Network, of Dr A.Q. Khan, Pakistani nuclear scientist, 369
Khanua, Battle of, 168
Khanzada, sister of Emperor Babur, 165
Kharadar, Karachi district, 300
Kharijites, 34, 37, 55, 411
Khayzuran, w/o Ababsid Caliph al-Mahdi, 61-62
Khedive of Egypt, 259-62
Khizr Khan, founder of Sayyid Dynasty of the Delhi Sultanate, 161
Khudabanda
Khudabanda, Safavid ruler in Persia, 201-3
Khurasan, 45, 49-50, 56-57, 59, 61, 63, 65, 70, 74, 77, 199, 206, 209-10, 279
Khurram, aka Emperor Shah Jahan, 182-83
Khusrau Mirza, s/o Mogul emperor Jahangir, 182
Khusrav Khan, slave of degenerate Khilji, Sultan Mubarak, 157
Khwarezm Shah, 79, 130, 150
Kiazim, lieutenant of Ataturk, 247
Kiev, 130
King Abdul Aziz, 241-43, 255, 264, 267-73, 275, 323-24
King Abdullah University in Saudi Arabia, 273
Kingdom of Castile, 120
Kingdom of Saudi Arabia, 270, 274-75, 310, 351, 403
King Faisal of Saudi Arabia, 244, 312-13, 323, 328, 344, 396, 405
King Farouk of Egypt, 263, 298, 313-14
King Fuad of Egypt, 262, 314
King Idris of Libya, 354
King John of England, 118

King Philip III, of Spain, 123
King Philip of Macedon, f/o Alexander, 138
King Roderic, Visigoth king of Spain, 52
King Saud, of Saudi Arabia, 319
Kirghizstan, 382
Kissinger, Henry, American statesman, 328, 405
Kitbuqa, 100, 135–36
Kleber, Napoleonic general in Egypt, 253
Klu Klux Klan, 396
Kohinoor diamond, 170, 193, 278–79
Koprulu, family of Ottoman grand vizier, 235–38
Korea, 129–30, 362, 369
Kosem Sultan, Ottoman, 233–4
Kosovo, 215, 413
KPMG financial consultants, 407
Kublai Khan, 145, 391
Kufa, 25, 31–32, 35, 37, 41, 43–44, 46, 48, 58
Kukoi Sanyang of Gambia, 356
Kurds, 125, 345, 349, 351–52
Kuriltai, Mongolian tribal council, 132
Kuwait, 268–69, 271, 312, 325, 346, 350–52, 403–4, 406–7
Kuyuk, 134
Kyrgyzstan, 389–90

Ladli Begum, aka Mihr-un-nissa, d/o Mogul Empress Nur Jahan, 182–83
Lady Mountbatten, Edwina, 304
Lady Willingdon, 301
Lahore, 82, 168, 171, 181, 212, 279, 303, 364
Lake Nasser, 321
Lashkar i Jhangvi, Sunni anti-Shia jihadist organization in Pakistan, 370
Las Navas de Tolosa, Battle of, 118
Laurent Kabila of Zaire, 356
Lawrence of Arabia, 271
Layla, mother of Umar II, 54

Lebanon, 35, 310
Lee Rigby, British soldier murdered by Islamic extremists, 394
Lenin, Vladimir, 5, 145, 310, 339, 381, 383
Leo Africanus
Leo Africanus, Berber Andalusia diplomat and author, 399
Leonardo Da Vinci, 72
Leon, Spanish kingdom, 70, 115
Lepanto, Battle of, 235
Lesley Hazleton, author, 3
LeT (Lashkar e Taiba), Islamic militant organization in Pakistan, 371
Liaquat Ali Khan, Pakistani prime minister, 302
Libya, 51, 117, 312–13, 325, 328, 350, 353, 355–61, 369, 398–99, 404
Libyan Islamic Fighting Group, 358
Lincoln's Inn, London, 300
Line of Control, military control line dividing Kashmir, 365
Lion of the Punjab, Ranjit Singh, 168
Lithuania, 284
LNG, liquefied natural gas, 381
Lodhi dynasty, 161
London, 71–72, 140, 300, 302, 347, 349, 386, 394–95
Lord Auckland, British governor-general in India, 283–85
Lord Crewe, British politician, 264
Lord Cromer, British consul-general in Egypt, 261, 414
Lord Mountbatten, last viceroy of India, 304
Lord Palmerston, British prime minister, 197
Lord Rothschild, British financial mogul, 259, 264
Lord Salisbury, British politician, 300
Lord Willingdon, British governor of Bombay, 301
Louis Farrakhan, leader of Nation of Islam in USA, 357, 360, 395

Louis IX, King of France, 97
Lucknow, 197
Ludhiana, 285
Lundi, city in Africa, 399

Ma'arra, Siege of city in the First Crusade, 23
Machiavelli, Niccolò, Italian diplomat and writer, 44, 71, 251, 254
Macnaghten, bureaucrat in British India, 283–84
madrassa, 116, 393
Madrid, 123, 394
Mafia, 59, 346, 379
Maghreb, 85, 99
Mahabat Khan, prominent Mogul general, 184–86
Maham Anaga, foster mother of Emperor Akbar, 176–77
Maharaja Scindia of Gwalior, 194
Mahdi, Abbasid Caliph s/o Mansur, 61–62
Mahdi of Sudan, Muhammad Ahmad, 399
Mahd-i Ulya, title for the mother of the Shah in Persia, 202
Mahmoud Abdul Latif, member of Muslim Brotherhood in Egypt, 319
Mahmud of Ghazni, 69, 81, 148
Mahmud s/o Mirwais 209–10
Mahmud the Reformer, Ottoman Sultan, 238
Maimonides, medieval Jewish philosopher, 70
Major Frank Holmes, first Saudi oil concession, 273
Major-General Iftikhar, Pakistani general, 366
Major Gerald Talbot, British businessman in Persia, 295
Malacca, Straits of, 207
Malala Yusafzai, Pakistani activist and Nobel Laureate, 414
Malaysia, 310, 312

Malcolm X, leader of Black Americans, 395–97
Mali, 399, 413
Malik Ayaz, King of Lahore, 82
Malik Mahmud, father-in-law of the Emperor Nader Shah, 211
Malik Mohsin, Governor of Kabul under Bachey Saqao, 289
Malik Shah, Seljuk Sultan, 82
Malta, 229
Mameluk, slave dynasty in Egypt 222
Mamun, 7th Abbasid caliph, s/o Harun al-Rashid, 62–67, 68, 72, 74–77, 84
Mandela, Nelson, South African President, 353, 357, 360, 368
Man Singh, Raja of Amber, general of Emperor Akbar, 179
Mao Zedong, 94, 321
Maqbul Khan, vizier of Firoz Shah Tughlak, 159
Maraj al debaj, Battle of, 22
Maratha, 192, 194, 280
Maratha Empire, 280
Marathas, 192–94, 212, 279–80, 309
Marble Arch, 395
Margaret of Austria, 120
Maria, d/o Ferdinand and Isabella, 120
Maria the Copt, w/o The Prophet, 10
Marj Dabij, Battle of, 102
Mark Antony, Roman general, 98, 253
Martial Law, 262, 304, 315, 320, 340, 398
Martinique, 238
Mathematics, 65, 67, 70, 246, 391
Mattei, Enrico, Italian oil magnate, 404
Mawlana Mawdudi, Pakistani religious scholar, 410
Maxim gun, 256, 305, 309
Maximillian, Holy Roman Emperor, 120
Maymuna, w/o The Prophet, 10
Mecca, 1–8, 11–12, 15–16, 22, 29–31, 44–49, 58, 61, 63–65, 84–85, 89, 97, 170–71, 177, 209, 222, 255, 266–67,

269–72, 274, 277, 391–93, 396, 398, 409–10
Medicine, 64, 67–69, 75, 385, 391
Medieval India, 21, 150
Medina, 2, 4–5, 7–8, 11–12, 14–16, 25, 27–32, 35, 41, 44–46, 49, 58–60, 63, 65, 76, 84–85, 222, 255, 265–67, 270–71, 410–12
Mediterranean, 68, 225–27, 247, 307, 401
Mediterranean Africa, 85, 398
Meerut, 195–96
Megawati Sukarnoputri, President of Indonesia, 413
Megrahi, Libyan Intelligence officer convicted for Lockerbie air crash, 361
Mehmed Ali Pasha, Khedive of Egypt, 238
Mehmed IV, 234
Mehmed the Conqueror, Ottoman Sultan, 214, 220, 240
Mehrunnisa, aka Nur Jahan, w/o Mogul Emperor Jahangir, 183
Merv, city in Central Asia, 30, 57, 65–66, 199
Meshed, city in Persia, 204, 206, 209, 211, 279
Michael Flynn, anti-Iran hardliner, aide of President Donald Trump, 417
Michael Jackson, American singer and entertainer, 359
Middle East, 69, 86, 99, 130, 135, 137, 143, 247, 262, 312–13, 321–22, 326, 328, 346, 352, 357–58, 361, 395, 402–4, 417–18
Midhat Pasha, Ottoman states man and vizier, 242–43
Mien Hessels, girlfriend of the young Sukarno, 374
Mike Pompeo, Trump's CIA Director, 417
Ming dynasty of China, 145
Miranshah, s/o Timur, 142

Mirs of Sindh, 280
Mir Sultan, interior minister of the Iron Amir, Abdur Rahman, 287
Mirwais, 209, 277–78
Mirza Ghiyas Beg, aka Itimad ud-Daula, father of Empress Nur Jahan, 182
Mirza-ye Shirazi, Irani religious scholar who issues a fatwa against smoking, 295
Mobil, major oil company, 404
Moghira
Moghira, shrewd early Muslim, governor of Kufa, 34
Mogul Emperor Akbar, 203
Mogul India, 117, 191
Moguls, 72, 77, 117, 162–63, 167–68, 171–73, 179, 183–84, 186–87, 192–94, 198, 203, 206, 277–79, 306, 309
Mohammad Mossadeq, 330–6
Mohammad Reza Shah Pahlavi of Iran, 330, 404
Mohan Lal, 281
Mongke Khan, grandson of Genghis Khan, 77, 99, 133–6
Mongolia, 129, 391
Mongols, 77, 79–80, 84, 100–1, 125–27, 130–31, 136, 139, 141–42, 151–52, 155–58, 391
Montazeri, *See* Ayatollah
Moors, 123
Morea, Peloponese peninsula in southern Greece, 256
Morgan Shuster, American financial consultant in Persia, 296
Moriscos, Muslims in Spain forced into converting to Christianity, 122–23
Moroccans, 393
Morocco, 51, 109, 112, 116–17, 313, 347, 356, 399
Moro Liberation Front, 357
Mortimer Durand, civil servant in British India, 286
Moscow, 77, 129–30, 321, 377, 382–85

Mossadeq, 312, 328, 331–35, 338, 340–41, 357, 404
Mossadeq's National Front, 332, 340
Mountbattens, *See* Lord Mountbatten
Mount Uhud, mountain north of Medina, 7
Moussa Koussa, Libyan foreign minister, 360
Mozaffar Shah, Qajar ruler in Persia, 295
Mozarabs, Christians in Muslim Spain who adopted Arabic culture, 122
Muawiya, Umayyad caliph, 12, 24, 27, 31, 34–47, 51, 107
Mubarak al-Sabah, ruler of Kuwait, 268
Muhajireen, first Muslims who emigrated with The Prophet from Mecca to Medina, 15
Muhammad Ali Jinnah, 299
Muhammad Ali Pasha of Egypt, 239–41, 251
Muhammad Ali, world champion heavy weight boxer, 255
Muhammad bin Abu Bakr, 27, 35
Muhammad bin Qasim, 50
Muhammad bin Saud, 255
Muhammad bin Tughluq, Sultan in Delhi, 158
Muhammad ibn Abdul Wahhab, founder of the Wahhabi movement, 265
Muhammad ibn Saud, 265–66
Muhammad ibn Tugh al-Ikhshid, Abbasid governor and ruler of Egypt, 84
Muhammad III al-Mustafki, Umayyad caliph in Cordoba, 114
Muhammad Shah, Mogul emperor defeated by Nader Shah of Persia, 212
Muhammad XII, Sultan of Granada, 119
Muharram, 46
Muizz, 4th Fatimid caliph, 85–86

Mujahedeen, 342
Mujahedeen e Khalq, Iranian Marxist political organization, 342
Mullah Omar, Taliban leader, 364
Multan, 40, 50, 142
Mumbai, 369
Mumtaz Mahal, aka Arjumand, w/o Emperor Shah Jahan, 182–83, 186
Muntasir, Abbasid caliph in Baghdad, 78, 85, 87, 89–91
Muqtadir, 18th Abbasid caliph, 62, 78–79
Murad Bakhsh, s/o Emperor Shah Jahan, 186
Murad I, Ottoman Sultan, s/o Orhan, 215, 234
Murad II, Ottoman Sultan, 216, 229
Murad III, Ottoman Sultan, 216, 229
Murad IV, Ottoman Sultan, 216, 234
Murad V, Ottoman Sultan, 216, 242
Murtaza Bhutto, 363
Musa bin Nusayr, Umayyad governor of North Africa, 40, 51
Muscat, 399
Musharraf, Pervez
Musharraf, Pervez, General, former president of Pakistan, 365
Muslim, 5, 7–10, 13, 15, 17–18, 20–27, 30–31, 41, 43–44, 49–50, 52–54, 56–57, 59, 67–70, 72, 75, 79, 81–83, 85, 89, 95–96, 99, 102, 104–6, 109, 111–13, 115, 117–23, 130, 136–37, 139, 148, 157, 160, 179–80, 187, 190–91, 194–96, 203, 206, 208, 212, 222, 226, 236–37, 243–45, 250, 252, 261, 263, 265, 271, 275, 294, 299–303, 305–10, 312, 315, 319, 357–58, 363, 369, 371, 373, 378, 381–82, 391–99, 401, 405, 408–11, 413–15, 417–18
Muslim Brotherhood, 263, 315, 319, 409
Muslim League, 300, 369
Muslim Republics of Central Asia, 381
Mustafa II, Ottoman Sultan, 237

Mustain, 78
Mustaqfi, 22nd Abbasid caliph, 79
Mutahdi, 14th Abbasid caliph, 78
Mutair, Saudi tribe, 274
Mutasim, 8th Abbasid caliph, 76–78
Mutassim s/o Gaddafi, 359–60
Mutawakil, 10th Abbasid caliph, 78
Mutawakkil, last Abbasid caliph in Egypt 68, 81
Mutazilites, school of theology in Basra and Baghdad in 8th to 10th centuries, 75, 77
Mu'tazz, 13th Abbasid Caliph, 62
Mutiny, Indian, aka The War of Independence, 196
Muttaqi, 21st Abbasid Caliph, 79
Muyyad, b/o Ababsid Caliph, 78
Muzaffar al Din Shah, Qajar ruler in Persia, 402

Nader Shah, Persian emperor and conqueror, 168, 187, 193, 210–18, 277–79, 281, 292–93, 309
Nadhlatul Ulama, Indonesian Sunni movement with million members, 378
Nadir Khan Afghan leader, 288, 290
Naguib, General, Egyptian President, 314, 316–19, 324
Nahas Pasha, Egyptian prime minister, 263
Naila, w/o Caliph Uthman, 33
Najaf, 338–39
Nanking, 391
NASAKOM, Sukarno's political concept, 376
Naser al-Din Shah, Qajar ruler in Persia, 294
Nasi, bootlegger of Salim the Sot, 232
Nasr ibn Harun, Christian vizier of Buyid Sultan, 81
Nassiri, General, head of SAVAK under the Shah, 334–35, 337
National Reconciliation Ordinance of

Musharraf, 368
The Nation of Islam, American Black Muslim movement, 396
Nawaz Sharif, Pakistani prime minister, 364, 369, 372
Nazarbayev, Kazakhstan President, 387–89
Nazi Germany, 121
Neauphle-le-Chateau, town in France, temporary home of Ayatollah Khomeini, 339
Nehru, Jawaharlal, Indian prime minister, 303–4, 319, 376
Nejd, 265–66, 269–70, 272
Neville Wadia, son-in-law of Muhammad Ali Jinnah, 301
New Zealand, 246–47, 273
Nile River, 86, 99
Nilofer, w/o Ottoman Sultan Orhan, 215
NIOC, National Iranian Oil Company, 332, 335, 340
Nixon, *See* President Nixon
Niyazov, Saparmurat, former President of Turkmenistan, 385–6
Nizam al-Mulk, 71, 74, 82
Nizamiyah of Baghdad, 112
Nizamnama, code of King Amanullah in Afghanistan, 288
Nobel Peace Prize, 414
Nobels, European business dynasty, 402
Nokrashy, 315
North Africa, 12, 27, 40, 45, 51–52, 80, 85, 100, 105, 111, 113, 117, 225–26, 262, 313, 392
Northern China, 130
North Korea, 369
Norway, 393
Nubia, 100
Nuclear Proliferation Treaty, NPT, 418
Nuqrashi, Egyptian prime minister, 263
Nur al-Din, ruler of Syria under the Seljuks, 91
Nurbank, large Kazakh bank, 388

Nurbano, w/o Ottoman Sultan Salim the Sot, 230, 232
Nuri Said, Anglophile prime minister of Iraq, 345
Nuristan, formerly Kafiristan, 287
Nur Jahan, w/o Mogul Emperor Jahangir, 179, 182–86
Nursultan Nazarbayev, President Kazakhestan, 382, 386

Obeidallah s/o Caliph Umar, 30
Odysseus, 43
Ogedei Khan, third son of Genghis Khan, 132–4
Omar Khayyam, Persian mathematician, philosopher and poet, 24, 36, 71
Omar Mukhtar, Libyan freedom fighter, 399
Omar Shaykh, s/o Timur, 142
Omar the Great, 187
One Thousand and One Nights, 20, 60, 64
Ong Khan, ally of Genghis Khan, 128–29
OPEC, Organization of the Petroleum Exporting Countries, 325–26, 328, 335–46, 357, 404
Operation Ajax, CIA coup in Iran to restore the Shah, 334
Orhan, early Ottoman Sultan, 215
Oriana Fallaci, author, 360
Osama bin Laden, founder of al-Qaeda, 93, 364, 370
Osman, founder of the Ottoman dynasty, 215, 233
Ottoman Bayezid, 199
Ottoman Empire, 102, 143, 149, 214, 216, 222, 231, 235, 240, 243–44, 256–57, 344

Pahlavi Foundation, 336
Pahlavis, Dynasty in Iran, 296
Pak-China, 368, 370
Pakistan, 81, 283, 286, 299–300, 302–4, 310, 362–64, 367–72, 386, 389–90, 406, 413–14, 418
Pakistan Peoples Party (PPP), 364
Pakistan Resolution, 303
Palestine, 20, 23, 35, 80, 264, 322–23, 333, 357
Panama leaks, 372
Pan-Arabism, 321, 323, 345
Panipat, Battles of (I: Babur defeats Lodhis; II: Akbar defeats Hemu; III: Afghans defeat Marathas), 162, 168, 176, 279
Pari Khanum, Safavid princess and temporary de facto ruler, 202
Paris, 69, 71–72, 252–53, 288, 297, 302, 339–41
Parviz, Mogul Prince, 184–85
Pashtunwali, 364
Patriarch Sophronius, 23
Patrick Cockburn, 361
Patriot Act of America, 398
Paul, Czar of Russia, 294
Pauline Foures, Napoleon's mistress in Egypt, 252
Payindah Khan, f/o Amir Dost Mohammad Khan, 282
Persia, 21, 25, 41, 45, 83, 94, 101, 125, 129–30, 135–36, 140, 166, 168–70, 187, 200, 203, 206, 210–12, 222, 228, 277, 279, 281–82, 292–98, 309, 332
Persian Empire, 12
Persian Gulf, 207, 271, 336
Persians, 1–2, 24–25, 50, 55, 57, 65, 77, 79–80, 184, 187, 193, 201, 209, 252, 265, 278–79, 306
Pertamina, Indonesian oil company, 380
Peter the Great, Czar of Russia, 210–11, 238
Petit, Sir Dinshaw, father-in law of Muhammad Ali Jinnah, 301
Philip II, anti-Muslim Spanish King, 115, 123

Piali, Ottoman admiral, 229
Pir Mohammad, grandson of Timur, 146
Plato, Greek philosopher, 68
PLO, Palestine Liberation Organization, 322
PNI, Partai Nasional Indonesia, 374
Pompey, Roman military and political leader, 112
Pope Leo X, aka Giovanni Di Lorenzo De Medici, 399
Portugal, 120, 306, 309
Portuguese, 102, 189, 207, 399
President Bush, George W., 245, 284, 366
President Carter, Jimmy, 406
President Clinton, Bill, 365
President Gaddafi, *See* Gaddafi
President Ghulam Ishaq, of Pakistan, 364–65
President Nixon, Richard, 328–9, 380, 418
President Obama, Barack, 371
President Rajai of Iran, 342
President Reagan, Ronald, 353
President Sukarno of Indonesia, *See* Sukarno
President Trump, 398, 417–18
President Yudhoyono of Indonesia, 381
Prime Minister Nokrashy of Egypt, 315
Prime Minister Shaukat Aziz of Pakistan, 367
The Prince, 44, 71, 134, 251
Prince Abdullah, later King of Saudi Arabia, 326
Prince Faisal ibn Musaid, assassin of King Faisal, 329
Prince Mahdi, 61
Prince Mahmud, Durrani, King of Afghanistan, 281
Princess Ashraf of Iran, 330, 334
Princess Fawzia of Egypt, 330
Prophet Muhammad, 1–18, 20, 24, 27, 29–31, 34–35, 37, 39, 42–43, 45–46, 49, 55, 57–58, 67–68, 80, 83, 98, 103, 109–10, 136, 160–61, 184, 190, 199, 206, 222, 265–66, 270, 276, 305, 307, 339, 393, 398, 408–14
Prussia, 241
Ptolemy, Greek mathematician, 68
Punjab, 168, 197, 279, 364, 368, 370
Puran Mal, Hindu Raja, enemy of Sher Shah Suri, 174
Pure Soul, Muhammad, great grandson of Hasan bin Ali, 59–60
Putin, Vladimir, President of Russia, 383, 395

Qabiya, Ottoman Sultana Valida, 62
Qadi al-Numan al-Tamimi, historian, 86
Qadisiya, battle of, 24
Qahiba, Ottoman Sultana Valida, 78
Qahir, 19th Abbasid Caliph in Baghdad, 79
Qajar, Persian dynasty, 293, 296–97, 330–31
Qalawun, Mamluk general in Egypt, 101
Qanun, the Law of Ibn Sina, 69
Qarmatians
Qarmatians, renegade sect which sacked the holy cities, 85
Qatar, 394, 402, 404
Qatr al-Nada, 'Dewdrop', Egyptian princess, 84
Qaynuqa, Jewish tribe in Medina, 7
Qazvin, Persian city, 203
Qing dynasty of China, 391
Qizilbash, warriors in Safavid Iran, 200–5
Qum, city in Iran, 337, 339
Quran, The holy, 3, 9–10, 13, 30, 32, 36–37, 47, 49, 65, 69, 75, 145, 151, 160, 217, 220, 284, 323, 326, 354, 409, 412
Quraysh, The Falcon of the, Abd al Rahman in Spain, 107, 411

INDEX | 453

Quresh, dominant tribe in Mecca in the 17th century, 15
Qureyz, Jewish tribe in Medina, 8–9
Qutayba bin Muslim, Umayyad commander and governor of Khurasan, 49
Qutb, Syed, Egyptian Islamic intellectual, 409
Qutbuddin Aybek, founder of the Slave Dynasty of the Delhi Sultanate, 148–50
Qutuz, Mamluk Sultan in Egypt, 99–100

Rafsanjani, Akbar Hashemi, Irani politician, 341, 344
Raheel Sharif, Pakistani general, 368, 370
Raja Jai Singh, Hindu general of the Moguls in India, 190
Raja Jaswant Singh, ruler of Marwar in Mogul India, 190
Raja Puran Mal, Rajput ruler in Mogul India, See Puran Mal
Rajput, 168, 179, 191
Rakhat Aliyev, Kazakh politician and son-in-law of President Nazarbayev, 388
Rakmonov, President of Tajikistan, 390
Raleigh, Sir Walter, 306
Rana Sanga, King of Mewar in Mogul India, 167–68
Ranjit Singh, 283
Ranjit Singh, leader of the Sikh Empire, 168, 282, 284
Rashid al-Din Sinan, aka 'The Old man of the Mountain' Ismaili assassin leader, 93
Rashidian Brothers, British agents in the 1953 coup in Iran, 334
Rashidov, Communist Party leader in Uzbekistan, 384
Rastakhiz, party in Iran, 336
Raushanara, d/o of Mogul Emperor Shah Jahan, 186, 188
Raytheon, major US defence contractor, 324
Rayy, old Persian city, 65
Razia Sultan, d/o Iltutmish in India, 413
Razmara, 332
RCC, Egypt Revolutionary Command Council, 318–19, 347, 349
Respublica newspaper, 389
Revolutionary Guards, Iran, 343
Reza Khan Pahlavi of Iran, 296–7
Reza Shah, 298, 312, 330–31, 404
Reza Shah Pahlavi, 292, 297, 310
Ridda Wars, 16–17, 28
Riyadh, 265–69, 272
Robin Hood, 289
Rockefeller, John D., 402
Roderick, Visigoth King of Spain, 105
Romanos, Byzantine Emperor, 82
Rome, 1, 113, 252, 334–35, 338
Rommel, German general, 129, 262, 403
Roosevelt, 249, 270, 274–75, 312, 333–35, 376, 404
Roqayya, d/o The Prophet, w/o Caliph Uthman, 7
Rothschilds, Jewish Business dynasty, 402
Royal Dutch, major oil company, 404
Rub al-Khali, Saudi desert, 269
Rubayat of Omar Khayyam, 71
Ruhollah Khomeini, 336–44
Rumaila oil field, 351
Ruqaiya, w/o Akbar the Great, 176
Russia, 129–30, 132, 134–35, 137, 210, 238–41, 247, 282–84, 294–96, 310, 319–21, 324, 339, 369, 377, 387, 389–90, 393, 402, 418
Russian, 145, 223, 225, 247, 277, 283–84, 294, 296, 346, 363, 381–83, 385–87, 395
Russo–Persian Wars, 294
Rustam, Persian general, 24–25

Rustem Pasha, grand vizier and son-in-law of Suleiman the Magnificent, 224, 228, 231
Ruttie, w/o Jinnah, 301–2

Sa'ad bin Abi Waqqas, companion of The Prophet, 24–5
Saad ibn-Muad, 9
Saadi, Persian poet, 360
Saad Zagloul, former Egyptian prime minister, 260, 262
Saddam Husain, 91, 312, 334, 339, 342, 344–53, 397, 401, 407
Sadozai, Pashtun tribe, 281–82
Safari Club, 408
Safavid Sheikh Khwaja Ali, 199
Safavids of Iran, 198
Safiyah, w/o The Prophet, 10
Safiye Baffo, Ottoman Sultana Valida, 232
Said, Egyptian Khedive, 258–9
Saif al Arab, s/o Gaddafi, 360
Saif al Islam, s/o Gaddafi, 359–60
Saints and Sinners, 349
Sajida, w/o Saddam Hussein, 345, 349–50
Saladin, aka Salah ad-Din Yusuf Ibn Ayub, 21, 23, 80, 83–84, 91–97, 99, 101, 252, 345
Salafists, 411
Salima, cousin of Akbar the Great, 176, 181
Salim III, Ottoman sultan, 238
Salim the Grim, Ottoman Sultan, 81, 101–2, 199, 220–21, 227, 251–52
Salim the Sot, Ottoman Sultan, 225, 228–29, 232
Samarkand, 49, 72, 102, 125, 136, 138–41, 145–46, 165–67
Samarra, 77
Sancho the Fat, King of Leon, Spain, 70
Sandinistas of Nicaragua, 357
Saparmurat Niyazov, 382
Saray Khanum, w/o Amir Timur, 139

Sardar Akbar Bugti, 368
Sardinia, 227
Sassanids, 21
Saud, 255, 264–69, 272–75, 312, 319, 324–28
Saud al-Kabir, 267
Saudi Arabia, 244, 255, 264, 270, 272–75, 310, 312–13, 323, 325, 329, 333, 351, 366, 393, 403–5, 407
SAVAK, Irani secret police, 335–37
Sawda, w/o The Prophet, 9
Sayyid
Sayyid, dynasty of India, 161, 295
Sayyid Jamal al-Din Afghani, 295
Scargill, Arthur, 357
SEAL, 'Sea, Air and Land' teams of the US navy, 371
Second Anglo-Afghan War, 285
Second World War, 240, 245, 262, 274, 298, 303, 310, 374, 403
Senegal, 413
Sephronius, Patriarch of Jerusalem, 23–24
Serb, 215
Serbia, 219
Serbian, 231
Seville, 115, 118
Shaban the Brainless, Tehran street-gang leader, 334–35
Shafii, one of the four major schools of Islamic Jurisprudence, 75
Shaghab, powerful grand lady and mother of the Caliph in the Abbasid court, 62
Shah Abbas of Persia, 72, 184, 201, 203–9
Shah Alam II, weak and blinded Mogul Emperor, 193
Shah Alam, last sultan of the Sayyid dynasty in India, 161, 194
Shahbaz Sharif of Pakistan, 20
Shah Hussein, s/o Shah Suleiman, Safavid ruler in Persia, 277
Shah Ismail, Safavid ruler, 166, 200,

221
Shah Jahan, Mogul Emperor, 168, 179, 182–89
Shah Mahmud, 281
Shahnawaz s/o Zulfiqar Ali Bhutto, 363
Shah Reza Khan, 403
Shah Rukh, grandson of Nader Shah, 142, 146, 292–93
Shahryar, youngest son of Mogul Emperor Jahangir, 184–86
Shah Shuja, s/o Mogul Emperor Jahangir, 186, 281–85
Shah Sulayman, Safavid Shah, 209
Shah Tamasp, Safavid Shah, s/o Shah Ismail I, 168, 170, 200, 210–11, 228
Shah Zaman, Afghan King, 281
Shaibani Khan, Uzbek ruler, 165–66, 169, 199
Shaikhally, foreign minister of Iraq under Saddam, 345–48
Shaista Khan, Mogul general, 183
Shajar al Durr, Egypt, second female Muslim monarch in history, 84, 413
Sharia, 243, 267, 288, 298, 307, 336, 408
Sharifs of Mecca, 269
Shaukat Aziz, 367
Shawar, vizier of the Fatimid Caliph during the time of Saladin, 92
Sheikh Ali, Safavid Sheikh, 199
Sheikh Mohammad of Dubai, 20
Sheikh Rashid of Dubai, 343
Sheikh Safi al-Din founder of the Safavids, 198
Sheikh Zahid, Sufi mystic, 198
Sheikh Zayed of Abu Dhabi, 405
Shell, major oil company, 329, 404
Shepherd's Hotel, Cairo, 315
Sher Khan, aka Sher Shah Suri, 169, 172–73
Sherlock Holmes, fictional detective, 242, 245
Sher Shah Suri, 21, 169, 171–75, 201
Shia, 16, 43, 46, 55, 59, 74–75, 79, 81, 84–85, 95, 111, 166–67, 176, 192, 199–201, 203–4, 206, 211–13, 252, 272, 287, 300, 338, 343–44, 351, 371, 402, 418
Shia Buyids, dynasty in Persian, 79
Shia Fatimids, dynasty in Egypt, 111, 252
Shia Hazaras of Mongolia, 287
Shia Safavids
Shia Safavids, Persian dynasty, 206
Shiraz, 140
Shirkuh, uncle of Saladin, 91–92
Shivaji, Maratha warrior king in India, 192
Shuja, Mogul prince, b/o Emperor Aurangzeb, 188–89, 281–82, 285
Shukri Ghanim, Libyan economic administrator, 359
Shukuk ala alinosor, aka *Doubts about Galen*, treatise by al-Razi, 69
Shurahbil, Muslim army commander under Caliphs, Abu Bakr and Umar, 23
Siberian, 387
Sibilla, 274
Sicilian, 85
Sicily, 227
Siffin, Battle of 35, 37
Sikandar, Lodhi, Sultan in India, 161
Sikandra, burial place of Emperor Akbar, 181
Sikhs, 193, 284, 304
Silk Road, 277, 369, 391
Sinai, 329
Sinai Peninsula, 322
Sindh, 50, 179, 212, 279–80, 363
Sindhis, 364
Sir Alexander Burnes, British Intelligence officer in Afghanistan, 283, 285
Sir Dinshaw Petit, father-in-law of Muhammad Ali Jinnah, 301
Sir Ian Hamilton, 247
Sir John Lawrence, British

administrator in India, 168, 197
Sir Lee Stack, 262
Sir Stafford Cripps, British politician, 303
Sir Stratford Canning, British ambassador in Ottoman Turkey, 241
Sirte, city in Libya, 360
Sir William Hay Macnaghten, British administrator in India, 283
Six Day War, 313, 322–23, 328–29
Siyasatnama, of Nizam e Mulk, 70, 82
Siyurkuktiti, aka Princess, w/o Tolui Khan, 132
Slave dynasties, 149
Slave Kings, 149–53
Smyrna, 246
Socal, oil company, 274, 403
Socrates, great philosopher, 133
Sokollu Pasha, 231
Somnath, temple in India, 82
Song dynasty of China, 391
Songhay, Muslim empire in Africa, 399
Soraya, w/o King Amanullah of Afghanistan, 288, 330, 335
Souk al Manakh, financial market in Kuwait, 406
Southern Russia, 100
South India, 309
South Korea, 362
Soviet Union, 336
Spain, 40–41, 51–52, 58, 68, 70, 72, 78, 80, 104–9, 111–23, 226–27, 306, 309, 393, 398–99
Spanish, 105–6, 117–18, 121–23, 204
Spartan, 6
Sri Lanka, 365
Stalin, 246, 324, 346, 348, 382, 386
Stanley Lane-Poole, historian, 88, 147
Steppes, 101
St Helena, 128
St Petersburg, 145
Subha, m/o Saddam, 345
Subh, w/o Caliph al-Hakim of Spain, 112

Subotai, general of Genghis Khan, 125, 127–31, 133
Subuktigin, founder of the Ghaznavid dynasty, 81
Sudan, 89, 116, 243, 255–56, 260, 262, 356, 399
Sudanese, 87, 89, 256
Suez Canal Company, 259, 261, 320
Sufyan, Abu, 7–8, 10–11, 24, 39–40, 43–44
Suharto of Indonesia, 374–75, 378–81
Sukarno, President of Indonesia, 310, 312, 319, 374–79
Suleiman Pasha, French-born general of Muhammad Ali Pasha in Egypt, 257
Suleiman the Magnificent, aka Qanuni, Ottoman Emperor, 122, 201, 208, 220, 222, 225, 240, 242, 307
Sultan Abdul Hamid, Ottoman Caliph, 230, 238, 260
Sultan Ahmed, Ottoman ruler, 233
Sultana Shajar al Durr, Egypt, second female Muslim ruler, 84
Sultana Valida, 61, 149, 151, 230, 235, 238–39
Sultan Buhlul, 161
Sultan ibn Humaid, Saudi rebel chief against King Abdul Aziz ibn Saud, 274
Sultan Mahmud of Ghazni, most prominent ruler of Ghaznavid Empire, 69, 81
Sultan Muhammad Khan, ruler of Bihar in time of Sher Shah Suri, 173
Sultan Nur al-Din, Zenghid ruler of Syrian province of the Seljuk Empire, 92
Sultan of Kilwa Muslim ruler in medieval Africa, 399
Sultan of Oman, 399
Sultan of Tripoli, 226
Sultan of Zanzibar, 399
Sultan Qutuz, Sultan in medieval Egypt at time of Mongol invasion, 99

Sultan Razia, d/o Iltutmis, first female Muslim ruler, 151
Sultan-ul-Adil, the Just Ruler, aka Sher Shah Suri, 173
Sunni, 55, 75, 79, 81, 87, 95, 166, 192, 201, 212, 344, 370-71, 396-97, 402, 418
Sunni-Shia, 75, 402, 418
Sun Tzu, Chinese military strategist and philosopher, 130
Supreme Court of Pakistan, 372
Swat, 414
Sweden, 393-94
Swedish, 384
Swiss, 252, 350, 384, 389
Switzerland, 5, 331
Sword of Allah, aka Khalid bin Waleed, 8, 10, 17
Syed Qutb, Islamic scholar, member of Muslim Brotherhood, 49
Syria, 8, 12, 20, 23, 31, 34-35, 43, 56, 58-59, 66, 80, 85, 91, 93-94, 106, 243, 255-57, 267, 310, 321-22, 325-26, 350, 356, 394, 398, 401-2, 411
Syrian, 45-46, 94, 106, 323

Tabari, *See* al Tabari
Tabriz, 125, 140, 199-200
Tahirids, descendants of Tahir ibn Husayn, 77
Tahir, Tahir Ibn Husayn, Abbasid commander of Caliph al-Mamun, 65-66
Tahrir Square in Cairo, 319
Ta'if, 11, 115, 143, 266, 272, 274
Taifa, independent Muslim principalities in Spain, 116
Tajik, 289
Tajikistan, 383, 389-90
Taj Mahal, 183, 186, 188, 302
Taj Mahal Hotel, 302
Talal, bin Abdulaziz al Saud, Saudi prince, 326
Talas, Battle of, 381

Talat, member of the Young turks triumvirate, 245
Talbot, Major Gerald, British businessman in Persia, 295
Taliban, 77, 121, 363-64, 366-67, 370, 384, 409, 414
Tamasp, *See* Shah Tamasp
Tamerlane, aka Amir Timur, 17, 72, 77, 102, 124-25, 137, 164, 229, 277, 381, 383
Tanker War, Iran-Iraq, 343
Tansu Ciller, 22nd prime minister of Turkey, 413
Tanzania, 397
TAPI, Turkmenistan-Afghanistan-Pakistan-India Pipeline, 386
Tardi Beg, Mogul general in India, 176
Tariki, *See* Abdullah Tariki
Tarzi, Mahmud Beg, Afghan intellectual and foreign minister, 287-88
Tashkent, 145, 385
Tatars, 139, 144
Taufiq, Khedive of Egypt, 259, 261
Taymiyyah, ibn, Sunni theological scholar, inspired Abdul Wahhab, 265, 409
Tehran, 296, 328, 333, 340, 404
Tehran Agreement, 328
Tehran University, 340
Tel el Kabir, Battle of, 261
Theodora, Byzantine princess, w/o Ottoman Orhan, 215
Third World, 102, 155, 262, 319, 321, 344, 348, 362, 376, 398, 406
The Thirty Year War, 307
Tibet, 392
Tikrit, city in Iraq, 91, 345-46, 349
Timbuktu, 399
Time magazine, 329, 331, 378
Timur, 17, 137-46, 160-61, 165, 196, 199, 216, 280-82, 383
Timurids, 166
Timurtash, minister of Reza Shah of Persia, 297

Tito, Yugoslavian President, 319
Todar Mal, finance minister of Mogul Emperor Akbar, 179
Toghrul, *See* Ong Khan
Toktamish, Descendant of Genghis Khan, Chief of the Blue Horde, 139–42
Toledo, city in Spain, 109
Tolui, s/o Genghis Khan, 132
Topkapi, palace of the Ottomans, 214, 219
Torquemada, first Grand Insquisitor of Spain, 120
Tours, Battle of, 53, 106
Trans-Arabian Pipeline, 328
Transjordan, 271
Transoxonia, 49
Treaty of Lausanne, 248
Trigonometry, 70
Tripoli, 27, 235, 354, 356, 360
Truman, Harry S. US President, 331
Trump, Donald, *See* President Trump
TTP, militant terrorist organization in Pakistan, 367–68, 370, 409
Tudeh Communist Party of Iran, 340
Tulip Revolution in Kyrgyzstan, 390
Tunis, 252
Tunisia, 51, 111, 117, 356, 360
Turakina, w/o Ogadei Khan, 134
Turk, 79, 87, 91, 100, 125, 257, 262, 391
Turkestan, 130, 392
Turkey, 76, 135, 198, 208, 240–41, 246, 248–50, 260, 276, 287, 297, 313, 338, 413
Turki ibn Abdallah, founder of the second Saudi Kingdom, 268
Turkish, 76–79, 81, 87, 89–91, 97, 111, 113, 149, 214–15, 219, 226, 229, 239–42, 247–49, 260, 284, 287, 314, 338
Turkish War of Independence, 248
Turkistan, 245
Turkmenistan, 76, 135, 382, 385–86

Turkoman Qizilbash, 201
Turks, 55, 69, 76–81, 89–91, 103, 139, 141, 143, 157, 205–7, 210–11, 222, 225–26, 236–37, 239–40, 244, 246, 256, 262, 265, 269–71, 392–93
Two-Nation Theory, 303–6

UAE, United Arab Emirates, 407
UAR, United Arab Republic, 321
Ubaidullah al Mahdi Billah, founder of the Fatimid dynasty in Egypt, 85
Ubaydallah bin Ziad, governor of Iraq, 46
Udaipuri Mahal, Hindu wife of the Mogul Emperor Aurangzeb, 190
Uday, eldest son of Saddam, 349–50, 352
Uhud, Battle of, 7–8, 11, 17, 35
Ulayyah, sister of Abbasid Harun al-Rashid, 64
Ulugh Beg, 146, 385
Umar II, Umayyad Caliph, great grandson of second Caliph, Umar ibn Al-Khitab, 40, 54
Umayyad dynasty, 24, 39, 45, 47, 58, 110
Um Kulthum, d/o The Prophet 21,
Umm Habiba, d/o The Prophet, 7, 413
Umm Kalthoum, International famous Egyptian singer, 327, 354
Umm Kulthum, d/o Caliph Ali, w/o Caliph Umar, 20
Umm Salama, w/o The Prophet, 9
UNESCO, 348
United Kingdom (UK), 247, 333, 335, 369, 392, 398
UN, United Nations, 323, 332, 342, 348, 358, 360, 377–78
Uqba bin Nafi, Arab general serving the Rashidun and Umayyad caliphs, 21, 27, 40, 51
Urabi, *See* Colonel Urabi
Urumchi

INDEX | 459

Urumchi, capital of Xianjiang, Northwest China, 392
USA, 321, 323, 326, 328–29, 335–36, 351, 359–60, 364, 376–77, 384, 396–97, 418
US–Afghan war, 386
US army, 352, 371, 397
US embargo, 342
US Embassy, 341, 394
Usmanli, aka Ottoman, 237
US SEAL, *See* SEAL
USSR, 76–77, 310, 346, 358, 363, 381–83, 385–87, 391, 393, 409, 418
USS Stark, American navy frigate, 343
USS Vincennes, American navy guided missile cruiser, 343, 361
Uyghur, Turkish ethnic group in Central Asia and northwest China, 392
Uzbek Beys, 280
Uzbekistan, 76, 135, 260, 382–85
Uzbeks, 175, 199–200, 203, 205–6, 211, 383–85
Uzbek–Safavid war, 206

Valencia, 118
Vasco da Gama, Portuguese explorer, 102
Velayat e faqih, Rule of the Jurists in Iran, 339, 342
Venezuela, 325, 333
Venice, 219
Vienna, 236–37, 359, 388
Vietnam, 397
Vinnell Corporation US military supplies company, 324
Visigoths Germanic tribe, medieval ruler in Spain, 52
Vitkevich, 284

Wafd Party, 262–63
Wahhab, *See* Ibn Abdul Wahhab
Wahshi, killer of Hamza, 8, 11–12, 18
The Wailing Wall in Jerusalem, 405

Waldorf Astoria Hotel, 326
Walid ibn Uqba, b/o Caliph Uthman, governor of Kufa, 31
Walid II, 55
Wallada, Andalusian princess and poetess, 114
War of Independence, 196
War on Terror, 362–372
Washington, 328, 347, 351, 365, 405
Water Carrier, 289
Waterloo, 23, 210
Wathiq, Abbasid caliph, 78
Waziristan, 367
Wellington, Duke, Arthur Wellesley, defeated Napoleon at Waterloo, 23, 238
Western Europe, 53
West Papua, 379
White Revolution, Irani reforms of Shah Mohammad Reza Pahlavi, 337
William Hodson, British major of cavalry during Indian Mutiny, 197
Winston Churchill, 274, 310, 331, 344
Wives of the Prophet, 9–11
WMD, Weapons of Mass Destruction, 401
World Bank, 362, 377, 389
World Trade Centre, 358, 366, 397
World War, 245–46, 261, 264, 270–71, 287, 301, 303, 311–12, 322, 344

Ximenes de Cisneros, grand inquisitor of Spain, 120–21
Xinjiang, autonomous territory in Northwest China, 391–92

Yacub, Abbasid vizier, 61, 86, 285
Yamani, Ahmed Zaki, Saudi oil minister, 326, 328–29
Yamuna, river in India, 153
Yaqub ibn Killis, converted Jew, Fatimid finance minister, 86
Yarmuk, Battle of, 17, 22
Yassa, secret code of law of Genghis

Khan, 127, 131–32, 134
Yasser Arafat, former chairman of PLO, 313
Yathrib aka Medina, 2
Yawaddud, talented and expensive slave girl, 64
Yazdegerd, early Persian ruler, 25
Yazdi, historian of Timur, 137
Yazid bin Muhallab, Umayyad governor, brother-in-law of Hajjaj, 50–1
Yazid II, s/o Abd al Malik, 55
Yazid III, 1st Caliph born of slave mother, s/o Walid, 55
Yeliu Chutsai, Principal advisor to Genghis Khan, 131, 133
Yemen, 107, 310, 326–28, 360
Yesugai, f/o Genghis Khan, 126, 129
Yildiz, 244–45
Yom Kippur War, 328–29, 404
Young Turks, political reform movement in Turkey, 244
Yuan Dynasty, Mongol dynasty in China, 136, 145
Yuri Churbanov, son-in-law of Leonid Breshnev, 384
Yusuf ibn Tashfin, Moroccan Almoravid leader, 115–16

Zab, Battle of, 56
Zade Koprulu, Ottomon grand vizier, 237
Zagloul, 262
Zahedi, 333–35
Zainabadi Begum, aka Hirabai, Hindu dancing girl, love of Emperor Aurangzeb, 190
Zainab Begum, Aunt of Shah Abbas, Safavid emperor, 206
Zainab, w/o Abu Bakr Ibn Umar, Almoravid general, 116, 206, 412
Zaman, Shah, Durrani Afghan King, 281
Zam Zam water from Zamzam Well in the masjid al-Haram, 2, 85
Zand, Persian dynasty, 292–93
Zarang, town on Afghan-Iran border, 140
Zardari, Asif, Pakistani President, 364, 368
Zayd Saidov, opposition leader in Tajikistan, 390
Zaydun, poet in Andalusia, love of Wallada, 114
Zhang He, Muslim admiral in China, 391
Zia, *See* General Zia ul-Haq
Zinat, w/o Bahadur Shah Zafar, 194
Zionism, 327–28
Ziryab, singer poet and gentleman of fashion in Andalusia, 109
Zoraya, aka Isabel, w/o Abu al Hasan, King of Granada, 119
Zubayda, w/o Harun al Rashid, 62–65
Zulfiqar Ali Bhutto, Pakistani prime minister, 362
Zulu, 385

Rep9
I.T.S.11/23